Also by Devon Monk

Magic to the Bone
Magic in the Blood
Magic in the Shadows

Magic
on the
Storm

Devon Monk

A ROC BOOK

ROC
Published by New American Library, a division of
Penguin Group (USA) Inc., 375 Hudson Street,
New York, New York 10014, USA
Penguin Group (Canada), 90 Eglinton Avenue East, Suite 700, Toronto,
Ontario M4P 2Y3, Canada (a division of Pearson Penguin Canada Inc.)
Penguin Books Ltd., 80 Strand, London WC2R 0RL, England
Penguin Ireland, 25 St. Stephen's Green, Dublin 2,
Ireland (a division of Penguin Books Ltd.)
Penguin Group (Australia), 250 Camberwell Road, Camberwell, Victoria 3124,
Australia (a division of Pearson Australia Group Pty. Ltd.)
Penguin Books India Pvt. Ltd., 11 Community Centre, Panchsheel Park,
New Delhi - 110 017, India
Penguin Group (NZ), 67 Apollo Drive, Rosedale, North Shore 0632,
New Zealand (a division of Pearson New Zealand Ltd.)
Penguin Books (South Africa) (Pty.) Ltd., 24 Sturdee Avenue,
Rosebank, Johannesburg 2196, South Africa

Penguin Books Ltd., Registered Offices:
80 Strand, London WC2R 0RL, England

First published by Roc, an imprint of New American Library,
a division of Penguin Group (USA) Inc.

First printing, May 2010
10 9 8 7 6 5 4 3 2 1

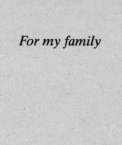

For my family

Acknowledgments

Writing is only part of what brings a story to its final form. Without the many people who have contributed time and energy along the way, this book would not have come to fruition. Thank you to my agent, Miriam Kriss, and my editor, Anne Sowards, two consummate professionals and awesome people who make my job easy.

All my love and gratitude to my wonderful first readers, Dean Woods, Dejsha Knight, and Dianna Rodgers. Your speedy and loving support and brilliant insight make this possible. Thank you also to my family, one and all, who always offer unfailing encouragement and share in the joy. And to my husband, Russ, and sons, Kameron and Konner, who are the very best part of my life. I couldn't do this without you.

Last, thank you, dear readers, for letting me share this story and this world with you.

Chapter One

Two months of self-defense classes, mixed martial arts, and weapons training did not make it hurt any less when I was thrown over my opponent's shoulder and slammed into the ground.

Yes, I should have tucked and rolled. Would have too, if he hadn't kept hold of my arm and twisted at just the right instant to knock my balance off and make me sprawl like a dead jumper waiting for my chalk outline.

"Give up?" he asked.

My right wrist still locked in his grip, I stretched out my left hand and grabbed his ankle, leveraged to pull down, and twisted. I broke his hold on my wrist and rolled up onto my feet. I got off the mat and out of arm's reach quick.

"I'll take that as a no, then?" Zayvion Jones asked. He was a little sweaty, a lot relaxed, standing halfway across the mat from me. Barefoot, he had on a pair of jeans that, if there were any justice in the world, would not let him flex and move and stretch the way he did in a fight, and a nice black T-shirt that defined the muscles of his chest, his thick, powerful arms, and his flat, hard stomach.

He was every kind of good-looking in the dictionary.

"Take it as a hell no," I said sweetly.

That got a grin out of him, his teeth a flash of white

against his dark skin, his thick lips open enough that I suddenly wanted to drop this whole I-kill-you/you-kill-me act and kiss the man.

Instead, I rolled my shoulder to make sure my arm was still in its socket—Zayvion Jones played for keeps—and tried to come up with a game plan to tip the fight to my advantage. He might have bendy denim on his side, but I had something better. I had magic in my bones.

My shoulder sore but still attached and functioning, I stepped back onto the mat.

I could use magic on him. It might be worth ending up in bed with a fever just to take Mr. Superpowerful-Guardian-of-the-Gates down a notch during a practice match.

The void stone necklace, a chunk of rock caught up and caged between silver and copper whorls and glass beads, rested against my sternum and made the magic in me lazy and slow. I could still use magic, but it took a little more effort when I was wearing the stone.

If I'd known about void stones, I'd have found a way to steal one months ago. Not that they were common knowledge. The Authority had lots of tricks up their sleeve that they didn't like the common magic user to know about.

"Is there a particular way you'd like to end up on the floor this time?" he asked as he shifted his stance and waited for me to attack. "Or do you just want me to surprise you?"

"Gee, if I get a choice, how about if I end up on top this time?" I gave him that slow blink–smile combination that always got him into bed.

He licked his lips, and a flash of uncertainty narrowed his eyes. "I thought you said you wanted to fight."

I strolled up to him and paused. Out of arm's reach—I'm not dumb. "I thought you were asking me how I wanted this to end."

Zay studied me, his brown eyes just brown, no hint

of the gold that using magic always sparked there. As far as I could tell, he hadn't been using magic for the past couple months. Ever since my test to see whether I could become a part of the Authority, and the craziness with the gate between life and death opening right in the middle of the test room, things had been quiet.

And I mean quiet. I'd Hounded only a couple magical crimes for Detective Paul Stotts. My dead father, who had taken up residence in my head, seemed to be so distant, he mostly appeared in my dreams. And my training—both physical and magical—with members of the Authority had been exhausting, but a long way from life threatening.

Things were actually pretty good. I liked that. Liked not having to worry whether I'd survive the day. And it wasn't just my life that was better for the downtime. Over the past several weeks I'd watched Zayvion change from a somber, tightly controlled, dutiful man, to someone a little surprised he was enjoying life.

Time off from his duties with the Authority looked good on him. Sexy.

"I wasn't talking about ending this," he said, and it took me a minute to remember what we were talking about. Oh yeah, the fight. "But we can call it a day. Since you're surrendering and admitting you lost. Again."

As if I'd give up that easily. I glared at him.

Light poured in through the windows, casting warm coffee-colored shadows beneath his high cheekbones and jaw. His hair was always short, but he'd recently buzzed his dark curls, which somehow only enhanced his beautiful eyes and strong, wide nose. The look of worry that I only occasionally glimpsed through his Zen mask had been absent for weeks. He smiled more. Laughed more.

And it made me realize how hard I'd fallen for him. I didn't want what we'd had for the past few weeks to change or disappear. But I'd lost too many people in my life, and too many memories along the way, for me to think things would always be this easy between us. The idea of losing him made it hard to breathe.

I tried to push that fear away, but it clung like a bad dream.

"Allie?" Zay was no longer smiling. "Are you hurt? Your shoulder?" He came closer and put his wide, warm palm on my shoulder.

That touch gave me the faintest hint at what he was feeling: concern that he'd torn my arm out on that last flip, which, yes, he could have, but no—I wasn't that fragile.

And that reminded me of what this little get-together was all about. Fighting. Training. Becoming strong enough to hold my own against anyone. Even the legendary Zayvion Jones.

I knew I shouldn't do it. But hey, a girl has to take what opportunities present themselves, right? I had my game plan.

I stepped into him and turned my hip, sweeping his foot out from under him. He went down, rolled, but I was there, got in close, getting his arm back, my arm through it, and the other over his throat.

"Give," I said. We were in close contact, but I was too busy staying on the winning side of the tussle to have brain cells left to concentrate on what he might be thinking.

"No," he grunted.

Even though I am a tall woman, Zay still had me on sheer muscle. He flexed and managed to break my hold, twisting over and onto his back, his legs scissoring to catch mine.

No way I'd let him do that.

I followed him, using his momentum to roll over him and then behind. I huffed out air, got to my knees, and tried to keep his arm pinned.

He shifted, rolled. I ended up kneeling with him beneath me. Boo-ya! I was on top.

I had one knee planted beside him and the other foot braced on the opposite side. Forget about his arm—I wrapped my hands around his throat, knuckles at his windpipe.

He pressed his palms flat against my hip bones and tilted his hands inward so his fingers stroked upward beneath my T-shirt. I glared at him as the heels of his hands slid over the bullet scar on my left side and the smooth skin on my right. Then up and up. His thumbs tracked slower than his fingers over my stomach, pausing to dip and press at my navel. Then he fanned his hands outward, upward, and rested them beneath the curve of my breasts, supporting the weight there.

I raised an eyebrow. "You do notice I'm choking you?" I squeezed a little harder in case he thought I was kidding around.

He grunted.

I most certainly was not kidding around.

He shifted his grip. Tried to pull me down and rolled one hip to throw me. No chance. I braced my heel to stay out of the roll and pressed harder.

"Mercy," he whispered.

I relaxed my grip. "Say I win."

"I win," he managed.

I retucked my thumbs against his windpipe. "What? You win? Is that what you said? I must not have heard you correctly."

"Draw," he whispered.

"Oh, sweet hells, Jones. You have got to be the most stubborn man I know. You lost."

"I agree," he said.

Huh. I hadn't expected him to give in that easily. I pulled my hands away, rested them against his chest.

"I am the most stubborn man you know." He rubbed at his throat with one hand. Grinned at me.

I smacked his other arm. "My honor's at stake here. You lost. I won. If you can't admit that, I'm not sure our relationship will survive."

He snorted, grabbed my shirt, and pulled me fully on top of him. His fist, in the valley between my breasts, was a hard pressure between us.

"Nothing's going to get in the way of our relationship." His gaze searched my own, and the slightest fleck of gold sparked there. "So long as we want this, nothing can stand in our way."

Damn. Could the man get any more romantic?

I tipped my head down and caught his lips with my own, soft, thick, hungry. He instantly responded, then licked gently at my mouth until I opened for him. He tasted of deep, warm mint, and his pine scent, peppered by sweat, carried the memory of the countless times we had touched, loved.

I explored the textures of his lips, his mouth, savoring him slowly, and he did the same, his tongue stroking a delicious heat through my body. I moaned softly and gave in to the liquid fire burning through me.

I wanted him. And it was very clear he wanted me.

He flattened his fist and released my shirt, then wrapped his arm around me, holding me tightly, as if he were afraid I might disappear.

A little too tightly. Claustrophobia tickled the back of my throat. It was suddenly hard to breathe.

I exhaled and pushed back enough that he knew to loosen his grip. I lifted my shoulders and chest and took a deep breath. There was plenty of room here, plenty of room for us to be this close.

He drew his arms off from around me, his hands at my ribs instead, helping me stay half raised above him. My right hand on the floor next to him did the rest to support my weight.

With his free hand, he tucked my hair behind my ear, a gesture that was becoming habitual and endearing.

"Okay?" he asked quietly.

I nodded. Just that much space, that one deep breath, cleared my head and pushed the claustrophobia away.

I wove my fingers between the thickness of his and pulled his hand out to the side. I eased back down on him and caught his other hand, and drew it outward too, so that we lay body against body, spread wide upon the floor. My breasts, stomach, hips, thighs, melted into the length and hardness of him beneath me. I wanted more of him. All of him. I kissed the side of his neck, bit gently. His hands clenched, and his body responded to my unspoken invitation.

I sucked at his neck while his heartbeat grew stronger and faster beneath my breasts.

"Allie," he begged. Electricity rolled through me, and I caught my breath.

It had been two months, and it still felt like I couldn't get enough of him.

I want you, he whispered in my mind. We kissed again, his tongue tracing the edge of my bottom lip. I felt his desire burn through me like a hot wind, making my skin prickle with tight heat.

Soul Complements, they say, can cast magic with each other, matching and blending exactly how they use magic, work magic. Soul Complements, they say, can become so close, they hear each other's thoughts. Soul Complements, they say, can become so close they lose their sense of identity and go insane. That made Soul Complements an unmeasured power, a combination that could change magic, break magic, make it do things it should not do.

Zay and I could hear each other's thoughts when we touched. We hadn't cast magic together, which was a little strange. I thought the Authority would have wanted to know what kind of strength or liability we could be for them. But Sedra, the leader, refused to allow us full testing.

We hadn't pushed for it. Maybe we were both worried it would feel too good. Would make us need it too much. Maybe we were afraid if we got too close, we'd never be able to let go, no matter the price.

Yeah, that last thing was pretty much it.

But what they didn't say was that sex, when you could feel your partner's pleasure, when you knew exactly what his body craved, was awesome.

I rocked my hips against his and nipped at his earlobe.

Ask me real nice-like, I thought.

Zay paused, swallowed. I pulled up, gazed down at him. His eyes held more gold than before, as if he was resisting the need to use magic. He slid one leg between mine. "Or what?" he asked.

Didn't he know I couldn't ignore a challenge?

I propped my forearms on his chest and tried to look unconcerned.

"Or we could call it a day and go get lunch."

"Hmm." He brushed my hair back again, tucking it behind my right ear. He traced the whorls of magic that started at the corner of my right eye and flowed like metallic ribbons down the edge of my cheek, jaw, neck. I shivered at the cool mint that licked behind his touch.

His finger stopped at the pulse point at my throat, even though the marks of magic continued down my arm to my fingertips.

"Are you hungry?" he asked.

I was. But not for food. "Yes."

A rock hit my arm.

I twisted, my palms up, ready to cast a spell.

Zayvion was way ahead of me. One elbow braced beneath him, he rolled, putting me partially behind him, his right hand already outlining a glyph in the air, though he didn't pour magic into it yet.

Another rock, a wet rock—no, an ice cube—hit my

hip. More ice hit Zayvion's shoulder, clattered down his chest to the mat in front of him. Ice rained down around us in handfuls.

Shamus Flynn stood at the door halfway across the room, a bucket of ice tucked between his arm and chest, and a grin on his face.

"Thank God I got here in time." He tossed another volley our way. "You might have gone up in flames. Burst into sex at any minute."

"Shame," Zayvion warned. "Put the ice down."

"Like hell. No need to thank me. It's what friends are for." He tossed another cube at Zayvion's head. Zay didn't even blink as it whizzed past his ear.

Boy had good aim.

Zay didn't take his eyes off Shame, but he shifted so that we were no longer tangled.

"Do you remember what happened to you the last time you threw ice at me?" he asked calmly.

Shame shook his head. "Doesn't ring a bell."

"It had something to do with you not walking straight for a couple days."

Shame grinned. "Oh, you mean what Chase did to me. *That* I remember. Girl's got no sense of humor. And she kicks like a mule. Bad combination."

"The bucket?" Zay held up his hand where he still held the glyph between ring finger and thumb. "Down."

Shame pulled out a piece of ice and stuck it in his mouth. He chewed it—noisily—as he strolled over to us.

I swear he had a death wish.

Shame did a fair job at that goth-rocker vibe. Black hair cut with the precision of dull garden shears shaded his eyes. Black T-shirt over a black long-sleeved shirt on top of black jeans, black boots. Even his hands were covered by black fingerless gloves. But behind all that black was a man who wasn't as young as he looked. A man whose eyes carried too much pain to be hidden by that sly smile.

"That was your last warning." Zayvion tensed, ready to pour magic into the glyph.

"Do not burn your best friend to a crisp," I said, sounding more like a babysitter than a girlfriend.

Zay just kept staring at Shame. "He's won't burn long. Not with all that water on him."

Shame laughed. "Bring it on."

"No one's going to bring anything on." I stood, and took turns glaring at Zayvion and Shamus. "No magic fights in the gym."

Right. Like they'd do what I said.

Time to change tactics. "How about food? Zay and I were just going to do lunch," I said.

"Lunch?" Shamus said. "Is that what you kids are calling it these days? Back in my day we called it fucking."

"Shamus," Zayvion said, "may I have a word with you?" Zay let go of the spell and stood up in one smooth, graceful motion that showed just how many years this man had spent sparring.

Shame didn't have time to answer because Zay closed in on him, fast and silent as a panther. He wrapped his arm around Shame. It looked friendly enough, but both of Shame's arms were pinned and Shame was tucked tight against Zay's side.

"You want a word with me, or you want to date me?" Shame asked. "'Cause if it's the second thing, you're buying me more than lunch."

Zayvion forced him toward the far side of the room.

I shook my head. Those two acted like brothers, even though they were physically about as opposite as they could get. I glanced at the door, wondering if Chase, Zay's ex-girlfriend, might have come along with Shame. No one was there.

My shoulders dropped. Chase and I were not exactly friends, even though we'd had to work around each other the last couple months. She wasn't done hating me for what happened to Greyson, the man she dumped Zay for. And I was more than done explaining to her that I hadn't turned him into a half-dead beast.

What can I say? My relationships were complicated.

I found the water bottle I'd left on the floor, picked it up, and took a drink. Zay and Shame were far enough across the room I shouldn't be able to hear what they were saying. But Hounding for a living meant I had good ears. There was a chance I'd be able to spring into action if Shame needed me to save his life or something.

"...ever throw ice at me again, I am going to beat you with that bucket. Do you understand me?"

"Oh, please. Like I should take you seriously. You haven't raised a finger in two months."

"Listen." Zay paused, lowered his voice. "This is different than Chase and me. More than ... that ever was." He paused again. "I need you to respect what we have, or you and I are going to have real problems."

"Respect?" Shamus asked, just as quietly. "I'm filled with envy."

"Then stop being an ass."

Shame snorted. "Better to ask the rain not to fall."

"Rain," Zay said, squeezing Shame a little harder. "Don't fall." He released his hold.

Shame got out of arm's reach and shook his hand, probably trying to get blood back into it. Like I said, Zay played for keeps.

"Can't remember the last time you and I had real problems." Shame stuck his hand in the ice bucket and dug out another frozen chunk, popped it in his mouth.

"It'll come to you."

From Shame's body language, I could tell it had. "Yes. Well. Let's not go there again."

Then Shame raised his voice, obviously talking to me. "Aren't you going to ask why I came by?"

I shrugged the shoulder that didn't hurt. "You need a reason to harass Zay?"

"Hell no. But I'm not here to talk to Zay. I'm here for you." He strolled across the room toward me.

Zayvion paced over to where he'd left his water bottle. The man was so quiet that if I weren't looking at him, I wouldn't think there was anyone in the room except Shame and me.

"What's up?" I asked.

Shame stopped and held out the bucket. "Ice?"

"We're going to lunch, remember?"

"You were serious about that?" he asked. "Huh. Well, you might want to eat quick. My mum wants to see you." He glanced at the clock on the wall behind me. "In an hour, the latest. At the inn."

"Did she say why?" I asked.

"Officially?"

"At all."

"There's a storm coming," he said, all the joking gone now.

Zayvion stiffened. I watched as the relaxed, laughing man I'd spent the last few weeks with was replaced by an emotionless wall of control, of calm, of duty.

"What kind of storm?" I asked, even though I was pretty sure what the answer would be.

"Wild magic," he said. "And it's aiming straight for the city."

Dread rolled in my stomach. The last time a wild storm had hit the city, I'd tapped into it and nearly killed myself. Ended up in a coma. Ended up losing more memories than I wanted to admit. Like my memories of Zayvion.

"And what does that have to do with me?" My voice did not shake. Go, me.

Wild-magic storms were violent and deadly, and messed with the flow of magic that powered the city's spells. But that's why my father invented the Beckstrom

Storm Rods. Every building in the city was outfitted with at least one storm rod to catch and channel strikes of wild magic.

"Maybe nothing," he said. "She might just want to go over details from your last session with her." He nodded toward the void stone necklace around my neck. "See that things are going right with you and all."

Lie. Lie. Lie. Shamus knew more. Knew what Maeve wanted. Knew why I was being called upon.

I looked him in the eyes. Raised my eyebrows.

He just shook his head.

Okay, whatever it was, he wouldn't or couldn't tell me. It was hard to remember that Shame was a part of the Authority too. He reported to Jingo Jingo, and above him was Liddy Salberg. They all used Death magic, which was unknown to the average magic user, and for good reasons. Maybe Jingo had told him not to talk.

More likely his mother had told him to keep his gob shut.

I'd only taken a handful of classes with Shamus's mother, Maeve, but she treated me like a cub who needed protecting from the other senior members of the Authority, people like Liddy; Jingo Jingo; Zay's boss, Victor; and especially the leader, Sedra.

She was wrong to think I needed protecting. But over the last month or so, I'd discovered the one thing the members of the Authority had in common. They were all suspicious as hell. Not a lot of trust going around for a group of people who relied on one another's discretion to stay in business.

"For that, you couldn't just call?" I asked, trying to lift the mood.

"What, and waste a perfectly good bucket of ice?"

"Tell your mom I'll be there in an hour." I picked up my gym bag and headed to the women's locker room. "Zay, you still on for lunch?"

"We have time. I'll take you out to Maeve's afterwards."

Shame followed Zay into the men's locker room, his voice drifting back to me. "Oh, what's with the face? Mad your vacation's over? When was the last time you did any work, you lazy git?"

I heard the muffled smack of a fist against flesh and an "Ow!" as I closed the door.

I was the only one in the locker room, and Zay and Shame were the only other people in the gym. The gym wasn't advertised—as a matter of fact, it was fairly hidden, and not by magical means. It was located on the bottom floor of a fabric store, and no one suspected there was a modern workout facility here.

Zay had told me it was only one of several places in the city set aside by members of the Authority for members of the Authority. It was like they had an entire hidden city shoved into the pockets and cracks of Portland. And no one got in those pockets if they weren't part of the Authority.

The whole exclusivity of the Authority was a little odd to me. I still wasn't one hundred percent down with the I'm-on-their-team bit, because I wasn't sure they were on my team.

Yes, the members of the Authority had magical knowledge up the wazoo, and used more magic in more ways than I could imagine. Yes, I loved learning how to control the magic that filled me. Not that I had been top of the class in the execution of everything they tried to teach me.

But the price for all this knowledge was that I could never speak of it outside the Authority, never abuse the trust they placed in me, and never use magic in the hidden ways in public. And the public included the police.

Which made my day job of Hounding illegal spells for Detective Stotts a difficult combination of remembering what I should know and, more important, what he should know I knew.

I shucked my T-shirt, and traded my exercise bra for something I could breathe in. I didn't look in the mirror until I'd pulled on my jeans and boots. I dug the brush out of my bag and did a quick once-through on my hair. My hair was dark and short enough I could tuck it pretty easily behind one ear, and I did so on the left side. The right I let fall free, hiding the metallic whorls magic had marked me with.

Since it was winter in Oregon, there wasn't a natural tan in town, and I was no exception. My pale skin made the glass green of my eyes look like chipped jade. I held my breath and braced myself for the shadow of my father in my eyes. Nothing but me staring back at me.

Good.

If my dad never spoke to me again—better yet, if he faded away into death like a decent dead person—that would be fine with me. I did not like being possessed.

I shoved my workout clothes into my bag, zipped everything, and put on my hoodie before strolling out of the locker room. Zay and Shame stood by the door. Shame cradled a cigarette and lighter in one hand—neither lit.

"So, where to?" I asked.

"The River Grill's on the way to Mum's," Shame suggested.

"You're coming with us?" I asked.

"Like you're surprised. Free lunch, right?"

"Wrong," Zay said. "It's your turn to buy."

I opened the door and stepped out into the hard, cold air. The sun lent the day no warmth, but it was sunny and the sky was a shock of blue that hit my winter-weary soul like a cool drink of water.

Zayvion followed behind me. Shamus paused to light up.

"You going to tell us the rest?" Zay asked over his shoulder.

Shame exhaled smoke. Finally got walking.

"The rest of what?"

We'd made it to the car, and Zay unlocked the passenger's side and touched my arm before walking around to the driver's side. Shame, still smoking, paused near the back of the car. He'd gotten here on his own—I assumed his car was in the parking lot somewhere.

Zay turned and gave Shame a look that said more than words.

One corner of Shame's mouth curved upward. The wind stirred his hair, pushing it closer over his eyes, and taking his scents—cigarette smoke and cloves—away from me.

"Sedra called in the crew from Seattle."

"Terric?" Zay asked mildly.

Shame just took another drag off the cigarette. His shoulders were squared, tense, his free hand fisted. He looked like someone who had more pain in him than he had breath left to scream it out.

"Of course."

"Have you seen him yet?" Zay asked.

"Nope. And if luck holds, I won't see him at all." Maybe it was supposed to come out funny, but his voice dropped into a growl, even though he was smiling. Whoa. There was a lot of fury behind that smile.

"Come to lunch," Zay said.

Shame tossed the cigarette to the damp concrete, then clapped his hands together as if brushing away dirt, his fingerless gloves muffling the sound. "Not going to talk about it."

"I know."

Shame nodded, then strolled off to his car, whistling a punk rock song from the nineties.

I looked over the roof of the car at Zayvion. He

watched Shamus with such intensity, it was like he could see the man's bones, his soul.

Who knows? Maybe he could. There were a lot of things about both of them I didn't know.

Shamus, walking away, couldn't see us. Still, he must have felt Zay's gaze. He lifted his hand in a dismissive wave.

Zayvion inhaled, his nostrils flaring. When he looked back at me, he was calm. Zen Zay. Private Zay. Controlled. Deadly.

"Vacation's over, isn't it?" I asked.

Zay shrugged one shoulder. "I think we have time for one last lunch."

"As long as lunch involves coffee, I'm on for it." We both got in the car, and at least one of us, namely me, wondered how long it would be before the storm really hit.

Chapter Two

The River Grill was on the Oregon side of the Columbia, and should have been swank if the real estate
surrounding it had any sway. Instead, it looked pretty
much the same as it did back in the day when the lum-
beryards were still going strong—a squat, wide building
with plenty of windows facing the water, mostly clean
tables, and food that was hot, filling, and cheap.

It was three o'clock, a little late for lunch, and a little
early for dinner, so the place was mostly empty.

Zay and I took a table by the window and Shamus
strolled in behind us. He plucked a menu off the stack
by the cash register, and read it while walking over to
the table.

"Think it's the burger today." He sat in the remaining
chair and folded the menu.

"Big surprise," Zayvion said over the top of his glass
of water.

Shame held up one hand, and caught the waitress's
attention.

She was over in a jiffy, took our orders—burgers and
sodas all around—and then was off.

Shame cracked his knuckles. "So, how did sparring go
today?"

"She's improving," Zayvion said.

"She won," I said, clearly.

Zay just smiled. I really was getting better. Good enough I knew I could hold my own in a fight. Good enough I was doing more than just knife training—we'd moved on to the machetes Zay and his crew use to hunt down magical nasties. Zay had let me work with the katana, a beautiful blade, heavy with the weight of old magic. Training, being aware of every muscle in my body working in concert to my command of magic, made me feel powerful. And I liked it. A lot.

"Very nice, Beckstrom," Shame said. "Zay's a hard man to take down. Not that he's much of a challenge for me, of course. I could take him with one spell tied behind my back. And now that he's all soft from his time off, he'd go down in a hot second."

"Are you done?" Zay asked.

"Done?" Shame said.

"Not talking about Terric."

Shame glared at Zayvion. Zay sipped his water, patient as time. Shame finally gave up, and rubbed his mouth across the palm of his fingerless glove. With his other hand, he cast a very subtle Mute spell. The people around us, not that there were many, wouldn't be able to hear our conversation. Handy, that.

"Mum said Sedra's calling . . . them . . . down. Said it's about the storm, but I think there's more going on."

Zay folded his fingers and propped his elbows on the table. He stared at Shamus, waiting for him to talk.

"I think there's something wrong with the wells," Shame said.

Zayvion's eyebrows rose. End of reaction. "All of them?"

Shame took a drink of water. "Like I know? I don't have access to all of them. But the one beneath Mum's place . . ." He shook his head.

Zayvion did not look pleased. Then he pulled on the somber mask of Zen, of calm, of duty, and simply looked emotionless.

Well, that was helpful.

"Want to tell the new girl what can go wrong with the wells?" I wasn't a complete idiot. In the time I'd been taking classes from Victor, Liddy, Maeve, and Jingo Jingo, I'd realized that Portland has four natural wells of magic beneath the ground. That was unusual. Other cities had wells—usually one. Sometimes two. Rarely three. But the Portland area had four wells, one of which was beneath the Flynns' inn, which Shame's mother ran, just on the Vancouver side of the river, and all of which were a hard-guarded secret.

The waitress hurried over, three plates balanced across her arm. She placed everything on our table, plunked down a carrier of condiments, and left us to our meal.

"So?" I asked. "What can go wrong with the wells?"

Shame took a huge bite of burger, pointed at his mouth, and gave me a shut-up-and-let-me-eat look while he chewed.

Closers such as Zayvion, Chase, and, apparently, Terric could take away the memories of any people they judged were a harm to themselves or others when using magic. Judge, jury, and executioners, Closers had the final say about what people remembered about magic. It made me uncomfortable. Shame told me once that Closers take away Hound memories if Hounds stumble across magic they shouldn't know about.

I'd asked him and Zayvion if I'd ever been Closed. It would explain a lot. It would explain why I randomly lost my memories when I used magic.

They'd both said no. Shame told me he didn't think anyone in the Authority was really interested in me before my dad's death. And while Zayvion hadn't exactly agreed with that, he said he had never seen or heard of anyone being ordered to take my memories.

I wasn't sure if I was glad about that. If my memories were taken by a person, there was still a chance I could get them back. If they were taken by magic, I could kiss those parts of my life good-bye.

Still, I didn't know what could go wrong with the wells that the Closers couldn't handle. They could just erase any memories about them if someone outside the Authority found something out.

I looked at Zay. "Well?"

"If Sedra is calling in more Closers, it might have something to do with the gates, not the wells," he said.

"They're closed, right? No openings in the last two months? Since my . . . test?" What I didn't say was since there had been a huge fight, and Cody Miller's spirit had sacrificed himself to close the gateways between life and death.

"Wild storms can blow the gates open," Zayvion said.

"Neat. So you Closers have some work ahead of you, but it's not a big problem, right?"

"It is very, very difficult to close a gate during a storm," Zay said. "Magic doesn't work right in wild storms. It can be hard to access, or come too quickly and foul or mutate spells. And if the wells are also affected by the storm . . ." He shrugged.

"Can enough Closers contain it?" The Authority was tight-lipped about membership. I wasn't even sure how many people were a part of the Authority in Portland, much less other cities, or the world. And I had no idea how many of those members were Closers.

Shame shoved french fries in his mouth, mumbled, "Lunch," and gave a nod toward my plate. "Save the world on a full stomach."

Fine. If they didn't want to talk about it, I'd find out when I went to see Maeve later. I took a bite of my burger. Juicy, hot, nothing fancy, but as soon as I got a bite of it, I discovered I was starving.

The door opened, letting in the brisk wind and a man and woman.

The man was at least six feet tall and wide as a foot-ball field, his long, shiny black hair pulled back at the base of his neck. He wore cargo shorts, flip-flops, and a black and red Blazer jacket, even though it was February and cold, and moved with that island-warmth vibe of his birthplace. Detective Mackanie Love.

With him was a blade of a woman. Thin, unsmiling, dark and cool as a rainy midnight, she was wrapped in a gray coat and gray scarf that did nothing to soften her angular but pretty features. Detective Lia Payne.

I used to run all my Hounding jobs that dealt with illegal use of magic past them before Detective Stotts and the MERC, a secret branch of the law that dealt with magical crime, came into my life. We were maybe not fast friends, but friends just the same.

Just as I spotted them, they spotted me.

I smiled and waved.

"Tell me you did not just wave down the cops," Shamus whispered.

"Tita!" Mackanie strolled over, a smile on his face. He took in my company, with what seemed to be friendly interest.

Zayvion Jones looked Love in the eyes, but had slouched into his slacker-drifter bit he did so well, and Shame motioned under the table, breaking the Mute spell before Mackanie got too close.

"Food any good today?" He stopped between Zay's and Shamus's chairs.

"Good enough that it's almost gone," I said. "Have you met Zayvion Jones and Shamus Flynn?"

"Jones and I have met." He nodded at Zay.

"Detective Love," Zayvion said.

"I don't think I've had the pleasure, Mr. Flynn." He held his hand out to Shame. They shook.

"Pleased to meet you," Shame said with very little tone inflection. He'd fallen into his sullen goth-boy act pretty fast. What was it with these two and the cops?

Oh yeah. Most of what they did would probably be considered illegal if the world ever knew magic could do what they could make it do.

"So, you talked to Stotts today?" Love asked me.

"Should I?"

"He knows how to find you, yah?"

"He has my number. There a case he wants me on?"

"Not sure. He's got your number, you got no worries. But that warehouse of yours. There's a worry. I hear they're gonna condemn it."

I grinned. That warehouse of mine was the building next to Get Mugged. Grant had decided to buy it, and agreed to let me lease two of the floors for an office, a meeting space, a couple bunks, a kitchen, and a workout room for the Hounds. To say it had been a learning experience was a serious understatement. I'd never repaired or renovated anything in my life. Yes, I hired a contractor to do the big fixes, but then I dragged as many Hounds into manual labor as I could.

Not one of my brighter plans. Hounds are loners. Working together was so far out of their natural tendencies, it was laughable.

And with how much I'd spent doing it, I think it would have been cheaper to just knock the place down and build from scratch. But Grant loved the "vintage" feel of it, and so did the ghost hunters who were renting out the bottom floor. Therefore, the old building remained as it was, standing proudly. Well, leaning proudly, anyway.

Plus the location—right next door to my favorite coffee shop—was pretty hard to beat.

"Too late to condemn it," I said. "Paint's dry by the end of the week, and the landline's being hooked up tomorrow."

"So you got emergency response plugged in, in case of trouble?"

"No drug use allowed on the premises. No guns. No brawls. No troubles."

He just stared at me. Yeah, we all knew that things went to hell when too many Hounds got together for too long.

"Fine," I said. "Yes, I've set things up."

"Good, then, good," he said. "You Hound, Flynn?" he asked Shame.

"Wash dishes at my mum's restaurant, Feile San Fhomher."

"Maybe that's where I've seen you, yah?"

He shrugged. "Unless you worked juvie a few years back."

I turned and stared at Shame. He had a record?

"You have a record?" I asked. See how tactful I could be?

"Did some tagging when I was fourteen."

How come I figured it was a lot more than that?

"Gang?" Love asked.

"Just art and anger."

"You get that out of your system?" he asked.

"Let's just say I'm not fourteen anymore."

Love grinned. "Yah, live and learn. I got some eating to do, though this place's got nothing on your mom's blackberry cobbler."

Maeve's inn was a working restaurant. Which meant a lot of people went there, including cops who had no idea she was one of the voices in the Authority and her entire inn and restaurant was built over a secret, hidden well of magic.

This kind of stuff gave me a headache. There were layers and layers of who knew what in this city. Zayvion said he had a spreadsheet to keep track of what secrets were spoken where. I had yet to see it.

Every time I thought these things out, I was more impressed that the Authority hadn't been discovered yet. Of course, they had one ace in the hole no one else in this city had. Closers, who could get in your head, make you forget anything they wanted you to forget—like a secret you shouldn't have heard or maybe how to use magic. They could Close away your desire to stay in the city. Take away your life, and give you a new one if they decided the situation warranted it.

Kill you, if you got in their way.

I glanced at Zay. He was drinking his Coke and trying hard not to look over at Love's partner, Payne, who sat in the booth across the room. She was staring at him.

She caught my gaze and gave me a considering look, her mouth pressed together in a thin line. I wondered how, exactly, she and Zayvion knew each other. I remember Mackanie Love being there when Frank Gordon had dug up my father's body and tried to kill me. Zay had been there too. So it was possible that their only connection was Zay being a witness to that crime. But if I remembered right, Love and Payne had been looking for Zay prior to that.

Interesting.

I stretched my foot under the table and rested it against the side of Zay's tennis shoe.

The contact let me concentrate on his emotional state: tense, which was not at all what I'd have guessed from his body language, with a side order of worry and dread.

He must have sensed my curiosity because he gave me a sideways look and sat up, pulling his foot away from mine.

Like that would stop me from finding out why he was all worked up over Payne.

Even though it had taken only a couple seconds, I'd sort of lost track of the conversation Love and Shame were having. I had a hard time listening in to Zayvion's emotions and listening to the real world at the same time.

I tuned back in just in time to hear Love say, ". . . lunch. Later, Tita."

"Bye," I said, wondering if I'd just made a lunch date with him.

Love rambled over to Payne. She stopped staring at Zayvion and stared at her menu instead.

"You don't like the police, do you?" I asked Shame.

Shame flicked up a couple fingers in a dismissive motion. "They do good work. I just like them better when that work has nothing to do with me."

"Juvie?" I asked.

"It happens."

"Would have thought your mom had some pull to keep you out of there."

"She did," Zayvion said. "So did his dad."

Shame looked up at me. He didn't grin, but there was a sparkle in his eye. "They let me sweat it out for a week. Said it'd help me rethink my priorities."

"Did it?"

"Yes. I decided my first priority was not getting caught."

"You are a man of questionable morals, Shamus Flynn," I said.

"You have no idea. Well, then." He stood, stuck one hand in his jean pockets, and brushed hair out of his eyes with the other. "Thanks for lunch. I have to run. See you soon."

I had a mouthful of fries. Zay was finishing his too. I held up my hand to tell Shame to stop, but he spun and was across the room, weaving between a noisy crowd of college kids pouring into the place. He was out the door before I could call his name.

The waitress saw my hand and came over with our ticket. Zay reached for it, but I got it before him. "You cover next time."

"How about we just make Shame pay for a month?" he said.

"Does he ever pay for anything?"

Zay finished off his Coke. "Nope. That's one of his special talents."

I pulled out the cash, left it and the ticket propped next to the condiment basket. I stood. "Ready?"

For a second, just the briefest of moments, a wave of dizziness hit me. The entire building felt like it shuddered, like a liquid earthquake rumbled far beneath my feet, and echoed up my body and rolled through my head.

"Allie?"

I rubbed at my temple and the sudden headache. "Headache." But it couldn't be from magic use.

The last time I'd used magic was two weeks ago. A Hounding job that had nothing to do with the police or Detective Stotts. I had tracked back a spell for a lady in my building to make sure no one was putting Attraction on her car. Turned out no one was. The parking tickets and the speeding and seat belt violations were all nonmagical and all her.

Maybe this was just a regular headache? Regular people did get regular headaches. I was regular people too.

Zay put his hand on my arm and I walked with him out the door. The headache hung on despite the cool air. By the time we were halfway across the parking lot, the pain was less, and I felt stable on my feet. Normal.

Zay's hand was still on my arm. I didn't have to concentrate to feel his concern.

"I'm okay," I said. "Just a little dizzy. It's gone."

He didn't let go of me until we were next to his car, which he unlocked. "Maybe you should stop wearing the void stone."

I hadn't thought of that. "Can it make me dizzy? Give me headaches?"

He shrugged. "No one holds magic in their body like you do. It's hard to know what the long-term effects are." He paused, looked at me over the top of the car. Probably saw my panic as I scrambled to get the necklace off.

"It won't bite," he said.

"Right." Visions of the stone sucking magic out of me like a leech filled my mind. "Nothing about you secret magic users or your secret magic toys is dangerous."

I tugged the length of leather off over my head and held it out in front of me like I had a snake by the head. The void stone swung in the breeze, a dark heart wrapped in copper and silver wire like fire and moonlight, glass beads flashing like stars.

Zay grinned. "Want me to tie it in a knot or kill it and put it in the trunk?"

"Shut up." I ducked into the car and plunked the thing down into the empty cup holder.

Magic stirred in me, a tingling warmth that grew hot, flushing across my skin, then sinking back down, warming my bones and filling me. It moved within me with promise, with desire. I closed my eyes, wanting to lose myself to it. Wanting to use magic in every way I could.

But that would be bad. I had enough magic inside me, I could burn down a city.

And I didn't want to do that. I liked the city.

I took a deep breath and worked on letting the magic move through me without me touching it. *I am a river and magic is the water. It pours through me, but it does not change me.* I closed my eyes and repeated that litany until the magic backed off and settled like a layer of lead over my bones.

Several minutes had passed. Zay had already started the engine and was heading toward Maeve's through traffic that was starting to thicken up for pre–rush hour. It was still light out, and a misty rain ticked against the windshield and roof. Other than the rub of the windshield wipers and the hum of the engine, it was quiet in the car.

I knew Zay could Ground me to help me keep the magic at controllable levels and could ease the pain I carried from using magic. But ever since we'd stepped into each other's minds, we'd tried not to use magic together.

Grounding was extremely difficult and carried twice the pain for the user—in this case, Zay—as other spells did. It was one of the spells I'd never been good at.

No, let me be blunt: I sucked at Grounding. Always had, and it looked like I always would.

Zay could Ground like he was strolling through daisies.

It would be easy to ask him to Ground me, but I had to do this, learn to quiet the magic inside me on my own.

"Hint?" I finally asked.

"You learned it with Victor."

Okay, Victor was Zay's boss. Head of the Closers, who followed the magic discipline of Faith. Tall, elegant older man. Cultured, intelligent, and ruthless. He had a sort of calm and deliberation about him that I liked. It was a little like Zayvion's Zen mode, and I wondered if Zay picked up that particular habit from him.

I may not fully trust Victor—issues; I have them— but other than Maeve, who taught Blood magic, he was my next-favorite teacher despite the fact that he taught Faith magic.

Faith magic was the same magic Dr. Frank Gordon had used to dig up my dad and try to kill me. Well, Frank had used a lot of disciplines, Faith, Life, Death, Blood. He'd probably used everything he could to try to open the gates between life and death. Wanted to control dark magic. Sacrificed a few innocent girls to do it.

I did not regret that he was dead.

"Allie."

Oh, right. I was supposed to be dealing with the magic that was trying to burn its way out of me.

Victor. What had he taught me? That magic was a river, a constant flow. But it could be thought of as shape and form too. As glyphs. And every glyph had a beginning and an end. Every glyph had break points, corners, places where you could block and stop magic.

So what I needed to do was think of the magic in me as a glyph, find a corner, a break point where it flowed through me, and block it.

Good thing using magic was so easy.

Not.

I imagined myself as a river. Magic flowed up through my feet, filled the pool I held inside me—the small magic I was born with that was now a raging sea—and then magic poured out, too slowly, through my fingertip and into the ground again.

Where was there a break in that?

"Another hint?" I asked.

Zayvion placed his hand high up on my thigh, his long fingers curving downward. I sighed as cool mint washed along all the rivulets and pathways magic had torched through me. Swallowed and tasted mint on the back of my throat, and breathed deep to make room for Zayvion to tap into the magic I carried. I wanted to close my eyes and savor the feel of him within me. I licked my lips, shifted in my seat a little, and drew my fingertips up the back of his hand.

"Hey," I said all breathy-like.

"Hey. Are you going to pay attention to what I'm doing?" he asked.

Spoilsport.

I rolled my head to one side and looked at him. I didn't draw Sight. Using magic right now was sort of the opposite of what I was trying to do.

Still, there was that whole soul-to-soul thing between Zayvion and me. When we touched, I could sense him. I concentrated on that, felt what he was doing.

Sweet hells, the man put the multi in multitasking.

He held himself in a very disciplined, meditative frame of mind. He had sort of opened himself up, a lot like how I breathe deeply to let magic move through me.

But instead of just making space for magic inside him, he had made a channel.

He had drawn a glyph, mentally. The glyph of Grounding wrapped through him like cold steel cables. He concentrated on feeding magic into it. I'd never seen this spell worked on a purely mental level.

Probably because I'd never seen any spell worked on a purely mental level.

Zayvion Jones kicked magical ass. I wondered if even my father, who was one of the most powerful magic users I'd ever known, was as strong as Zay.

"Wow," I breathed.

That got a small smile out of him. His eyes squinted, laugh lines edging the corners.

"Thank you. Can you see how it's channeled?"

"Other than magnificently?"

We stopped at a red light. He looked over at me. "Other than that, yes."

I stared into his eyes, at the gold burning hot and deep there. All that did was make me want to touch him, kiss him, pour so much magic into him he'd be begging me for mercy.

Magic rolled in me, deep in my stomach, and I worked hard not to moan with the need to have him.

"You are not winning," he noted.

"No kidding," I gasped. Right. The idea here was to not give in to magic. Or, apparently, my need for Zay.

I pressed my fingers against my eyes. My right fingers were hot, and my left were cold, positive and negative from the magic pouring through me. I took a second to breathe in again and clear my mind.

When I looked again at Zayvion, he was paying attention to the road, taking us across the bridge, calm, unconcerned. And he was Grounding like mad on the inside.

All I had to do was find a way to slow magic pouring into me. That meant a glyph that would track back and forth at the beginning, loop and loop so that magic had a long way to travel before it could add to the pool I already carried. I could do that.

I thought.

"Victor said I could use any of the spells that slow magic, right?"

"Yes."

"Okay." I didn't care how good Zayvion was—I was absolutely certain I could not just mentally draw a glyph and expect it would work. I used my right hand and traced a liquid, curvy glyph for Linger in front of me. These kinds of spells were used inside stores, restaurants, and salons. They gave off a comfortable, relaxed feeling. If they were particularly well drawn, they made shoulders drop, smiles come out, and people spend way more money and time in their vicinity.

I pinched the glyph between thumbs and two fingers of both my right and left hands. Instead of pouring magic into it, I was going to push the spell into me, so the magic in me would be forced to follow it.

I had no frickin' clue how to do that.

"Uh," I started.

"You can do it."

"A little help?"

"I'm watching."

"I wanted help, not an audience."

He just gave me a look.

Okay, fine. I recited my go-to mantra, the "Miss Mary Mack, Mack, Mack" jingle, to clear my mind. Then I pulled the glyph into me, toward my chest, concentrating on it wrapping around the flow of magic, the speed of magic, the pressure of magic.

My heart stuttered. Whoa. Not good. I concentrated harder on the spell. *Magic, not heart. Find the magic. Just the magic.* I released the spell. It sank like a rock toward my feet, then settled beneath my feet and pressed against my arches and heels. It rested there like a layer of sand

and stone and soil, soaking up the magic, filtering it, and giving it a place to stretch out before it trickled up into me at a much slower pace.

My head cleared. I broke out in a sweat.

"Holy crap. Good?" I asked Zay.

He nodded. "Not how I would have done it, but effective. So yes. Good. You have control?"

Oh, right. That was the other half of this deal. I cleared my mind again, calmed my thoughts, and pressed back on the magic rolling within me. Magic fluttered, pressed once again, tempting me to use it, to fall to its siren call.

Nope. La, la, la. Not listening.

Magic quieted.

"Very nice," Zayvion murmured. "I'm impressed." He drew his fingers slowly up my thigh, then away, leaving the lingering cool warmth of mint and his touch behind.

"Are you still dizzy?" he asked.

"No. I feel pretty good."

Oh, screw it. I felt powerful. Proud. That had been a fine little piece of magic using I'd just done. Yes, I'd probably pay for it with a walloping headache, but right now, I didn't care. "I'd feel even better with a hell-of-a-job kiss."

"So that's how it's going to be? One elementary-level spell and you get naked?"

"First, that was not elementary level. High school at the very least. Second, tell me you don't like the idea of me being naked."

"How about I tell you I don't like the idea of driving off the road. Which means your clothes stay on you." He stopped at a light, then added, "For now."

"Chicken."

He grinned. Zay had a good profile, a strong, wide nose, high cheekbones, and a slant to his eyes that I thought was incredibly sexy, and that spoke to his mixed heritage. Under that ratty coat and jeans was a very fine, very fit body.

But he was also a man full of secrets. Even though we'd been officially dating for a couple months now, I still hadn't gotten much about his past out of him.

I didn't even know where he'd grown up.

"Did you do time with Shame in juvie?" I asked.

"That's what you were thinking about when magic was trying to burn you up?"

"No, it's what I'm thinking about now."

"Shame?"

"Your past."

"Hmm."

We were on the other side of the bridge and making our way southeast along the Washington side of the Columbia River. The sun pushed through cumulus clouds on their way to the Cascade Range, where rain would cover the mountains in snow and keep the skiers happy.

"Well?"

"I never got in trouble with the law when I was young."

"So why was Detective Payne staring at you?"

He glanced over at me, then back out at the road.

He drove for a while, silent. I'd learned to give him his space. I didn't know if it was life or if it was just second nature to him, but he was the most private person I'd ever met. I didn't even know if he had a middle name.

"She helped me out once."

I waited. I didn't want to, but I did it. Go, me.

"I was twelve. Fostered to a family that . . ." He closed his mouth, inhaled through his nose. "She caught me digging in Dumpsters for food. Made me give her my foster parents' names and address. Things got better after that."

"Is she part of the Authority?"

"No." He paused again. "The past is the past, Allie," he said. "I'd rather not go over it."

I just shook my head, but didn't push him. Strange. There was so much of my past that I'd lost—memories magic had taken away from me—moments I wished I could have back. It was odd to hear someone choose not to remember. Maybe I'd been that way once too. It was hard to say. Magic had done a lot of damage to my life. Maybe it had done a lot of repair to Zayvion's.

We made it to Maeve's and pulled into the gravel parking lot between the inn and the scrap-metal collection site beside it. Both buildings were tucked off the main road, and close enough to the Columbia that I could smell the algae and green off the river as I stepped out of the car.

The inn used to be an old train-station boardinghouse and restaurant. The track didn't run past here anymore, but the building remained much as it was when it had been built. Fresh white paint, and glittering rows of uniform windows, gave the Feile San Fhomher a welcoming, homey feel.

Zay stood on the other side of the car, silent. I knew why. Something was wrong here.

There was an immense sense of emptiness, as if something huge, solid, and familiar had been removed.

It took me a second; then I finally placed what was missing: the well. I couldn't even catch a scent of the magic I knew roiled beneath the ground.

"Do you not feel that?" I asked.

Zayvion nodded, then walked silently across the gravel to me. He looked calm, but when I touched his wrist, I could feel the heightened awareness of his senses. He was calm. He was also ready for a fight.

I took a second to check our surroundings. The parking lot was about half full and the rush of cars over the bridge and freeway hummed in the distance. The river on the other side of a thin line of trees gave off that clean, rich green scent, and far off, I heard either a boat horn or a factory whistle.

It seemed like a normal evening.

And it most certainly was not.

"The well," I said, somewhat unnecessarily.

He placed one hand on the side of my face, the other on my hip, and pulled me close. I pressed against him, wrapped one arm around his back, the other up around his neck.

His mind was obviously not on the well. Neither was mine.

He tipped my face up, and bent to me. His lips were soft, catching at my lower lip, pressing, then opening, inviting. His tongue dipped sweetly at the corner of my mouth, then drew into the heat of my mouth. Electric tingles warmed me, and made my toes curl. I pressed tighter against him and kissed him back, taking my time, sharing a long, lingering kiss that made me want more.

He finally pulled away, reluctant, then rested his lips against my ear. "Hell of a job," he murmured.

I leaned into him, my cheek against his chest, and smiled. I loved a man with good follow-up.

We pulled apart. Holding hands, we crossed the parking lot and walked up the steps to the covered porch that wrapped the building. Zay pulled the door open and we stepped inside.

The delicious sweet, buttery smell of pies baking, and something savory, maybe sausage, greeted us. Even though I'd just had lunch, my mouth watered, and that had nothing to do with magic. Maeve knew how to cook.

Light poured down from the high-vaulted ceilings, making the large dining room feel even bigger than it was. The tables to the left were filled with the early dinner crowd. I knew the arched doorway beyond them led to private rooms, and the well-warded study where Maeve tutored me.

Upstairs were bedrooms, and down in the basement, a grand ballroom with the well pulsing just beneath its marble floors.

Here on the main floor, the girls behind the lunch counter to the right of the room were brewing coffee and plating pies.

"Coffee?" Zayvion asked.

"Sure." I didn't know if we had time, but I wasn't one to go into any situation undercaffeinated.

He strolled off toward the lunch counter and I unzipped my hoodie, scanning the room for Shame or Maeve.

Maeve strode through the arched door to the left. Her red hair was pulled up in a loose bun, ringlets touched with gray falling around her face. She wore a dark green blouse, a tan skirt, and a pair of riding boots, all of which gave her the look of a woman who knew how to use a whip. Which, coincidentally, she did.

She carried a stack of menus in her arms, and gave me a smile and a nod as she walked my way.

"Allie. It's good to see you. Tea?"

"Coffee, thanks. Zay's getting it. How are you?"

"Busy. Beautiful weather, today. Walk with me a minute?"

"Sure." I matched her stride and crossed the room to the lunch counter, where she handed the menus to one of the girls there.

"I have a job you might be interested in," she said. "Hello, Zayvion."

"Mrs. Flynn." He handed me a cup of coffee. No, more than coffee. A latte, which the girls had poured to leave the image of a four-leaf clover in the foam.

Very nice.

"Why don't you come along, Zayvion?"

It wasn't really a request. We both knew that. Still, to any outsider, it sounded like chitchat between her son's best friend and his girlfriend, who Hounded for a living.

We strolled along and Maeve took the time to say hello to a few people at tables and ask them if they were enjoying their meals. I knew those people weren't a part of the Authority. Despite being involved with supersecret magic users, Maeve was also a successful restaurateur.

She led us through the arched doorway, down the hallway a bit, and into the first sitting room. It was decorated in velvets, wood, and brass, love seats and chairs huddled to make comfortable conversation nooks, heavy curtains on the windows giving the room a deep sense of privacy.

She held the door open as we walked through, and then locked it behind us. With one quick wave of her hand, she cast a ward and activated the Mute spell worked into the wallpaper.

"Thank you both for coming." She gestured to the seats, and we sat. "Shamus did talk to you?"

"He didn't tell us much," I said. "There's a storm coming, Sedra has called other people from Seattle, and there's something wrong with the wells."

She brushed a tendril of hair back up toward the bun, even though it just fell back down to her face. "There will be a meeting tonight among the members of the Authority. To exchange information. To plan for the storm."

Zay, lounging on a love seat, took a drink of his coffee. I could feel every muscle in his body ratchet tighter and tighter as Maeve spoke.

She walked over to an empty chair and sat. She looked tired. Worried.

"The storm is still a day or two off. At least we think so."

I opened my mouth and she held up one finger to tell me to shut up. I didn't know what it was with her and her fingers. She had that motherly no-bullshit way of using her hands as a second communication device and I always fell for it.

I drank my coffee and made a note to ignore her fingers.

"We can't track them like weather fronts," she said. "Wild storms are sorely underresearched. One theory is that wild-magic storms are a combination of how the magic in the earth is being accessed and released into the world, and how magic, all disciplines, dark and light, is being used. When things swing too far out of neutral, magic can rise and gather into a storm front—and ride upon a real weather front.

"The other theory is that the magic is wild to begin with, a mix of dark and light that causes nothing but chaos and destruction when it is used.

"You can imagine it has been difficult to test either theory on a large scale in secret. In any case, we do believe a wild storm is coming our way."

"The gate Mikhail opened?" Zay asked quietly.

"That could be it. There are more things happening in the world that could have accumulated or triggered to set it off."

"Wait," I said. "So magic is a ticking time bomb and as soon as someone shakes the nitrogen a little too hard, or mixes in the wrong elements, we get explosions?"

She frowned. "No. It's a combination of factors. Magic on its own is a part of the natural world. No more destructive than wind, rain, and fire."

Which was like saying no more destructive than hurricane, flood, and inferno. Spiffy.

"We'll go over how to handle the storm at the meeting tonight," she continued. "I want you both there. And Zayvion, if you see Shame, make sure he comes."

Zay nodded. "I'll get him there."

She brushed her hair back again. "Now, what I most needed to talk to you about, Allie, is the well. I want you to look at it. To tell me what you see in the magic there."

"You want me to Hound the well? Really? For illegal magic use? You people don't even recognize the law on magic use, so I'm sure you're not using it illegally."

She gave me a steely gaze and I wiped the innocent look off my face.

Note to self. Do not be a wiseass when your Blood magic teacher is stressed-out.

"Right. I can Hound the well," I said. "Not a problem."

"Zayvion, I'd like you to be there too, please," she said.

He rubbed his palms across his jeans and stood.

I finished off my coffee and left the empty cup on the table.

Maeve led us down a long hallway to a set of stairs that jagged down and down.

I'd been in the lower level of the inn just once before. When I'd had to stand in front of members of the Authority and fight for my life. I hadn't expected to get out of it with my memories or magic intact.

I wanted to take Zay's hand and hold on like a little girl as we descended the stairs, but I refused to. There was nothing down here I couldn't handle on my own. I'd already proved that.

The last flight of stairs spilled out into a room that looked like it should be the receiving room of a castle, a ballroom, a grand theater for a grand ceremony, instead of the basement of a railroad boardinghouse.

The floor was tiled with marble that washed from the purest white through grays, then sank into the deepest black. The ceiling rose up two stories, huge pillars spreading out at the ceiling into wings that arched up to meet in the center. Glyphs shaped and carved the pillars, the arch of wings, the ceiling, and the walls. Magic drawn in lead, glass, iron—a powerful network of holding spells, warding spells, most I still didn't know—surrounded the room and the well that pulsed like the earth's heart beneath the marble floor, deep underground.

There was one thing out of place since I'd last been here. A cage stood in one corner of the room. Built of steel, four-sided, it looked mobile and was placed over the purest white marble tiles.

In that cage was a beast of a man, a nightmare creature caught between life and death. Greyson.

Chills rolled up my spine and I could not take my eyes off the cage, nor the man who was still too much beast within it. Covered by a blanket, he hunched in the corner of the cage, his too-long arms crossed over bent knees, his mouth resting against his forearms so that only his eyes, animal yellow, glowed from within the shadow of the blanket.

I smelled his magic, twisted, dark, burnt-blackberry stench, mixed with the old wax and polish perfume of wood that had been cleaned for centuries. And I smelled blood.

Greyson had a good nose too. He turned his head, just enough to show a flash of fang digging into his arm and leaving a trickle of blood behind.

Something in my head flickered, rattled, and scratched behind my eyes.

I knew the feel of that. Even though I hadn't felt it for two months. It was my dad. Then my father's voice, clear as if he were standing next to Greyson's cage instead of in my head, whispered, *Come to me.*

Chapter Three

A hand landed on my left shoulder.
I yelled, pivoted, and swung.

"Holy shit!" a voice said.

My fist whiffed through empty air. That was because Shamus Flynn was fast. He ducked and skidded down two steps, neatly avoiding a broken nose.

He laughed. "You have got to lay off the coffee, Beckstrom. You're all twitchy and whatnot."

"I thought . . ." I was breathing hard. Felt a little sick too. Didn't know if it was from the overwhelming smells, the half-beast killer guy staring at me, my dad's voice seeming to come from the half-beast killer guy, or the feeling of my dead dad scraping at the backs of my eyes again.

Why choose? It was all of the above.

Greyson, back when he was just a man, had been one of my father's murderers. I'd seen that memory from sharing my head with my dad. And since Greyson had one of dad's experimental disks stuck in his throat, it was a pretty easy leap to guess that someone had stuck it in his neck and used it to keep him in his current state of half man, half beast. The disks could hold magic, and somehow the disk in Greyson held both dark and light magic, and whatever spell worked into it made him the half beast.

My guess was that Dr. Frank Gordon had done it to

him, probably around the same time he'd dug up my dad's grave and tried to possess my dad's spirit to open up a gateway to death and draw dark magic into the world. Things hadn't gone the way Dr. Frank Gordon had wanted them to go. Namely, instead of doing what Frank wanted, my dad had possessed me.

Then Greyson had hunted me. Well, not me. He wanted my dad's spirit. I didn't know why. Maybe revenge—that seemed like the easiest answer. What I did know was that letting Greyson get his hands on my dad's spirit, and maybe my dad's knowledge of magic, fell squarely in the middle of my Bad Things list.

And to make it all worse, Greyson used to be Chase's boyfriend, maybe even her Soul Complement. She had dumped Zayvion to be with Greyson before Greyson had gotten so screwed up.

I closed my eyes, trying to regain my calm. I was okay; everything was okay. The cage would hold Greyson. Why did they have him caged?

Why was Dad talking from way over there? My dad wasn't in Greyson. He was in me. Maybe not the best thing, but certainly better than the other options.

"Allison," Maeve said. "Come down the stairs." She didn't put Influence behind it, didn't even make it sound like a command. Just calm, gentle, Motherly.

If I remembered correctly, I wasn't listening to her motherly commands.

I opened my eyes. Zayvion, Shame, and Maeve all stood on the bottom step, looking up at me like I was about to burst into flames.

"Sorry," I said. "I just. It's just." I took a step. My knees went wet-noodle and I had to hold the rail to keep from falling. What the hell was wrong with me?

I gritted my teeth and pulled my shoulders back. I could do this. I could walk down these stairs without falling. Did it too. Stood in front of Maeve, breathing a little too hard, sweating a little too much.

She put one finger under my chin and looked up into my eyes.

The good thing? One look from her and Dad stopped scraping at the backs of my eyes.

The bad thing? Greyson growled. Not quite a howl. It was more of a low moan-yell. The hairs on my arms pricked up, and goose bumps tightened my skin.

Allison, I heard my father whisper. Yes, from outside my head. Again.

"I don't think ..." My breath gave out, so I tried again. "I don't think you need to look," I managed. "He's there. And in Greyson. I think he's in Greyson too."

Maeve's eyes flicked back and forth, probably seeing more inside me than I really wanted her to.

Greyson howled as Maeve looked deeper in my mind for my dad. He wanted the rest of my dad's spirit in me. The cage shook. I hoped the steel bars could hold him. I hoped the magic in this room could hold him.

"We have been through Greyson's mind," Maeve said. "Jingo Jingo has been through his mind and has seen nothing, no trace of your father in him."

Yeah, well, Jingo Jingo had been through my mind and said my father wasn't there either. I'd already told her that a dozen times. She never believed me.

"You know what I think about Jingo Jingo's ability to sense my father." It came out calm. Reasonable. Strong.

Go, me.

"I do. Jingo Jingo is an expert at sensing the dead. You are not."

"Jingo Jingo isn't the one who's possessed."

We stared at each other for a couple seconds.

"He could be wrong," I pressed.

Maeve was a woman made of stubborn. So was I.

"Can you feel the well?" she asked, suddenly switching subjects.

I held my breath, trying to keep from yelling. The well was the least of our problems. The caged killer Necromorph half-beast dude over there, who had a part of my father in his head that no one else could see, and a desire to drag the rest of dear ol' dad out of me even if it meant killing me, was something I thought we should all be a little worried about. "Why?" I asked.

"Just answer me." She was not amused. Not playing games. Not happy.

Yeah, well, that made two of us.

I leaned back on one foot and glanced at Zayvion. He watched me, fists clenched at his sides belying that oh-so-Zen mask. He'd been helping me keep my dad blocked in my mind. Taught me a few spells that seemed to be working to keep Dad quiet. Until now.

I raised one eyebrow, to let him know I could handle it.

Shame, however, was pacing across the room away from us, like a man walks on rice paper. His head was tilted down at an odd angle, as if he were listening to his footsteps. His hands were lifted slightly above his waist, fingers spread. He was trying to hear something, sense something. Something beneath the floor.

He was listening for magic.

I realized I couldn't feel it like I had before. The deep strumming heat of it beneath the room, beneath the tiles. Outside the inn, the well was usually no more than a faint presence, but down here, the well radiated power.

Or at least it had the day I'd taken my test. And now the well felt—not empty, but certainly less strong, less radiating, less full.

"It's different," I said.

Shame paused over tiles that were gray going on black. He knelt, stuck his fingertips against the marble. Took a deep breath, let it out, then rocked back on his heels. "Damn."

He patted the pocket of his jacket, looking for cigarettes, found them, tapped one out.

"Don't smoke in here," Maeve said. Then to me, "How is it different?"

I glanced at Zay. He had moved silently to stand next to Greyson's cage. Maybe he didn't want to influence me. Maybe he wanted to pound Greyson.

He wasn't the only one.

"You want me to Hound the room?"

"First I want you to tell me what you feel. What you sense."

I'd learned that when Maeve asked me to do something in her teacher voice, she wasn't really asking. Normally, it bothered me and I gave her lip for it.

But there was something very wrong about the well and the magic here. Something that made me want to go home to my apartment, home to my stone gargoyle, and stay as far away from the Authority and magic as I could.

Like ducking for cover before a storm hit.

Who was I kidding? Even if I went home, I couldn't get away from magic. It flowed under the entire city, through the conduits and Gothic glyphed cage work that wrapped every building. And it flowed through me.

I tucked my hair behind my ear, my hand trembling. I walked across the room until I stood in the center of it, and stopped just short of where Shame knelt.

The same down-the-throat horror that I usually got from enclosed spaces skittered through my brain and set fire to my nerves. My heart was pounding too hard. I wanted to turn back. I wanted very much not to do this.

Shame watched me from his position on the floor. He placed one hand on the tiles, palm flat. I hoped he wasn't planning to Proxy or Ground me. I was shaky. I wasn't sure how magic was going to respond to my cast, or if it would respond at all.

I stopped, spread my feet so I had a chance of staying on them if things got bad. I resisted looking behind me to see what Maeve, Zayvion, and Greyson were doing. Instead, I calmed my mind: *Miss Mary Mack, Mack, Mack . . .*

I licked my lips. Instead of tracing a glyph in the air, I tipped my head up to the angel-wing ceiling, dropped my hands at my sides, fingers wide and open, and drew the glyph for Seek at my side. I reached out with my senses, using a little magic from inside me to seek. I sent my mental fingers deep, deep into the earth beneath me.

The well was not there. I frowned, reached deeper, sent my magic farther. Finally felt the well, a glow of magic, a heat, yet so far away. The magic was there, still pooling, still flowing, but it was like an ocean at low tide. Or like someone had punched a hole in the well, and magic was draining away. I didn't feel it filling any other space, didn't feel it creating new channels, new rivers. Didn't feel it pouring out through the iron and glass conduits that channeled the magic that flowed freely beyond the well.

Something, or someone, was draining an enormous amount of magic out of the well.

Holy shit.

Magic inside of me went cold and sticky. I wanted to puke. Okay. That was enough of trying to touch the well. I let go of the small Seek spell and tipped my head back down.

Shame watched me with a grin on his face. *Nice*, he mouthed.

I took a couple breaths, maintaining eye contact with him until I was confident my panic didn't show. How could he be so calm? Maybe the well emptied out like this all the time. Maybe I was overreacting.

I turned back to Maeve and Zayvion. "Do you really want to talk about this here?"

Maeve frowned. "Why?"

"Greyson."

"He is contained. Controlled. He cannot hear us. Or see us."

I glanced over her shoulder. Greyson glared at me from amid the shadows of his cage.

I was pretty sure he saw me.

"Isn't there a better place to keep him?"

Maeve folded her arms over her chest. "This is the safest place for him exactly because he is near the well."

I did not believe her. This was a bad idea. A really bad idea. People who use magic to murder should not be anywhere near magic, much less a well of it. How did she not get that?

"What did you feel?" she asked.

Fine. I'd do it her way. But I wasn't happy about it.

"Something is draining the well."

I didn't think Maeve could get any paler. The freckles on her cheeks suddenly seemed darker, and a greenish hue lined her lips.

"The storm?" Zay asked.

"It must be," she said. "Allie, you hold magic inside your body. Can you sense anything unusual about it within you?"

Other than that it was cold, sticky, and giving me the creeps? "It's usually warm, or hot. It feels cold. Kind of sticky."

Shame snorted.

I made a mental note: smack him when his mom wasn't looking.

"Has it ever felt that way before?" she asked.

"That I can remember? No."

"Do you feel magic being drained out of you?"

I took a second to concentrate on the magic inside me again. It felt strong right now, just . . . wrong. "No. It's still there."

"That's good news." She didn't smile. "Shame, come stand with us," she continued as if this were class. "Allie, I'd like you to Hound the room, to see if there are any unusual spells here."

She was such a kidder. Every spell, ward, and glyph worked into this room was unusual. Still, I knew what she meant. She wanted me to look for predatory spells,

Drains, Siphons, anything else that might be used to screw up the well.

It might help if I knew how the well worked, or how the spells and wards and glyphs normally reacted to being so near it. Nothing like throwing the new girl into the deep end of the magic pool and telling her to dive for pearls.

Good thing my lack of knowledge had never stopped me from doing stupid things before.

I calmed my mind, used my little jingle again, and chose which price I would pay to use magic. My standard pain lately had been muscle aches. Don't get me wrong: it still hurt to use magic, but since I was working out and hurting anyway, and had the funds to get a massage and soak in the steam room or hot tub every once in a while, I figured muscle aches made the most sense.

I set the Disbursement for muscle aches, then drew the glyphs for Sight, Hearing, Smell, Taste.

Spells keyed to life beneath my vision. Pale fire in rainbow metallics crawled up the columns, across the walls. Shadow glyphs, glowing in deeper tones than those on the walls and ceiling, burned like dark ghosts shifting beneath the marble tiles.

Wow. It wasn't just glyphs worked into the room. The entire room, including the winged arches, was a glyph, carved and constructed to carry magic, to channel it, to hold it, keep it, hide it, tap it.

The art, the vision, the intimate knowledge of architecture and how spells blended, contrasted, strengthened, and weakened, were stunning. I didn't know who had created this room, but whoever they were, they were brilliant. Genius.

"Allie?"

It was Maeve. I licked my lips and realized I'd been standing there and staring, transfixed by the beauty and power of the room, instead of Hounding.

Embarrassed much?

I paced to the wall opposite the stairway, and made my way along the perimeter of the room. I dragged my fingertips across the wall as I went. The soft, ancient wood, carved and placed here long before this was a train station, long before this was even a building, thrummed beneath my touch. Magic darkened and rippled away from me, like water beneath a soft wind.

The glyphs shifted from one discipline to another as I made my way around the room. Faith, Death, Blood, Life. Nothing seemed strained, strange, or out of place. All magics flowed and merged in harmony I'd never seen before. All magic working together as one.

If something here was draining the well, I didn't think it was in this room.

I stopped next to Zayvion, in front of Greyson's cage. I had every intention to Hound that cage. I wanted to know that it could really hold him. The binding, holding, and ward spells were strong, but there was a hint of something, a darkness beneath them, that worried me.

I wondered if the spells were being drained like the well. I reached out to touch the cage. The spells were strong. Whole.

Greyson growled, animal gaze fixed on my face.

He saw me. Or my dad in me. I was sure of it. And I was sure Greyson was not blind to what was going on in the room.

"You are mine." His voice was little more than shadow scraping skin, but I felt it to my bones.

"Like hell," I whispered. I pulled my hand away and I released the magic, letting my senses snap back into more normal ranges. I walked away from the cage, away from the murderer in the cage, even though doing so made me want to run. Got three steps before I found Zayvion stood so near me, I almost ran into him.

"Not good," I said quietly.

He frowned, then brushed his fingertips down my

cheek, tracing the whorls of magic and wiping away the sweat.

Sweet hells. Hounding the room hadn't been as easy as I thought. I was exhausted. I blinked, my eyes staying closed a little too long, and realized if I blinked again, I'd be asleep.

Zay's hand ran over my right arm, a warmth, a comfort. He drew me farther from the cage, and a little bit of his strength flowed through our connection and into me. I felt more awake.

Still, I wanted to take his hand and tell him we had to leave now. Before the cold, sticky flow of magic inside me got worse. Before Greyson got better at seeing me. Before that cage fell apart. Before the storm hit.

But I did not do that.

He stepped away from me, and I did from him too. We had business to take care of. Maybe even a city to save.

Like superheroes.

Right.

"I don't see anything out of place," I told Maeve. "But I've never Hounded the room under normal circumstances. If you were bringing me in to see if someone had cast a spell to purposely change the flow of magic in the well, I didn't see anything that could accomplish that."

She visibly exhaled. Oh, she had been very, very worried about what I would find. And that worried me. If she thought it was that likely someone would come in here and mess up the well, I was more than a little terrified at their security measures.

"It's a start. Thank you." She strode across the room to the staircase, and Zay and I followed.

"Did you think someone broke in?" I asked.

"No, but not all members of the Authority have the same agendas. There is always the chance someone has played their hand."

Why can't the secret, powerful magic users all just get along?

"The meeting is at ten o'clock," she said. "Upstairs. I want all three of you there."

Shame scoffed.

"Yes, even you, Shamus Flynn. You'll not shirk your duty this time."

This time? That sounded interesting.

Still crouched in the center of the room, Shame straightened, then strolled toward the stairs. He wasn't looking at his mom, or at us. His eyes were on Greyson. And Greyson's eyes were still on me.

Shame frowned, tipped his head to get a better angle on Greyson's gaze. Followed it. Right to my eyes. Raised his eyebrows when he found Greyson's gaze ended at me.

Yeah, I didn't like it either. And the less time I was in Greyson's eyesight, the better. I turned and walked up the stairs.

Weird, weird, weird.

Only my tennis shoes and Maeve's boots made noise. Zay was Zay. Silent. Brooding. When he carried himself like that, he was a force, a darkness, a power.

I was glad he was on our side.

Once at the top, Maeve called down to Shame. "Come up, now. Jingo Jingo will be by soon to look in on Greyson. I don't want him to find you poking at that cage."

More stairs, and some doors; then we started down the hall.

I rubbed at my arms, trying to banish the image of Jingo Jingo with Greyson.

"Why is Jingo coming by?" It was none of my business, and I really should learn to shut my big mouth and let the senior members of the Authority deal with the big problems. Like the storm. Like the well. Like Greyson.

"He has been working with Greyson. Trying to diagnose exactly how Frank Gordon implanted the disk.

Trying to see if there is any mercy in breaking the spells worked into him."

"You mean trying to turn him back into a man?" I asked.

Maeve gave me a look that said more than words ever could. "He is trying to find a merciful answer to the question of him," she said.

Shame clunked up behind us. For a man who had just been moving silently across the marble floor like it was made of thin glass, he sure could make a lot of noise.

"Chase been by?" he asked.

Maeve frowned. "I haven't seen her in a few days."

"Huh," he said, then, "Anyone else thirsty? All that hard work watching Allie Hound deserves a beer, don't you think?" He moved past his mom, and exchanged a short glance with Zayvion.

I didn't think the two of them could actually hear what the other was thinking, but I was positive they had a secret code. Zay had even hinted as much, saying he always knew when Shame was up to trouble.

And that look had been more than just a look.

"Ten o'clock, Shamus," Maeve called after him.

"I heard you the first time, didn't I?"

Maeve tapped one fingertip against her lips, and watched him go. "He knows something," she decided. "Is up to something. Zayvion, you'll watch that he doesn't stir too much trouble, won't you? I do not need any more problems right now."

"I'll do what I can," he said mildly.

"When that son of mine gets a wild idea in his head, it never ends well."

She sounded angry, but her body language said more. It said she was worried. Worried she was about to lose something precious to her. Maybe her son.

"He'll be here tonight," Zay said. "Sober. He knows this isn't a game." I wondered how many times he'd told her that over the years.

"Terric will be here," she added more quietly.

"He knows."

Maeve brushed her hair back again. "I thought as much." She shook her head. "Well. What will be will be. I'll see you both this evening." She strolled off, her bootheels clacking across the old wooden floors.

The moth-wing flutter scraped at the backs of my eyes, pressing harder, insistent. It made me think of Greyson, of him watching me, wanting me and my dad in me. I swallowed and tasted wintergreen and leather— my dad's scents. Great.

I suddenly really wanted fresh air, a shower, hells, to be anywhere but here right now.

My creep-out quota for the day was officially maxed.

"I need air." I strode past Zay, not waiting to see if he followed. It wasn't exactly tactful, but he'd watched me fight my claustrophobia before. Stayed out of my way. Boy had smarts.

Maeve had turned the opposite way down the hall, so she wasn't in my flight path either. I took the first opening I could and walked right out into the main dining area again.

The noise was up, every table filled. The smell of food and drinks and people—perfume and soap and cigarettes—closed in on me.

Out more. I needed much more out more.

I did not run, because I am composed even in full-throttle panic mode. But I made quick work of that room—long legs had their use—and straight-armed that door open.

The evening wind hit like a sharp slap to the face, and I inhaled a huge lungful of cold, misty air.

I didn't stop at the porch. There was too much roof on the porch, too many railings around the porch, too much building behind the porch. I clattered down the stairs, and jogged across the gravel, looking for out, for space, for air.

"Afraid of the dark?" a voice asked from one side of me.

Okay, yes, I was freaking out from claustrophobia. And yes, I was already a little freaked-out over the whole cold-magic weirdness and empty well. Add to that Greyson staring at me out of his magic-blocked and warded cage, and my dad, or maybe only half of him, shuffling around in my head—or even better, him spending time-shared brain space with Greyson—and what I really needed was just a few seconds of normal.

Instead, I got Chase.

"Chase," I said, relatively calmly too, considering. "Did you hear about the meeting tonight?"

Zayvion's ex-girlfriend was nearly my height. If I had seen her walking down the street, I'd think she was a model, not a Closer. Her pale skin was almost luminescent in the low light, and her eyes belonged to a cat, framed by the blunt wedge of dark brown bangs. I'd never seen her use makeup, not that she needed it. I'd never seen her dress in anything other than jeans, T-shirt, and flannel.

Tonight was no different.

"I heard about it." She took a step toward me, her hands very obviously held with fingers spread, as if she was looking for a spell to grab hold of.

A sound behind me made her look up. She bared her teeth in a semblance of a smile. And not a very pretty one.

"Hello, Zayvion. Still babysitting all the troubled children for Mommy Maeve?"

"I do what I can," he said. Unconcerned. Zen. "Are you done running away?"

"Running away from what?"

"Greyson."

Chase held very still. Something moved across her eyes, a shadow, sorrow, pain. Maybe fear. Maybe hope.

"I've never run from him," she said. Flat. Emotionless. What she didn't say, what none of us was saying, was she still loved him. And she blamed me and my father for changing him into a monster. I was pretty sure she'd do anything to get him back, to see him be a man again.

I know I would feel that way if it were Zay in that cage.

"They wouldn't let me see him," she said. "Not without Jingo Jingo being there."

Zayvion crossed his arms over his chest and strolled closer, his footsteps silent across the wet, noisy gravel. "You're going to listen to them, aren't you?"

"Be a good girl and do as I'm told?" She raised one eyebrow. "Have I ever done anything else?" It was a challenge.

Zayvion didn't reach out for her, but his voice was softer. "It will work out, Chase. We'll find a way to help him. Trust that."

That tone got through. She swallowed and looked off over his shoulder. "Trust. Just like that."

"You've been doing it for years. Don't stop now."

I could see how much it cost her to look back at him. Could see the emotions she was fighting back. Looked a lot like rage and grief. "No, that's what you've been doing. Trusting. Trusting it will all work out. No matter how blind or stupid that makes you."

"Trust isn't a weakness," Zay said.

"So says the man who begged for the chance to be the hero, the keeper of the gates, user of all magic, light and dark, no matter how much it destroys him. Do you get off on taking the fall, Jones, or are you just too stupid to know that's what they're using you for?"

"Are you done?" he asked, a hint of fire rising behind that ice.

She glared at him.

He ignored her. "You joined this fight for a reason. You joined this fight to make the world better for the people you cared about. Not for me, not for them, but for who you love. Who do you love, Chase? Other than yourself?"

"Fuck you."

She took a step, but he moved, silent and swift, to stand in front of her. They weren't touching, weren't drawing on magic. Yet.

"That's over. Remember?" he said. "You ended it. Ended us. For him. For Greyson. And now you're going to have to risk a little trust to save him. I think that's a small price to pay, not even a price at all. Or maybe you're just looking for an easy way out again."

"You have no right—," she said through clenched teeth.

"Yes, I do. Don't turn your back on him. Don't turn your back on the Authority. Don't choose that ending."

And that threat, that anyone in the Authority, even a Closer, could be Closed, got through too.

She unclenched her fists and shook her bangs out of her eyes. "I'd do anything to have him back," she yelled. She looked down, swallowed a couple times, as if trying to get the rage down. Then she looked back up at him. "I don't turn my back on anything I love." She looked at me, then back at him. "But you wouldn't understand that, would you, Jones?"

She strode off toward the inn, leaving Zayvion and me alone in the rain.

Chapter Four

I touched Zay's arm and jerked back as if I'd been burned. The anger seething under the surface of his calm was rivaled only by the pain he felt for Chase. I'd always assumed their breakup had been bad, but now I knew it.

There are moments, emotions, that we really don't want to share with other people. Things we shouldn't have to share unless we want to. Unless we choose to. This was one of those moments. I shoved my hand in my pocket and tried to pretend I didn't know how he really felt.

"Are you okay?" I asked. "Do you need to go talk to someone?" *Punch someone*, I added silently.

Zay licked the rain off his lips and tipped his head down so that he stared at the gravel. He inhaled, slowly, then exhaled, pushing his shoulders down from the rod-straight fighting angle, his hands relaxing out of the stiff, magic-ready spread.

Caught in the overhead lighting, he was a study of neon blue and black shadows. The rain on his ski cap glittered like tiny blue stars, and rain trickled a slick line from his temple, across the arc of his cheek, then down to the stubble along his jaw. I waited.

Finally, he seemed to notice the rain, the night, and me. "I'd be better out of the wet," he said.

He headed for the car and so did I. I wanted out of the wet too. Exhaustion was sucking my reserves. I'd spent a couple hours sparring, then come over here to Hound the well. Even though I'd had a late lunch, and a good latte, I was hankering for a hot, strong cup of coffee.

"Home?" Zay asked.

"Home." Because home is where the coffeepot is.

He started the car and I thought about sleeping on the way to my apartment, but every time I closed my eyes, I saw Greyson's gaze and remembered my father pushing around in my mind.

"Greyson saw me in there," I said. "I think he might have seen Dad in me."

"I know."

"You want to tell me why no one else believes me? Why don't they believe Dad is in me and maybe in Greyson too?"

"Jingo Jingo is the expert. The Authority trusts him on these kinds of things."

"You don't believe him."

"I should. I can't think of why he would lie about it."

"So you don't believe me?"

"I do believe you. I just don't know why Jingo Jingo would lie."

Because he's a freak? I thought. Then, out loud, "Maybe he thinks he has a good reason. Some kind of behind-the-scenes mumbo-jumbo politicking or something."

Zayvion exhaled. "That could be." We stopped at a light. "Ever since just before your father's death, tensions in the Authority have been building. Each discipline seems to think they have a corner on how magic should be used. Each person believes their view correct."

He glanced over his shoulder and merged into the next lane. "The heads of the Authority—all the leaders, not just Portland's—are having a hard time responding to the problems fast enough. We had to deal with

Dr. Frank Gordon, Greyson, your father's murder." He was quiet a moment. "We're good at emergencies. Still, we didn't do enough, fast enough. I don't think anyone, especially not Sedra nor the voices within the Authority, expected things to come to this—to the war that's brewing—nor knows what to do next."

"I'd start with the Necromorph doing the Hannibal Lecter thing in the basement," I said. "Fix Greyson. Make him into a man again and then put him on trial for my dad's murder."

"It isn't that easy. The disk in his throat, and the spells trapping him as both man and beast, have affected his mind. Mercy," he said quietly, "would be to end his life."

Silence again. I thought about Chase, how she would deal with Greyson's death. Not well.

"And even a merciful death wouldn't be easy," he said. "Death magic mixed with Blood magic, dark and light magic." He frowned. "Impossible to Close, and hard to kill."

"What about Chase?" I asked.

"She wouldn't Close him. I don't think she could kill him."

"Creepy, but not what I'm asking. What happens to her if they Close Greyson, or, uh, kill him?"

"Her memories of him would be Closed."

I rubbed at my eyes. "Is that your answer to everything? If it might cause pain or inconvenience, just take the memory away?"

"Sometimes it is the only thing that can be done," he said. "Sometimes people don't want to remember the pain, Allie." He glanced at me, his eyes flecked with gold. He was still angry. Angry at Chase, or Greyson, I didn't know.

I opened my mouth, but my phone rang. I dug it out of my hoodie pocket.

"Hello?"

"Allie, this is Grant."

"Trouble?"

"Is that really the first thing you ask when someone calls you?" he asked.

I took a breath. Remembered Grant was from the part of my life that had little to do with angry magic users or stolen memories or secret organizations. Grant was from the part of my life that had to do with afternoons in a coffee shop, reading the paper, and really good scones.

"Sorry. It's been a long day and I haven't had nearly enough coffee."

"Take care of half of that for you."

"The long day?"

"Don't I wish. Listen, I know we haven't really discussed this part of you leasing the warehouse, but you have a couple visitors waiting for you in my shop. I don't mind the business, but I thought you'd want to know people are looking for you."

"Do you know who they are?"

"I think one of them is a Hound. Looks sick. The other two, a man and a woman. I haven't seen them here before."

"Okay, I'll be there soon."

"If I'm going to be your secretary, or spy boy, I'd like two weeks' vacation and an office with a view. Oh, and a watch that dispenses dry martinis."

"Sure thing," I said. "I'll get right on that. Thanks for calling."

I said good-bye, and filled Zayvion in.

"Still want to go home first?" he asked.

I thought about it. I was damp and hadn't gotten a shower since before the gym. But if someone was looking for me, especially if it was a Hound who was hurt, I didn't want Grant to have to deal with that.

Note to self: set up a schedule for other Hounds to hang out at the warehouse and take in the strays. I refused to spend every night down at Grant's dealing with Hound crap.

I groaned. "Get Mugged," I finally said. "Do you have time?"

"Until the meeting tonight, I do."

It didn't take long to get to Get Mugged. The old coffee shop stood on the corner like a beacon in a grimy city. Yellow light spilled out from two stories of windows, and the street around it was lined with cars.

Zay found a place to park in the open lot next to the warehouse.

I couldn't help it. Looking at the warehouse that still leaned a bit but—as we were told by inspectors and code officials—was sound, and knowing that a part of the building was mine, made me feel good.

I'd promised Pike I'd look after the Hounds for him. It was his idea to bring the Hounds together so we could watch one another's backs. It was his idea to keep track of Hounding jobs and support the police through contract Hounding. He wanted better for Hounds, who too often died trying to escape the pain of using magic.

Just like his granddaughter who hadn't survived her brush with the Blood-magic and drug dealer Lon Trager a few years ago. I'd helped Hound that case to throw Trager in jail. But when Trager got out, Pike had taken him on, alone. He hadn't known Anthony, the kid he was trying to set straight, was being used by Trager. Didn't know Trager was being used by Dr. Frank Gordon, the grave robber, to bind my father's soul. Didn't know there was a whole lot of secret-magic-user stuff going on in the background of this city.

Gruff, fair, blunt, Pike was a good man, and my friend. I still hurt when I thought about his death. The warehouse was a physical manifestation of my promise to him.

Pike had gotten his den.

I scanned the street as I got out of the car and made my way over to the sidewalk. A few people walked by, hoods up, or, that rarest thing in Oregon, an umbrella furled. Traffic drove past slowly, tires hissing against wet pavement. It felt like a pretty normal February night.

I inhaled, got that welcome-home scent of deeply roasted coffee, and something salty, like hot cheese and garlic. Grant had started serving homemade soup and sandwiches along with his baked-from-scratch pastries. If he didn't watch out, he was going to become a sensation.

We strolled up the sidewalk to the front door of Get Mugged and stepped in.

Get Mugged was a lot bigger on the inside than it looked on the outside. An open loft took up the back half of the building, and the bottom floor was a combination of bricks, wood, and well-placed lighting. Tables filled the room, clustered by love seats and couches. The tables nearest the windows were plain dark wood, a little scuffed up. Homey.

No music played, or if it did, it was drowned out from the thrum of conversation. People sat at tables with coffee, tea, food, laptops, and handhelds, content to call Get Mugged their second living room.

I grinned. Noisy, crowded—I loved it here. Even though it was smaller than the dining room at Maeve's place, it somehow managed to feel cozy, not claustrophobic. Plus, having the best coffee in town went a long way toward securing my affections.

Grant was at the end of the room, his back toward me as he bused a table. He wore a tight gray T-shirt with a dish towel thrown over one shoulder, dark jeans, and cowboy boots. Had good arms, a nice ass, and a strong, trim build.

When he turned, he gave me a howdy-baby smile.

Or more likely he gave it to Zayvion, who glided in behind me.

I walked toward the counter, pushing the hood of my jacket down and then unzipping it. I wished I'd thought about taking a heavier coat to my workout.

Grant swung behind the counter, his hands filled with plates and mugs, which he carried into the back room. He deposited the dishes with a quick comment to another employee there I couldn't see before he came out to stand behind the cash register.

"Allie. Good to see you, girlfriend. Hey there, Zay. What can I get you two?"

"Sixteen-ounce, black," I said, "and the freshest scone in the case."

He grinned. "My scones are always fresh. Last out of the oven was lemon poppy seed. Is that okay? And for you, Zay?"

"Just coffee. Black."

"For here?"

I shook my head. "To go would be better."

He plucked a couple paper cups off the stack beside him.

"So who's looking for me?" I asked.

"The man at the back of the room near the stairs to the loft. The woman who was with him is in the bathroom."

Okay, I am not a spy. I'm pretty sure I would fail spectacularly at spy school. So instead of trying to make it look all accidental, I just turned and looked at the guy.

Light hair, big eyes that were sort of puppy-sad, chin too narrow, he was the kind of man who spent his life disappearing in crowds. No one would guess he was a part of the Authority, a magic user, and a damn good one too.

He was also my stepmother's bodyguard. Kevin Cooper.

Well, so much for being followed by bad guys. Violet probably just wanted to talk about Beckstrom Enterprises. Business. Or maybe she had news about the baby she was carrying—my only sibling.

I didn't even have to ask Grant who the Hound was. I could smell his scents among the people in the room, though the subtleties of his scent had changed. No more sweet cherries, which was good. That meant he hadn't been around Blood magic lately.

Hunched against the wall to my right, close enough he wouldn't have to push many people out of the way to get to the door, was Anthony Bell. The same kid Pike had been trying to help.

My heart did double speed for a minute. The last time I'd seen him, he'd been beaten to a bloody mess on the floor of the warehouse where Dr. Frank Gordon was trying to raise my dad from the dead. Dr. Gordon had used Anthony as a Proxy and made the kid pay the price for the magic Frank threw around. I'd heard Anthony survived it. Spent some time in the hospital. Then in the courts. I hadn't followed his case, not much caring whether he would be convicted of the charges of working with Lon Trager and dealing in illegal Blood magic, kidnapping, murder.

I hated following the media when it came to things that touched me personally. I'd never been much of a spotlight lover when I was growing up in my very influential father's spotlight-filled life.

Still, another Hound, Davy Silvers, had told me Anthony got off pretty easy, since he was a minor and hadn't had an actual hand in kidnapping the girls. He'd gotten some counts on forgery of a magical signature, he'd spent some time in juvie, and, last I heard, he was doing community service.

Didn't seem like a fair trade for Pike's life.

"Coffee," Grant announced, as he placed the cups on the counter. "Scone."

I looked away from Anthony, put a few bucks down, and picked up my cup and the scone Grant had put in a small bag. When I looked back at Anthony, he was staring at the table. Had his hands in his pockets, and there was no cup or plate in front of him. I looked over at Violet's bodyguard again, and he gave me an imperceptible nod.

Right. Violet could wait. I'd go take care of Anthony first.

But before that, coffee. I took a drink, savoring the heat and rich, dark flavor. So good. No one in the city roasted beans like Grant.

"You're a doll, Grant," I said.

"A doll without a martini dispenser," he said.

I grinned, then started off toward Anthony. Zayvion followed. "You sure?" I asked. Hounds were my responsibility, my trouble. I didn't want Zayvion to feel like he had to get into this mess with me.

"I was there," he reminded me, like maybe I didn't remember he had been the one who untied Anthony and tried to get him out of the warehouse.

I did remember, but it was nice of him to remind me anyway.

Anthony looked up, scowled when he saw both Zayvion and I were headed his way.

I stopped next to his table, between him and his easy escape to the door. Power play? Me?

"You looking for me?" I asked. I didn't mean for it to come out quite so flat and angry, but hey, this kid was part of what got Pike killed. Sue me.

"I got some things I should say," Anthony started. His tanned cheeks flushed a deeper red. Boy was sweating this one. I could smell the discomfort on him, could tell it was taking every fiber of his will not to squirm, or maybe get up and get out from under my gaze.

Tough. I just didn't have it in me to forgive the kid.

"Say it." I didn't sit. Neither did Zay.

Anthony, to his credit, nodded, and pulled his hands out of his jacket. "You want to sit, maybe? You could sit. This is gonna take more than a minute."

I didn't want to. I wanted the kid to say he was sorry Pike was dead, and then I was going to tell him I wouldn't accept his apology, and to never talk to me again.

Zay hooked the leg of a chair with his foot, and scooted it out.

His shoulder brushed mine as he took the extra seat, and I felt a flash of his curiosity, his sense of compassion.

It was strange. Zayvion went through his life taking away people's memories, sometimes taking away their lives, without qualms. I didn't expect him to have a shred of compassion for a kid like Anthony.

Hells.

I took the other seat. "Talk."

Anthony licked his lips. His gaze skittered over my face, finally settled somewhere around my chin.

"I've tried to think of how I should say this, and I can't." He raised his eyes, met my gaze, then looked away. Ear this time. "I'm sorry. For those girls getting hurt. For what I did to Pike."

"You killed him," I said. "You might not have held the gun, but you sold him out, and you killed him."

Anthony's eyes went narrow. It looked like he was trying hard not to yell. I could smell the heavy stink of guilt on him.

"I know what I did," he said. "If you can't forgive me, it doesn't matter. I just had to say it. Counselor told me." His looked back up at my forehead, his gaze steady, flat.

I couldn't forgive him. And there was no way I would ever trust him. I wanted to tell him to go away and never talk to me again. But I had a pretty good idea what would happen if I handed the kid his ass. Sometimes it takes only one word to send someone into a spiral they never pull out of. Then how many deaths would he be responsible for? And how many would be on my hands?

"I don't trust you, Anthony, and I don't like you. But Pike saw something in you. Get clean. Get your life together and make something out of it."

"I want to Hound. I want to be a part of the pack."

Sweet hells. What was I supposed to say to that? I sure as hells wasn't going to be his babysitter. I was nowhere near as nice as Pike.

"Have you even finished high school?"

"I'm doing online classes."

"Does your mother know you want to do this?"

"We don't talk much."

I took a drink of coffee to keep from yelling at the kid. He was what, sixteen? And already taking his life back down a path that had almost killed him the first time.

No sense.

Of course, most Hounds didn't have any sense.

Me included.

This was a bad idea.

"This is a bad idea," I said.

"So you're saying no?"

I'm sorry, Pike. I can't do it.

"I'm saying no."

"That's what I thought you'd say."

Kid was angry. But even if I let him join the pack, no one would work with him. Plus, I was pretty sure Davy would kill him if they ever got in the same room together.

"You want to be part of the pack, you have to earn it."

"Pike wouldn't—"

"I suggest," I said over the top of him, "you don't quote me on what Pike would or wouldn't do. Ever."

Kid wasn't the only one who was angry.

He shut his mouth. Good.

"Finish school. Get clean. You give me your counselor's number so I can check in on you. You don't Hound—at all. You got me on that, Bell? Not for the cops, not for a friend, not for anyone, until you're straight and clutching a diploma in your hand. You do that and I'll give you a try."

"Fuck that shit," he said. "I don't need you."

"No," I said, "you don't." I stood. "And one more thing—I'd avoid Davy Silvers if I were you. He's not as forgiving as I am."

Pike had been my friend, but Davy had worshipped the man. I waited a second to see if Anthony had anything else to say. He didn't. So I turned and walked off.

Anthony swore again behind me.

Kid didn't know it, but I was doing him a favor. I was giving him a chance at a life without pain. Well, with less pain anyway. I think that's what Pike would have really wanted—for the kid to have a second shot at a clean life, regardless of the dumb things he'd done.

Anthony had that chance. I hoped he made good use of it.

I strolled over to the table where Kevin and a noticeably pregnant Violet waited for me. Zayvion, surprisingly, stayed seated for a few more seconds. He said something to Anthony, but even with my good ears, I couldn't catch it over the noise of the crowd.

Rats

"It's good to see you," Violet said once I was close enough.

I smiled, even though Anthony still had my hackles up. "Good to see you too." I took the extra seat. "Is it okay if Zayvion joins us?"

Violet nodded, the low lights of the room flashing across her tasteful wire-rimmed glasses. She had pulled her red hair back in a plain ponytail. She wasn't wearing any makeup, but had that beautiful glow pregnant women were supposed to always get. I used to think the whole glow thing was a bunch of baloney before watching Violet go through the last few months of carrying my dad's child.

Yes, it was weird to see someone younger than me pregnant with my dad's baby. Family issues. I have them.

"Why didn't you just call?" I asked.

Violet pushed her glasses back on her nose and shifted to sit up straighter. Kevin pulled a Mute spell out of his sleeve. I mean literally. He tugged his rucked-up shirtsleeve back down on his wrist, and somehow in the middle of that put up a very subtle Mute that even a good Hound would have a hard time tracking.

Like I said, he was very, very good at that sort of thing.

"I didn't want the call traced," Violet said.

Wow. The woman knew how to set a mood.

"Someone's tracing your calls?"

"There are members on the board of Beckstrom Enterprises. They represent a faction of shareholders. They are displeased with the amount of resources going into the lab and technology development, and the lack of results. They insist I show them classified documents of my progress."

"Okay," I said, trying to get my head around the problem. "What classified documents?"

"The disks. They want to know about the disks."

The same disks that were stolen. The same disks that were implanted in Greyson's neck and used to turn him into a beast. The disks that would make magic portable and nearly without price. Disks that would change how everyone accessed magic and be used for as much bad as good.

That was a problem.

Zayvion strolled over, made eye contact with Kevin, and then sat in a chair next to me without ruffling the Mute spell. Very nice.

"Are they members of the Authority?" I asked. I knew some of the people in my father's company were in the Authority, like his accountant, Mr. Katz, but it wasn't like anyone had ever done a roll call for me.

Note to self: get a roll call.

"No," she said. "The disks are proving to be too dangerous when not in the right hands, which is such a shame considering how much good they can do in the right hands. I'm working on ways to limit how much magic a disk can hold, and how many times it can be recharged. There are pros and cons as to creating fail-safes for compatibility between disks. We designed them to be compatible. But ever since the robbery at the lab, and then Daniel's death . . ." She paused.

In my head, my dad stirred and pressed outward, like he was leaning against a wall of glass. He scratched at the backs of my eyes, and a melancholy need that was not my own filled me.

"Since his death," she continued, "I haven't been pushing forward on that project as hard."

Which made sense. James Hoskil, one of the people involved in my dad's murder, had admitted using disks with Blood magic. Violet didn't know it, but Greyson had a disk implanted in his neck, holding him permanently between life and death, neither man nor beast.

As far as I could tell, the disks had only ever been used to harm.

"What happens if you don't release the documents to the shareholders?" I asked.

"There are legal actions they could take." She picked up her cup, the steam giving up the sweet perfume of licorice. "They've threatened locking me out of the lab, seizing my files, closing down the facility . . . and . . . other actions. We've had some interesting mail. Threats." She gave me a small smile and I saw a flash of anger in her eyes before she took a sip of her tea. Violet was no fainting flower. I'd come to believe she had matched my moody father's intellect and stubbornness point for point.

"The attorneys are involved, but these kinds of people don't always go through legal channels. Which is why

I wanted to talk to you. I'm going to move in with Kevin for a little while. Just while the condo is being remodeled for the baby, and retrofitted for security measures."

I couldn't help it. I stared at Kevin.

Kevin didn't show a scrap of concern. Didn't give off a single vibe that he was happy or sad about the arrangement. I'd seen the two of them together enough to know he was in love with Violet, even though she had no clue, and as far as I could tell, he was not willing to admit it to her.

But living together. Seriously?

"Seriously?" I said, because I am clever like that.

Violet nodded. "I could have rented a second condominium for a while, but the security may have been a problem. Kevin suggested I stay at his house, which is well guarded, magically and technologically, and since he has a guest room, I agreed."

Kevin picked up his nearly empty coffee cup, took a drink, his gaze meeting mine over the top of his cup.

The man was hard to read, even for me, and I make a living off reading people. The only page I could read in the book of Kevin was that this was none of my damn business.

Maybe he was right. But I wasn't going to let that stop me.

"You don't care what the tabloids will say when they catch wind of this?" I asked.

"I've put some people in place to make sure that doesn't happen."

Well, well. Look at who knew whom to bribe and how. Violet was good at playing this game. "All right, then. So don't try to reach you at home, is what you're saying?"

Violet twisted, as much as she was able, and dug into the purse hanging on the chair beside her. "Yes. Here's the address, and the number at Kevin's. My cell phone remains unchanged. If you need me, just call. And if they do tap my phone, I'll find a way to let you know."

She produced a piece of paper and handed it to me.

I tucked it into the back pocket of my jeans.

"Thanks," I said. "How are you feeling?"

"Other than being as big as a house?" She laughed.

"You are not," I said. "You look beautiful. Doesn't she, Kevin?"

The man could set a stone on fire with that look. I just smiled innocently. Yes, I am cruel like that.

But as soon as Violet looked over at him, Kevin turned down the inferno and went back to Mr. Plain and Mild. I had no idea how he kept all those emotions he felt for Violet behind the proper, impersonal attentiveness of a bodyguard.

"You do," Kevin said. "You look beautiful."

Violet rolled her eyes, but she blushed. "You're both crazy. Or blind. But thank you." She patted Kevin's hand. She didn't see what that simple touch did to him, because she was looking at me instead.

I kept my gaze off Kevin. No need to torture the man. "So when's the big move?"

"Last week," she said.

Correction. She was very good at playing this game. I hadn't even heard a hint of a rumor.

"I would have contacted you earlier, but on top of all this, I've been trying to get everything ready for the baby. I know I still have three months to go, but I don't want to put it off to the last minute, just in case."

"Oh." I wasn't the maternal type. I had very little idea of what a baby needed. Blanket, bottle, diapers. Was there more to it? Nola, my best friend, never had kids. And my lack of social life hadn't afforded me many baby showers.

"Do you . . . uh . . . need me to do anything for you, for that?" I asked.

"No, no, I've got it. There's still a lot of time; I'm just putting my nervous energy to good use. Making lists. A lot of lists. I like lists."

"Do you know if it's a boy or girl?"

"Nope. And I won't until he or she takes their first breath of air." She picked up her cup again, took one last drink. That reminded me. I hadn't finished my coffee, or even opened the bag with the scone yet.

"I do need to be going, though," she said. "I have an appointment with the lawyers. If you need anything, or have any problems, I'd like you to let me know." She stood, and I marveled at how her petite frame could be so rounded in front and otherwise look exactly the same.

Kevin was already on his feet, holding her coat out for her. All the sounds from the room came rushing in like someone had pulled plugs out of my ears. Kevin's Mute spell was gone.

"I'll call you when I move back into the condo, or if I hear anything about the legal actions." Violet put on her coat. "And you call me if you are contacted by anyone, stockholders, members of the board, anyone. I want to know if they are offering you anything . . . interesting in return for favors."

"Like I'd have anything to do with this political business maneuvering crap," I said.

"We all have our price," she said pleasantly.

"Did you just tell me I'm going to sell you out?"

"I don't think you would, no. You're . . ." She paused and gave me a critical look. Her eyebrows dipped. "What have you been doing lately, Allie? You look good."

"Remodeling. Next door for the Hounds. Oh, and the whole three-meals-a-day thing is catching on." Not lies. But not the whole truth. I'd been training my butt off. Physically and magically. And it showed. In all the right ways.

"Still seeing a self-defense teacher?"

"Yes."

She nodded, but I had a feeling she didn't think I was telling her the whole truth.

Note to self: tell my sibling never to lie to her.

"You were saying?" I prompted.

"Oh, right. Don't get pregnant. It ruins your short-term memory."

I was the last person she needed to explain memory loss to.

"Keep a journal," I suggested, with as little sarcasm as possible.

She actually laughed at that. "I can't believe I said that to you." She pressed her fingertips against her lips. "Pregnant makes me a little stupid. I'm sorry."

"At least you won't be pregnant forever." I gave her a crooked smile to take the sting out of my words.

"True. True. And I was saying you do have a price. We all do. It's human nature. But you're not easily bought." She nodded. "You're like your father in that. Unbreakable morals."

I swear she and I had not known the same man.

My father, in my head, exhaled a moan, and the need, the loneliness, swelled in me.

"Take care, okay?" I said. "And let me know if you need anything. Anything I can do for you." It came out soft, concerned. I didn't know how much of it was me, and how much was my father.

Probably mostly me. When he tried to take control of my mouth, I got shoved into the back of my head and had to fight to regain control.

"I'll be fine." She looked around like she was missing something. Kevin handed her purse to her.

"Thank you," she said. "I would have completely forgotten it. What would I do without you?"

He smiled back. Polite. Friendly. But I watched how he held his breath, how his shoulders tensed, how his fingers spread open as if trying to catch or hold something fleeting.

Something inside me hurt. That something was my father.

And yes, it worried me. My father was not a nice man when he was in pain.

"You're welcome, Mrs. Beckstrom," Kevin murmured.

"Good night, Allie," she said. "I'll see you soon. And I'll call if I hear anything has changed with the . . . project."

"Night, Kevin," Zayvion said. Zayvion had been so quiet, I'd almost forgotten he was sitting there. This, I decided, was what it would be like to date the invisible man.

"Night," he replied. "Coffee on me next time."

"Let's make it a beer," Zay agreed. "Shoot some pool."

"Pool sounds good. Give me a call, okay?"

I was pretty sure they weren't really talking about coffee and pool. It wasn't just Zay and Shamus who had a secret code.

Before Violet could open the door to let herself out, Kevin was there, bending over her, smooth, unhurried, holding the door for her.

They both stepped out into the night.

"What was that all about?" I asked.

Zay shrugged.

"Pool?" I asked. "You play pool?"

"Why do the most mundane things about me surprise you?" he asked.

"Because you never tell me any of this stuff."

A corner of his mouth quirked up. "I play pool. Shoot hoops sometimes too. Any other sport you're curious about?"

"Hockey? Polo?"

"Simultaneously. Trick is to keep the horses on their skates."

I rolled my eyes. "Forget I asked."

"No, I'll show you sometime."

"Deal. Horses on ice skates, Jones. Now, what were you and Kevin really talking about?"

"Business. Someone doesn't like the idea of your father's latest wife running the company."

"I know that. She told me that. I mean the other thing."

"What other thing?"

"Beer and pool."

He lifted one eyebrow. "It's beer and pool. One's a drink. The other's a game. That's all. Ready to go?"

I let it slide since I didn't want to cast a Mute spell when we could just talk about it at my house in a couple minutes. The coffee shop had quieted some. Enough I could hear the music, something that had a country beat, and a sitar. I took a quick look at the people still in the shop.

And noted Anthony was gone.

"When did Anthony leave?"

"After you sat down with Violet."

"Did he say where he was going?"

"The warehouse. To see if Davy was there. He wants to apologize."

"Are you serious?"

"Always."

Great. If Davy was there—and I thought he'd mentioned he was going to check on the place this evening—there'd be blood on the floor before I could dial 911. I rubbed at my eyes, thinking maybe I shouldn't have promised Pike anything. Hounds were nothing but trouble.

"Listen," I said, "if you want to head out, you can. I'll go up there and mop up the blood and call the cops on someone."

"When are you going to stop that?"

"Stop what?" I asked.

"Telling me to go away."

"I don't do that."

"You do." He caught one of my hands. His fingers were warm. His touch radiated a sense of peacefulness, of calm.

I, on the other hand, radiated nerves. Too many things were going wrong: Dad, Greyson, Chase. And now Violet was in trouble over the disks. The whole Anthony-Davy-Pike's-death thing was one more hassle I didn't need.

"I'm staying right here, with you," Zayvion said. "Because I don't want to be anywhere else in the world."

I inhaled his words, felt the assurance of that promise reverberate through me.

"Me too," I said. And I meant it. Zayvion and I had an agreement that we were going to give this relationship everything we could. And that included trust, faith, and honesty.

Not a single one of which was among my strong points.

He gave me that sexy smile that usually got me in bed, then pulled away. It had been a few seconds, us touching. But the absence of him, of the awareness of him in my mind, rolled through me like a cold chill. I took a deep breath to keep from reaching out for him.

Being Soul Complements made letting go difficult.

Understatement of the year.

Zay didn't appear to have the same problem. He lifted his ratty jacket off the back of the chair, then gathered his empty coffee cup.

But I'd been around him enough to know he was gliding through those motions. Like a mantra, the ordinary actions guided his muscles and body, helping to clear his mind. I knew there was a storm inside him. And that storm was sparked by a need for me.

I liked that I could ignite that kind of heat in the man.

But right now I had to see if Davy had thrown Anthony out a window.

I finished my coffee and waved to Grant, who waved back. Zayvion and I left Get Mugged and strode to the warehouse next door.

Chapter Five

Zay and I let ourselves into the warehouse through the side door. There was an elevator inside, but I took the stairs behind the door.

Grant leased out the second and third floors to me. I wasn't sure what I was going to do with the third floor yet, but liked the view and the strange architecture enough to keep it.

At the top of the second-floor stairway was a door. I pushed it open, out into the wide hall that split the entire floor in two. Half the space nearest Get Mugged was reserved for my office, a dojo, and a smaller kitchen/living area that had enough locks and wards, I could keep the Hounds out if I needed to. The other side of the building was set up as the main living quarters for the Hounds. Bunks would eventually line one or two walls, and there were a couple bathrooms, showers, and a larger kitchen. A few couches, a TV, computers, and a space cordoned off for meetings.

It wasn't a home, but it was a roof and walls, and a place out of the weather.

Right now, it was open loft space with bits of furniture here and there. Which meant it was easy to hear who was here, and easy to find them.

I planned on keeping it that way.

Davy Silvers, arms crossed over his chest, leaned

against one of the walls on my side of the floor, between the windows that overlooked Get Mugged. Anthony was halfway across the room from him, about dead middle of the space, his hands out of his pockets, empty. No guns, spells, or blood yet.

"Hey, Davy," I said. "Anthony. You boys figure things out?"

Davy spoke. "He said you okayed him being here. Hounding." It came out low and soft. Even though it had been several weeks since Davy had been mauled by Greyson and betrayed by his girlfriend, Tomi, he still hadn't fully recovered. A few weeks ago, we'd found out Tomi left Oregon. Went back to California to stay with her grandmother. Ever since Davy had heard that news, there was something different about him. Something broken inside him.

And out of that breakage poured a cold anger I'd never seen in him before. I figured it would just take time for him to get his footing again, to feel normal without Tomi. And I figured he did not need Anthony rubbing salt in his wounds in the interim.

I wandered over to my desk, letting my oh-so-casual body language wet-blanket as much fire out of their standoff as I could. Davy was my secretary and right-hand man when it came to Hound business, and had been indispensable during the renovations. He'd put a few files on my desk for me to look through. I opened the first one, and pretended to read it.

"I told Anthony he has to get his act together before he can be a part of the pack," I said.

Davy shifted his fists to crack his knuckles against his ribs. "I don't like him," he said. "I don't want him here."

"If we only opened our doors to Hounds who got along, there'd never be more than one of us here at a time." I closed the folder. Looked over at the boys.

Still hadn't moved. Still looked like they were ready to attack.

"Did I mention the new rule? No killing each other. If you two can't be in each other's presence, then I don't want you in the same room."

To my surprise, it was Anthony who listened. "I should go. I just wanted to say—"

"Good-bye," Davy said. End of conversation.

Anthony looked over at me. I nodded. Kid had guts. No smarts, but plenty of guts.

"See you around, Anthony."

He looked down at his shoe. He walked over to me, head still down. Davy tensed with every step Anthony took.

Me too, but I hid it better.

"Here." Anthony handed me a piece of paper. "Like you said, right?"

I glanced down at the note. It was a name and a number. His counselor, I assumed. "So far," I agreed. "Go on home."

He hesitated. "I was trying to tell him, you know, the same things I told you."

"Fuck," Davy whispered.

"Go home, Anthony," I said a little stronger. "While you can do it walking. This isn't going to get solved in one night."

He hitched one shoulder and gave me the angry gaze. Didn't like me much. Yeah, well, I already had friends.

"Good night," I said.

"Screw this." He strode across the room and out the door without once looking back. When it was clear he had taken the elevator down, I opened the file on my desk for real.

"You staying here much longer?" I asked Davy.

He finally shifted away from the wall and walked over to me. I kept my eyes on the paper but out of my peripheral vision paid attention to how he moved. He wasn't limping anymore, which was good, but still looked a little stiff, as if something inside hurt every time he took too deep of a breath.

He sat in the chair on the other side of my desk, leather, comfortable—hey, I had some money. "I was just headed out when Bell showed up. You could have warned me."

"Sorry. I didn't know he was coming up here. He was down at Get Mugged. Wanted to apologize. Wanted to join."

"And you're gonna let him?"

"He screwed up, Davy. We all know that. I can't forgive him for what he did to Pike. But I won't throw him under a train. If he can pull his life together, I'm not going to get in his way."

"You don't understand."

"I do. I understand what Pike would have done for him."

Davy scowled, his eyes narrowing, his teeth showing.

"Pike saw something in Anthony," I said. "He stuck with him even when the kid was being an ass."

"And it got him killed." Davy stood. "I'm not that stupid. I didn't think you were either."

"Lon Trager killed Pike," I said. "Not Anthony. You know that."

"I know Pike wouldn't have gone down to Trager alone if Anthony hadn't used his blood to frame Pike."

"Pike went there alone because he was a stubborn old man. I told him the police would go with him, with us. He wouldn't listen. Sometimes Hounds make stupid, stupid choices, Davy. Just like Pike did, just like Anthony did, and just like Tomi did. She almost killed you. And if she came walking in here, telling me she was clean and had pulled her life together, I'd give her the chance to prove it to me too."

Davy's face flushed red. The thin scar that still hadn't healed over his left eyebrow and down his temple turned white.

"Leave Tomi out of this."

"Listen—" I stopped. Took the volume out of my

voice. "What I'm saying is, Hounds make bad decisions. It comes with the territory. I think you have to be willing to do stupid things if you're going to Hound. We're hardwired that way. Pike understood that. I think if he were still alive, he'd probably give Anthony the ass-kicking of his life, and then take him in, and teach him so he never made that kind of mistake again. It's up to Anthony to pull his life together. There's a good chance he'll find something better than Hounding, safer than Hounding, before I let him in the pack."

"You think that's how Pike would want you to run this place?"

"I think that's how I'm going to run it. When someone wants to take over, they can run it their way. Until then, I make the rules. If you don't want to follow those rules, no one's saying you have to stay."

I leaned back. "I hope you won't leave. Not over Anthony. He's not worth it."

Davy gritted his teeth again and looked out the window. Not much to see out there, just the roofline of Get Mugged and a few lights shining through the rain.

I waited. Gave him some space to think, some time to breathe.

Zayvion, who had been silent this whole time, stayed where he was, sitting in one of the couches behind Davy, in my line of vision, watching Davy, me, and the door, without looking like he was doing any of those things.

The rain pounded harder, wind kicking it across the window. It felt suddenly much colder in here, as if night had crept unnoticed through the seams of the walls and sunk down into all the shadows of the room.

"Things aren't . . . aren't what I want," Davy said quietly.

"Hounding?"

"Everything."

"You want some time off?"

He shook his head. "More time only messes with my

head. I can't even sleep, well, not enough. Not really. Not since . . ." He stared out the window, and I watched his eyes shift, as if he could see someone there.

"Sometimes I think I can feel her."

I didn't let my surprise show. "Who? Tomi?"

He nodded. "When she's hurt. I think when she's cutting. . . ."

"That seems a little strange, doesn't it?" I asked gently.

He laughed, a short huff. "You think?" He looked back over at me, gave me the half grin that I hadn't seen in weeks. "Just a little strange?"

I had no idea what to say to that. Davy didn't know about the Authority. He just thought Zayvion was my boyfriend, who sometimes hired out as a bodyguard. Since Davy didn't know about the Authority, he also didn't know about the kinds of magic the Authority kept hidden. And other things, like the magically half-man, half-beast Greyson, who had been using Tomi to try to trap me, and dig my dad out of my brain. Zay was careful not to use much magic around Davy, and I was trying my best to keep who knew what straight.

Blood magic had been used to hurt Davy. And Blood magic was . . . intimate. It dug into your body and senses, deep and hard, and offered you pleasure—so long as you did everything the caster wanted you to do. It tied you to the caster in ways other magic disciplines did not.

There was a reason people mixed it with drugs and sex.

And there was a reason it was illegal.

Davy might know some of that, but I couldn't tell him that Blood magic could be mixed with dark magic to do very bad things. Things that were done to him. Things that stained your soul.

I glanced over at Zayvion. He was frowning, staring at the back of Davy's head. I was pretty sure he couldn't actually see inside Davy's brain, but for a minute I kind of wished he could.

"You gonna call the psych ward?" Davy asked.

"What? Why would I do that? You're no crazier than the rest of us."

Davy relaxed a little.

I couldn't believe he'd really been worried I'd do that.

"Blood magic is pretty rough stuff," I said. "And Tomi was using it. That . . . man she was working for made her use it. I know she doesn't remember that." I didn't tell him I knew she couldn't remember what she had done to Davy—what Greyson had made her do to him— because someone in the Authority had taken away her memory of it. "But I'm the one who found you in the park, and there was definitely Blood magic involved. It can take a while for the effects of that to fade."

This is where living three different lives is tricky.

Spreadsheet. Still needed one. Because a woman with as many holes in her memory as I have should not be allowed to try to juggle all these secrets.

"You think that's it?" he asked.

"Yes. I mean, it's possible you're just the sensitive sort, lonely and all that."

He grinned. "Right."

"It's more possible magic messed you up a little. Tomi hit you pretty hard. Magic hasn't been in use long enough for us to know everything it can do to a person. You might be sensitive to Tomi, to her pain for a while.

"If you want, I could find a doctor who might have some experience with this," I said. "There's no end to what my father's fortune can buy."

"Maybe. I'm not ready to mess with it . . . yet."

He meant he wasn't ready to give up feeling Tomi yet. Poor kid had it so bad for her that even if all he could feel was her pain, he was going to keep it.

I guess Anthony wasn't the only one who needed counseling.

I wondered if anyone in the Authority would know

why he was able to feel Tomi's pain. I made a note to ask. I knew there were doctors in the Authority who specialized in magical wounds.

"Sleep might be a good idea," I said.

He ran his hand back over his hair, leaving it stuck up on one side. "Yeah. That's not working so good right now."

"How about sleeping pills?"

"I hate pills."

Funny, for a Hound who used booze to cut the pain from magic, it was a little high-handed for him not to want to take a drug that might actually be good for him.

"Then try some warm milk. Eight hours. Sleep."

"Warm milk? What are you, my mother?" He smiled again, looking for a moment like the Davy I knew.

"I'll know if you lie about it," I said.

"Would I lie to you?"

"If you thought you could get away with it."

I stood and so did he. "You staying?" I asked.

"No. I've had enough of this place for one night. I'm going home. I have sleep to catch up on, apparently."

Zay stood too, and we all walked out the door and were down on the street in the rain in no time. We didn't say anything else, even though a hundred things were going through my head. All one hundred were things I couldn't tell Davy.

"Night," Davy said.

"See you," I said.

Davy hunched his shoulders, and crossed the street to his car. Zay and I made it to the parking lot, and managed to get under cover before we were soaked.

"Home?" Zay asked, after starting the car.

"How much time do we have before the meeting?"

"It's only seven o'clock."

I groaned. "Feels like midnight. Home. I want to eat my scone." I held up the wrinkled, slightly damp bag I still had in my hand. Maybe I'd get a chance at a shower too, or maybe Zayvion would crawl into bed with me for a little bit.

The void stone necklace was still in the cup holder where I'd left it. I had worried it was making me dizzy, sucking magic out of me too quickly. But right now I was feeling a little edgy, the magic in me uncomfortably hot. The whole thing with Anthony and Davy bothered me, but even worse was the problem with Violet and the disks.

As soon as I thought about her, my dad scratched at the backs of my eyes. Like I needed a constant reminder of things out of my control.

I could ask Zay to Ground me again. Could recast the Linger spell that had apparently worn off. Or I could put on the necklace.

Right now, I wanted easy.

I put on the necklace, and sighed as it settled against my skin. Magic cooled, slowed. Dad stopped scratching. I felt like I'd just taken a painkiller.

Nice.

I watched Zay drive, city lights and shadows sliding down his dark skin, highlighting his strong features. The windshield wipers kept a steady beat. Zay didn't look happy.

"Everything okay?" I asked.

"Ask me after the meeting tonight."

Right. There was another thing to worry about. "How does the Authority usually handle storms like this?"

"Not well."

"Ha-ha. I'm serious."

He looked over at me. His eyes sparked with gold, with magic. It was a feral look, the eyes of a killer.

"So am I. Magic doesn't follow the rules when it's being thrown around in a storm. If a front is big enough, and organized enough that they know it's going to hit Portland, and if the wells are somehow being drained by it . . ."

He shook his head and flicked on the turn signal, changing lanes.

"A lot of things could happen. We'll just have to deal with things as they come." He eased the car into the parking lot behind my apartment and parked.

"That's it?" I asked. "But this isn't the first wild-magic storm that's hit the city. Every building has a storm rod to channel magic strikes. Dad knew what he was doing when he invented those."

"They help. But if the storm is big enough, the storm rods won't be enough." Zay turned off the engine and twisted in his seat toward me. "We'll handle it. It's just different this time."

"Why?"

"Because you're going to be there." He smiled a little, as if his own honesty surprised him. "These are the sorts of things I didn't think through when I was lobbying to get you accepted into the Authority. But now, knowing you'll be a part of our fight, of our struggle, against magic . . . that you could get hurt—" He glanced away. "I don't know. I know you're a fighter, Allie. I just wish you didn't have to be."

Actually, that was sweet of him. "I wish you didn't have to be too."

He chuckled, and I liked how his eyes curved into crescents. "I'd fight even if they told me I couldn't."

"We're a lot alike that way. You know I never back down from a challenge."

He reached over, brushed my hair back, and tucked it behind my ear. "Not the safest way to go through life."

"Maybe not. But it's my way."

He searched my face, his hand paused to cup the edge of my jaw. I knew he wanted to say something. I could feel his concern like a hard palm against the base of my spine.

I was suddenly aware of our connection, of our shared need for the other to be safe, and our knowledge that it was unlikely either of us would go through life safe and unscathed. It was hard to face how much we both dreaded the thought of the other in pain.

I drew away.

"You know what I'd really like right now?" I said, changing the subject, and trying to change the mood in the car. "A hot shower. Want to join me?"

He leaned his wide shoulders back against his seat and stared out the window for a second or two. He nodded. "Hot shower sounds good."

A wave of cold prickled over my skin, a slow, biting chill. Zay rubbed at the back of his neck. He felt it too. Magic. Pulling, twisting. Magic moving as if stirred by a wind, as if unsettled by a storm coming over the horizon. Magic that we'd have to deal with soon.

Chapter Six

Time. We needed it. The Authority thought we had it. A day or two before the storm hit. Which was good. Because I really did want that shower.

Zay and I walked up the stairs and I paused in front of my apartment door—habit. Didn't hear anyone moving around in there. I was on my way to a several-month streak of people not breaking into my apartment, and I wanted that streak to continue.

I unlocked the door and stepped in, switching on the hall light.

"Stone?" I called out.

A familiar coo, half pipe organ, half vacuum cleaner, answered me from the corner of the living room. Stone, the gargoyle I couldn't get rid of, slipped out from beneath the fall of my curtains, stretched his big, batlike wings, and tipped his wide head to one side, his ears perked up in perfect triangles.

"Hey, boy. You ready to get up for the night?"

Stone was big as a Saint Bernard, but had a heck of a lot more teeth and muscle. He clacked, his bag-of-marbles happy sound, and trotted over to me. He was heavy enough that I felt the vibration of each footfall. He pushed his flat snout under my hand, then angled his head for a scratch.

Even though he was made out of stone and was alive

via magic, he was warm to the touch and loved getting scratched. I rubbed my fingers behind his ears.

He clacked—happy—then dropped me cold for Zayvion, who knelt and gave his head the rubbing of its life.

Stone cooed.

"I see how you are," I said. I shrugged out of my coat, hung it on the back of the door, and carried my gym bag with me into the bedroom. My answering machine wasn't blinking—no messages waiting for me, which was a little strange. I had expected something from Stotts, since Detective Love had made a point of telling me he was looking for me.

"Want a shower?" I called back to Zay. I unzipped my bag and dug out my notebook. Tugged the cap of my pen off with my teeth and opened the book to a blank page.

It took me less than thirty seconds to note what had happened today, but I wanted to update it before I spent more time around mega magic users tonight. Magic hadn't wiped out many of my memories lately. I didn't know if I was just getting better at setting Disbursements, or if maybe having my dad take up residency in my brain had done something to help with that.

And with all the training I'd been doing, physically and magically, I was getting more and more nervous that magic was just . . . I don't know . . . saving up to take a huge chunk of my life away.

Maeve said the void stone necklace might help block that price magic extracted from me. Or that my training was helping with the memory loss.

Whatever it was, ever since I'd started training, I'd kept my memories.

Personally, I wondered if it had something to do with being lovers with a Closer. Zayvion was good at taking people's memories. Maybe he was good at helping them stick around too.

"Ready?" Zay said it softly, but I jumped anyway.

Boy was too damn quiet. I glared at him from just inside the bedroom door.

"Make some noise, will you?"

"I've got a better idea," he said all low and sexy-like. "How about I make you make some noise?"

I smiled. "I thought we were taking a shower."

"That's a good place to start."

"Okay, magic boy. You're on. First person to cry mercy folds the laundry."

"After you." He stepped aside so I could walk past him, and I did too, without freaking out or even having to hold my breath even though there just wasn't enough room in the hall for me and him in the same place.

Of course my bathroom was even smaller.

And it was currently filled with a half ton of living rock who was flushing my toilet and watching the water circle the drain, his wings quivering in excitement.

Great. When had he learned to flush the toilet? My water bill was going to be sky-high.

"Stone," I said. "Out. Go play with a lathe or something."

He swiveled his head and looked at me over his shoulder, one five-fingered hand still resting on the tank plunger.

"Window, boy. Go to the window. It's dark out. Nighttime. You could go. Out. Go fly."

He clacked doubtfully and looked back down at the water.

"Need some help?" Zayvion asked.

"I got it." I walked into the bathroom, squeezing around Stone, and giving myself the willies.

I put my hand on Stone's head and stared straight into his intelligent, round eyes. "Out." I pointed my other hand at the door, and tipped his head that way.

He cooed happily at Zayvion, who leaned one wide shoulder against the doorway and took up all the remaining space and air.

"Getting out of the way would be nice," I said to Zayvion.

"Oh. Sorry about that," he said, clearly not at all sorry.

He backed into the hallway and snapped his fingers twice. Stone's ears flicked back, then pricked up when Zay snapped his fingers again. Stone looked at me, clacked, in a why-didn't-you-say-so way, then lifted up on his two back legs and waddled out of the bathroom.

He clattered like a bag of marbles being shaken, and Zayvion treated him to another head scratching and told him he was a good boy.

Fine. Let him play with the statuary. I was taking a shower.

I started the water and stripped, throwing everything but my bra—which wasn't wet, wonder of wonders—into the hamper. I did not look at myself in the mirror, because right now I didn't care how many scars I had, nor if my father was going to be looking at me through my eyes. Hot water was calling me and nothing was getting in between me and the steam.

I shut the door so Stone wouldn't wander back in, took off the void stone, and put it on the sink, then stepped into the shower. I dunked my head under the strong, hot spray and moaned. I hadn't even gotten a chance to shower at the gym this morning.

"No fair starting without me," Zayvion said.

Man was too damn quiet.

But I did hear him taking off his shoes, and then just one clack of his belt buckle being undone.

The thought of him, of his body, in the shower with me, made me wish I hadn't agreed to this little bet.

"Don't flatter yourself," I called out.

He pulled back the curtain at the head of the shower, caught my arms in his wide, strong hands, and pulled me in for a kiss.

I sputtered and laughed against his lips as he manhandled me to one side so he could step into the shower. He tried to pull me out of the water so he could get in and soak, but I planted my feet.

"Get your own hot water, cowboy," I said, holding my own under the showerhead.

Zay drew his hands down my arms, his fingers leaving my wrists to caress my stomach and hips. He stroked back over my ass, and pressed against me full-body.

Yum.

"What if I like your water?" he asked.

"Then you're going to have to work a heck of a lot harder for it."

"Fair enough. I think I'll start here."

He leaned down again. This time his mouth found my shoulder. He kissed me there, his tongue licking over the marks magic had left on me, stroking and urging the magic inside me to rise to his touch.

I bit my lip on a groan. Magic flared in me, licking hot, and I didn't even try to hold it back. Thought, for just a moment, that I should have left the void stone necklace on. And then I didn't think about anything but Zayvion, and what he was doing to me.

Zayvion's other hand slid up my butt, pressed at the small of my back, while his mouth moved down to the edge of my breast.

Okay. I was done with the shower. Done with being clean. All I wanted was him.

"Say mercy," he murmured.

What? Oh no. Hells, no. I wasn't going to lose.

"You say mercy," I said. I pulled his head up, my thumbs beneath the scratchy stubble along his jaw, and then pivoted so his back was against the wall and the shower fell on both of us.

He smiled, wet, hot, gorgeous, and leaned his shoulders back, giving me all the time I wanted to take in his dark, hard body.

I spread my legs for balance. He gasped at that move,

which made me grin. Then he swallowed, his eyes sparking gold. He reached out to pull me in closer, but I held my ground, even though his need washed through me. I had plenty of need on my own, thank you.

I knew what he wanted. He knew what I wanted.

I held eye contact. "Mercy, Jones." I pressed my hand against his thigh, and slowly kneaded my way upward. "Say it."

He closed his eyes, tipped his head back. "Allie," he breathed. "M-my God, woman. Come here."

Close enough. I couldn't wait any longer either.

We embraced, giving in to the passion we could no longer contain. I drew him into me with aching sweetness, his body familiar and right. Water slipped hot fingers down my shoulders, back, thighs, licking, searching, finding every inch of my skin that was exposed, wrapping me in wetness and heat.

Inside me, Zayvion's emotions rose and raged like a summer storm. His need licked beneath my skin, warring with the magic I held inside me, pushing it up and up through me, where he caught it in his mouth, drank it from my skin, my soul.

More. I wanted more. Wanted him to take more, wanted to give him more.

I called on magic. Pulled it through me, and let it pour out, a wild flood of power and passion and raw need, into him.

His muscles, his body, stiffened, hardened, arms clenching me tighter, caught in a burning overload of pure magic that lifted to my call, answered my desires, and rushed swiftly as glyphs pulsing in the air, into him.

He drank the magic down, changed it, and thrust it back into me.

For a moment, everything went black. Silent. Still.

There was no beginning to him. No end to me. There was only the heat of our nerves, the thrum of our heartbeats, skipping, catching, pounding in rhythm to the magic that gave and took, from him, from me, to him, to me, building and falling, and building again.

We were more than man and woman. Magic took control and drew through us glyphs and spells flashing lightning and fire and heat through my mind, his mind. Our soul.

Burning us together as one.

We cried out for mercy with one voice, one need.

It took time, maybe too much time, for magic to release us. Too much time until one of us finally pulled away.

Time while Zayvion convinced me that we were not one, but two people, two bodies, two minds, his kisses gentle, slow, his lips and fingers reminding me of my own skin, my own body, separate from his. Reminding me of the rightness of that. The rightness of being me.

I opened my eyes, blinked from the light. Not magic, just plain electric light.

"It's okay," he said, and I knew it was. I also knew he was worried. I could still feel his emotions as if they were mine, could taste his worry like sour rinds at the back of my throat.

"Allie," he said, his fingers splayed against both sides of my face. "Do you remember where you are? Who you are?"

No words could kill a mood or bring me crashing back into my own mind, my own body, faster.

I had memory issues. That was something I would never forget.

Checklist: we were standing in the shower. The water was off. I didn't remember washing the soap out of my hair, but I knew I had. I didn't remember turning off the water, didn't know how long we had been in the shower.

But yes. I knew who I was. Allison Beckstrom. Hound. Newly a member of the Authority, filled with magic, and Soul Complement to Zayvion Jones.

And I was just as sure that for some time, I had forgotten all those things, and had instead been content to be more. Had been a part of Zayvion, joined. One.

"Me—my place," I finally answered him. "How long?"

His relief rained through me and I tasted candy melon. "Maybe an hour," he said. "I'm not sure." Which meant he'd lost track of reality too. That I'd made him forget who he was.

Was it wrong for me to love, just a little, that I could do that to him?

His eyes shifted back and forth between mine.

"I'm fine," I said. "Light-headed. What exactly happened?"

"We made love."

I frowned. "I know that." Eloquent. My middle name.

"Soul Complements," he said, as if that covered the rest of what I should know.

He stepped out of the shower and I stepped out with him, unthinkingly needing to stay in contact with him, to move in tandem with him, to be no more than inches apart from him.

He handed me a towel. "We fell . . . fell too far into each other. Magic drew us in, and we didn't let go."

I took the towel and stayed where I was while he purposefully took two steps away. The need to follow him and limit the distance between us was still there, but it was fading. I dried myself off in silence.

He rubbed the towel over his hair, and mopped off, the towel wadded in his hand. He shook the towel out, and wrapped it around his waist.

"What did we do wrong?" I asked.

"We lost control."

"You say that like it's a bad thing," I said.

"Too far, too long, and we won't want to be who we are without also being the other person." He said it without emotion, as if he were reciting a textbook. "We'll lose ourselves. Lose what we are as individuals. That's a problem."

He was right. I wanted that closeness, that awareness of every inch of him. Wanted him, wanted us, bound together, burned, melded by magic. There was a power in it. I could sense it, could almost taste it. A power I'd never felt before.

And knowing I could never have it again, that we *should* never have it again, made me hollow and empty, even though he was only a few steps away, and closer to me than any man in my life.

"You don't think this will happen every time, do you?" I asked.

"Every time we have sex, or every time we take a shower?" He smiled.

I knew he was trying to change the mood, push away the seriousness of what had just happened, of how bad it could have been. I tried to follow his lead, to let go of the fear.

"I don't think the shower had anything to do with it," I said. Yes, I sucked at letting go of fear.

Zay shrugged one shoulder. "I wouldn't say it was entirely innocent. All that warm, wet water touching us everywhere. And the soap definitely had ulterior motives."

I wrapped the towel around me, tucking it tight at the top. "That career in comedy? Walk away now, Jones."

"And give up on my dreams?" He gave me a grin, and carefully avoided touching me while he picked up his jeans and shoes and carried them into the bedroom.

I rubbed my hands over my arms, needing contact, needing his touch, but firmly staying right where I was. Zay could make jokes. I'd just do what I always did—endure.

Zay had been staying with me enough lately that he had a spare change of clothes and a dresser drawer of his own.

"I've always thought if the magic thing didn't work out," he called from the bedroom, "I could give comedy a try."

Comedy. Right. The last thing Zay had on his mind was a career in stand-up. "I thought you had the whole ice-polo thing to fall back on." I dug in the drawer beneath the sink and pulled out my brush.

I could do this. I could be just me. See me being just me? I was hella good at it.

"I like to keep my options open," he said. "You know how the girls love an athlete with a good sense of humor."

I left the brush on the sink and put on the void stone necklace again. Magic settled in me, taking the edge off my discomfort. I walked into my bedroom. Zay had already put on his boxers and jeans. He was half bent, digging through the laundry basket for a T-shirt.

I was done pretending. "So this magic and Soul Complement thing. You think we'll be okay?" I asked.

He stood, the T-shirt in his hand. "I have never once doubted us. Not once."

I walked over to him. He had slipped back into expressionless Zay, Zen Zay. He wasn't giving off much in the way of body language except for patience, and I was trying my best not to listen in to his emotions. "Not even when you wrote me that Dear John note?"

He grimaced. "That was me doubting myself. Doubting if I could keep you safe."

"How about if you let me keep me safe?" I gingerly placed my fingertips over his heart, felt the soft rhythm there, felt the rise and fall of his chest. But nothing more. No emotions, no thoughts.

"Are you blocking your thoughts and feelings?" I asked.

"Just trying not to project. You?"

I shook my head. "So this is okay?" I dragged my hand down and around his rib cage, my fingers sliding along the waistband of his pants. I wrapped my arm around his back, leaned into him. Still had my towel on too. Go, me.

I felt the tension drain out of him as he exhaled. "This is very okay." He put his arms around me, pulled me close.

I tucked my head, resting it against his smooth, hard chest. He tipped his head down, not far, and kissed my hair. "Good?" he asked.

I nodded, and rubbed my hand down his spine, massaging the muscles of his wide back as I went, until I finally slid my fingers into the back pocket of his jeans, to keep my hands off any other tempting part of him.

He smiled. My hair caught in the stubble along his jaw.

"Very nice," I mumbled.

I stood there and savored the sound of his heartbeat, of his breathing. Stood there longer than I should have, and still didn't want to part. But I didn't feel trapped with him, and didn't feel apart from him. I felt like I belonged here. Felt like I was home.

I yawned, and finally pulled away. I didn't know if it was the whole magic thing, or just the long day, but I was tired. "I need a short nap before the meeting." I tugged off my towel and let it drop to the floor as I walked over to the bed.

Zayvion inhaled behind me. Oh, right. Naked me, plus half-naked him, plus bed equaled one thing.

I looked over my shoulder.

From the fire in his gaze, I knew exactly what he was thinking.

"A nap," I repeated, crawling under the covers quick. "I'm tired. You should be tired too."

Zayvion stalked over to the bed. "Maybe I'll make it worth your while to stay awake."

"No. No way. You said we should be careful, remember? You said we might get too close and mixed-up and stuff, remember? Sleep, Jones. Sleep is good."

He grabbed a fistful of my comforter and tugged. "Promise I'll be good."

"Zay . . ."

"Or, if you'd rather, I'll be bad. Either way works for me." He tugged a little harder on the blanket, exposing my shoulders and chest. I was losing ground quickly. I scooted down the bed a little and tugged back.

"Here's an idea," I said, shifting tactics. "Why don't you take a nap with me? Nice warm blankets. Nice soft pillow. We could get some sleep. Rest up before the big storm meeting tonight . . ."

His smile faded and all the sexy on-the-prowl was gone. I shouldn't have brought up the meeting, shouldn't have let the real world back into this small moment we were sharing.

"I'm sorry—"

"No, you're right."

He let go of the comforter and rubbed at the back of his neck. A sound of something falling in the living room made us both glance out into the hall. It was just Stone stacking the alphabet blocks I'd bought him. I knew Stone wasn't a child, but I was tired of coming home to find all the cups dragged out of my kitchen and stacked in precarious pyramids in the living room. Plus he liked the blocks enough I'd bought him three sets of the things.

They kept him busy.

Stone usually stayed in the apartment during the day. But at night, he came and went as he pleased—opposable thumbs meant doors and windows were not a problem for him. I didn't know what magical statuary did at night, but since I hadn't heard of any gargoyle sightings in the news, whatever it was he did, the big lug was discreet about it.

When Zay looked back at me, some of the seriousness was gone. "Move over, woman."

He crawled under the blankets and hogged the bed.

Note to self: explain that the bed was mine, and I should get more than half of it just on principle alone.

He hadn't put on his shirt, but still wore his jeans, as if knowing we'd be out of bed soon. I shifted closer to him, and judiciously placed a sheet between us, because a half-naked man in my bed—especially if that man was Zayvion Jones—was going to ruin my control.

"How long do we have?" I asked.

"Forever," he said.

I savored that thought. It was a nice fantasy, anyway.

"Maeve's at ten, right?"

"Mmm." He shifted so I could throw my leg over his, and rest my head on his shoulder, his arm snug down my back. "An hour or so."

"Need the alarm?" I asked.

He shook his head. "I'll be awake."

I was going to ask him about that. Ask him why. But I really was tired, and it took only a few breaths before I slipped off into deep, blissful darkness.

Chapter Seven

Zay didn't have to wake me up. The cold air coming in from the window did the trick.

I shifted away and elbowed up. "Stone," I groaned. "Go out or stay in. Don't just stand there with the window open. You're killing my heating bill."

Stone stood on his hind legs, half his body out the open window, backlit by the streetlights below. His head was tipped upward. He seemed to be watching the sky. Probably fascinated by the moon. He was smart like that.

He made that bag-of-rocks happy sound, and pulled back into the room, dropping on all fours. He, of course, did not shut the window behind him.

He clacked some more, his ears perked up, his wings tucked tight against his back. He seemed happy I was awake. So happy he trotted over to my side of the bed and stuck his big freezing-cold head in the middle of my chest.

I yelped. "Too cold, you dummy." I pushed at his face and he just ducked under my hand, begging for a scratch.

Zay chuckled.

"You're no help," I said.

"He's your yard ornament."

Fine.

"One scratch." I rubbed the ridges of Stone's eyes. He pulled his lips back in what I could only guess was a smile, even though there were a dozen too many sharp teeth involved.

"Now go. Shut. Window." I gave him a little shove, and he rubbed the side of his head over my hand for one last scratch, then tromped back to the window, cooing a sort of out-of-tune hum.

"All engines ready to go?" I asked.

Stone clacked.

"Runway clear for takeoff?"

Stone stuck his head out the window again. Cooed, vacuum cleaner–style. His ears were straight up, and his wings quivered. This was a little game we played. I liked it much better than the chew-on-the-chair-legs game.

Zay snorted. "You think he understands you?"

"I'd sing him show tunes if it would make him shut the window. Ready?" I said. "Five, four, three, two, one. Blast off! Go, go, go!"

Stone gathered himself, his back legs dropping, his arms braced outside on either side of the window. He had gotten pretty good at launching himself out the window, his wings tucked tight. With one big push, he shoved out into the night air, his wings catching like a parachute, then beating, stronger than they looked. Yes, they were made of stone and didn't look aerodynamic, but somehow, he did it—the big lunk of rock and magic really could fly.

And the big lunk of rock and magic did just that.

But the big lunk of rock and magic did not close the window.

Hells.

I groaned. Zay just snorted.

Dragging the comforter with me, I scooted off the bottom of the bed, and shoved the window shut. I thought about setting the lock so the beast wouldn't be able to get in, but decided against it. I was pretty sure Stone would find a way into my apartment, lock or no lock. And I didn't want to have to pay for repairs.

Zay stood, stretched, and shook out his arm and hand.

"Arm asleep?" I dug through my closet looking for a sweater. It was freezing in here. How long had Stone had that window open?

"Can't feel it from my elbow down. You never moved."

I pulled one of my favorite sweaters off a hanger. With the blanket still wrapped around my legs, I shuffled to the dresser, found panties, bra, and jeans. Didn't take me long to get into all of them, plus a nice thick pair of socks.

"You could have shoved me off if you didn't like it." I found my boots, put them on too, and strode to the bathroom to fix my hair.

"True," he murmured.

For once, fortune was on my side. My hair wasn't sticking straight up. I brushed it back, tucked it behind my ears, and took a look at my eyes. Green, but too dark to be just my own. Someone else was looking back at me.

"Dad?" I whispered.

A weight shifted in my head and the entire room slid downhill sideways. I grabbed the sink, braced my feet, and tried not to fall down or throw up as dizziness tumbled through my head.

The storm, my father's voice said, quietly, as if he were speaking from far away. He sounded concerned, but calm. The same way he had sounded when I was seven and broke my wrist and he'd told me going to the doctor was going to hurt a little. The same way he'd sounded when he told me my mother had left me, left us, for good, but everything would be fine.

Nothing they say will change it; nothing they do will stop it.

I was on my knees now, still holding on to the sink, still trying not to fall down while the room spun and spun. I wondered where Zayvion was, if he was sliding down this dizzying slant too.

They will try to use it. Madness.

What? I thought. *Who?*

I must have said it out loud, because Zayvion was suddenly there, in the doorway to my bathroom, his smile quickly gone.

He reached for me. The moment he touched my shoulder, the world snapped back into place.

I was sitting on my normal bathroom floor. With my normal dead father silent and distant in the back of my mind.

I looked up at Zayvion. "Did you feel that? The dizziness?"

"I felt magic flux. Not hard, though."

"Dad pushed at me."

He exhaled, and knelt in front of me. Even though he took up too much room, I didn't feel claustrophobic. I wanted him near.

"He must have tried to use magic's fluctuation to shove me out of the way. Started talking."

I rubbed at my arms, trying to scrub away the cold. Zay placed his hands over mine and I realized I wasn't rubbing— I was digging. Like somehow I could dig the cold wrongness of magic out of me, out of my bones. Long red scratches lined my arms, but didn't ease the magic gone to ice in my blood, biting, stinging, burning.

I leaned the back of my head against the sink.

"What did he say?" Zay asked.

"He said they can't stop the storm. And that they'll try to use it, but it's madness, and that they'll fail."

Zay straightened and offered me both hands. "Huh."

I took his hands and he helped me up on my feet. "You cannot be calm about this."

He walked out of the bathroom, still holding my hand.

"It's not the first time in my life someone's told me I'm going to fail. I decided a long time ago not to believe them. Worked pretty good so far."

The living room table was taken over by an alphabet-block sculpture. Stone had stacked the blocks in a decent replica of the dual-spired convention center, with something that looked like fork tines stuck up out of the top two blocks. If that big lug was de-tining my cutlery, I was going to take a belt sander to his claws.

I tugged Zayvion off toward the kitchen. I needed coffee.

"Do you think Dad knows something we don't?" I filled the coffeepot with water while Zayvion pulled the bag of fresh grind—straight from Get Mugged—off the shelf.

"As far as I know, your father couldn't tell the future when he was alive." Zay scooped coffee into the filter, and the warm, earthy smell of the grind blended with his pine scent. I loved this, small things like this that reminded me we were a part of each other's lives, moving like we belonged in the same space, sharing simple things, like we'd been doing this together for years.

With the coffee brewing, I leaned back against the counter. "So you think my dad's just trying to scare me? I would be perfectly fine if your answer was yes."

"No."

Great.

"But we should tell Jingo Jingo about it," he said. "About you hearing him now, and about you hearing him near Greyson."

I shuddered. Jingo Jingo was one of my teachers and had been Shamus's teacher for years. He taught the ways of Death magic just beneath Liddy Salberg, who was the mousy woman I'd first met at my dad's funeral. I didn't mind learning about Death magic, but I did not like Jingo Jingo. Sometimes, when I cast the spell for Sight, I saw other things clinging to his heavy body, to his bones—the ghosts of children. And every time that happened, it creeped me the hell out.

"I've already told Jingo Jingo about my dad."

"And you'll tell him again."

"Sure I will." Rock, meet stubborn place.

He just stood there, quiet. Finally, "You'll do what's right. Even if you don't like it."

"Don't be too surprised when you find out you're wrong. Jingo gives me the creeps."

I pulled a couple mugs out of the cupboard, peered inside them to make sure there wasn't rock dust in there. Not that Stone shed or anything, but he was getting sneaky about putting away the things he played with while I was gone.

I poured us both coffee.

"Allie—"

"Yes, fine. I'll tell him. Again." *Not that it will do me a damn bit of good*, I thought. "And it's time for us to go."

I grabbed my heavy coat off the back of the door, because it was obviously freezing out there, and took the time to stuff my journal in the pocket. With coffee cups in hand, we left the apartment, locked the door, and were down the stairs and outside in short order.

We ducked inside Zay's car and headed off. We both held on to our coffee cups tucked against our palms. It was cold, February still dipping below freezing, but not quite cold enough for ice. There was something about the cold in Oregon that sank in deep and didn't let go.

"Maybe I'll just talk to Shamus instead," I said, carrying on the conversation from the kitchen.

"Shame can't look in your head as well as Jingo Jingo can."

"We don't know that," I said. "We haven't tried."

"True." Zay took a drink of coffee.

I thought it over. Shamus was good. I had a hunch he was a lot better at Death magic than he liked people to know. The first time my dad, through my eyes, had seen Shamus, he'd said he was a master. I think the slouchy goth bit was just so he could get out of doing work. Stay beneath his mother's notice, maybe, or stay beneath his teacher Jingo's notice.

Shame could probably do the job, but he might not want to.

"Jingo Jingo is a good teacher," Zay said.

"I didn't say he wasn't." I drank coffee and stared at the wet city lights through the window. "I just don't like him in my head."

Zay nodded. "He is . . . thorough."

I would have said *creepy*, *dangerous*, maybe even *disturbed*, but I still hadn't figured out why Zayvion felt the need to defend him. Shamus willingly admitted to thinking Jingo Jingo was a freak. Zay kept any strong opinions about Jingo Jingo to himself. Of course, Zayvion kept most of his strong opinions to himself.

"I don't think I can do much to help with the storm," I said, switching subjects. "I'm probably the least trained out of everyone."

"It isn't just training that makes a person good with magic."

"True. Blind stupidity and a high pain tolerance helps. Still don't think I'm going to be all that useful."

We were on the other side of the river at Maeve's inn. The drizzle had let up, and the sky was covered by clouds turned webby and gray by the city lights. Zay parked near the tree line by the river.

He didn't look at me, just stared out the window into the darkness. "You channeled the last wild storm. You tapped into its magic, and used it to heal me. And you didn't die."

Oh. Right. That. Magic had taken all my memories of that storm, but Nola—and later, Zayvion—had sort of filled me in on the basics. I may not have died, but I very

nearly did. A month in a coma is not a successful magical event, though. I'd paid for that like hell.

"They're not going to ask me to do that again, are
they?"

He breathed in, his nostrils flaring. He still didn't
look at me, didn't move. "I'm asking you not to do that
again."

I laughed, one hard choke. "Like I would."

That wasn't enough for him. He finally looked at me.
"I'm asking you to not step in. Not to help. Even if you
think you have to."

I raised an eyebrow and opened my mouth, but he
kept going.

"I know you'll do whatever you want. But there will be
many storms in the future. This is the first time you'll be
involved. The first time you'll see what we can do when we
all work together and what damage the storm can do, even
if we're at our best. I am asking—" He paused, thought it
over. Maybe he noticed the challenge in my gaze. People
didn't tell me what to do. He of all people should know
that by now. "I am asking you, Allie. Don't be a hero."

Hero. Was that what he was worried about? "Trust
me, I'm the last person in the world who will put on the
tights and cape."

The muscle at his jaw clenched. And I don't think he
was trying to hold back a smile.

"I will," he said.

"Put on the tights and cape?" I thought about that.
With a body like his, he'd look damn fine. "How about
leather instead?"

"No. I'll trust you."

Oh. That was nice too. I nodded. I wouldn't promise
to stand by and do nothing. But I wouldn't be stupid. I
knew how dangerous magic could be. After a couple
months of learning with the Authority, it was clear just
how much more I still had to learn.

A tap at Zay's window made me jump. Shame's pale face bent into view. "You two kids done bumping boots?"

Zayvion hadn't turned to look out his window. He didn't even twitch. What he did was smile. Then he opened the door so quickly, I thought for sure Shame would land flat on his back. Shame sidestepped the move, and made a little tsk-tsk sound.

"So slow," he said. "You're getting soft, Z."

"Want to try it again?" Zay asked.

They, apparently, had done this before.

Zay got out of the car and I did the same.

"You won't believe who's at this thing," Shame said.

"Try me," Zay said.

The two of them walked around the car, shoes grinding in the wet, loud gravel. Well, Shame's shoes, anyway. Zay moved like he always moved. Silent as an assassin's shadow.

"Okay, so, Sedra, Mom, Victor, Jingo, Liddy, you know, the regulars." Shame nodded at me. "How you feeling?"

"Why?"

"After the well-Hounding bit earlier today. You still look a little ... tense." Without waiting for my answer, he turned to Zay. "Jones, this woman is tense. I thought you were supposed to take care of that for her. Getting soft in more than one way, buddy?"

"Shut up, Shame."

"Just trying to be helpful. I'm here for you. To talk it out, if you need. Or to get you pills for what ails you."

"Done telling me who's here?" Zayvion asked. We were at the porch now. My bootheels made a solid thunk as I climbed the stairs and walked to the door.

"Well, for one, Hayden Kellerman is in."

Zay paused, just a second, a half beat in his normal stride. "Huh. Who else?"

"Oh, you know, some of the Seattle branch." Shame said that with a little too much forced cheer. "The Georgia girls, Romero, Pham. Maybe a dozen people."

"Terric?" Zay asked.

Shame smiled, like he'd come down with rigor. "Wouldn't be a party without him."

I opened the door and stepped through a ward that had been cast upon the doorway. The ward would probably make me stop cold if I didn't have an invitation to enter the room. Not exactly screening the participants, so much as letting whoever cast the ward—which, by the sweet Earl Grey tea taste on the back of my throat, I assumed was Victor—know who was coming in, and if they belonged here.

Even in the off-hours, I'd never seen the main room of the inn so quiet.

It wasn't that it was empty. There were maybe thirty or so people standing or sitting at the eight round tables with clean white tablecloths, arranged so that the area to the left, where a longer table was placed, held the room's focus. The lunch counter to the right was empty.

I had met half of the thirty or so people present, and could only assume the others were the Seattle contingent. Everyone had a drink: water, or coffee, tea, soda. There didn't seem to be any alcohol present. Ample baskets of bread and cheeses and olives were ready at each table.

It was clear there wasn't a regular customer, a non-Authority-sanctioned magic user, in the room. And it was also clear that no one much liked one another. Body language was tight and tense; expressions bordered on civil at best. People were grouped in four sections, probably shoring up with whichever faction they were sided with. Zayvion had been telling me for months that there was a war brewing among the Authority, and that it would break any day. Looking around the room made me wonder if it was going to break tonight.

The last thing I wanted to do was enter a room of angry, trigger-happy magic users. And that was exactly what I had come here to do.

Welcome to the bigs.

Chapter Eight

Most of the people in the room turned to look. Not at Zayvion, who stood to my right, not at Shamus, who stood to my left, but at me. Or more likely, at Daniel Beckstrom's daughter.

I met each of their gazes. A brief blur of faces, of eyes, of expressions: judgment, curiosity, and blatant hatred.

Yeah, well, I was thrilled to meet them too.

Maeve appeared from one of the doorways, walking beside a giant of a man, easily six inches taller than me or Zay, and almost as wide-shouldered as Mackanie Love. Black hair, dark beard with a dust of gray cut close to his jaw. He wore an old bomber jacket complete with wool collar over a T-shirt, jeans, and lumberjack boots. He smiled as he talked with Maeve. He gave off an easy, ready-for-a-fight kind of vibe, like he was in the company of old friends and old enemies and would be more than happy to take either down.

Some of the tension in the room shifted. Not that it was much better; it was just different.

Zayvion started off toward Maeve and the big man. I glanced out of the corner of my eye to see if this, perhaps, was Terric. But Shame's fake smile had turned into something introspective. Wicked. Boy was planning something. I didn't know what he was thinking, but anytime I'd seen that look on his face, it had been trouble.

"Who's that?" I asked as I strode toward an empty table in the exact center of the room, not caring who was staring at me, nor what faction I might be sitting down with.

Shame followed. "Hayden Kellerman. One of Mum's old friends. Might be my new da, the way she's looking at him." He yanked a chair out from the table, grinding the thing across the wooden floor, and then slouched down into it, scowling.

"You don't like him?"

"Are you even in the same room with me?" He gave me a brief, sideways look. No smile, but plenty of twinkle in that eye. "I thought you were good at reading people."

"So you do like him. What? Don't want your mom to know?" I took the other chair, and sat with a lot less noise, thank you.

"Better that way. For some reason she doubts the purity of my intentions when I give her pointers on her love life. Especially when it comes to me handing out her phone number."

"Doubts your purity? Can't imagine why."

He kicked my foot under the table, not hard, and went back to his sullen scowl.

I'd missed dinner, so checked out the cheese, chose a few squares, and popped one in my mouth. Very good. Mild and a little smoky. I watched Zayvion make his way across the room, pausing to talk and shake hands with at least a dozen people as he slowly strolled toward Maeve and Hayden.

"He's popular tonight," I noted.

"Guardian of the gates," Shame said like that explained it all. "I think he's been in Alaska."

"Zay?"

"Hayden."

"And?"

"And. Nothing." He picked up a glass of water, took a

drink. He looked much more relaxed, or maybe he had been relaxed and I just hadn't been paying attention. This many powerful magic users in one room made me jumpy.

No, it made me want to stand up and walk out. But that wasn't the way it worked. Once a part of the Authority, you didn't leave without checking your memories at the door. And I planned to keep hold of as many of my memories as I could.

I watched Zayvion work the room, all Zen and smooth, deadly confidence. Looked good on him. And it made an impression on the other people in the room too. Made them sit back, calm, or sit forward, anxious, reactions that were interesting in and of themselves.

For the first time, I realized Zayvion was a respected, or maybe even feared, member of the Authority. Not just a student. Not just a man who patrolled the streets looking for bad guys. But a very dangerous man who used all forms of magic—Life, Blood, Death, Faith, light, and dark—to guard the gates, to keep magic in the way the Authority intended it to be kept, and the people of this city safe. Even if it meant opposing fellow members of the Authority.

"Shame?" I asked, keeping my gaze on Zay.

"Mmm?"

"Am I dating royalty?"

"You tell me."

I smiled. "King Jones. Doesn't sound very royal."

That got a chuckle out of him. "He's a beauty, though, isn't he? Especially when he's working. Can make a mountain bow down to the sea."

I sat back to enjoy this. Maybe I'd get a good look at a part of Mr. Private I hadn't seen before.

Zay finally made it over to Hayden. I was right. Hayden was about six inches taller than Zay, and twice as broad at the shoulders. He made Zay look tiny, towering over him like that. Hayden would make a hell of a

Viking, swinging a battle-ax or carrying a cannon over one shoulder as he stormed the castle gates.

He shook Zay's hand, then wrapped him in a huge bear hug, slapping him on the back so loud, I winced as it echoed through the room.

"Good to see you, boy!" Hayden's voice carried over the rest of the conversations filling the place. "Looks like you're about to be put through your paces! Think you're up for it?"

Zay stepped back and answered, but his response was so quiet, I couldn't pick it up, not even with Hound ears.

Still, Hayden laughed. "That's what I like to hear. Got some new kind of fire burning in him, doesn't he, Maeve? What you been doing to this boy while I've been gone?"

"Excuse me," said a man behind Shame and me. "Are you Daniel Beckstrom's daughter?"

Danger. That was all I knew. Shame tensed from head to foot, both hands off the table now. The cheese knife was missing.

I inhaled, taking in the stranger's scents—the plastic of too much hair gel, and a deeper note of something faintly metallic. He was not familiar to me. I turned.

He was maybe midthirties, shorter than me, looked like he knew his way around a gym, and gave off that professional broker, banker, doctor vibe. Wore a Nike T-shirt under a Windbreaker, and jeans with tennis shoes. Clean haircut. Clean-shaven. Small, close-set brown eyes. I'd never seen him before in my life.

"Your father was a good man. I'm very sorry for your loss."

If he thought my father was a good man, my opinion of him just took a dive. Still, I had manners. "Thank you. And you are?"

"Mike Barham." He held out his hand. I didn't take it.

"Nice to meet you," I said. "If you'll excuse us, I don't want to miss out on the main event."

He glanced at Shamus and gave a halfhearted attempt to look surprised. "Shamus Flynn," he said. He didn't sound angry, but hate radiated off the man. "I didn't know you were in town. Still living with your mother?"

Shame didn't turn. Didn't twitch, didn't look at him.

Mike's smile slipped. He walked around to stand next to Shame, which did not seem like a very smart thing to do. "You still mad at me about the position up north?" he asked. "You know the best man won. Plus, you'd never make it out there without your dear mother to protect you. It's dangerous out in the real world."

Something inside Shame coiled and burned, ready to leap. One more word out of Barham, and I was pretty sure Barham would have a cheese knife stabbed in his throat.

"Blow me, Barham," Shame said.

Barham shook his head. "You are a spoiled little boy, Flynn. Your father used to tell me you were his biggest disappointment. He used to tell me he had wanted a son, not a fag."

Shame rolled his head back and smiled up at him. "Tell me more about my father, Mike. Please do."

I'd never heard that tone out of Shame. It was sweet, nice. And scared the hell out of me.

"You," I said to Mike Barham with enough Influence to stun a rhino, "move away. Now."

He jerked, and glared at me. He opened his mouth.

"Go," I said.

He did as I said, because he couldn't not do it. Under my Influence, he turned and walked away. He ended up across the room, where he sat at another table, and threw me angry looks.

Whatever. I was not going to just sit there and listen to him insult my friend.

It took Shame a full five minutes to finally let go of the cheese knife under the table, and place it back on the table. He didn't look at me. He didn't say anything. Just rolled his head down and stared off on some middle distance.

"So, he's a prick," I said. "Want to talk?"

He shook his head imperceptibly. I didn't push him on it. I'd always thought Shame was straight. Not that it mattered. If Mike had wanted to make Shame angry, he'd done a bang-up job of it.

I glanced around the room, looking for Zayvion. He was absorbed in a quiet, intense conversation with another man I'd never met. The man with Zay was slender and tall, wore black slacks and a black turtleneck, and held himself with an elegance that made me think of historical movies with sword fights and aristocrats. His hair was so blond, it was white, and long enough it fell between his shoulder blades, pulled back and banded. He and Zayvion were both turned half toward us, talking quietly, but also with hand gestures, as if they had a lot to say, and not enough time to cover it with words alone.

Hoping to change the mood, I nudged Shame.

"So who's Zay with now?"

Shame blinked and seemed to come back from a long, long distance. He inhaled, and looked in the direction of my gaze.

"Terric," he breathed.

It wasn't the sound of a man who hated another man. No. In that one word, in that one name, was longing, need, the sound of something precious lost.

I didn't realize they had been intimate. Or maybe they hadn't. Maybe the draw between Soul Complements wasn't about the sex. Maybe it was just about magic. Using it, having it, letting it use you, immersed and joined by it in ways unimaginable. Power.

Whatever it was, Shame's body language was that of

a starving man using all his strength not to yield to the poisoned feast before him.

I thought about putting my hand on his arm to console him, and decided against it. Shame was keyed up and I didn't want to get a cheese knife in the throat.

"Zay and him friends?" I asked instead, trying to draw Shame down.

"We all were once." Saying that seemed to help. He closed his eyes a moment. Maybe he realized he was sitting on the edge of his seat. He relaxed in stages back into his normal slouch and rubbed his gloved hand over his eyes.

"Balls," he said. "It's gonna be a long night."

"Were you and Terric lovers?"

"No." He sighed behind his gloves. "I'm not gay. But that man . . ." He pulled his hand away from his eyes. "Soul Complements. It's . . ." He just shook his head. "Him and me . . . and magic? No. It doesn't—can't—work."

"Did you refuse to be tested to see if you and he were Soul Complements because you were afraid you might want sex with him?" Yes, I am tactful that way. And also stupid.

He stared at me for a moment. "It's good you and I are friends, Beckstrom," he finally said "Because I'm willing to ignore that ridiculous nonsense that just fell out of your mouth. It doesn't have a damn thing to do with sex, okay? There were other reasons, other . . . bad things."

"Like?"

"Like I'm done talking about it. And like I wish Mum had ponied up a bottle or two of wine right about now."

"I can see why she wouldn't want to serve alcohol to a roomful of trigger-happy magic users," I said.

"She doesn't have to feed it to the magic users. She could just feed it to me."

"I'll buy you a beer if you give me a who's who on the rest of the people here."

"Done." He sat and leaned his elbows on the table. "The three women laughing over there? Dark wavy hair, coffee skin, and beautiful matching sets of big, lovely—"

I slapped him on the arm.

"Hey. Eyes. I was going to say eyes. What were you thinking? They're the Georgia sisters. Life magic. The blonde next to them, about Mum's age in the biker jacket who looks like she can wrestle an alligator? Darla. Death magic."

He shifted in his seat a little. "The Russian underwear model over there is Nik Pavloski, and the family man next to him is a sweet-hearted killer named Joshua Romero. Faith magic—that means they're both Closers. At the table near the wall is the ass wipe, Barham. Life magic, and the woman sitting next to him who looks like she hates him—petite, pale, black hair with a red streak, and a knockout scowl—Paige Iwamoto. She's Blood magic. Stab him, baby—you know he deserves it." Shame licked his lips and stared at Paige, as if he could will her to wield the cheese knife.

"Shame," I said.

He looked away from Paige and Mike, giving the room a subtle glance while he reached for a piece of bread. He would make a good spy.

"You know the rest of the people in the room, I think."

I looked around, the remaining people standing and sitting at the other tables: Kevin Cooper, Violet's bodyguard; Sunny, whose demeanor was the exact opposite of her name; Ethan Katz, who was my dad's and now my accountant; the twins Carl and La, whom I'd seen briefly at my test; the ex-quarterback-looking dude whom I'd also seen briefly at my test; and a few other suits—two women and a man—board members from Beckstrom Enterprises I'd met over the last couple weeks. The rest of the people I'd seen off and on at Maeve's, but hadn't been officially introduced to.

"Pretty much," I said.

"You're welcome," he said. "Now, about that beer."

"If I could please have your attention."

I glanced at the front of the room. Victor, trim and gray-haired, stood behind the long table, an open laptop in front of him. His suit jacket hung on the back of the chair, along with his tie, and his shirtsleeves were rolled up to the elbow. Even from this distance, I could see that his eyes were bloodshot. He looked like he'd just been through the longest meeting of his life, and been elected to stand up and give everyone the bad news.

Maeve, looking more composed and refreshed than Victor, sat to his left. Next to her was Liddy Salberg, a quiet, mousy woman, who took plain to the extreme. I'd first seen her at my dad's burial. She'd also been at my test, and she'd since been my teacher in Death magic. I never seemed to get a good read off her body language. That mousy exterior hid something else—I was sure of it—though I'd never seen her be anything but polite and professional.

Still, I got the impression that she didn't like me, or that I made her nervous.

At her left was Sedra, the head of the Authority in Portland. Always cool, always portrait-perfect, her unchanging expression and porcelain complexion made her look like she was carved out of marble. Only her blue eyes gave her a hint of life. Her bodyguard, Dane Lannister, stood behind her, looking how he always looked: relaxed and deadly. There was something about him that made me pause, like a bad taste in my mouth, but try as I might, I couldn't think of what it was about him that bothered me.

Instead, I wondered who usually filled the empty seat next to Sedra, wondered if perhaps it had been my father.

Interestingly, Jingo Jingo, who usually made himself a part of any gathering, was nowhere to be seen.

Weird.

"Please be seated, so we may begin," Victor said.

Everyone made their way to seats, filling the tables ahead of us, and behind us.

"Please, please, please," Shame whispered so quietly, I wasn't sure if he said it or I imagined he did.

Zay and Terric walked toward us, a study in opposites, and yet both powerful, calm, confident. Terric angled to take the seat next to Paige. Zay sat next to me, shifting his chair so he could better see the front of the room.

"Exhale before your head explodes," Zay said quietly. "He's not coming to the table."

Shame exhaled.

Victor began speaking. "As many of you have heard, we have an unprecedented warning that a wild-magic storm will be hitting the Portland area soon. We think it will strike within the next forty-eight hours. That gives us some time to coordinate our efforts and work together against this threat."

He paused, taking the time to make some eye contact. I'd seen my dad do that when he was facing a hostile audience. While Victor did that, I glanced at the body language within my range of sight.

Tight. Pensive. Maybe not explosive but damn close. Pretty much the same as when I'd walked in.

I'd already figured that these people were secretive and suspicious. But until this moment, I hadn't realized that these people barely tolerated one another.

Neat.

That brewing war? I'd put my bet on the table that it was done brewing. All it needed now was a spark to set it off.

My stomach clenched as I realized the war might already be on, and lines might already be drawn as to who should use magic, and how it should be used. And I had no idea who wanted what, nor whose side I was on.

I reached back in my head to see if Dad had something to say about all this, but he had been quiet as a corpse—ha, not funny—ever since I walked through that door.

I had the feeling he didn't much want to give Liddy or Jingo Jingo or anyone else an excuse to go digging around in my head looking for him.

Victor was done with the eye-contact pause.

"Our largest concern for the citizens of the area is that the wild magic will interrupt, or warp, the spells already in place in the city. We've compiled a detailed list of businesses and services that we will monitor and protect, and prioritized them from the most vital to the least, and divided that by the quadrants of the city. Since St. Johns has no conduits for magic, we'll just need to cover four of the five quadrants."

He glanced down at the laptop, then back up. "I know many of you have . . . vested concerns in the way magic is made available to the public. Here in this city, and in others. Now is not the time to push those agendas forward. Loss of life has never been the Authority's goal, and certainly now, more than any other time, a significant loss of life at the hand, influence, or neglect of a member of the Authority would carry dire consequences to any and all involved."

Threats. There's a neat way to ruin friendships and attract enemies.

"We've put together a suggested list of which businesses and services we'd like members to monitor. It's been an . . . exhausting few days." He took a drink of water.

"This list isn't perfect. I'm sure there will be changes. We'll distribute it in a moment. Are there any questions so far?"

There were. About forty-five minutes of questions, most of them dealing with things I did not understand. It was like everyone had suddenly switched to a foreign language, half of which sounded like it dealt with magic, and the other half sounded like some kind of underground lingo.

"Should I be understanding any of this?"

Zay leaned back a bit. "It's pretty standard elbowing and power plays for who gets to do what."

He didn't look concerned, so I took his lead and passed the time trying to remember names and what kinds of magic the people in the room preferred to use.

The gathered members of the Authority were pretty evenly split between the four disciplines—well, five if you counted the mix of magic and technology my dad had pushed into use.

But watching how they spoke to one another, or more so, how they didn't speak or look at one another, I could see the tension, the cracks and fractures, between them, divided not by what magic they used but rather by who should use it, and how.

And I found it fascinating—no, frightening—that no one had mentioned that there was the very real possibility that the well was already being affected by the coming storm. The magic in it was being drained—maybe by the storm. Seemed to me that we had two potential disasters on the horizon.

Perhaps that went without saying.

It sucked to be the newest kid in the club. And I hadn't even earned my decoder ring.

Sedra stood. Everyone watched her, waiting. It wasn't exactly reverence, but more a shared acknowledgment that she would make the decisions they would all have to live with. For good and bad.

"We will set spells in place to further monitor vital systems and services throughout the city," she said, her musical voice at contrast with her strict demeanor. "But until the storm hits, we wait."

You couldn't have quieted a room faster if you'd shoved a sock in every mouth.

Zayvion looked Zen on the outside, but inside he burned with anger.

"I thought it was agreed we would coordinate our efforts," he said, his quiet voice filling the room.

"That," Terric said, "is what I also understood. We would plan for the worst, and meet it head-on. We have time on our side for once. We can plan how to mitigate the magical onslaught."

With every word Terric spoke, Shamus hunkered into himself, his hands tucked into his pockets, one shoulder hitched as if he could deflect the pain.

Sedra gave both men a cool, emotionless gaze. "Closers," she said, like it was a dirty word she didn't want in her mouth, "will need to watch for gates opening, for breaches between life and death. I expect you are willing to do your duty and abide by the wisdom of the Voices of the Authority?"

Voices. She meant the highest-level magic users: Maeve, Victor, Liddy, and Sedra herself. My father too, once, though no one had yet taken his position.

"I will do what is asked of me," Terric said.

"Zayvion?" she asked. "Will you abide by the wisdom of the Authority?"

Okay, I was starting to dislike her imperious, overly formal, condescending tone. Oh, who was I kidding? I hated the way she high-handed people. I'd watched it over the last couple months. When this woman said *jump*, everyone asked her when they should come back down.

Yes, she was the head of the Authority. But there was something unrelenting about the woman. As if she had to work hard to cover her hatred for everything and everyone around her. And I knew Zayvion Jones, the gate-guardian-do-my-duty-until-death, would bow to her just like everyone else.

"I'll do everything in my power to keep the city safe," Zayvion said.

Well, well. Not exactly a "yes, ma'am." I wondered whether she would let it pass.

"So let me get this right," Hayden said. The burly giant was standing by the door, arms crossed over his wide chest. If Zayvion's voice had been loud, Hayden's was thunder. "No pre-spells, no triggers, no traps, filters, no backup conduits or overload lines? How exactly are we supposed to keep these places, hospitals, prisons, nursing homes, warded from the effects of the storm?"

Victor nodded. "We've decided to approach this with as little magic use as possible because of how powerful the storm appears to be. Too many spells and too many members supporting those spells, managing the pain— even with Proxies—will limit how quickly we can react when the storm hits."

"The big plan here is to wait and see how bad we're beat before we start fighting?" Hayden chuckled. "There's a winning strategy."

Victor glared at Hayden, but the big man just put his hand out, as if to say it wasn't his bright idea.

"All considerations have been addressed, Mr. Keller-man," Victor said. "We work together, as we have worked together in bygone times. If we fight each other, there will be consequences that will benefit none of us."

"Well, then." Hayden clapped his hands together and so effectively broke the tension building in the room, I wondered if he'd cast a spell. "Sounds like all that's left is to gut and clean. What part of town am I covering?"

He strode across the room toward Victor. As he passed, people sort of shook off the intensity of the meeting. Smaller conversations cropped up again, and people stood, stretched. Shame was on his feet, and heading to the lunch counter and bar at the back of the room. I turned to watch him. I wasn't the only one.

Terric shifted in his chair, and stared at Shame's back. His expression seemed calm, but the tightness at the edges of his eyes, in the angle of his jaw, spoke of restraint. And desire.

Interesting.

Shame slipped behind the lunch counter and dug around for something. I heard the thick clink of beer bottles; then Shame reappeared, three beers caught in the fingers of one hand, the fourth already pressed to his lips.

He lowered the beer, grinned at me, and then strode over, changing his gaze to meet Terric's straight on.

Boy didn't run from trouble. That was sure.

Terric stood and walked over to our table. Looked like he didn't run from trouble either.

Zay turned to face Shame too. Shame was still grinning. Since I was not about to be the only person sitting if this was going to turn into a brawl, I stood as well.

"Allie." Shame offered me a beer. "You still owe me."

I took it even though I didn't like beer.

"Zay." Zayvion, behind me, reached over my shoulder and took the beer Shame offered.

"Terric." Shame extended the last beer to him.

Terric took the beer. "Think you owe me more than a beer, Shamus."

Shame's heartbeat rose, but I didn't think the other men noticed. They weren't Hounds. They didn't have to live off instinct and the subtle shifts in the people around them to survive.

"Well, today you're getting a beer," Shamus said. He tipped his and gave us all a half nod. "To the hunt. To the kill. Till the world stands still."

"To the hunt," Zay and Terric said.

I just raised my beer and took a tiny sip. Nope. Still didn't like the stuff.

"I heard about Greyson," Terric said.

Shame nodded. "Have you seen him?"

"I just got in a couple hours ago."

Shame glanced around the room. "It's not like they'll let us out of this, but we've got a few minutes. Want to see?"

Zay took another drink of his beer. He wrapped his hand around my hip and hooked his thumb in my front pocket, the heel of his hand pressed against my hip bone. This close, I could feel his worry and anger that did not show through that Zen exterior. I didn't know exactly what he was angry about.

Terric paused, just a beat too long, before answering. "I'm sure you have somewhere else to be," he said to Shame. "I know I do." He took another swig of the beer, looked Shamus right in the eyes. "Thanks for the beer."

Shame nodded. Looked easy. Casual about the whole thing. But that response was a slap in the face.

Terric turned to me. "I'm sorry I haven't had the chance to meet you, Ms. Beckstrom. I hope to remedy that in the future."

"We'll figure it out," I said.

Terric made brief eye contact with Zay. Something changed in his expression. Sort of like ice breaking under pressure. He turned back to Shame. "Don't take me being here as anything other than it is. Authority business."

"Wouldn't think of it," Shame said.

"We have an understanding, then?"

"Hatred, with a heaping side of grudge?"

Terric smiled, a fleeting thing that seemed to warm through the ice, flicked to life by Shame's agreement. "That should cover it. Except for one thing. While I am here, you and I will not get in each other's way."

"You know me, Terric. I'd rather be almost anywhere than near you."

"Shame—," Zay said.

"No." Terric held one hand toward Zayvion. Then to Shame, "We stay out of each other's way. Tell me we're clear on that."

"Twenty-twenty," Shame said.

Terric nodded. "Good. I'll speak with you soon, Zay, Allie." He strode off toward the front of the room where people were poring over Victor's laptop and maps. I realized I'd been holding my fingers spread and ready to cast a spell. I closed my hand and stuck it in my pocket.

"You didn't have to be an ass," Zayvion said.

Shame tipped his beer up to his mouth again. Empty.

"You know I love you, Jones," he said, "but stay the hell out of my business." He didn't wait for Zay's reply. Didn't have to. He'd known him long enough he could give himself whatever speech Zay had planned.

Shame turned and walked away, to the bar again. He slipped behind it, found another beer, then stormed out the doors there, putting his pockets for a smoke.

Zay leaned into me a little more, or maybe he pulled me back toward him.

"They'll be okay." I tried to say it as a statement, but it came out all question.

Probably because Zay's doubt and concern washed through me. He hurt for Shame like a brother who knew there was nothing he could do to fix the pain Shame had gotten himself into.

"Terric won't try to hurt him, will he?" I asked. "He's a good guy, right?"

"We're all good guys," Zay said.

Yeah, he believed that as much as I did.

"Zayvion?" Victor was making his way across the room, looking like a man who knew how to wield a sword. And since he was one of my teachers, in magic and in physical defense, I actually knew he could swing a sword. Very well, as a matter of fact.

Zay pulled away so we no longer touched.

I'd never seen Victor looking so ragged. His eyes were bloodshot, and his usually clean-shaven face shadowed a beard.

"I'm going to go over the quadrants and coverage with the Closers now," he said. "Would you join us, please?"

"What about Chase?" Zay asked.

"She's here."

Zay took a second to find her in the crowd. I did too, since I hadn't seen her earlier. I spotted her walking in through the archway at the front of the room. Beyond that arch was the hall that led to sitting rooms and a stairway to the basement, where her ex-lover Greyson currently resided in a cage. She looked angry, shellshocked, sick. Like she'd just seen something, or done something, very, very wrong.

Yeah, I didn't think I'd be doing any better if it were Zay in that cage. Chase was handling this a lot better than I would, even if she hadn't come to see Greyson before now. And it didn't take a genius to know she had just come from seeing him.

The woman radiated a don't-fuck-with-me vibe stronger than any Repel spell she could have cast. It worked like a charm. Everyone steered a wide berth around her and left her alone.

Another person detached from the shadows beyond the archway and walked in behind Chase.

I'd wondered when he was going to show up.

Jingo Jingo was a big man, not like Hayden, who had height to balance out his width. Jingo was just heavy. There was something about him that made him seem even bigger. He had an immensity that took up more room than his bulk justified. He radiated a dark presence as if shadows and other, haunting things clung to him. The light, pouring down from the high rafters, couldn't clean the room of it.

He bothered me, even when he was laughing like he was everyone's friend. I didn't trust him. I didn't like him.

He rambled over to Chase, right into her leave-me-alone zone.

Fire, meet oil.

I thought for sure Chase would give him hell. But when he neared, she seemed to cool down, her fire snuffed to ash, her anger suffocated, gone dead as he reached out and stroked her arm reassuringly. Her shoulders slumped, her head fell back to rest against the wall behind her, and she closed her eyes. She looked exhausted.

And when he spoke—a low rumble I couldn't pull into words—she opened her eyes. She looked like a lost child, hopeful, maybe even desperate for his reassurance, his guidance. She did not look like the powerful, angry Closer I knew.

What was he doing to her? What was he telling her? What had they done down there with Greyson?

"Allie?" Zayvion said.

Right. He had been asked to do something. Look over Victor's plans or something.

"See you soon," I said.

Zay walked off with Victor, both heading toward Chase.

Even though Jingo Jingo did not turn around, as soon as Victor and Zayvion were on their way toward Chase, he dropped his hand off her arm.

Chase seemed to come to, and get her bitch back on. She scowled at Zay and Victor, and made it clear she didn't like following them to one side of the room where Terric and a small group of other people— Nik and Joshua and maybe three others, probably all Closers—stood.

Closers. People who could reach into someone's mind and take away their ability to use magic. People who took away memories.

Maybe I wanted to know what they were talking about. Especially if it had to do with the removal of memories—I had Hounds on the street I needed to look after.

Got halfway across the room too before Shame fell into step with me.

"Don't know what's stuck in your craw," he said, his breath heavy with beer and cigarette smoke and that clove scent that was all his own, "but you got company."

"What?"

I'd been so focused on studying the faces and body language of the group of Closers at the front of the room, I didn't notice everyone was looking over at the main door.

And standing in the doorway was someone who most definitely should not be here.

Davy Silvers.

Chapter Nine

Davy hadn't stepped through the doorway. He had good instincts. The ward on the door would push him out or knock him unconscious if he stepped in. But the room wasn't covered in Glamour or Illusion. Instinct might tell him not to step in, but his eyes showed him exactly what was going on.

People went back to talking, ignoring him, and acting like this was just a normal sort of meeting for some normal sort of business social.

I don't think Davy was convinced. But it wasn't the confusion on his face that I was worried about. It was the pain.

I turned and strode across the room, Shame ghosting me, and made it to the door in a few seconds flat, Davy's bad habit of following me around since Pike's death didn't make living three lives, all filled with secrets, and none of which could be shared equally, any easier. Every time my lives crossed, like now when Davy the Hound was sticking his nose into the secret business of the Authority, it set my teeth on edge.

"What's wrong?" I asked.

Boy looked like death on a bender. He didn't smell of alcohol. No, he just stank of sweat and pain.

"Where are you hurt?"

He shook his head.

"Hello," Maeve said, coming up beside us. "Can I help you?"

Davy squinted over at her, like the light in the room was too much. Migraine? Concussion? "I need to talk to you," he said to me, eyeing Shamus. "Allie. Could I talk to you? Now."

"Do you need help?" Maeve asked, a little less hostess, and a little more concern. I liked that she didn't immediately try to send him on his way. Maeve was one of my favorite teachers.

"This is probably Hound business," I said to Maeve. "I got it, thank you." I walked through the door and Davy backed off. The ward was good. Built to let the right people out and to not let the wrong people in.

Davy paced the porch. I reached back, intending to shut the door, but Shame was there, and stepped out with us.

"You want me to drive you to the hospital?" I asked. I'd long ago learned there was no use being subtle with Hounds. Too much substance abuse, too many overdoses, from dealing with the constant pain of using magic, for subtleties to get through to a reasonable mind.

"I didn't do it," he said, his voice tense, too high.

"All right. Do what?"

Davy turned, the yellow light of the porch lamp revealing his tortured expression. "I think it's Bea."

"What's Bea?"

"I think she's hurt."

My phone rang, and Davy and I both jumped.

I fumbled with my jacket pocket and pulled out my cell.

"Hello?"

"This is Stotts. I need you to Hound a case. Meet me at Third and Southwest Main."

"When?" I heard the sound of traffic behind him.

"As soon as you can."

I did a quick calculation. How long would it take me to drop Davy off at the hospital, or at least get him in the hands of someone else who could keep an eye on him? Like maybe over to the warehouse and have Grant look in on him, or, hells, back to his own apartment, not that I knew where he lived.

"Can you give me an hour?"

"Allie." Stotts paused, took a breath. "One of your Hounds is down. I've called 911. She'll be on her way to the hospital soon."

"She?" I glanced up at Davy, who had his arms crossed over his stomach and was standing there, rocking a little on his feet, miserable.

"Beatrice Lufkin," Stotts said over the sound of a siren growing louder in the background. "Whatever happened to her, there's a hell of a lot of magic involved. But it's fading fast."

My heart punched my ribs like a fist.

"I'll be there." I shoved the phone in my pocket. "Shame? Tell Zay—no, tell your mom that I had to handle a Hounding job. Thank her for inviting me to the get-together tonight." What more could I say with Davy listening? "I'll call her later tonight if I can. Tomorrow morning at the latest."

"Are you going alone?" he asked.

"No. Davy's going with me." Davy's head lifted at the mention of his name. His eyes, for the briefest of seconds, flashed red.

It might have been my imagination. Or it might have been magic.

Weird.

"You have the keys to your car?" I asked.

Davy fumbled in his jeans pocket, held out a set of keys with a plastic frame attached to it. In the frame was a picture of him and Tomi in one of those photo booths. They were kissing, Tomi's hand stretched out to try to cover the camera.

I put my hand on Davy's arm to help him down the porch steps.

"Stotts, right?" Shame asked.

"Yes." We were already on the gravel. "I'll have my phone on."

Davy walked with me, not nearly as light on his feet as he usually was. He breathed a little too hard, and was covered in sweat even though all he was wearing was a T-shirt and jean jacket in the below-thirty-degree weather.

We made it to his car, and he didn't even argue when I helped him slump into the passenger's seat.

I got in the driver's side, started the car, and got us across the parking lot and onto the access road.

"Talk to me," I said. "How badly are you hurt?"

His eyes were closed, his head against the headrest. He'd tried to buckle his seat belt, pulling it across his chest, but given up short of actually clicking it into place.

He didn't say anything until I hit the road that ran parallel to the river and would get me to one of the bridges and back across the river to Portland.

"Ever since I got out of the hospital, I've felt it," he said quietly. "When Hounds are hurt. I told you that, right?"

He had. Well, he'd told me he could tell when Tomi was hurting. But he sure as hell hadn't mentioned how debilitating it was to him. "You said you felt Tomi. You feel the other Hounds too?"

"Sometimes. When the pain's big. When it's magic."

"Is it always this bad?"

"No. Headaches. Muscle aches. But this . . . ." He was quiet for a little bit and I noticed his breathing was more even.

"It felt like I was on fire. And where there wasn't fire, I was numb. Freezing."

"You Proxying for anyone?"

"No."

"None of the Hounds? Not even Tomi?"

His breathing hitched, and it took him a little longer to answer. "No."

I didn't smell a lie on him.

"Where were you when this happened?"

"Here."

"The car?"

"Yes."

"Driving?"

"Parked outside the inn."

"Davy, how many times do I have to tell you to stop following me? That was a private business meeting between a lot of investors who want their interests in Beckstrom Enterprises kept quiet. If they find out I have a Hound on my heels, it could seriously damage my dad's company."

I'd kept that lie ready for months now.

He mustered a small smile, but still hadn't opened his eyes. "You don't like your dad's company."

"No, but I like Violet and her baby having enough income to keep them out of the poorhouse. Hells, everything I've done to get the Hound warehouse up and running was funded by my stake in that company. And my dad is dead. It's my company now."

"Like they'd kick you out if I followed you." This time he turned his head and opened his eyes. Red flashed there again, and I smelled a different scent on him. Something sweet like cherries, but different, muddied by other smells. Magic. That was certain. But whether he was using it, or it was being used on him, I didn't know.

How long could the effects of what Tomi had done to him last? It would help if I knew exactly what Tomi had done to him, but the only one who knew that was caged in the basement of the inn, and he was not the talkative type.

"Okay, I'll say it one more time," I said. "You have

to stop following me. There are personal things I don't want you involved in. Business things that, yes, would get me kicked off the board running Beckstrom Enterprises. These people don't see you as just a Hound. They see you as a possible information leak. As someone who probably does drugs to kick the pain, and who wouldn't take much to become desperate enough to sell what you know, what you've seen, for your next fix."

Yes, I was lying. And even though I was pretty good at it, because some of what I was saying was true and I'd been working on a bulletproof explanation for some time now, I was also hoping he was in enough pain, or distracted enough, he wouldn't scent the lie on me.

"Nice bunch of people you do business with," he said. His voice was a little stronger and he didn't seem to be sweating quite so badly.

"Business isn't about friendships. It isn't about nice," I said. "Everyone has their own interests to protect."

"And you're protecting your money." He rolled his head forward to look out the front window. "Sweet of you."

"No. I'm protecting the people I care about. Violet. My sibling. The Hounds. And that means you, Davy. But so help me, if you don't smart up and listen to me this time, I am going to report you to the police for harassment, stalking, and anything else that will keep you from getting in trouble. Or getting me in trouble. Do you understand that?"

"I heard you," he said. But from the set of his jaw, he wasn't listening. Stubborn, angry young man.

"I should take you home."

"Thought you had a job lined up with Stotts."

When I didn't say anything, he sighed. "You're such a hypocrite. All Hounds need a backup. Those are your rules. Yours. I'm your backup tonight."

"My backup can't stand."

"Since when do you need me to do jumping jacks?"

he asked. "I just need to watch. I won't get in the way. You know I'm good at that."

I didn't say anything.

"I want to see what happened to Bea. Want to know what I felt, if I really felt it."

We were on the bridge now, and traffic was light, since it was pretty late and there weren't any big games or concerts letting out.

"Please," he said. "I need to know I'm not going insane. That magic . . . that it didn't screw me up, permanently." And the last bit was quiet, wrenched out of him like he was angry with himself for even saying it. Or just very, very afraid it might be true.

Magic in me pushed, warmed under my skin, and left a prickly itch behind. The lights on the bridge flickered for a moment, went dark. The magical backup generators for the lights did not kick on.

Davy felt the drop in magic too. He grunted. "What was that?"

Lights, regular electric lights, flicked back on, burned bright.

"I don't know." I didn't. I had ideas. The storm was brewing. They didn't know exactly when it would hit. They thought we had a few days. They could be wrong.

We were on the other side of the bridge. Davy didn't say anything. Just waited as I slowed the car, weighing my odds of actually getting him home, out of the car, and locked in his apartment while I used his car to get to Stotts.

Wasn't gonna happen.

I headed into town.

"Thanks," he said. He didn't say anything else until it started raining.

"Wipers are on the left."

I flicked them on. Glanced at him. His eyes were closed again. Still tired, but the pain seemed to have passed. Maybe the pain was physical. Side effect from his head wound, from his collapsed lung. Appendix or something.

Magic wasn't the only way people got hurt.

"I noticed Zayvion was there," he said.

"And?"

"I didn't think he had an investment in your dad's business."

"He's my boyfriend," I said. "We have an investment in each other."

"And Shame?"

"Anyone tell you how nosy you are?" *And how damn observant?* I thought.

"No. I usually keep my nosy questions to myself."

"Shame's mother owns the inn. She used to know my father. They weren't friends, but she is a smart business-woman. If you were paying that close of attention, you also noticed he'd had a couple beers. I don't think he was there to enhance his portfolio. I think he was there for the free booze."

Davy smiled again. "My kind of guy."

"Do not make friends with him," I said. "He's trouble."

"And I'm not?"

"No, Davy," I said, angling the car toward Chapman Square. "You're a good kid. If you'd work on your pain-in-the-ass tendencies, you'd be real nice."

"Too bad that isn't going to happen anytime soon," he muttered. "Real nice doesn't get you very far."

"Real nice can keep you from getting beat up," I said.

He smiled. "Right. Maybe we should both work on it, then."

Like I said. Pain in the ass.

The blue and red lights of the ambulance glided over the dark, magic-caged buildings that surrounded the area. I spotted the MERC's cleanup van, and a few peo-ple who might have been Stotts's crew moving around in the shadows. The ambulance was just easing away from the curb, lights on, but no siren. I wanted to follow it, go to the hospital, make sure Bea was all right.

I briefly considered sending Davy along to do just that, but his eyes were closed. Kid was in no shape to drive. From the pace of his breathing he'd be asleep soon.

Police tape and traffic cones sectioned off part of the park, which as far as I could see was empty. I didn't know what job Bea would have been Hounding. Sometimes a Hound was hired by the city to make sure there wasn't any magical mischief going down on city property, but usually Jack took those calls. I searched my memory, wondering if he or Bea had mentioned going to Hound Chapman Square.

"Davy?"

He sucked in a quick breath. I'd just woken him. He blinked, sat a little straighter, got his bearings pretty fast, and glanced over at me. "Yeah?"

"Did Bea or Jack say they were doing the park?"

He looked out the window at the police tape. "No. Not at last week's meeting. Maybe a last-minute jobber?"

"Maybe." I parked the car a block away. "Stay here. Get some sleep. I'm going to be right over there with the cops—"

"The cursed cop," he corrected.

"Allegedly cursed cop," I said. "Stay here. Do not walk out on that street. Do not drive this car. You are too tired, and would probably get yourself killed if you tried to do either."

He shook his head. "You just can't give a guy a compliment, can you?"

It wasn't a promise. But it was all I had time to get out of him.

I left the keys in the ignition and got out of the car. I still wore the void stone necklace. I couldn't take it off and leave it with Davy. If he touched it, he would know it was a kind of magic unavailable to the common user, and then he'd start digging for answers. Luckily, I could cast magic while wearing the stone—it just made it a little more difficult.

The wind was stronger here, funneled by the buildings, and cold enough I was glad I'd worn my heavier coat. I pulled up my hood and made quick work of the sidewalk. Stotts stood at the end of the block, looking my way.

"Hey," I said when I got close enough. "Show me where you need me."

Stotts was a good-looking man. Latino heritage gave him soft eyes, heavy lashes and eyebrows, and an easy smile that had caught my friend Nola's heart and not let go.

So far, their long-distance relationship was working. But she lived three hundred miles away on a farm, and he was a detective. Stotts had gone out and visited her for a week, but other than that, it was all about the phone.

Well, that and the computer. Nola had finally given in and had a computer with Internet access installed in her old farmhouse. Love. It finds a way to make a person want to change.

Tonight Stotts was wearing what I usually saw him in—a trench and scarf, slacks, nice shoes. No hat.

Even before he said anything, I knew something bad had happened here. Something wrong. Really wrong. I'd felt this before. But I couldn't remember where.

"Over here." He started down one of the paths beneath the old elm and gingko trees. "That Davy Silvers with you?"

"Yes. He followed me to a business meeting. When I got your call, I made him let me use his car."

"Hmm. Any other Hounds out here?"

I shook my head. "I didn't even know Davy was following me. And Bea didn't say she was going to be here tonight. Are you sure she was Hounding?"

"Someone was throwing magic around."

He didn't have to point to where Bea had been hurt. I could feel it, taste it on the air.

Stotts didn't give me any more information. And he wouldn't. Police never wanted to influence a Hound's initial response and reaction to a magical-crime site. So I didn't waste my time asking him any more questions.

I cleared my mind, mentally singing my little "Miss Mary Mack, Mack, Mack" song to settle my racing thoughts. Magic pressed in on my head, a heaviness, like the air was thickening for the storm. It wasn't my dad, and didn't seem to be coming from the void stone.

Weird.

I set a Disbursement, my latest favorite—muscle aches—and then traced the glyphs for Sight, Smell, Taste.

Magic within me stuttered, like a smooth stone rubbing across my skin. It didn't hurt, but it wasn't comfortable either. I inhaled, exhaled, and urged magic up through my bones, my muscles, my blood. Magic stretched out slowly, thick, heavy. I traced the glyphs again, more to keep my concentration while I waited for magic to respond than out of need to redraw the spell. The heaviness in my head, in the magic, suddenly lifted and magic flooded through me. Too fast. Too much. Too hot.

The glyphs caught fire, wild jeweled colors of raw, deadly magic, licking down my arms, into my fingertips searing the glyphs into the night air.

Magic is fast. Too fast to see. But I wasn't the only one who saw it.

Stotts lifted his hand and traced a dampening spell— I think Smother or maybe Cancel.

"Wait," I said. But it was too late. He threw his spell at my spell.

There is a reason why people don't walk around throwing spells at each other, or getting into wizards' duels like you see in the movies. Every user casts magic differently from other users. Like handwriting, magic follows the form each user casts for it. When two forms clash, you never know if they will blend, extinguish, or go up like a barrel of gunpowder in a bonfire.

Right now, I was betting on the gunpowder thing. I didn't have control of the magic pouring out of me. I was a leaky powder keg, and Stotts's spell was a tossed match.

I clapped my hands, breaking the flow of magic. Yes, it stung. No, it didn't knock me unconscious. Thank you, training sessions.

Stotts's spell slammed into mine.

There was a terrific flash—a blast of green lightning— but no sound. Magic clashed and sucked all sound out of the air, leaving behind painful silence.

I inhaled, exhaled.

And then the night was just the night again. No thickness in the air from the encroaching storm, no strangely heavy magic. The night filled with sounds of traffic and, somewhere farther off, a train. I could smell the damp pavement and trees again.

"Allie?" Stotts said. "You're burned."

Wrong. I was angry.

"What the hell?" I wiped at the sweat running down the edge of my temple. I was suddenly very, very hot, and very, very cold. "Never get in the way when I cast magic. If you want me to Hound for you, you stay the hell out of my way and let me get the job done. You could have contaminated the entire scene." Or blown up the block. Or killed us.

I was yelling, or at least I thought I was. The other sounds, things like city traffic and air noise, still seemed rather distant now that I thought about it, like someone had shoved cotton in my ears.

Apparently angry, screaming women weren't something that fazed Detective Stotts.

"You were burning," he said calmly. He looked over my shoulder. "Call an ambulance." Stotts sounded a lot farther away than he should. Didn't matter. I was good at reading lips. The person behind me whom he was talking to, probably a cop, might have responded. I couldn't tell.

"I'm fine."

Stotts gave me a look that could melt the hinges off the doors to hell. "You are burned. And bleeding."

"I'm Hounding."

"No. You're not."

I took a step and Stotts grabbed my arm. Strong. He was a police officer, after all.

"You are dismissed from this case." He made sure to stand in front of me so I could see his lips moving. He was not a happy man. "I'll find another Hound to take the job."

Someone stepped into my range of vision. I hadn't heard Davy coming—ears—but he was close enough I heard him say, "I'll do it."

I scowled. Hounding for Stotts wasn't always a hard job. But Davy wasn't kidding when he said the man was cursed. A lot—too damn many—Hounds had died working cases for the detective.

"You're injured," I said to Davy.

He raised his eyebrows. "I had a headache a while ago. I'm good now."

Liar.

"No," I said.

Stotts let go of my arm. "That would be fine. Allie, step back."

I didn't step back, but I didn't move forward. Davy followed Stotts closer to the center of the park, stopped, traced a glyph in the air, and then pulled magic up from the network of conduits and lines that ran beneath the streets.

Easy. Like he'd been doing this all his life. Magic answered him, did exactly as it should—followed the lines of the glyph and gave him Sight and Taste and Smell. He paced a large circuit around a couple benches and trees, the wide half circle of brick steps just south of us. Nothing else in the park except the ashes of the old spell that I could only guess still lingered there.

My hands itched and stung, like I'd slapped them against stone. I wanted to cast magic so badly, it hurt.

Instead I wiped the thin line of sweat off my forehead again. Not sweat. Blood. Great. Stotts wasn't kidding I was hurt. Weird that I didn't feel it.

I gently ran my fingertips through my hair, searching for a cut. Found one just inside my hairline on the left. A scratch, but deep enough to bleed.

And finding that scratch made me realize how tight and sunburned the left side of my face felt. Which meant Stotts was right about that too. I was burned. But not so badly I couldn't have finished Hounding for him. Even my hearing was clearing up.

Fine, if I wasn't Hounding, I was backup. Which meant I needed to keep an eye on Davy. I paced over to Stotts, still angry enough to ignore the pain of the burn and the cut. "You watching?" I asked, meaning, of course if he was watching with magic.

Stotts had his thumb and middle finger pinched together, his hand held out in front of him. I knew he was holding another glyph there, probably something like what he threw at me.

"Not yet," he said. "I want to make sure he doesn't go up in flame. Once in a night is my limit."

I calmed my mind, set a Disbursement again, and traced the spell for Sight. Nothing fancy, nothing difficult. Magic lifted through me like morning fog, soft and easy, and filled the glyph.

It was like someone had turned on the sun. The park broke open into sharp colors and deep shadows. No watercolor people in sight. That was the one benefit of having my dad in my head. Somehow, his presence blocked my awareness of the Veiled—the imprints of dead magic users on the flow of magic—and better yet, he blocked their awareness of me.

I didn't think he did it on purpose. Knowing him, he'd rather not help me like that.

Davy finished pacing the circle. I'd never watched him work before. He was a good Hound, knew when to let go of a spell that wasn't giving him the information he wanted. Knew how to cast replacement spells quickly and quietly. The whole thing took all of two minutes tops. And in those two minutes, Davy should have gotten a full picture of what had happened magically, and who cast the magic that hurt Bea.

But even from this distance, I could recognize that spell.

A gate. Someone had opened a gate here, and closed it just as quickly. Fast enough the Closers back at Maeve's hadn't noticed. Unless it was a Closer back at Maeve's who had opened it. Could they open gates long-distance?

If they could, I didn't think they would be sloppy enough to hurt someone and leave a trace of the gate behind.

When Davy turned and looked over at us, I saw it again—the red flash in his eyes. The red eye flash had been happening ever since Tomi knocked him out and used his blood to open the gate in St. Johns that let the Hungers through. I kept hoping it was just an aftereffect of his blood being used to crack open the doors between life and death. I kept hoping it would wear off, and fade away. Didn't look like it was getting better, and it had been months since he was hurt.

Davy strode over, hands tucked in his armpits as if he was dodging a hard chill.

I let go of Sight, and Stotts released whatever protective spell he held at the ready.

"Bea didn't cast magic," he said. "It's not her signature here. But I can't tell whose signature it is." He shivered, looking a little tired again, and a lot cold. Why didn't he have on a warm coat?

"No idea at all?" Stotts asked.

Davy answered him, but looked at me. "I've never seen magic cast like that. The glyph is crushed in on itself. It shouldn't have worked at all, but magic followed it."

"Could you tell what kind of spell it was?" Stotts asked. "Or what it did?"

He shook his head. "It might have been a ward of some type. A lock? It doesn't make sense. Whatever it was, it's too tangled and fading fast, like someone crushed their own spell to get rid of it. Really fucking weird."

Stotts turned and stared at the area, as if he could see the magic with his bare eyes.

"Was there other magic involved, a mix of spells?"

He shook his head. "Don't think so. I can't tell. . . ." He glanced back over his shoulder. "It's gotta be a fluke. Magic doesn't work like that."

"Hmm," Stotts said. "I'll check into the conduits in the area, make sure none of the lines have been tampered with."

We all looked back over at the spot where Bea had been found. Her blood was still on the ground. But without Sight, there didn't appear to be any magic in the park at all.

"You saw no signs of attack?" he asked.

"No. There's traces of a few day-old spells, cheap Illusion, and maybe Mute, but that crushed spell is less than an hour old. And it's almost gone. It's like she got in the way of someone else casting. Was caught off guard and the magic hit her. How bad is she?"

"They want to look her over at the hospital. Hit her head, possible concussion. Backlash from magic is what they're most worried about. She was found unconscious. Disoriented. Couldn't remember what happened to her."

Davy nodded and nodded.

I worked hard not to give in to the panic that had me by the throat. Why would the Authority do this? Who in the Authority would do this? Why didn't they stop to help Bea?

"I'll make sure you're paid for your time," Stotts said. "And I'll need a sworn statement. Come by the station tomorrow. I'll be there."

"Right," Davy said.

"Allie," Stotts said, "I want you to get checked by a doctor. Do I need to make those arrangements?"

Yes, Stotts was my boss, but it was more of a contract-by-contract basis. He didn't have any real right to tell me what to do. Normally I would have reminded him of the boundaries of him sticking his nose up my business. But he was also my best friend's boyfriend. And I think it was more that relationship than our working relationship that was prompting his concern.

"Afraid Nola will read you the riot act?" I asked, faking calm and collected and getting damn close.

A soft smile curved his lips. "It came to mind. Plus, you are singed and a little bloody. A trip to the emergency room makes sense."

"I'm going to go by the hospital to check in on Bea anyway. Which hospital did they take her to?"

"OHSU. Need someone to drive you there?"

"I got it."

"Good." Stotts started toward the taped-off area again.

"What else aren't you telling me, Davy?" I asked once Stotts was out of hearing range.

I could smell the fear on him. "Nothing," he lied.

"Want another go at that?"

He licked his lips, looked at Stotts, who was talking to a police officer—no one I recognized—who stood nearby.

"I don't know how to explain it."

"Try words. If that doesn't work, we'll move on to interpretive dance."

Not even a faint smile out of him. "That spell was really strange. Like it was an Unlock or opening or something. Bothers me."

I didn't know what to say to that, because there was nothing I could say to that. Nothing he could know without having to be Closed. And I refused to let that happen to him.

Davy had gotten a lot paler and was shivering harder. It was time to get him back to the car, and probably to the hospital to have him checked out too.

I glanced back at Stotts, who was going through the procedures to reestablish the park for the public. Since there was no sign of magical crime, other than Bea being hurt, this would be treated a lot like a fender bender. Just an accident where the driver used poor judgment and got in the way of someone else's oncoming spell.

The wind shifted, bringing me the faintest scent of the spell. Blood, copper, and bitter burnt stink of blackberries. It was just a moment, the slightest hint. But I knew that scent.

Greyson.

Holy shit.

No. He couldn't have gotten out. They had a cage on him. And with the whole inn filled with powerful magic users, there would be no way he could access magic from there. This had to be something else. Someone else. I had to be wrong.

I inhaled again, sorting smells, searching for Greyson's. But the scent was gone, lost to the heavier scents of the city.

Davy looked worse than just a minute before. I think he'd been putting up a brave front so Stotts would let him Hound the spell.

He looked like he was going to puke.

"I think I'm going to puke." He stumbled over to some rhododendron bushes, and heaved.

The cops didn't even look our way. A puking Hound wasn't that unusual.

Stotts, however, noticed we were still there and came over. "I thought you were going to the hospital."

I waited for Davy to pull himself together. He stood back and wiped his mouth with the heel of his hand.

"We are." I hoped Davy had remembered to take the keys when he got out of the car. "If you need me," I said, "if you need someone else to Hound that, or if anything comes up, call, okay?"

"The spell's gone now," he said. "I think this is done."

When I didn't answer, he exhaled. "You want to tell me something?"

"Have you noticed anything strange about magic?"

"Other than you trying to burn the park down and Mr. Silvers telling me that was a spell he'd never seen before?"

Okay, maybe I shouldn't tell him. But I liked Stotts. Enough to give him at least a small heads-up. I know I had sworn to keep the Authority secrets secret. I wasn't going to tell him anything that would get my memory erased.

I hoped.

"I don't lose control of magic like that," I said. "Not with something as simple as Sight. But magic lagged when I tried to use it. Then it came pouring out too fast."

Stotts was not a stupid man. He had one Hound in the hospital, one barfing in the bushes, and one burned and bleeding in front of him. He knew how to put three and three together. They taught that sort of thing in detective school.

"We're checking into the networks and conduits here," he said. "Making sure no one hacked into them."

I hadn't really thought about people hacking the networks, but it made sense. "Maybe it's more than just the networks."

"You have something to back that up?"

I shouldn't. I really shouldn't. I should just close my mouth and not say a word. "I think there's a storm brewing. Wild magic. And it might already be messing with magic."

That, detective school must not have covered. No one had advance warning for when wild-magic storms hit.

"The coma," I lied. "After I tapped into that wild-magic storm, I think I'm sensitive to the storm coming in. Like a trick knee."

He paused, searching my face for a lie. The wind shifted again, cold. Too damn cold. And on it, I smelled the strange electric scent of lightning and something more. Magic.

"A storm is an entirely different situation," he said. He inhaled, glanced at the sky, then exhaled. I could tell he was sorting his options. Not that I had any idea of what he or his crew would do to prepare for a wild storm. "You sure you don't need a ride?"

Davy stood—well, swayed—next to me. "I'm good." I hooked my arm through Davy's. The poor kid was ice-cold and shaking. "I got it."

"Thanks," Stotts said. "And let me know if that weather knee tells you anything else, okay?"

"Will do."

Then Davy and I walked away, leaving the park, the police, and the glyph I hoped had nothing to do with Greyson behind.

Chapter Ten

I cranked up the heat in the car and made sure Davy was actually buckled in this time. I pulled out my phone and dialed Zayvion, trying to look nonchalant about it. The phone rang, but Zay didn't pick up.

That wasn't good.

"Are we going or not?" Davy asked.

"We're going." I pulled out into traffic and headed toward the hospital. Davy scowled out the window.

"Why aren't I driving my own car?" he asked.

"You're sick."

"And you're bleeding."

I wiped at my forehead. The blood had slowed. "Okay, try this. Because I said so."

He rolled his tongue around in his mouth and made a sour face. "Got any gum? Mints?"

"No. You going to hark again?"

He shook his head. "Mouth tastes like the bottom of my shoe."

I didn't ask him how he knew that particular flavor.

"Storm, huh?"

"What?" I merged across traffic, putting a little gas into it. Davy's car had good response, and I remembered how much I liked driving. Maybe it was time to get my own car.

"You told Detective Stotts you think a wild storm is coming."

"I thought you were puking."

"Not with my ears," he said. "So?"

"So what? I do. I think a wild storm might hit us. Just because they're rare doesn't mean they're unheard of."

"True," he said. "But there's a reason they're called wild."

"Right. Because the magic in them is wild, unpredictable."

"No, because they hit without warning. Without any sort of hint, sometimes out of a clear blue sky."

I glanced over at him. "Where did you hear that?"

"Everywhere. Everyone knows that."

"Well, everyone is wrong. Wild storms can be quantified. Maybe not accurately predicted, but there are indicators. You learn this in college." I gave him a hard look that didn't work. I'd never asked him if he'd gone to college or, for that matter, if he was old enough to go to college. And honestly, even if he had, magic was not a required course. He could have a degree in Wiffle ball for all I knew.

"So you do storm quantifying in your spare time?" he asked.

"I don't have to quantify them," I said. "I have a gut feeling, like I also said back there. I know there's a storm coming. I can feel it in my bones. Hounds are like that. We're geared to sniff out things other people can't sense."

He shut up, and it took me a second to figure out why. Oh, right, he had been feeling the pain from other Hounds.

"Have you talked to your doctor?" I asked.

"About what?"

"About the aftereffects you're still suffering from your injuries."

We were almost at the hospital now, the winding

twists up the hill between forest and jogging paths emptying out into a maze of twenty-story buildings and parking centers that gave off a little bit of vertigo, even though they were nestled back into the hill around them.

This late at night, the lights of Portland and the river below spread out between the trees like diamonds against velvet.

"It's not like that," he finally said. "Not a pain that medicine can fix."

"And you know for sure it's only when Hounds are hurt?"

He shrugged one shoulder.

"That's not an answer."

"Then what answer will make you get off my back?"

"The real one."

"Fine. I know it's only when Hounds are hurt."

"Can you tell which Hound is hurting?"

"Usually. I just . . . I just know. It's like their scent, their blood and pain, is imprinted in my head." He rubbed his face with his left hand. "I can tell when you're hurt too."

"Really? Right now?"

"No. It fades. I felt it when you got hit by magic back there. I don't feel it now. Are you still hurting?"

"Not much." I eased the car into the underground parking structure. "Is it only pain brought on by magic?"

That gave him pause. "I don't know. I haven't told anyone else about it, to, like, test it."

"Well, I'm not going to slam my hand in the door or anything." I found a parking spot—there were plenty open this time of night—and turned off the engine. "Did you tell Stotts the truth about that spell? You weren't just making it up?"

He exhaled a short breath. "That's the last time I try to do you a favor. Yes, of course I told the officer of the law the truth. Whoever cast that spell deserves to get slapped with a ticket or get thrown back into casting basics 101. That was weird magic."

"Just checking."

"What? That I know how to do my job?"

"That you're okay. Magic can do more than just mess with your body. It can mess with your head too." I meant it to come out nice. No luck. It sounded condescending.

Great.

Davy opened the door and got out of the car. "You can go to hell." He slammed the door shut.

I took a deep breath and rubbed at my eyes. That was stupid. But I didn't know what else I could tell him without putting him in danger of losing his memories.

And frankly, magic did mess with your mind. It took away my memories. I was pretty sure it had changed Davy in some way. Blood magic, in particular, left scars. I knew that because I had them.

Which made me worry about the other things magic might be doing to him, and doing to me. That flare of magic in the park had left me feeling a little shaky inside.

If magic was acting strange, something both Davy and I had felt on the way to the park, and if magic was draining the wells, then what did that mean for me? I carried magic inside me. How much magic was going to get sucked out of me?

I didn't know. But what I did know was I had been stupid to talk to Davy like that. And I needed to mop up the mess I'd made of our friendship.

I got out, locked the doors, and dialed Zay again while heading after Davy. I wanted to tell Zayvion a gate had been opened, and that I'd caught a whiff of Greyson at the park.

Davy stormed toward the elevators in the middle of the parking structure. There was no way I'd get in that tiny tin can on pulleys.

The phone rang in my ear, but Zay still didn't pick up.

Yes, that was beginning to worry me.

"Davy. Wait." I picked it up to a jog, and was happy to feel my body respond. After too many months of magic kicking my ass, all the workouts and training were finally giving me my strength back.

Davy did not wait. He punched the elevator button, his back to me.

The doors opened just as I reached him. I hung up the phone.

One look inside that wooden interior and all I could think of was nails in a lid. My palms broke out in a sweat and my stomach clenched. I couldn't stop myself from taking a step back.

Davy walked in, turned around, and gave me a flat stare.

"I'm sorry. I didn't mean it like that. It was a stupid thing to say. See you inside." It came out in one big nervous rush. Just looking at the elevator, with the added bonus of the parking structure's ceiling feeling like it was pressing down on my shoulders, was giving me the willies.

He didn't say anything. The doors closed and I shook my hands out, trying not to give in to the urge to shriek a little.

The faster I got into the hospital, the faster I got out of this crowded space.

I strode down the concrete ramp, and back up again, taking the route a car would take to get out of the parking deck. That put me on ground level pretty quickly. I saw a bus coming from farther up the hill, and made it across the street to the glass entry doors of the hospital. Unfortunately, the magic-trauma unit was on the thirteenth floor. I might be able to avoid the elevators in the parkade, but walking up thirteen flights of stairs seemed ridiculous, even to me. I knew I'd have to take the elevators. I hated that.

Davy was probably already on the skywalk four floors above me. Probably almost at reception to find out which room they'd put Bea in.

I wiped my sleeve over my face, dabbing away any blood that might be there. The cut had stopped bleeding, which was something at least, but my face still felt tight.

I made my way down the tile hallway, and past a few unmanned desks, carpeted waiting areas to my right and left edging the tile like manicured lawns, flat-screen TVs showing parks, waterfalls, and wildlife.

It was quiet tonight. I passed only two people, a man in scrubs and a woman with a backpack who looked like she hadn't slept for a few weeks.

I turned the corner to the elevators and pushed the button. While I waited for my own personal hell to creak to a stop, I recited my mantra to calm my mind. I took several deep breaths. Pretty soon, the floor swung a little under my feet. Right, hyperventilating did not equal calming breaths.

The bell pinged and the elevator door slid open. I could do this. I could step into that tiny space that didn't feel big enough for my legs, my chest, my lungs. I could duck down and not have the ceiling hit me, hold my breath, and squeeze in there between the walls, scraping my shoulders on either side.

Sweet hells, I hated this. I bit my bottom lip, and forced—and I mean literally forced—my foot to take a step forward. That got me two steps; then I closed my eyes, held my breath, and took the third.

I turned around, punched the button for floor thirteen, and positioned myself in the exact center of the elevator. I stretched my arms out to either side, so I could hold back the walls when they started closing in.

They started closing in on the seventh floor. Good thing the elevator was fast.

I was sweating by the time the bell dinged again. It felt like an eternity before the doors slid open. And I was there, pressed up against them, my hands out in front of me. As soon as the door started to open, I stuck my hands in it, pushing it wider, and stepped out, escaping.

I hated elevators.

I took a right and strode down the hall, not knowing where I was going, but needing to be a hell of a long way away from that damn elevator. I took the hall as far as it would go, until a set of double doors that were marked AUTHORIZED PERSONNEL ONLY showed up in front of me.

I stood there, breathing hard and sweating. Okay, I needed to pull myself together. It was just a (shudder) elevator. I could handle it. I could kick that elevator's gears into next year, if I had to.

I took a minute to calm the race between my heart and my head, then walked back the way I came, looking for the signs that would take me to the magical-trauma area.

Past the elevators, the only sound on this floor was my boots on tile, and the squeaky wheel of a custodian pushing a cleaning cart toward the elevators. It was a little weird that I hadn't run into Davy yet. I guess he made good time. I just hoped he hadn't passed out on the way up here. Anger aside, he hadn't been looking all that good.

I spotted a sign, and took another right. This hallway was beige and tea brown, the textures in the paint subtle glyphs, mostly blocking and guarding spells that would activate with a flick of magic. Also a lot of glyphs set up for absorption. It made sense, I guess, to cover all the bases on what kinds of problems could happen here. After all, all the patients in this section either came in with a wound inflicted by magic or still had the magic clinging to them.

Down at the end of this hall, with a decent view of the window and roof of the building below us, was a reception desk. A tiny elderly woman sat behind it. She wore a hat that looked like someone had gutted a Muppet, then used it to knit a cap. Way too many blue feathers, and I'm talking neon and fuzzy, with a big pink flower appliqué over one ear.

"Hello," she said. "May I help you, dear?"

I couldn't help it. I smiled. "I'm here to see Beatrice Lufkin? I think she was brought in an hour or so ago?"

"Let me see, now. Beatrice, you say?"

"I say," I agreed.

She tipped her head and looked down her nose, even through she wasn't wearing glasses.

"Oh, it's good you made it just in time."

"Just in time? Are they doing something to her?" Maybe Bea was worse off than Stotts had said.

"No, dear. She'll be going home soon. Her friend, a Mr. Quinn, is here to take her home."

"Can I see her?"

"It would be better if you waited. She'll be out soon. Go ahead, now, have a seat."

I tasted the slightest hint of honey on her words and suddenly wanted to sit down. Influence. Not strong, just enough to make me want to calm down. Even an old gal like her used magic.

It wasn't a strong push, so I just paced next to the chairs instead and dialed Zayvion.

I didn't have time to wait for him to pick up the phone. The doors clicked and I turned to see Jack Quinn pushing Bea, who was in a wheelchair. Jack looked like he always looked. A little like leather that had been left out to dry.

Bea, however, looked like she'd been rolled by a tank. She had a bruise over both eyes, and her lips were swollen. Her normally perky smile was gone, though her lips twitched up at the corner when she saw me.

"Hey." I closed the distance between us. "How are you doing?"

"Peachy." It came out a little slurred and I raised my eyebrows. I also found out the eyebrow on the left hurt.

"Pain meds," Jack said. "The good stuff."

Bea nodded, her eyes not quite tracking. "Nice to see you, Al," she said. "I miss a meeting?"

"No, you were out in the park tonight."

"Yeah?" she said.

"Do you remember that?"

"Not really. Downtown?"

"Yes. What happened?"

She licked her swollen bottom lip and lifted her hand to push back her wild curls, the wristband ID bracelet catching her hair. She didn't seem to notice. "I got a job. Last-minute contact. Was supposed to meet him there to get the specifics."

She paused. No more than that—she looked like that was all she was going to say.

"Did he show up?"

She frowned. "I don't remember."

Jack just gave me a look that said this was pretty much all he'd been able to get out of her.

"Did you cast magic?"

"I don't think so."

"Do you remember any other spell being cast?"

She shook her head.

"Do you remember being hurt?"

Again with the headshake. "I just—I don't know, Allie. I was there, and now I'm here. And all bruised up, you know?"

"Are you sure the doctors said you can go home?"

She held up a piece of paper. "Right here. I just want a shower and sleep. I think . . . Jack, are you taking me home?"

"Brought my car. Unless you want me to try to strong-arm the ambulance into a little door-to-door service."

She tried to smile, but didn't quite make it.

"You got any other questions, Detective Beckstrom?" Jack asked.

"Lots. Have the police talked to her yet?"

"No. But all her contact information is on her file. If they want to find her, they will."

We started toward the elevators. "You going to stay with her?"

"Thought I should. Unless you want me to call someone else?"

"No, it's fine. If you want to use the warehouse, it's open."

"I got that, thanks."

We made it to the elevator. Another question was scratching at the back of my head. "Jack, what were you doing in the park?"

"Didn't say I was in the park."

"So how'd you hook up with Bea?"

"Was downtown. On my own time, not a job. Saw the magic flare. Got curious."

"You saw what happened?"

"Not really. Saw a magic fire. Thought I'd check it out. Then there was Bea all banged up on the ground. Called 911. Got ahold of the ambulance and cops."

I studied his expression. Did I trust Jack? As much as I trusted any Hound. Which meant I expected him to have a highly developed sense of self-preservation and a somewhat stunted sense of morals and charitable leanings. Still, it seemed like he and Bea might have become friends over the last couple months. And who knew? Maybe they were more than friends.

But there was always the possibility that Jack hadn't just been innocently downtown doing nothing at the same time as Bea was hurt.

"Is that it?" I asked.

"You have a suspicious mind, Beckstrom," Jack said. "That look on your face. Anyone tell you that?"

"Daily."

"I don't want to rain on your neurosis or anything, but it was chance that had me in the same area as her. And if it'd been another Hound down, I'd be right here, doing the same damn thing. So stop trying to shove the black hat on my head, right?"

The elevator pinged and Bea jerked. "Oh," she said. "Scared the crap out of me."

Jack guided her chair into the elevator, pivoting it so that she was facing the doors.

"I'll call later to check in on her," I said.

"You're not her mother, Beckstrom. Get over yourself."

The door closed and the last thing I saw was Bea's eyes, a little too wide, her mouth open as if she'd just remembered something to be frightened about, and Jack's hard glare, his hand caught tightly on her shoulder.

Shit.

Why did I suddenly think I'd just handed Bea over to the wolves?

No, that was just me being jumpy. Jack had worked for Stotts once or twice in the past, and he'd shadowed several Hounds, and no one had complained. I was just overreacting, too keyed up. Bea would be fine.

And I'd call in an hour or two just to make sure, or maybe I'd send someone else over to her place to make sure everything really was on the up-and-up. What I couldn't figure out was where Davy had gone.

"Excuse me," I said to the receptionist.

Muppet-skin-hat-magic lady smiled. "Yes?"

"Have you seen anyone else come in? A young man, blondish hair, T-shirt, jean jacket."

"No. No one at all."

"Thank you."

So no Davy. That meant either he was passed out somewhere, or he'd ditched me.

"Do you need to see a doctor?" she asked.

"What? No. I'm fine."

She was still smiling, but pointedly gazed at the burnt half of my face.

That. Right. I walked to one of the windows and checked my foggy reflection. Still had all my hair. My skin was a little darker on the left—the burn—but I'd done a pretty good job blotting the blood off my face. It hurt, but no more than a sunburn.

And yet, I looked just dandy.

I pulled out my cell and called Davy. After eight rings he still hadn't answered.

What was it with my phone tonight?

Okay, there were other ways to find people in this town. The easy way would be to cast a searching spell and see if I couldn't Hound him down. But the hospital had a sign placed every five feet down the hall stating magic was not allowed inside the hospital.

Yeah, tell that to Muppet granny.

I didn't want to be responsible for screwing up someone's life-support system, or clashing with a surgery, so I'd just take it outside.

Magic. Kind of like smoking. Only in the approved areas.

"Are there stairs?" I asked as I pocketed my cell.

"All the way down the hall, to the left and to the left again. But the elevators are much faster."

"That's okay. I need the walk."

I took the hall fast, not jogging, but putting my legs to good use. Left and left. I straight-armed the door leading down and got ready for my thighs to start burning.

Three flights down and still going strong, my phone rang.

Finally.

"Yes?"

"Allie, where are you?" It was Zay, and he sounded worried.

"At the hospital. Bea was hurt. I Hounded for Stotts. Davy was with me. Didn't Shame tell you any of this?"

"Is Davy still with you?"

"No. Why?"

"You're alone?"

"Yes."

"Can you get around people, a crowd?"

"Zay, it's midnight at the hospital. There is no crowd. Especially not in the stairwell. What's wrong?"

"Get somewhere public. Get off at the next floor and tell me where you are."

"That bad?"

"Greyson is gone."

Chapter Eleven

A high-pitched ringing started in my ears. "Dead?" I asked, not at all ashamed at the tiny bit of hope that leaked into my voice.

"No. Escaped. He'll be hunting you."

With that as the option, I liked dead better.

"But what about the cage? All that magic holding him. He was supposed to be guarded, warded, blind."

"Magic fluxed. The wards fell apart. Greyson tore the cage into twisted bits of metal. He's out. And he's after you."

"You never tell me any good news, you know that?" I tried to make light, but the truth was, I was terrified. I turned the last corner and pushed open the door. "I'm on the ninth floor, by the stair exit. I'll go find a waiting room full of people."

"I'll be there in just a second. Hold on."

He made it sound like I was going to stop breathing or something. "Take your time," I said. My phone vibrated. I had another call coming in. "Hold on." I checked the caller ID. Davy Silvers. "Zay, Davy's calling in. I need to pick this up. I'll call you back."

I hung up before Zay could protest. I wasn't the only one Greyson had nearly killed. Davy had been right there on his fuck-up list, along with his girlfriend, Tomi.

"Davy, you okay?" I answered.

"Allie? Where are you?"

"Ninth floor. Where are you?"

"I'm downtown."

"What?"

"Took the bus. I'm going home. You pissed me off. But not enough to make you spend all night looking around the hospital for me. Plus, you have the keys to my car and I want them back."

"Are you crazy? Why did you do that?"

"Forget it," he muttered.

"No, wait. Listen. Davy?"

"Yeah?"

"There's someone out on the street who doesn't like me very much."

"And?"

Right, like that was news. "And I think he was part of the attack with you and Tomi in the park."

He took a minute. The sounds of the bus's engine filled in for his silence.

"Do you need my help?" he asked.

See, he really was a good kid.

"No, I'm calling Stotts. Zayvion is on his way. I'm probably going to go home and let the police take care of this." Lie. A big fat one. Good thing we were on the phone; otherwise Davy never would have bought it.

"I want you to go home, and stay there until you hear from me. As soon as I have an update from the cops, I'll let you know. And if you can't get home, then get to the warehouse and stay there."

"Oh sure," he said, "I'll just go home and sit there staring at the walls until you tell me it's safe to go out again."

"Davy, this is dangerous."

"And?"

"And I don't want you to get hurt. More. What I want is for you to see a doctor, but since you won't do that, you should at least go home and lock the doors. This is police business. Be smart. Stay home."

"Do you think I'll just do whatever you say?" Oh, that anger could boil the lead off my phone.

"No. I think you're my friend. I don't care how angry you are at me. Just do the safe thing for once. I refuse to beg you to listen to me like I begged Pike."

His breath caught. "That's low," he whispered.

"It's the truth." And it was. I'd begged Pike not to go find Trager, not to go take him on alone. I'd begged him to let the police take care of it. Begged. And I am not the begging type.

"Fine," he said. "I'll go to the warehouse. Lock up. Call me." It all came out short. A little like someone's hands were around his throat and he couldn't get enough air.

Yeah, I knew how he felt. I still really missed Pike too.

"Is Bea okay?" he asked.

Right. That was what we'd come to the hospital for. "She has a concussion, but she's going home. You were right. She got hit by magic. Can't remember what happened, and can't remember casting magic. Jack took her home." Silence. From both of us.

Finally, "Davy?" What more could I say? "Thanks for listening."

"Yeah." He hung up.

I hung up too and realized I wasn't paying attention to my surroundings. Oh, that was a great way to get myself killed.

I was in another hallway, this one wide and lit by fluorescents that weren't up to the job. I could smell coffee, so there was either a cafeteria nearby or maybe a coffee station. That was a good sign, right? Where there was coffee in Oregon, there would be people.

The hallway curved to the right and deposited me into a waiting area where six people sat. A little girl, maybe five years old, spun around and around, her pink skirt puffing up, her heavy snow boots scuffing the carpet.

"Becca, do you want to come read with me?" a woman, probably her mother, asked.

Becca just kept spinning.

I didn't take a seat. Being around people was not a sure way to stop Greyson from attacking me. And if he did show up here, I wanted to be on my feet and ready for him.

I'd been doing a lot of learning since he'd attacked me. I knew more physical self-defense, and I knew a hell of a lot more about magic. I hadn't had a memory loss for two months. That meant that right now I was pretty much at the top of my game.

A little part of me—okay, a big part of me—hoped he would try to take me down. Just so I could show that bastard what I was made of. Pay him back for what he did to Tomi and Davy. For what he did to my dad.

I paced, and kept an eye on both ends of the hallway. I didn't pull on magic, but I was good at paying attention to details, like whether I caught a whiff of the burnt-blackberry and blood smell of him. My cell rang again.

"Yes?"

"Ninth floor where?" Zay asked.

"I'm in surgery and admissions. By the windows. You?"

"Almost there. Anything?"

"No. Davy's going to the warehouse, I think. I need to tell you about the job with Stotts."

"I see you."

I turned. Sure enough, Zayvion Jones was striding my way, wearing that ratty blue ski coat and a dark blue ski beanie. He didn't look particularly concerned as he tucked his cell into his pocket, didn't look like a guy who could throw around enough magic to tear a city apart, raise the dead, and pull the heavens to the earth. Didn't look like he was on the hunt for a creature that had murdered, destroyed, broken the boundaries between life and death. Didn't look like a killer.

But he was all those things. And he was mine.

I hung up and strolled over to him. "We headed out?"

"What happened?" he asked.

I frowned. I'd just gone through all that. "Oh. My face?" I shrugged. "A spell kicked back on me."

He took a breath and looked like he wanted to tear something apart. The little girl stopped spinning and ran over to sit with her mother. Kids. They have great instincts.

"Just a burn?" he asked.

"It doesn't feel too bad. A little tight, like a sunburn." I decided not to tell him I'd also been bleeding. No need for the man to go ballistic and make the little girl cry.

"My car's outside," he said.

"So's Davy's," I said.

"We'll leave his car here. Should be fine overnight." He started toward the elevators and I followed. "Think you can do the elevator?"

Crap. No, I very much did not think I could do the elevator. But that wouldn't stop me. "Oh, I've been looking forward to it, thanks for asking."

He gave me a sideways glance, and wisely said no more. The elevator door opened, and an orderly maneuvered a patient in a wheelchair out, leaving the elevator empty.

Zay stood behind me. Probably blocking me from running away. Damn.

I took a deep breath, held it, and stepped in. Zay moved behind me like my shadow. I recited my "Miss Mary Mack Mack Mack" jingle, trying to calm the screaming in my brain. There wasn't enough room—it was too hot, too full, too small. Any minute the ceiling would slam down into me, crush me. I couldn't breathe.

"Breathe," Zayvion said. "Allie. Breathe."

Oh. No wonder why it felt like I couldn't breathe. I was holding my breath. I exhaled, but it didn't do anything to stop the panic. I inhaled too quickly, sucking in more panic than air, and the sound of my gasp only made things worse. I was going to die. Crushed. Smothered, suffocated.

In a damn elevator.

Zay took one step closer to me and a tight whine slipped out between my teeth.

"Don't," I squeaked, "don't, oh, *sweethellsplease* don't." If he got any closer, I'd run out of air. I'd freaking snap and scream my fool head off, then pound my way through those walls and into fresh air.

He didn't step closer. He reached out and pressed his fingertips down on my shoulder. Mint, cool, soothing, and familiar, washed through me. I didn't think Grounding was going to do anything for panic.

But my shoulders lowered away from my ears, I unclenched my jaw, and I managed to swallow that kicked-puppy whimper coming out of my mouth.

The bell pinged, and I waited an eternity, two, three. Then finally, finally, the doors opened.

I was out of there faster than a sprinter on fire. I didn't look where I was going. I didn't care. Away was all I wanted. Far away. And my feet were plenty happy to oblige.

I jogged only about ten steps before logic kicked back in, and I stopped.

Zay was still near the elevator, his hands loose at his sides. The casual observer wouldn't notice it, but I trained with him. I knew when he held his wrist at that angle, he was half a thought away from casting a whole lot of magic.

I stuck my hands in my pockets and started back toward him, blowing my breath out in a thin stream to try to stop the ringing in my ears.

"The car?" I asked, all dignified like I hadn't just been running away like a scared little girl.

"That way." He tipped his head to indicate the parking structure behind him.

"Sorry," I mumbled as soon as I was beside him.

"Don't be. It's kind of cute."

Lovely. Just what I want to be. Cute.

"Bite me, Jones."

"Anytime." He grinned.

We headed along the narrow concrete walkway that took us down into the parkade.

"Where's Davy's car?" he asked.

"Down a level. How did it happen?" I asked.

"What?"

"Greyson's escape. Maeve said he was safe there. Said that cage couldn't be broken or breached. How did it happen?"

"We don't know yet. The spells in place to record the area were tapped, tripped, and disabled."

"Hold on. The ancient order of powerful magic users who can make magic do anything they want got screwed by someone hacking their wards? Why wasn't there a camera in there? Why wasn't someone guarding him?"

"No cameras because we don't want any kind of recorded information about the well, Maeve's place, or Greyson. No cameras because magic has always been enough."

"Common sense. Would it hurt you to use it like the rest of us mortals?"

"You sound like your dad."

"Nice."

"His ideas for how magic should be regulated weren't all bad."

"So you have a man crush on the man I spent most of my life hating?"

"I didn't say I liked him. I said he had common sense when it came to magic. Backup systems, technological support, hands-on—he believed it could all go together, work together, instead of being sectioned and divided. Magic used by the few, technology used by the masses."

"Common sense didn't keep him from being murdered."

Zay fell silent. That brought us full circle. Greyson was one of the people who had killed my father back when Greyson had been a man working for the Authority. As far as anyone in the Authority could figure it, the murder was a multiple-person, complicated job. James Hoskil, my dad's ex–business partner's son, had been involved. And so had Cody, the gifted but mentally limited Hand my friend Nola had taken in to live on her farm in Burns, off the grid, and out of reach of magic.

There were probably more people involved. We still didn't know who.

A man leaned against Zay's car. I'd expected Shame, but this man was taller, his white hair a beacon beneath the fluorescent light.

"Hey, Terric," I said. "What brings you out?"

"An escaped Necromorph. You?"

"Injured Hound."

"Shame with you?" I asked. As soon as the words were out of my mouth, I wished I could take them back.

Terric frowned, and brushed the side of his nose.

"He's with Chase. Hunting."

I glanced at Zayvion, who opened the driver's-side door. "Get in. We need to get you somewhere safe."

I got in. Not because I was going to let them drop me off somewhere out of their way, but because it was cold and dark, and I preferred to win my arguments where there was a heater and comfortable leg room.

Terric slid into the backseat. It was a little strange to have someone other than Shame back there. Since I didn't know him very well, I distrusted him on principle. But Zay was perfectly comfortable with the man. Like he'd just had a work buddy return after a long absence.

"So who decided it's a good idea to let Chase hunt her boyfriend?" I asked.

The muscle in Zay's jaw clenched. Sore subject.

Terric answered. "She's one of the best people to look for him, don't you think?"

From how she was acting back at Maeve's I didn't think that was at all true. "I doubt she likes the idea of seeing him put back in a cage."

"Maybe not," he said. "But she knows that the Authority are the only people who might be able to help him."

"Or kill him," I said.

"That too. What is life without risk?"

"Long?"

Terric laughed, a sort of high whooping that made me—and Zayvion, much to my surprise—smile. Contagious. For all he had a serious exterior, Terric was the guy you'd want to sit next to at a funny movie, just to hear him laugh.

"So are either of you going to tell me why I can't come on the hunt?"

"You need to be safe," Zay repeated. Man did one-track mind like no one's business.

"And where do you suggest my safety will be found?"

"Maeve's."

"You mean the place Greyson broke out of?"

"With people guarding you," he went on over my remark. "There will be a new cage constructed for him. And if he comes to you—"

"Hold up. I'm bait?"

"Allie—"

"You have got to be kidding me. I'd be safer at home." I didn't say *with my gargoyle* because only Zay, Shame, and I knew the big lug had decided my apartment was his den, nest, quarry, whatever it was that gargoyles called home.

"No, you'll be safer at Maeve's," he said.

"You can't tell me what to do." Wow. I sounded just like Davy. Just like Jack. Spoonful of my own medicine. Yuck.

"I'm not telling you what to do," Zay said. "This is a direct order from Maeve."

"Oh, for fuck sake. I'm an adult. Maeve is my teacher, not my mother."

"You have met Mrs. Flynn?" Terric said from the backseat.

Just what I needed, another smart mouth in the car.

"You have to listen to her," Zay said. "Because she is your teacher. Until you are done training under her, she has say about where you should be in the event of magical emergencies."

"Was that in the contract I signed? Oh, no, wait. There was no contract."

"No, there was a test and a vow." Zay's voice didn't rise, but I could tell by how hard he was gripping the steering wheel that he was not a happy man. "If you break that, you are out of the Authority."

It had been at least two months since Zay had had to remind me of that. Still, it chafed. I hated knowing that one perceived misstep would mean my memories, and all the training I'd done, would be gone out of my head. Hells, if they wanted to, they could make me forget who I was. Take away everything.

If I kept training, if I gave in this time, I knew I would become strong enough that they'd never be able to mess with my memories.

The soft moth-wing flutter tickled the backs of my eyes. I actually rubbed my eyes trying to make it go away until I remembered it wasn't some kind of weird muscle twitch. It was my dad, in my head, reminding me that he was there.

We could be so much, he whispered. *So powerful together. Life and death. Light and darkness. And all magic will be ours.*

The only thing worse than my dad being in my head was him getting all creepy and poetical on me. I ignored him.

Zay had taken us down the twists of Terrwilliger Boulevard, and we were now headed into town, toward I-5 North.

"Where are Shame and Chase?" I asked.

"Hunting," Zay answered.

"No, I mean where? Which part of town do you think Greyson's in? You don't think he made it across the bridge to Portland, do you? Do you think he could have made it downtown to Chapman Square?"

"He's a Necromorph. He doesn't have to use just his feet to get around."

"So he could be in Chapman Square?"

Zay's nostrils flared. "Why?"

"Someone opened a gate in the park, closed it, and crushed the spell so all traces of it would disintegrate within a half an hour. I thought I caught Greyson's scent. It was faint. I don't think he's still there, if he ever was, but something happened there. Maybe around the same time he escaped."

Both men were dead silent. I tried not to look smug, because frankly, I was more aggravated than smug.

"I'm taking you to Maeve's. Then we'll look," Zayvion said.

"And I'm just going to wait at Maeve's for days until you find him?"

"Allie, don't," Zay warned.

"Listen, when Greyson was on the street before, you said people in the Authority were looking for him for months. Who found him?"

Nothing.

"Me," I said. "I found him."

"No, he found you," Zay said.

"Okay. He found me. So why not let me go out and find him this time? Let me be the hunter instead of the bait."

Terric spoke. "Taking you to Maeve's is a form of hunting. We're setting the trap, and he'll come for you."

Unlike Shame, who always stuck his head between Zay and me, Terric lounged, one arm over the back of the seat, half tucked against the corner of the door, his leg stretched out on the seat in front of him.

"He's not going to come for me there," I said. "Not at Maeve's. Not where there are magic users and the well, and the cage he just escaped. He might eventually be desperate enough to break back into his prison to get me. How long will that take? Weeks?"

Neither man said anything.

"He's not stupid," I added.

Still the silence.

"He remembers being in the Authority. He remembered my father, remembered how to used Blood magic and Death magic, and even bound Tomi and used her to cast those spells for him to hurt Davy and open those damn gates, and whatever the hell else he did. He is nowhere dumb enough to walk back into the place he escaped. Not even to get me."

Terric made a little *huh* sound.

Zay just looked angry. "What do you expect us to do?" It came out with enough volume, I knew he was pissed. Long fuse didn't mean the man never blew. "Do you want us to stand you out on a street corner with a sign?"

My shoulders tightened and I swallowed the need to yell back. Instead, I let a little silence soften the space between us, mostly so I could act calm. "Yes. I think something like that is a good idea. But we could be a little more subtle about it."

"An ambush?" Terric mused. "It has merit."

"No," Zay said.

"I won't be safe at Maeve's," I said for the millionth time. "Not really. It would just stall his attack."

"No," he said again.

I didn't say anything. Neither did Terric.

I watched the city roll by and did my own share of

controlling my urge to yell. Dad pushed at the backs
of my eyes, not hard, but enough to annoy. Like I'd let
down my guard now.

"I will do this, Zay," I said. "If not today with you,
Terric, Shame, and Chase, then sometime later, on my
own. I'll hunt him down. I'll face him. I'll make him pay
for what he's done. Do I think I'd be stronger with you
there? Maybe. But that doesn't mean I'm not plenty
strong enough on my own."

"She's right," Terric said. "Let it go."

Zay, that remarkable man, took a deep breath,
and let it out slowly. With it, he seemed to exhale his
anger. It was probably one of the most amazing things
I'd seen him do, and I'd seen him do a lot of amazing
things. I sucked at letting go of anger. Maybe all that
Zen training of his gave him a better control over his
emotions.

Yeah, well, that and the fact he had to be calm and
centered to work all disciplines of magic. Guardian
of the Gates. There was no one else as good at wielding magic as he. And the Authority hung their hope of
keeping magic in the right hands, and used in the right
ways—for good and life, not for destruction and death—
squarely across his broad shoulders.

A responsibility he bore without complaint.

"Call Maeve and let her know," Zay said.

"I'll do that." Terric dialed.

I reached over for Zay's hand, but he pulled away. He
didn't look at me, just straight ahead, as if driving suddenly took all his concentration.

"Maeve?" Terric said. "There's been a slight change
of plans."

"You know I'm right," I said while Terric talked.

"No. I don't." He pressed his lips together, as if he
wanted to say something more, but thought better of it.

"Zay—"

"Are you wearing the void stone?" he asked. All business now. No emotion. Okay, he was still angry at me. Too bad.

"Yes."

"Are you going to carry a weapon?" Flat.

"Of course I want weapons. Did you think I was going to take him on with my bare hands?"

"I don't know what you're thinking."

"I'm thinking you might have a machete I can use." I said sweetly.

"It's in the trunk. We're meeting Shame. You can get it then."

Terric hung up. "Well, that was interesting. Your teacher does not approve of the change in plans, but she understands our point. She's sending out some people to double-check Chapman Square."

"She's not going to throw me out of the Authority for this?" I asked.

"She is giving you one chance, until morning, to draw Greyson in. If he doesn't show up, you are to be taken to Maeve's, where you will be under constant observation, or you will be taken to your apartment, where you will be under constant observation."

"Nice to know I have options."

"You're welcome to try to negotiate with Maeve if you want," he offered.

Right. Shut up, Allie. This was as good as it was going to get. And if we did this right, if we were very lucky, we might be able to take care of this problem tonight.

A dizzy flux of magic washed through me again. I broke out in a cold sweat and wiped at the top of my lip. I glanced at Zay, but if he noticed, he didn't show it. The storm was coming, rolling closer, messing with magic, messing with me. I knew tonight would be our best chance to take Greyson down.

Chapter Twelve

We drove to the meeting point, a twenty-four-hour diner and truck stop. Shame's car was parked near the gravel back of the lot. Neither Shame nor Chase was beside the car. There wasn't enough light for me to make out who was inside it. Zayvion stopped the car several parking spaces away.

"Coffee?" Terric asked.

"Please," I said, "black." I dug in my pocket for cash.

"I got it. Zayvion?"

"No thanks."

"Back in a moment, then." Terric slipped out and headed to the restaurant without a glance at Shame's car.

Right. They didn't want to be around each other. Zay and I were currently fighting, Terric and Shame had been avoiding each other for years, and not only was Chase Zay's ex-girlfriend, but also, the guy she dumped him for was the murderer we were about to hunt down.

For cripes' sake. Could we be any more dysfunctional?

"Zay?"

"I need some air." He got out, slammed the door, and started walking toward Shame's car.

He was just the lord of pissy tonight, wasn't he? Fine. I was done apologizing for being right, for being strong, for being me. If he couldn't deal with it, then too damn bad.

I got out of the car. Noticed, in a distracted way, that it was sprinkling. Started over to tell Zay to suck it up and deal.

Zay slowed. He stopped, bent, and looked in the back driver's-side window.

Something was wrong.

I moved faster. "What?" I asked.

He held up his hand to tell me to stop, and I did. Strong, stubborn, capable, yes. Stupid, no.

He opened the driver's-side door. An arm fell out of the door and Zayvion leaned in to catch the rest of the body that followed.

Shamus.

I jogged the remaining distance, around the other side of the car to see if Chase was in the other seat. I looked in. Nobody. I opened the door and the stink of used magic hit me so hard, I had to turn my head to take a breath.

I recited my mantra and set a Disbursement, muscle aches one more time. I was going to be a head-to-toe cramp once all these deferred prices hit me. I traced the glyphs for Sight, Smell, and Taste. My senses burst open. Magic had been used inside the car. The ashy remains of Impact stuck like a huge brown and red spider, pulsing against the upholstery of the roof. An overpowering mix of so many other conflicting scents made me think someone had cast an extra spell full of scents just to throw off any attempts to Hound. There were too many smells to sort quickly, if at all. In those smells I caught the edge of Shame's blood and a hint of sweet cherry. Blood magic?

Tendrils of brown and red from the Impact hooked out the door and into Shame. Maybe in his mouth or chest. Zay had him on the ground, but was blocking my view.

I knew the signature of the spell. I knew who had cast this.

Chase.

Holy shit.

I straightened, turned a slow circle, looking for any sign of her, or which way she might have gone. A trail of magic, thin as a thread, spilled off toward the street. It was dissolving in the rain. I jogged across the back of the parking lot and through a row of bushes out onto the street beyond. The ashes of the spell ended. Chase had come this way. Whether she had continued down the street or turned around, Sight couldn't tell me.

I shifted my attention to Smell.

I knew Chase's smell—a musky vanilla perfume. I breathed in through my nose and open mouth, so I could get a taste of the air as well. Maybe just the slightest hint of vanilla, but the heavier smells from the truck stop screwed with the subtleties. I turned another slow circle, sensing for any hint of the way Chase had gone.

Nothing I would swear on.

Shit. I let go of magic.

Shame moaned. Zay was talking to him, telling him not to move. Shame, being Shame, was acting like a smart-ass.

"So you can kiss me? Not on a first date," he said as I reached them.

"It was Chase," I said.

Both men glanced up at me. Zayvion cursed.

"Chase hit you with Impact, Shame. Do you remember that?"

"Are you sure?" he asked. "We were just sitting here, waiting for you to show up. Well, not you, Beckstrom; you, Z., and then . . ." He frowned. "I thought. I thought I was tired. Did I fall asleep?"

"It was Chase," I said again to Zay.

"Are you sure?" he asked.

"I'd testify in court. That was her signature."

"Shame," Zay said. "Chase hit you with magic. I think she Closed you so you wouldn't remember."

"Well, fuck that little bitch," Shame said. "I'm going to have her roasted for that." He pushed at Zay's hands. "Let me up. I'm fine."

"You're bleeding."

"Might be Blood magic," I said.

"It's just my mouth where I hit the steering wheel," Shame said. "Plus I'm angry now. Does the body good. Move."

Zayvion stood, one hand down just in case Shame needed it to stand. Shame took his hand and pulled up onto his feet.

"Fucking fuck fuck of a fuck." Shame dug in his pocket for his cigarettes and lighter. His hands shook as he lit up.

"Eloquence, thy name is Flynn," Terric said from behind us.

Shame didn't even bother looking up. "Fuck you too," he said around the cigarette.

Terric was closer now. Close enough to see the details of the scene.

His expression turned into a very carefully constructed, pleasant smile. Okay, that was scary. I knew he was angry at Shame, and I figured he was also aware of the remnants of Chase's spell. Even a novice could sense it, and Terric was no novice. But that smile made him look like a nice guy, friendly and polite.

Note to self: when Terric smiles that friendly smile, be worried. He was really about to kill something. A lot.

"I'd love some details," Terric said, still all friendly-like, while handing me a cup of coffee.

"Chase did this," I said.

Terric's eyebrows shot up. "Come again?"

"I Hounded the spell that knocked Shame out. It was Chase's signature."

"How did it happen, Flynn?" His voice was a little

softer when he spoke to Shame, though I doubted either of them noticed.

Shame just shrugged one shoulder and took another drag off his cigarette. "Don't know," he said through the smoky exhalation. "She took my memory."

Terric the nice guy suddenly looked like Terric the killer. He stared at Shame, and Shame finally, finally, looked up, met his eyes, then looked away.

The pain and fear and anger in Shame's expression disappeared as he sucked on his cigarette, his long, ragged bangs falling to hide his eyes.

Yeah, I knew how he felt. It was hell to lose parts of yourself, to know someone or something had that kind of control over your mind. It made you feel vulnerable, in the worst way.

"Interesting," Terric murmured. He took a swallow of his coffee, and when his cup came back down, he was Terric the nice, smiling killer guy again.

Well, I saw no need to be polite about this. "This is bullshit. She has no right to do that to him. Do you remember what you and she were talking about, Shame? Did she say anything before she attacked you?"

"I got nothing."

"Zay," I said. "Can you think up a scenario that makes Chase innocent?"

"Not at the moment."

"So we hunt Chase?" I asked, realizing that I liked the idea of kicking her ass a little too much. She'd bitch slapped me something fierce when I'd found Greyson back in St. Johns, accused me of turning him into a Necromorph. She and I hadn't ever been on friendly terms, and it pissed me off that she would hurt Shame.

I liked Shame. I'd always thought she'd liked him too.

"We hunt Greyson," Zayvion said.

"Are you kidding me?"

He finally looked at me, his eyes more gold than

brown, a different storm of magic roiling there. "Because where we find Greyson is where we'll find Chase."

I'm not kidding—that made chills run over my skin.

Magic fluxed again, sucking at my feet like a starved leech. A wave of vertigo teeter-tottered the world, then slowly stabilized. It was a lot like when magic had fluxed and I'd fallen in the bathroom.

The storm was coming closer.

Damn.

"Allie?" Zay asked.

I took a drink of my coffee. Buying time for me to pull myself together.

"Are you hurt?" He raised his hand to cast a spell, probably a form of Sight.

So much for hiding the effects of magic's fluctuations on me.

"Magic," I said. "It's a little . . . weird."

Zay waited, hand still raised.

"I keep getting dizzy. When magic fluctuates, it pulls on me. I'm guessing it's from the storm, right?" Why it was affecting me and not them probably had something to do with me being the only one stupid enough to tap into a wild-magic storm and get thrown into a coma. But that didn't mean I couldn't be a part of the hunting crew.

I looked him right in the eye. No lies for me, Mr. Jones. No sirree. Nothing but the truth. I'm in plenty good enough shape to hunt.

He believed me enough to nod. "If you feel dizzy again, tell me. We'll be on foot for some of this."

"Are we wearing wrist cuffs?" I asked.

"No," Shame and Terric said simultaneously.

Zay glared at both of them. "Yes," he said. "We are." He walked over to his car and opened the trunk.

I followed, leaving Shame and Terric behind. That didn't last long. Even though Shame was hurt, and it obviously concerned Terric, they still didn't like being alone with each other.

I'd gone out hunting with Zay and Shame only once before. Chase had been there too. We'd hunted Hungers, magic-eating, killing creatures that found their way into our world through the gateways between life and death and preyed on magic users and innocents alike. We'd fought the Hungers and, on the way, found Tomi being used by Greyson, and then Greyson himself.

But that time we'd been tucked away off the main roads, our cars covered by the trees and bushes. It was more than a little strange to be standing in the middle of a parking lot, even this late at night, with an open trunk filled with magical weapons. Most of the weapons could pass off as everyday items.

The machetes, for instance, might pass as yard tools. Lots of wild blackberries and ivy in Oregon meant lots of machetes in Oregon. And the knives could just be knives, the chains, just chains. But there were weird bits in the trunk too. Things that looked ancient. Archaic twists of metal and glass and leather that channeled magic, enhanced magic, did almost anything you could think of with magic, if they fell in the right user's hands.

It gave me nightmares to think of what they would do if they fell in the wrong user's hands.

Zay cast a subtle Illusion spell, just enough that people might think we were digging in the trunk for a spare tire or something. Then he started unloading the goodies.

I got a knife, the same one he gave me every time something like this went down.

"Isn't that your blood blade?" Terric asked Zay.

"Yes." Zay handed him a set of axes. Terric took them both in one hand, and finished off his coffee, then crushed the cup in his hand.

"What do you want, Shame?" Zay asked.

"Got a flamethrower in there?"

"Take a look."

Shame threw his cig on the ground and dragged the

toe of his boot across it. Then he stepped up and started digging through the trunk like a kid going elbow-deep in a candy bin.

"Lord, Jones, you've stocked up. What'd you think, we were taking down a fucking army?"

That perked Terric's interest. He stepped up next to Shame. "Well, I'll be shitted," he said. "That's an impressive toolbox."

Zay shifted out of the way. Shame and Terric gleefully dug around in the weapons. They each proclaimed their finds much better than the other's, and ended up—I am not joking—doing a round of rock, paper, scissors over something that looked like a cherry bomb, swapped a few other things, and actually laughed a little.

Forget the flowers. Forget the cards, or a nice dinner. Apparently deadly magical things were the best way to bring people together.

And they did look good together. I didn't know how to explain it. Like shadow and light. They belonged in each other's space. They even moved in unison, strapping on blades, and tucking other gear under their coats with an unconscious rhythm that echoed each other's movements.

I looked over at Zay. He was watching them too, a thoughtful, sad expression on his face, like he was trying to solve a puzzle that had long ago lost its pieces.

I stretched my hand out and took his. He didn't look down at me, but he wove his thick fingers between mine, and squeezed my hand gently.

Our fight suddenly seemed like a small thing.

Think they could at least be friends again? I thought.

All things break, all things end, he thought.

Maybe. But some broken things grow again. Like trees. And hope.

Soul Complements? He wasn't asking me the question, so much as just asking. I didn't know if that could ever grow between them again.

Shame laughed, I mean a deep chortle, and Terric hooted along with him. I didn't know what they were laughing about, but it sounded dirty.

Maybe it never died in the first place, I thought. *Maybe they just don't know it yet.*

I felt Zay's quiet acceptance. His willingness to give them time, to be patient. To hope for them, even if they couldn't hope for themselves.

It made me love him even more.

At that thought, he turned, looked at me, and smiled. "What were you just thinking?" he asked.

Since I knew I was blushing, I let go of his hand. I'd had quite enough of thought sharing. "Something about trees."

We hadn't said we loved each other yet. On-again, off-again magic had destroyed the likelihood of us ever having a normal relationship. It never seemed like the right time to tell him that I loved him. Or maybe it never seemed like the right time to admit it to myself.

How normal could a relationship be when at a casual touch you could hear the other person's thoughts?

Zayvion stepped into me, put his hands on both sides of my face, his fingers sliding back through my hair. His palms were warm and callused, and I inhaled the sweet, familiar pine scent of him.

We kissed, letting our lips, our tongues, our bodies, say what our words dared not. He didn't think anything while we were kissing, and neither did I. We didn't have to.

He ended the kiss with soft, small kisses at the corners of my mouth, and pulled away, his arms still embracing me. He held me against him a little longer. "Be safe," he breathed. "I don't ever want to see you hurt again."

I licked my lips, tasted the echo of him on me, in my mouth. "I'll be fine. I promise."

"Oh, for the love of all that's holy. Get a room," Shame said, "or I will bring out the ice."

We stepped apart. "You throw any more ice at me, Shame," Zay said as he stalked over to the trunk of the car, "and I will shove it up your hole."

"No, no." Terric said. "Flynn likes that."

"Bite me, you flaming prick," Shame said with absolutely no heat.

Terric grinned, and Shame flipped him off. They were both smiling.

I intended to keep it that way.

"Let's leave our issues, and ice, at home," I said. "We have hunting to get done."

I stepped up on the other side of Zay, and took the machete he offered me. It was a good thing I'd brought my heavy coat, because otherwise I didn't know how I'd hide this much steel.

And not just average steel. The wicked blade only mimicked a machete. It was really a bladed, deadly length of razor-edged metal and magical glyphs. One swing with this baby, and the right word or two, and you could cut an old-growth oak down with one smooth slice.

Next, I pulled a thin chain over my neck and felt the tongue-on-battery tingle of it rattling down around the void stone and resting against my skin. Not so much a weapon as a sort of enhancer for defensive spells, blocks, wards, those sorts of things.

I didn't like to carry anything else. Had never gotten the hang of the bladed whip Zay wielded like he was skipping rope. Didn't like the double axes that Chase, and apparently Terric, preferred. For me, a knife, a machete, and a magic chain were all I needed for a good time.

What could I say? It's the simple things in life that make me happy.

"Right, then," Shame said, lighting up another cigarette already. "That's it. Who calls shotgun?"

"That is not it." Zayvion pulled a cloth package out

of the trunk and carefully unwrapped the contents. The contents were several leather wrist cuffs in small, glyphed boxes that were probably ancient and worth millions. He pulled out four round amulets. They weren't the same size and heft of the disks my dad and Violet had invented, but I was pretty sure they had given my dad the idea that magic could be contained in something similar to these things.

Unlike the disks, these amulets could be used for only one thing—sensing the heartbeat of another person who wore the amulet. They were all carefully carved from a stone that had been found hundreds of years ago in China, I think. It was the stone itself that had been shaped by magic, infused in such a way to make it sensitive to itself and to the living things in contact with it.

Dad's disks were pure technology that could hold magic, raw, uncast magic, for any amount of time, be used, and then, with the right spell, be reloaded again.

The disks Dad invented would make magic portable. They would allow magic to be called upon out at sea, or in unnetworked lands, and act as a battery for people like doctors and rescue crews who needed to access magic quickly, sometimes in out-of-the-way places, to save people's lives.

Plus, there was absolutely no price to pay once the magic was in the disks.

That meant I could pay the price of casting the spell to charge the disk—probably something little, like a runny nose, or itchy scalp. But Zay could then use that magic to burn down a house—something that would usually carry a high magical cost.

It was an amazing advance for magic and technology.

And scary as hell.

Zay held out a leather cuff for each of us, and then gave us each an amulet. I snapped the amulet into the circle carved in the leather cuff and it fit into place with a heavy thunk I felt at the back of my teeth. The faintest scent of moss filled my nose. I strapped the cuff to the inside of my right wrist, snug against my pulse.

Everyone else did the same, but I felt only two other heartbeats. Terric and I both looked at each other. We'd never hunted together before, so I, at least, needed to touch him once to attune the cuff so I could feel his heartbeat too.

I stepped over to him. "Mind?" I held my palm out toward his chest.

"Help yourself," he said.

Charmer. I pressed my palm against his chest and concentrated on the rhythm of his heart. Strong, a little fast. I also caught the faintest hint of his emotions. Anger. Sorrow. I looked into his eyes, and he gave me the convincing, friendly smile. But behind that were a lot of emotions. Emotions I knew were for Shame.

"Thank you," I said.

He nodded. At the edge of my peripheral vision, Shame stood smoking, his back toward us. If I focused on him, I would feel his emotions too.

One look at his body language told me how he felt.

Terric placed his fingertips lightly in a small circle just below my collarbone, and above my heart. One of the bullet scars I carried was right there, and even though he couldn't feel it through my thick coat, it still made me a little uncomfortable to have him touch me there.

He smiled, a real smile this time, something that looked a little like an apology, and drew his fingertips away. He'd probably gotten a sense of my discomfort.

"Sorry," he said.

"It's fine," I said. "Just twitchy about my scars."

"I know the feeling," he murmured.

Right, that was more of the issue stuff we weren't going to get into right now. "Shame," I said, "give me your keys."

"What? No." He turned. "Wait—let me rephrase that. Hell no. I'm driving."

"Don't be an idiot," Terric said. "You were unconscious less than ten minutes ago."

"And you were a dick. One of us got better."

Terric the nice killer smiled. "A man with a concussion should not drive."

"And you think a woman who's having fainting spells should?"

"Wow. Could you two give it a rest?" I asked. "I'm driving."

Shame looked over at Zayvion like calling the ref in for a replay. "Are you seriously going to let her drive?" Shame asked.

"No."

Shame flipped his hands out in a told-you-so gesture.

"Terric's going to drive," Zay said. "Give him your keys."

At Shame's look, Zay added, "We don't have time. Just get in the damn car—your car—and let Terric drive."

If his words didn't clue Shame in, Zay's heartbeat, pounding strong, impatient, would.

Terric held his hand out to Shame.

You would have thought Shame was removing his own spine for the look on his face, but he finally dropped the keys in Terric's hand.

The keys hit his palm, and Terric glanced down. I caught a glimpse of a man's ring, gold and silver and glyphed, on Shame's key chain. Terric's eyebrows shot up in surprise. He looked up at Shame.

Okay, maybe I was wrong. Maybe there was more between them. Shame said he wasn't gay, but that ring could mean something else. A brotherhood-of-magic or class-ring sort of thing.

Shame just gave him a steady stare. The kind of look that started bar fights.

"Okay," Terric said softly, as if he was trying to regain his breath. He closed his hand over the keys. "Where are we going?"

They all looked at me.

"Seriously? How were you people going to track him down if I wasn't here?"

"Through a process of elimination," Zay said.

"Why doesn't anyone in the Authority Hound?" I asked.

"Huh," Terric said. "She's right. Why is that?"

Shame just exhaled smoke.

Zay shook his head. "I don't know. It's probably a part of the history."

"No," Terric said. "There used to be Hounds. A couple of them. Remember? Theo and Kaida? Back when Mikhail was the head of the Authority. What happened to them?"

"I wasn't involved," Zay said, "Wasn't old enough, or around then. Neither were you. Do you think you can Hound Greyson, Allie? If not him, Chase?"

"Chase ran down that road. I know that. But if she got in a car, and wasn't casting magic, I won't be able to find her."

"Do you swamp-walk?" Terric asked.

Color me impressed. I didn't think anyone in the Authority kept up on those kinds of things. Swamp-walking was pretty woo-woo, even for people who threw magic around on a daily basis.

"I can. Do any of you have something that belonged to her? Or that she's recently touched?"

"How about a car?" Shame suggested.

Yes, I was full of smart tonight. "Yeah, I think that would work."

I crossed the parking lot to Shame's car and felt the gossamer caress of Zay's Illusion sliding away from me. The night felt colder outside that spell, outside his touch.

I opened Shame's car door again, but instead of casting spells for my senses, I simply knelt down and placed my fingers on the seat of the car. I could still smell too many scents, and still smell Shame's blood and sweet cherries over them all. I wondered if they'd gotten into a magic fight before she knocked him out.

I pulled on the magic inside me and drew a glyph for finding, then concentrated on it, letting the magic pour through my fingertips and wash over the seat of the car. It picked up on the high emotions Chase had left behind, picked up on her energy—not on a particular spell like Hounding.

That was another problem with swamp-walking. The emotions any person left behind on any object were transitory at best. If the person was in a high-enough state of emotion, a good swamp walker could sense at least something of which way that person had gone before the emotions faded away.

Chase had very high emotions. The magic Ouija'ed my fingers east, and I got the faintest impression of green. Lots and lots of green. Like Forest Park.

"East," I said. "Maybe Forest Park. Would she go there?"

Zay, who had been pacing behind me, started off toward his car. "We'll find out."

Chapter Thirteen

I jogged back across the lot to Zay's car, glancing over my shoulder once. True to their word, Terric was driving, and Shame got in on the passenger's side.

"Forest Park?" Zay said. "That's a lot of ground to cover."

"Get me there, and I'll try to Hound her. Or him." Once we were there I could use a Seek spell. Seek had a pretty limited range, so we'd need to be close for it to do us any good.

Zay put the car in gear and with Terric following, we made good time heading through the city, then up along Highway 30 to Forest Park. Ahead and to our right, the Gothic arches of St. Johns Bridge flashed with red and white lights, the broad oubles scalloping the skyline. St. Johns lights were electric yellow and white, without fancy magical enhancements. Since St. Johns was off the magic grid, it looked like it belonged to an entirely different city from Portland.

Zay pulled off in a gravel lot in front of a spooky old brick building with a clock tower and enough peaks on the roof, it looked like it belonged to another century. The old Portland Gas and Coke had been abandoned for years.

"Here?" I asked. "We can't get into the park from here."

"Best to check again before we go in." He paused, and the headlights from Shame's car slid across his face.

"Don't trust my swamp-walking abilities?"

"I don't trust Chase."

Right. I got out of the car. Still no rain, only clouds clotting the dark sky. I saw a spark of a star against the black, before the gray snuffed it out.

Terric killed the engine. He and Shame got out. Zay walked with me, though he gave me plenty of room.

I cleared my mind, something that always seemed a little easier when I was close to St. Johns. I didn't know what it was about that part of town, but it always made me feel better.

I set a Disbursement, then drew the glyphs for Sight, Smell, and Taste. I drew magic out of my bones and blood and poured it into the glyphs.

The world came into hard focus, every color brighter, every shadow sharper.

I looked for magic. I looked for Chase. I looked for Greyson. And I looked for signs of blood and violence. Spells pulsed against the chain-link and barbed-wire fence that cut the forbidden building off from street access. In that building was something else. Something magical. I couldn't tell what it was. But none of that magic, not the ward spells nor whatever magic lay crouched in that building, smelled, tasted, or looked anything like Greyson or Chase.

"Not here. Not them," I said. "Something, though, but not them." I walked along the road. Scented, maybe, just the slightest hint of vanilla and blood up ahead.

Crazy. This was no way to track someone. I could try Seek, but if they were in Forest Park, they'd be out of the spell's range. I returned to Shame's car.

"Shame, ride with Zay," I said. "Terric, I'm going to swamp-walk, and you're going to drive."

And, wonder of wonders, all the men listened.

I let go of the sensory spells and got in the passenger's

side of the car. I closed my eyes and pressed my fingers down on the seat next to me, focusing on the emotional residue there to sense Chase. Got a flash of Shame, angry, and, strangely enough, hopeful. But there was still a hint of Chase's emotions beneath that, her emotions vibrating even higher than Shame's, high enough for me to follow.

"Okay, we're going in the right direction. Right. Turn right."

"Over the bridge?"

"If that's a right." It was hard to sense the subtle tugs of the swamp-walking in a moving car with quickly fading emotional energy.

I heard the sound of tires on the bridge. Just as Chase's energy faded for good, I felt a tug to the north.

"Shit." I opened my eyes. "That's it. All I got was a slight shift north. Where are we?"

"St. Johns," he said. "Does she have a place out here?"

"I have no idea." I didn't feel like I had been much help at all. As a matter of fact, I might have just led us on a wild-goose chase. I needed something more. Something that was still connected to her. And the only thing I could think of was Zay.

"Stop the car, okay? I need to regroup."

Terric found a grass and gravel stretch along the road, and Zay pulled up next to us.

I got out of the car and jogged over to Zay's window. He rolled it down.

"Listen, I lost the trail. I need something else that Chase has touched, some other way to connect to her, and I have an idea."

"What?"

"I want you to call her."

Zay's eyebrows rose. "Because?"

"I'm going to try to follow the connection."

"Have you ever done that before?"

I wanted to say yes. Wanted to tell him I could track down people by cell phones in my sleep. "No."

"Then we do it my way."

"What—get out the search-and-rescue team?"

Zay ignored me. He pulled his cell out of his pocket. "You think she's in this area?"

"This is as far as I could track her. She may not still be here. Does she have a house here? Family?"

"No, but this is the only place in Portland off the grid. It's a good place to hide. Except she knows we know it's a good place to hide."

He pressed a button on his phone. I was pretty sure my phone didn't have that button. Then he chanted, pulling the tiniest bit of magic up from five miles away, on the other side of the railroad track. And he did it like it wasn't as hard as sucking water out of stone.

The glyphs encasing his phone rolled with silver light, then went dark.

"She's not close," he said.

And then his phone rang.

Zay frowned at the caller ID. "It's Chase," he said calmly.

"Chase," he said.

He didn't tip the phone so I could hear. He didn't have to. I was a Hound. I had good ears.

"I knew they'd send you out to look for me," she said.

"Where are you?"

"I'm safe. I know where Greyson is."

"Are you with him? Are you hurt?"

"You don't understand. You just believe everything they say. But it's not true. Lies. It's all lies. You're on the wrong side, Zayvion. You can trust me on that. Don't come looking for me."

Zay's lips pressed in a thin line. Chase sounded a little hysterical, and out of breath.

"Tell me where you are." Zay traced a glyph in the

air, drew a circle and line through it to cancel it, turned south, did the same thing, until he had drawn four spells, one at each compass point.

Chase's voice changed, went down a little, trying for normalcy. "Don't do it. Don't look for me. Or him. You can't . . . I don't want you mixed up in this. Two of us is enough. This is war, Zayvion. War."

The connection ended and Zay put the phone in his pocket.

"Anything?" Shame asked.

"She's on the other side of the river. Vancouver," Zay said.

So it had been a goose chase.

"Goddamn it," Shame said. "Let's go."

"Are you sure?" I asked.

"Can you sense her here?" Zay asked.

I shook my head. "I thought so. Nothing I'd swear on, though."

"She's good, Allie," Zay said like I shouldn't blame myself. "One of the best."

That was what I was worried about. If she was good enough to get us out here, she'd be good enough to lead us to where she wanted us to be.

Shame stayed where he was in Zay's car. Terric nodded to me, offering a ride again.

"We're better than her, right?" I asked Zay.

"We are." He hesitated. Nodded. That worried me, but I didn't tell him so.

I got into Shame's car next to Terric.

"How good is she, really?" I asked Terric once we were on the road and speeding to Vancouver.

"I haven't worked with her for a couple years." He was silent for a minute, navigating traffic. "She is very good. I've always thought Zayvion was better."

"Is he?"

"He is if he doesn't pull his punches."

"Which means?"

Terric rubbed the side of his nose, then brushed his hair back, even though it was banded at the nape of his neck. Boy had a lot of nervous twitches. I wondered if he was always like this or if this kind of thing made him nervous.

Wondered if I should get my worry on too.

"What does that mean, Terric?"

"They used to be lovers."

"And?"

He glanced at me, maybe glad I already knew that. "How easy do you think it would be to kill someone you've loved?"

A knot in the pit of my stomach clenched. Memories of Zayvion flashed through my mind, his smile, the easy sense of humor that he kept so carefully hidden under his dutiful exterior. His touch, the weight of him next to me, in me. Could I kill him if I had to? If he did something stupid like what Chase was doing?

"He doesn't have to kill her," I said a little doubtfully.

"Maybe not. But he might need to." Terric shifted his grip on the steering wheel, and pushed his shoulders down as if settling an uncomfortable weight. "It is always possible when you're a Closer."

"To kill?"

His eyes were a darkness in the night. "To destroy the ones you love."

Creepy. Sad. And so not what I wanted to deal with. "We'll all be there. Enough of us to stop her and find Greyson, and what? Does the Authority have a jail?"

"There are . . . places. Out of the way. Guarded. Betraying the Authority doesn't always end in your death. There are worse punishments."

There he went with the creepy again.

"So that's where they'll take Greyson. And her?"

"That's where I'd put them."

We were on the other side of the river now. Ever

since magic had been found and piped, Vancouver had become Portland's darker sister. Maybe it was because there were so many wells in the area, or maybe it was just geographic luck, but somehow all the light seemed to shine on Portland, while Vancouver huddled in Portland's slick, dusky shadow.

We were following Zay. He drove like he knew exactly where she would be. Terric and I didn't say much. Zay took the exit right on the other side of the Interstate Bridge that dropped us immediately on the other side of the river.

Fort Vancouver spread out to our right, a collection of historic buildings in brick and clapboard, with barracks and winding neighborhood-like streets, huge oak trees, and fields surrounded by split-wood fences.

Zay stopped by the brick three-story buildings down in Officers Row. It was late. There were no lights on, no one out on the street. Zay killed the engine and got out of the car, striding, then bolting into a run, heading between two of the big brick houses. I couldn't see where he was running, but I felt his heartbeat, kicking strong against my wrist. I felt his emotions, grim determination with the heady thrill of the hunt. Shame was out of the car too, not running.

He walked a short distance from the cars, turned on his heels, spinning so he faced the cars while he walked across the street. He had a lit cigarette, and held it in his mouth, the cherry glow of it marking his place in the shadows.

He motioned with one hand for us to get out of the car.

"This is it," Terric said. "Ready?"

"Always."

He didn't give me flak, just got out, paused as if scenting the air, then headed to the left of where Zayvion had gone, breaking into a jog.

Shame waited until I was next to him. He hitched his

hands forward, which drew the sleeves of his jacket off his wrists, and flicked an Illusion over the two cars so that they faded from casual observation.

He grunted, and swayed, his heartbeat under my wrist missing a beat, then pounding hard to make it up. I reached over and caught his elbow. He was shaking.

"What's wrong?" I asked.

He pulled the cig out of his mouth. The cherry trembled and jumped as he tried to push his hair out of his eyes. "Just. Fucking tired. I'm okay."

And that was when I smelled the pain on him, and the blood.

"Bullshit. She hurt you, didn't she? Where? How?"

He gave me a considering look, noticed I was fuming mad. He exhaled. "My gut. I'm fine."

I gripped his elbow tighter and dragged him back to his car. "No, you're not."

"What part of the language don't you understand, Beckstrom?"

The very fact that I could actually force him to walk with me told me just how badly he was hurt.

"You need a doctor?"

"No."

"Stitches?"

"No."

We passed through the Illusion he had cast, the slippery green scent of aloe filling my nostrils and throat. I opened the front door of Zay's car. "Get in."

"For Christ's sake," he started.

"Duck." I pushed on his shoulder at the same time I shoved him into the car.

He gave in, or more correctly, his knees gave in, and he folded down into the seat. Groaned.

"Let me see."

He turned his pale face in my direction. "I'll call my mum. Honest." He pulled out his cell phone and flipped it open. "You go make sure Z. and . . . Make sure Zay's okay."

He looked sick, greenish even in the low light. Casting that spell must have exacerbated his wound.

"How badly are you bleeding? Don't bullshit me, Shame."

"She stabbed me once. With a knife. I remember that." Dead serious. What did you know? The man could tell the truth without going up in flame. "The bleeding isn't too bad. She planted a Blood glyph and when I cast that spell, it started bleeding. It's not enough to kill me—you can trust me on that, Beckstrom. But she is seriously fucking up my fun."

"Show me."

He scowled. Gave in. Lifted his jacket. Even in the low light, I could see the glyph of Blood magic spread out across the width of his flat stomach, just catching on his hip bone. It bled—not badly—from one edge, probably the entry of the wound. The rest of the glyph snaked out under his skin, like deep red ropes. Blood magic was strange stuff. The glyph formed itself to the caster's will like a time-release capsule after the incision was made.

He pushed his shirt back down.

"You'll call your mom?"

He held up the phone again. "Go. No one's gonna find me under this Illusion, and if they do, I'm not without weapons. And a phone."

I nodded, and shut the door. Shame tipped the seat back a bit, and I saw a brief flash of the phone's blue light against his cheek and jaw before I was out of the umbrella of the spell, and then couldn't see the car at all.

I started off in the direction Zayvion had run, concentrating on the heartbeats at my wrist. Shame's was slow, labored, but even. I was glad he'd stayed behind.

I shifted my focus on Terric's heartbeat, fast, like he was running. His emotions: angry, but calm.

Then Zayvion. His heart beat in the steady rhythm of a marathoner or an athlete. Someone who was used to this kind of exertion. But his emotions hit me like a brick wall falling. Surprise. And fear.

Something was wrong.

I broke out of my jog and into a run. The concrete beneath my feet gave way to soft soil, well-tended grass wet from all the storms and the night's dew. Zayvion was near. I could feel him, like a heat beneath my skin.

And he was in trouble.

I broke out from between the buildings to the grounds in the back. Trees and outbuildings cut my view into bits.

The acrid scent of a Confusion spell burned like black pepper at the back of my sinuses. I couldn't tell which way I should go. Didn't even know which way I had come from.

Okay. This wasn't the first time I'd been hit with Confusion. I knew what to do.

I stopped, closed my eyes, because you can't do anything if you're staring at Confusion. I took a deep breath to calm myself. It didn't matter how good I was—there wasn't anyone who could cast magic in high states of emotion. Even Zay, whose fear I could feel in the tattering heartbeat at my wrist, still gave off a calm focus and determination.

Sometimes casting magic meant you had to be of two minds, or two emotions, at once.

I set a Disbursement—I was tired of muscle aches and went instead for a headache. I muttered a few lines of a coffee-commercial jingle to clear my mind. With my eyes still shut, I drew Cancel with my right hand and Sight with my left.

Cancel should wipe out the Confusion. Sight should show me what other magic was being used.

I opened my eyes. Cancel worked wonders. I didn't even smell the pepper anymore.

Sight showed me magic burning like carved fire on the buildings around me. I actually hadn't made it all the way through the alley between the buildings, even though it felt like I'd been running for blocks.

Confusion spread a sticky spiderweb between the structures, but now that Cancel was in effect, hovering like a shield over my head, the tendrils of Confusion were no longer touching me.

I took a second to focus on the heartbeats again. Zay and Terric were near. Very near.

I walked past Confusion, and stopped short.

Just on the other side of the spell and buildings, the grounds opened up. It was too dark to see how far back the grounds reached, but somewhere back there were trees and shadows, and flickering lights in the distance.

What I could see, very clearly, was the battle.

Terric glowed like a slice of moonlight, his hair gone silver, his skin pure white except for where dark glyphs shifted and moved across his features. His eyes burned an eerie blue while he chanted, the words falling from his lips in a lyric prayer. He had his feet spread, hands out to either side, holding a Containment spell that covered a twenty-yard circle.

And in that Containment spell were two people: Zayvion and Chase.

I'd never seen them even spar before. Chase hadn't been around during any of my training sessions. And the only time I'd seen her fight was when the gate opened during my test. She'd been fighting Hungers then, beasts from the other side of death.

Now she was fighting Zayvion.

Even with Sight, watching them hurt my eyes. Still, I didn't let go of the spell. Zayvion was a seven-foot tower of black flame, silver glyphs whirling over him in liquid ribbons, glowing the same metallic shift of wild colors as the marks magic had left on me.

He wove a spell with his left hand, heaved it at

Chase like it was made of lead, and lunged, the machete in his hand pulsing with dark jeweled lights, a different kind of magic, dark magic, coursing through the blade.

But Chase was good. Unlike Zayvion, even through Sight, even throwing magic around—and she was throwing a shitload of the stuff around—Chase looked like Chase. Pretty, a little gaunt, pale-skinned, dark hair pulled back in a braid, black jeans, and a black turtleneck.

Except for one thing. Her eyes glowed red. It wasn't just the light from magic. It was something else, something more, something dark, like the Hungers, like the Necromorph, burning out from within her. And it was not human.

It scared the hell out of me. Instinct told me to run, to leave this place, to go somewhere where magic didn't do what they were making it do.

Yeah, well, instinct would just have to suck it.

Chase, knife in one hand, caught the weight of Zay's spell on the edge of her blade and tore it apart. She redrew and recast that magic into something else, flicked it low at Zay's feet.

He dodged. The spell burned after him. He tucked and rolled over the spell, sliced it apart with the machete, and was on his feet again.

In Chase's other hand was a sword. Not a machete, no. This thing was beautiful, slick, graceful, powerful. Maybe a katana. It burned, not with flame, but with darkness. The air around it seemed darker than the night, and wavered as if heated.

Chase cut a spell into the air with the tip of the blade.

Zayvion closed the distance.

Blades and magic met, clashed. Fire exploded on a viscous wind. Terric, standing inside his Containment spell, turned his face away from the blast, adjusted his grip on the spell, and did something that extinguished the fire.

Silent. I heard nothing. Smelled nothing. Felt nothing but the hard-hitting heartbeats at my wrist. The Containment Terric held was amazing. It made it seem as if there were no one on the grounds, no fight, no magic. Nothing but a quiet night in a quiet field.

Zayvion pressed Chase, chanting, even though I couldn't hear him, the machete in his hand flicking like a rapier, then slashing out like a broadsword. The blade changed as he used it, and used magic to morph it, a wicked weapon of speed, power, steel, and magic.

Chase gave ground, breathing hard. She was bleeding—at least I think it was her blood that left a dark trail on the grass behind her.

I'd fought with Zay. I knew the punishment he could inflict on the practice mats. And that had been sparring. I had no idea how Chase endured his assault.

Why didn't she give up? What did she think? That she could beat him down? And then what? Kill him with Terric standing by? Kill Terric too? Run? It didn't make sense. Zayvion was the best at what he did. And it didn't look like he had any trouble not pulling his punches.

Chase was not stupid. She was a Closer. She certainly wasn't foolish enough to take on Zayvion and Terric alone.

The soft moth-wing flutter of my dad in my head brushed behind my eyes. Then snapped so hard, I gasped. Stars flickered at the edge of my vision, and my dad's awareness pressed down on me like an avalanche.

Something was wrong. Something was wrong with this whole thing.

Zay had said where we found Chase, we'd find Greyson. So where was he?

The flutter behind my eyes flicked hard again. Pain snapped at my temple. *Allison*, Dad breathed. *Behind you.*

I turned, and dropped Sight just as the man—no, not man; Shame—lifted his hands and threw the world at my head.

Chapter Fourteen

I dodged, and wove Block. As I crouched, Block surrounded me in a defensive shield.

Shame's spell burned past me, leaving a scorched
stink of burnt cherries in its wake. While one part of my
mind was pulling out the swearwords, the other couldn't
understand how he could have missed. Shame dealt
Death magic. He was a master at it. If he wanted to hit
something, that thing got hit.

I pulled my machete, to block his next attack.

Instead of attacking, he stood there, breathing hard,
his hands clenched into fists in front of him, head tipped
down so that I could not see his eyes.

But it was the smell of sweet cherries that told me
exactly what was going on. Blood magic.

Chase had marked him, cut his gut. Bound him to her
with blood. Now she was using him.

Holy shit. I'd thought he was going to call his mom.

Shame's fists shook and the fingers of his right hand
slowly opened, one at a time.

"Don't," he said, one ragged word. "Don't let the
bitch."

He groaned. His hand jerked into the beginnings of
another glyph. The grass beneath him was drying up,
going brown as he drew on Death magic to fight her
control over him.

Or—and this would be on my list of bad things—maybe she drew on Death magic through him to use it on me.

Shame tipped his head up, eyes burning with hatred. Sweating, teeth bared in a growl. Furious.

"Fuck her hard," he said through clenched teeth.

To do that, I'd have to knock Shame out. He knew that. And he was buying me time.

I dropped Block, and stood back up while calmly reciting a mantra. I drew a spell for Sleep.

Not an angry spell, something a parent would use on a fussy child.

It's always the simple things that no one expects to work.

Of course, I put so much magic into it, Shame would be out hard and fast.

His eyes narrowed, but I thought I saw him nod.

I finished the spell, and hurled it, filled with all the magic burning in my body, my bones. I threw it at Shame with everything I had.

He jerked, but didn't lift a hand to block. He held his ground and let the spell hit him full force.

Gutsy. Like staring down a heat-seeking missile.

I felt an echoed flash of pain at my wrist, his anger—and that man knew how to hate—and then his eyes rolled back in his head. He crumpled to the ground.

Terric's heartbeat sped up, his worry bleeding through.

Okay, maybe there was a downside to being connected to one another.

Greyson, my father said in my mind, his voice growing louder. *Find Greyson.*

For once, I was already ahead of him. Let Zay deal with Chase; let Terric cover our tracks. I was going to handle the real problem here—Greyson.

And since I had my dad, at least part of him, in my head, and Greyson very much wanted to get his slathering jaws on him, I was pretty sure I could find him easier than anyone on this side of death.

I glanced at Zay and Chase and Terric. They were gone. Nothing but an empty field met my gaze. Right. I'd let go of the Sight spell.

Okay, let me add awesome Illusionist to Terric's qualities. I drew Sight again, and sucked in a hard breath.

Terric pulled in a huge amount of magic from deep beneath the ground to fuel the Containment. He was breathing hard and steady, like a man enduring a brutal run. I knew he wasn't about to drop, but I also knew there was a limit to his endurance.

Zayvion beat Chase back against the Containment. She stabbed her knife into the wall of magic Terric had created and drew the magic out of it, channeling it directly at Zay.

Not a spell. Not a glyph. She sent a raging stream of magic burning at Zay like a flamethrower.

Zay held one hand out, palm forward, blocking the flame like some superhero in a movie. Magic poured around him, flaring and sparking metallic colors, filling the Containment space. But it could not get through the walls Terric held.

Zay should cast a spell to knock her out. He should smack her with the blade, hell, punch her, tackle her.

Instead, Chase yelled. I couldn't hear what she said, but I guessed it was a spell.

And the Illusion that Chase had been casting, holding this entire time, shattered.

Fast. Too fast.

One heartbeat: Chase fell to her knees.

She redirected the stream of magic. Past Zay, who ran now, toward her, trying to stop her.

Magic poured past him. Just like she wanted it to.

Poured into the shadowy figure who ran on all fours, liquid, faster than any man, even Zayvion, at Terric. It was Greyson. Greyson running toward Terric.

I whispered a mantra. Maybe it was a prayer. Pulled on as much magic as I could contain.

Greyson leaped at Terric.

Terric raised one hand. Slow. Too slow.

Zay twisted. Threw a spell at Greyson.

Chase was talking, singing, chanting.

Giving her magic, feeding Greyson.

And waiting.

For the second Zay's back was turned.

For this second.

She threw her knife.

I yelled. Cast Hold. End. This had to stop. Something had to stop this. I had to stop this.

Greyson tore into Terric, knocked him down, sank teeth into his shoulder.

Magic slid under my feet, skipped, skittered, and was gone. The storm did it again—pulled magic out of my reach.

It was like someone had hit an off switch for me personally. I was empty. The magic I cast fizzled out before it even reached them.

I ran.

Chase's knife found its target, buried hilt deep into Zay's back. He yelled. And I heard it. Because Terric's Containment was down.

Chase chanted. Fast, guttural. She was crying. And she was casting a spell.

The bitch.

Apparently magic was still working for her.

Zay stumbled, touched the ground with one hand, and pushed back up. Running. Pounding forward.

He was almost on Greyson. Spells and steel. He swung the machete.

Thunder rolled, a hard, crushing crack I felt in my bones. A gate between life and death burned into the air, yawned open between Terric and Zay.

Chase was a Closer. She knew how to close gates. She knew how to open them too.

Greyson let go of Terric, and lunged at Zayvion.

He leaped through the gate. From one side to the other. Onto Zay.

Terric rolled up on his knees. Raised a hand, threw magic at Greyson, at the gate.

Zay swung his sword, chanting a spell of pain and death.

But it was Greyson I heard. His growl. His howl. As he drank down all the magic, everything Terric threw. Everything Chase offered. Everything Zay swung. Sucked it all in. Then howled as Zay's machete sliced into his ribs.

Except there was no blood.

What there was, was Greyson. Standing. More man than beast now. Muscled, naked, angry. Insane.

He cast magic, in exact and perfect rhythm and beauty with Chase.

Soul Complements.

Beautiful, battered, she moved up behind Zayvion, holding him trapped, the magic from her hands, the magic from Greyson's hands, caging Zay and burning into his skin.

Burning into me.

Soul Complements. Rarest of the rare. We shared each other's pain.

Just because Chase and Greyson hadn't tested didn't mean they weren't meant for each other. Didn't mean they couldn't use magic together. Didn't mean they couldn't make magic do things it was never meant to do.

Didn't mean they couldn't become one person, one caster, one soul.

With one desire.

Kill Zayvion Jones.

I was almost there, almost there. My heart ran faster than my feet. My mind spun.

Greyson and Chase cast, chanted, bent magic to their will. Made it beautiful. Horrifying. And tore Zayvion apart.

Hold on, hold on, hold on. A chant, a fear I could not contain. Spilling out of me. With my breath. With his blood.

I could feel Zayvion's heartbeat slowing. Too slow. Thudding. Heavy. Gone. Watched him fall to the ground. For a second, a moment, I saw him, on the ground, but also standing next to himself—seven-foot-tall warrior clothed in nothing but black flame and silver glyphs. Freed from his body, he still carried a shadow of the machete.

He swung it at Greyson's head.

Just as Chase cast another spell, and threw it at the gate.

Greyson roared, a yell, more beast than man. The gate exploded, tendrils of magic whipping out tentacles, like fire, like a nightmare I could not stop, could not reach, could not end.

"No!" I yelled.

But the tendrils hooked into the dark warrior spirit of Zayvion and dragged him into the gate.

Something huge, fast, ran behind me, ran past me. Shame?

No. Stone. Howling like a freight train from hell, he launched at Greyson. Wings pumped the air, and he came down, crushing the Necromorph into the ground.

Chase screamed. Fell to her knees. Lost hold of magic.

With her spell no longer feeding it, and Greyson's spell no longer feeding it, the gate closed.

Zayvion did not move. Did not breathe. I felt the absence of his heartbeat like a ragged pain emptying me of everything—thought, heart, breath.

Emptying me of everything except anger.

I strode across the remaining distance, my sword drawn. Terric lay in a bloody heap to my left. I could still feel his heartbeat against my wrist.

Greyson snarled and squirmed beneath the crushing weight of Stone. Chase knelt, not far from both the gargoyle and the Necromorph, hands over her face, as if she endured, or maybe even Proxied for, the beating Greyson was receiving.

There was no magic in me. The approaching edge of the storm had sucked it out. I couldn't access the magic deep in the earth. I didn't know why.

But I had a backup. The magic I'd always had in me, the magic I was born with. A tiny flame no bigger than the flicker of a birthday candle.

I had just enough magic to cast one spell. And I was not going to waste it.

"Stone," I said. "Tear him apart."

The big bruiser snarled. Greyson and Chase screamed in unison. Music to my ears.

I knelt next to Zayvion. Bloody, bruised, he was mostly intact. A trail of blood tracked down his forehead, slick over his closed eyes and his nose, and filling the valley of his soft, thick lips.

I didn't have to press my hand against his neck or wrist. I knew he had no heartbeat.

And I knew I had only a little magic.

I closed my eyes, calmed my mind. Focused on the small magic within me. I placed my hand on his chest, over his heart.

"Live," I whispered. "Breathe."

The magic spooled out of me like a thin thread. No spell. I didn't need one. I knew what I wanted magic to do, knew what it had to do for me. I sent it to wrap around his heart, to make it beat, to squeeze his lungs, to make him breathe.

"Live." No longer a request. Now a demand. Soul to soul.

If I could give my heart to replace his, I would. My breath for his, I would. My life for his, I would.

"Please," I whispered.

Nothing. Nothing. I inhaled. And so did he. Shallow. His heart beat one slow thud.

I exhaled.

And so did he.

I don't know how long I sat there, able to do nothing more than inhale and exhale, his heart a hesitant beat that followed my own, but a beat nonetheless. But I knew I would do this until the end of time if it meant he was alive.

A hand slid over the top of mine. I didn't open my eyes. I knew who it was. The rough brush of fingerless gloves belonged to Shame.

"Keep doing that," he said gently, his voice low. "You're doing fine. Just keep breathing for him."

Live, I thought, I begged. Because a body needed more than breath to be alive.

Another hand fell upon my right hand. Cold, trembling. The unfamiliarity almost made me lose concentration.

"Positive and negative," Terric said, and I knew it was he who held my other hand.

I don't know what they did, don't know how they did it. I couldn't access magic, but they did. Magic, a pure, even stream of it, poured in through my hands. And I sent that magic, willingly, carefully, gently into Zay, told it to knit, to mend, to fill, to support.

"Heal," I said.

And magic leaped to my desire, rushing through Zayvion's body and mind with a pure wave of healing.

He inhaled. Without me.

His heart beat. Steadied. Caught and lifted by magic, magic Shame and Terric accessed, magic I sent to blend with the small magic I carried. Magic that healed.

His heartbeat fell into a solid rhythm. Another

breath. Another. The rhythm of his heart beneath my hand, against my wrist, beat stronger, strong.

Alive.

I opened my eyes.

Zay didn't stir. There was more blood covering his face. He was breathing, though, on his own. With my hands still on his chest, with Shame's hand still on my left, and Terric's still on my right, I bent, and kissed Zay, his blood salty against my lips.

He didn't move. I didn't sense a flicker of his emotions, his thoughts. It was like kissing a hollow doll.

A new fear washed over me, so like claustrophobia, I swallowed back a whimper. "Is he alive? Shame? Is he alive? I can't feel him. Can't—can't feel him." My voice was ragged, too high, too fast.

I wanted this nightmare to end. But I couldn't make myself wake up.

Shame's other hand turned my face so I was looking at him. "He's alive." Fierce. No Influence, but the power of his conviction was a slap across my mind.

"Hurt," he said, "but breathing. Alive. Panicking will make it worse. Got that?"

I blinked, nodded. Those words, his anger, was like pulling blinders off. I could see the world around me again, could smell again, could feel my body, my feet numb beneath me, the rain falling cold and hard against my head, face, hands.

The rain, at least, had arrived. How much longer until the wild-magic storm hit?

Shame, drenched, squatted on his heels next to me, one hand on mine, the other releasing my chin. He smelled of sweat, blood, cigarettes, and fear.

On the other side of me, of Zay's prone body, was Terric. I thought Shame looked bad. Terric sat tailor-style, his hand still on mine. His head hung so that his heavy hank of shock-white hair fell over his left shoulder. And his hair was sticky, wet with more than just the rain. He did not look up, did not move. If I hadn't felt his heart-beat at my wrist, I wouldn't have thought he was alive.

"Stone?" I asked.

Shame shook his head. "I don't know."

I looked over where Greyson had been. Where Chase had been. Where Stone had been.

Nothing. They were all gone.

"When I got here," Shame said, "it was just you and Zay and Terric."

"We need to find them," I said. "They can't just do this and disappear. I want them dead."

"First Zay," he said. "Then we find them. Then we make them dead."

Rain fell in a steady stream into his eyes. He didn't seem to notice. There was a darkness in him that burned hot, strong. A killing hatred.

I liked it.

"Do we carry him?" I asked. The very mundane me-chanics of getting Zayvion out of the rain and safe were suddenly more complicated than I had the brain to han-dle. Using magic, all that I had, all that they gave me, had left me weak, shocky, and not thinking straight.

Of course Zayvion dying might have something to do with it too.

"No," Shame said. "They're coming."

And it was like magic words. Because I suddenly real-ized there were people walking toward us through the rain.

Even in the low light, even through the rain, I could make them out. Lean Victor, wearing a trench coat and carrying a sword that slicked silver and black in the rain. Next to him, tiny Liddy wrapped in an ankle-length coat that kicked open to show the whip she carried strapped to her hip.

The twins Carl and La strode step in step, heads up, moving as if the rain didn't exist, curved scythes clenched in Carl's right and La's left hands. Other people too—short and fit Mike Barham, who wore glowing, glyphed gloves; Sunny, dark, angry, knives in both hands; the Georgia sisters, who each held a staff.

Maeve had pulled her hair back in a stark ponytail. She wore stiletto boots and a leather full-length jacket, two blood daggers strapped to her boots, her hands in her pockets. The hulking mountain of Hayden strolled behind her with a rolling gait, big as the world. I was wrong—he didn't carry a battle-ax or a cannon. He carried a broadsword over one shoulder and a shotgun over the other.

Last was big Jingo Jingo, wool coat and fedora, his voice a low, soothing murmur, maybe a song, maybe a prayer, as they came. All of them. Toward us. To save the day.

This was not a funeral procession—Zayvion was still alive. This was the cavalry arriving a little too late.

As soon as they reached us, time, which had felt like it slowed, suddenly snapped up to normal speed.

I sat there while voices—while people—investigated spells, checked the area, made plans. I sat there, Zayvion's heartbeat beneath my palm, while Victor and Maeve and Hayden came over. Maeve helped Shame to his feet, and Victor helped Terric. And lastly, big Hayden picked up Zayvion, like he was a child, and carried him to a gurney, then to a waiting van.

I pushed up on my feet, swayed. It was Jingo Jingo, of all people, who was there for me, his wide, warm hands catching under my arms, holding me upright while I breathed heavily and waited for my knees, my muscles, to start working again.

I would not cry. Not now.

I tried not to think about the ghosts of children who clung to Jingo like a winter cloak. Tried not to think about how much he bothered me. I focused, instead, on his strength—and he had a lot of it—on his warmth and his calm. I focused on his voice, low, soft, comforting.

"There, now, Allison, angel. You're gonna be just fine. Take a step for me. That's good. Good. You're something, aren't you? Yes. Yes, you are. And it's gonna all work out. Keep going; you're fine."

I did as he said and walked, following Zayvion, because Jingo Jingo was one of my teachers and he was here for me, helping me. Even though he was a freak.

"You're not gonna have to worry about tonight," he said, and his words sank into my head and body with the weight and warmth of wine. A spell, I thought. Or maybe I was just exhausted and he was telling me what I wanted to hear.

"You've done enough for the night. Kept Zayvion alive." He said it as if he hadn't expected I would do it. "Done all you could. More than that. Rest now. Rest."

And my knees, which were working, suddenly felt like they were made of water. I slumped against Jingo, fought not to pass out, not to sleep.

As he picked me up, I wondered why he had cast the spell on me. And wondered why behind every gentle word, I could sense his fear.

Chapter Fifteen

Voices, talking in hushed tones, woke me. I opened my eyes to an unfamiliar ceiling—plaster and dark wood beams—and an unfamiliar, narrow bed. I took a deep breath. The honeysuckle and lemon-polish scent of this place told me where I was.

Maeve's inn.

The hushed tones were coming from outside the room, the quiet murmur of people nearby. I glanced around the room—or as much of it as I could see from the bed. White plaster walls, window curtained to block all light, small lamp on the dresser in the corner, not nearly bright enough to break the shadows down, and another narrow bed next to mine.

In that bed was Zayvion Jones. Sleeping, I thought. Breathing. Thankfully, breathing.

Medical equipment hooked into him, something that silently flickered with green light, an IV, and a few other things I couldn't see clearly. Gina Fisher, the Authority's doctor, had been here to see him.

The reality of what had happened, the fight with Chase and Greyson, hit, and I moaned softly.

"He's alive." A voice, Shame's, from the shadows by the window.

I pushed up, sat. My bones felt hollow, ached, empty of magic. It was a strange feeling, like I had somehow lost a part of myself. Maybe it was just that I couldn't feel Zayvion, couldn't sense his emotions, his thoughts. If I weren't staring at him, I wouldn't even know he was in the room.

I still had on my shirt, though someone had gotten me out of my jeans and boots and replaced them with something that felt like sweatpants, or maybe pajama bottoms. A cool weight shifted against my breastbone and I realized I was still wearing the void stone.

No wonder magic was so silent in me. Maybe that was blocking it.

"How long have I been asleep?" I asked.

Shame shifted in the chair. I couldn't make out his features in the shadows of the room.

"It's evening the next day. You've been asleep sixteen hours."

"Zay?" I asked. It was only one word, because I couldn't get my head around all the other words, and all the fears they contained.

"He's been seen by the doctors. They've done everything they can for him. Medically. Magically."

"He's okay, right? He's going to be okay?" I didn't like the tremor in my voice, so I swallowed and clutched the void stone in my hand, hoping it would calm my mind along with my magic.

Shame stood, slowly, I noted. He walked over to the foot of my bed, where he sat. Light finally revealed him to me.

I bit down on a gasp. "What happened?"

Shame looked like hell. His skin was pale and greenish, sunk in, all the bones of his face showing through too sharply. A red welt ran from the edge of his jaw, following the line of his jugular down his neck to disappear in his black shirt. His eyes were dark, more black than green, and carried something: pain, hunger, or anger, I couldn't tell. He looked like he was on his way to corpsedom. He also wore a void stone at his neck, a black stone wrapped in silver and lead on a leather cord, choker-tight so that the stone pressed against his throat and moved when he swallowed.

"We, my friend, were fucked." He smiled, a flash of humor in a face of pain. My heart caught. That was like him, though. Given the choice to laugh or cry, Shame always laughed.

"Do you remember us hunting Chase?"

I nodded.

"Do you remember us fighting her?" He said that a little quieter, but steady, as if ready for me to react.

It took me a second—then I realized why. Shame had tried to kill me.

"I remember Chase carved you up with Blood magic. Is that why you look like Death?"

Tact. I have it.

Shame's shoulders relaxed, and he sat back, crossing one leg over his knee. "Don't like the new look? Sort of death-chic, don't you think?"

"Undoubtedly the new fashion trend."

He smiled again. "You want me to give you the run-down of what happened?"

"Sure." With a memory as spotty as mine, I had learned to never say no if someone wanted to recap events.

Shame went through the time line, starting with us finding him knocked out and Closed by Chase in the car in the parking lot.

I, surprisingly, remembered all of it, and added in some details about Zay and Chase fighting, and Greyson being cloaked in Illusion the whole time.

"And Stone showed up."

Shame grinned. "Thought so. They found footprints—well, more like craters—at the scene. You call him?"

"No. He likes to follow me around at night."

"Did you see what he did to them?"

I thought about it. I remembered Stone attacking, remembered him pinning Greyson. And I remembered

Chase fell to her knees. I hadn't watched the rest of it, too angry, too afraid for Zayvion. But Chase had knocked Stone out once before. Maybe she had done it again.

"I didn't pay attention." I couldn't believe how stupid I'd been. "I should have done something. Should have stopped them."

Shame gave me a steady look. "No. If you had done anything differently—anything—Zay would be dead."

I don't know if he was telling me the truth or just trying to make me feel better.

"You kept him alive, Allie," he said quietly. "I think you sat there, breathing for him, living for him, for some time before I came to. Nice Sleep spell, by the way. Remind me not to piss you off."

"Don't piss me off," I said distractedly. "What did you do, Shame? What did Terric and you do? I remember you added something to my magic. Helped Zay."

He held his breath, just the slightest tensing of his body. "Death magic, mostly. Channeling magic, taking a little of our . . . life and giving you and Zay something more to work with."

"Oh, Shame." I didn't know what else to say. How could I pay him back for that sacrifice? "How badly are you hurt?"

"I'll be okay. So will Terric. I know how much to give before things get dire. We'll recover from this. Eventually."

There was more to it.

"And?" I asked.

"And it worked. Enough." He glanced over at Zayvion, and I did too.

"What else, Shame?" I felt like I'd woken up too soon, and into a world that wasn't the way it should be. It wasn't just that I was tired and sore. It wasn't just that Zay was injured and Shame looked like he was on death's door. There was a deep wrongness about everything that triggered panic in my gut. I wanted to get out of this bed, take Zay—hells, take Shame and Zay and Terric—and get somewhere safe before whatever I was feeling, before the fear that scraped around inside me, got out and became real.

"Magic's gone," he said.

"Excuse me?"

"Gone. Maybe just off. Certainly not accessible. The backup spells, which carry time-delay triggers—kind of like batteries to keep the city going—are in effect, keeping things like the hospitals and prisons limping along." He tipped his head toward the window. "The backup spells won't last long. Then it's all going to go to hell out there. Soon. Real soon."

Maybe it was the fact that he said it so calmly. Maybe it was just that he had finally put a name to my fear. Whatever it was, I suddenly felt calm. Reasonable even.

Have I mentioned I am good under pressure, and can handle stressful situations well? Consider it mentioned. Well, at least I wasn't the only one who couldn't access it now.

"Has this ever happened before?" I asked.

"Which part of it?"

"Magic being gone?"

"Brief flickers. Usually before storms."

"So it's not unheard of."

"No, but it's usually just a pause. Magic's been out for hours now."

"And are there standard procedures the Authority implements when this happens?"

"We've done them. All the things Sedra has allowed."

"Do I want to know more about that?"

"She doesn't want any of us screwing with anything more until the storm hits. It makes some sense. When magic is this unpredictable, adding fuel to the fire can be disastrous."

"Explain disastrous."

"Magic channels through all the spells set throughout the city, hits hard, blows the network, destroys Proxies' brains, burns the city down. For starters."

"So the plan is to do nothing?"

He shrugged one shoulder. It looked like it hurt. "That's what Sedra wants. She's been"—he looked over at the door as if expecting someone to walk in— "different."

The latch clicked and Maeve pushed the door open, letting in the golden glow of light beyond the room, and the smell of lemon wood polish and something more savory that made my mouth water. Clam chowder, I thought. Maybe bread.

I blinked in the raised light. Shame got to his feet and headed over to the shadows again as if even that small amount of light coming near him burned.

"I thought I heard voices," Maeve said. "I brought food. For both of you," she said pointedly.

She expertly maneuvered a large tray with bowls, bread, and glasses of water on it over to the dresser, where she set the whole thing down. "How are you feeling, Allie?" She turned, a bowl of soup and hunk of bread on a plate in one hand, a glass of water in the other.

"Can you move the tray?" she asked.

I broke out of the hypnotic trance the food had me in—I was starving—and reached for the medical tray next to the bed that slid on wheels until it was over my lap.

Maeve placed the food and drink on it, adjusted the tray height without spilling a drop, and put her hands on her hips, giving me a motherly stare. "Headache?" she asked.

I already had the spoon in one hand and had gotten a mouthful of the creamy, rich, salty, buttery soup down. Still, I frowned. I didn't have a headache. I didn't really hurt at all, though I should. I'd used a lot of magic, and using magic always meant paying the price in pain.

"No headache," I said. "I should, though."

She nodded. "If there were magic flowing right now, under the ground, or inside you, you'd feel the pain. That's why you still have the void stone on. As soon as magic kicks back on again, there's a chance we'll all suddenly feel the price of using."

Didn't that sound like fun?

"Any idea when that might happen?" I asked. "I like to plan for when I catch on fire."

She turned back to the dresser. But Shame had already scuttled from the shadows and taken his share of the food. He was back in the chair in the shadows by the window, bowl in one hand, slurping it down.

"Utensils, Shamus," she said.

"Mmm." He pulled the bowl away long enough to get the hunk of bread involved.

"Magic will revive when the storm hits," she said, "maybe sooner. It's difficult to know. These things don't calendar well."

She walked to Zayvion's bed, brushed her fingertips across his forehead. She had done that a hundred times for me in the last few months I'd been training. Her touch brought a sense of soothing, an ease of pain. She said it wasn't so much magic as it was a knack. A little like my father and I have a knack for Influencing people, she said, she and her kin had a knack for settling the mind, soothing the body, easing, just a slight amount, the pain magic made you pay.

If Shame had the knack, I had no idea. I'd never seen him use it.

Zayvion didn't move, didn't so much as stir at her touch.

"He's in a coma, isn't he?" I asked quietly.

Maeve nodded. She folded her hands in front of her,

fingers twined. I'd never seen her look helpless. "We think he'll come out of it. When magic stabilizes."

I was pretty sure she was trying to convince herself of that, because I wasn't buying it. I'd seen Zay fall. I'd seen his spirit, his soul, get sucked into the gate. And I didn't think magic coming back was going to fix that. Fix him.

Well, unless it blew open a gate. And if Zayvion was still capable of finding his way home through that gate, maybe that would work.

"He went through the gate," I said.

Maeve looked over at me. I'd never seen that expression on her face before, but I knew what it was: horror.

"He what?"

"Went through the gate. Chase and Greyson opened it. I watched Zayvion's soul cross over the threshold."

It sounded like I'd just said he died. And in a way he had. But he was still breathing. He was right here in the room with me. Still fighting to live. I refused to give up on that.

"I see," Maeve said, no more than a whisper. "That changes things."

"How?"

She just shook her head. "Let me talk to some people first. When I know, I'll tell you. Right now, you should rest. I want you to stay here until you are feeling better."

"I'm fine."

She raised one eyebrow.

To prove how great I was feeling, I pushed the tray away from the bed and then the covers away from my legs. Pajamas, plain blue, flannel. Not mine, but nice not to be in nothing but panties.

I stood, and brushed my hair back behind my ears. My hands didn't even shake. Much. And the good thing? I wasn't dizzy.

"You want to leave?" she asked.

"I'm not staying in bed." I took a few steps. My body

didn't ache, really. Other than the hollowness of magic not in me, I didn't feel like I'd done much more than work out really hard.

"Can I do anything for him?"

Okay, I'll admit it. I was afraid to touch Zay. Afraid that if I did, I would have to come to grips with him not being there, not being present in his body. That I'd realize he was little more than a breathing corpse.

No. I pushed that thought away.

Maeve wove her fingers together again. "I don't know."

Three words I didn't want to hear.

"So there's not a lot about this in the histories?"

She shook her head. "Did you see him go through the gate with your bare eyes, or were you using Sight?"

"I don't remember. I don't think I was holding magic. It all happened so fast."

She sighed. "I'll talk to Sedra. To Liddy. To Victor. To Jingo Jingo. We'll contact other members of the Authority outside the city. See if anyone has experienced this before." She was suddenly all business again. Busy was her default mode when she was faced with an emergency.

"In the meantime, you'll stay here. Not because I don't think you are well enough to leave. We may need you once magic flares again, once the wild-magic storm hits. It would be easiest for us if you were nearby."

"I'll stay awhile," I said.

"Good." Maeve looked over at Shame, who had been sitting quietly, head back, eyes closed, for most of the conversation. It didn't take magic to see how her body language changed once she looked at him. She was worried for him. She was afraid for him. I'd never seen her doubt Shame's strength. Not even when magic had taken him to his knees.

"Will you sleep?" she asked like this had been a point of contention.

"Not yet."

"Terric sleeps."

Shame nodded, though he did not open his eyes. "I know. Why do you think I'm awake?"

I gave Maeve a questioning look and she only shook her head. Okay, fine. If she wouldn't tell me what was going on between Shame and Terric, I'd make Shame tell me.

"Eat again, soon," Maeve said. "I'll bring you something in an hour or so."

Shame didn't move. Didn't say anything.

With one last brush of her fingers over Zayvion's hand, Maeve turned and walked out, shutting the door behind her.

I stood there a minute, trying to make sense of everything. Zayvion had been killed—no, sucked through to death. Magic was gone, or at least not accessible. Shame was half dead. I didn't know what was up with Terric.

And Chase and Greyson, as far as I knew, were still on the loose.

It didn't look like the good guys were winning.

Well, I sure as hell wasn't going to wait around for magic to bail my ass out. I could take care of this without magic.

"You have some problem with light?" I asked.

Shame frowned, opened his eyes. "Why would you even ask that?"

Because you look like a vampire or a corpse, I thought. But I said, "Yes or no?"

"No."

"Then open the curtain. I need to see Zayvion better." And find my clothes, my shoes, and my gear. It was time to go hunting.

Shame pushed up on his feet. He moved like every muscle in his body was on fire.

"Maybe you should be in bed too," I said.

"Maybe you should keep your opinions to yourself."

He grunted softly as he tugged the curtains over to one side of the window.

Evening light poured into the room. I hadn't expected it to be that late. But it was still bright enough that the cool gray light revealed the room—white plaster walls and dark wooden beams and floor. Even better, I could see Zayvion.

He was breathing normally, deeply, as if he were sleeping. The IV attached to his arm was wrapped with gauze that I thought might have a spell woven into it. He looked like he was sleeping. Just sleeping.

I reached over, gently brushed my fingers across his lips.

The awareness of Zayvion, of his soul, his mind, his emotions, was absent.

Fairy tales said all it took was a true love, a kiss, a tear. But Zay wasn't enchanted. He was gone. Dead. And I didn't think there was a fairy tale that could make this turn out happily ever after.

The tight tension of sorrow made me swallow hard. I was not going to cry. Because I didn't need a fairy tale. All I needed was one beauty and a beast—Chase and Greyson.

Zay had sat by my side for two weeks not knowing if I would recover from magic that had nearly killed me. I wasn't about to give up on him on the first day.

I let my fingers wander, knowing I could never give the gentle comfort that Maeve could, but needing him to know I was there, I was with him. I traced his forehead, eyelid, cheek, and down the rough edge of his jaw. Nothing. Nothing stirred within him. He was empty. Silent.

I bent and kissed him, then rested my forehead against his. "I'll make it right," I told him. "Don't give up."

Then I straightened. I pushed my hair back behind my ears again and looked over at Shame.

He leaned against the wall, arms crossed loosely over his chest.

"Nice," he said. "How exactly are you going to make it right?"

"By finding Chase and Greyson. And doing whatever it takes to get Zayvion back."

Like gasoline catching a spark, Shame suddenly seemed much more awake. An anger, an animalistic hunger, flared in him. I wondered if he'd given up a little of his sanity too. Wondered what happened when an untested Soul Complement used magic with his possible Soul Complement—Shame and Terric. What happened when that magic involved Death magic, and a good friend dying?

Just what kind of man was Shame when he was this angry and this wounded?

"Whatever it takes?" he asked a little too casually.

"Yes."

"Doesn't that sound like fun?" he murmured.

I looked away from him because I didn't like his smile. I searched for my jeans and sweater—found them folded, obviously laundered—in the dresser drawer.

"So what's going on between you and Terric?" I asked.

"What do you mean?"

I straightened, huffed out a breath. "Are you still angry with each other? Did using magic together make things worse? Have you killed him and buried him in a box somewhere?"

"I don't think that's any of your business," he said.

"I do. Listen, I've been paying attention to things. Things like Soul Complements, which are supposed to be this rare and wonderful joining of magic. But so far all I've seen is tragedy. Chase and Greyson, you and Terric, and now Zayvion and me."

"And Leander and Isabelle," he added.

"Who?"

"Old story. Old, sad story."

"Fine. Leander and Isabelle too. I'm beginning to think once you find your Soul Complement, someone or something does everything in its power to destroy that bond. I want to know what happened between you and Terric. What really happened."

He just scowled at me. Sullen.

"It would help me believe Zay and I have a shot at this. Please," I added.

It took him a while, but he finally spoke.

"It was a long time ago," he said quietly. "About five years. We'd been sent out on a job, Zay, Terric, and I. Something had slipped the gates, and we were after it.

"We were good friends. Mates, you know? Did a lot of our schooling together. Z. and Terric were both after the job of guardian of the gate. Not that you can just fill out a form and get picked for the position. But for a while there, it was anyone's guess which of them would be best at handling all disciplines of magic. Which of them wouldn't crack under the pressure of using all magic.

"Terric's no slouch. He could have had it. But . . ."

He shook his head. "So we were hunting. It was night, and I'd had a drink or two. Stupid, I know. Zay caught a scent of something down an alley. Terric and I went up a block to try to block its escape."

He paused, licked his lips. He wasn't looking at me anymore, his eyes focused on the past. "It was a hot night. Summer. We were fast. Quiet. The plan was for us to pin it in the alley, then take it down. Easy pickings . . .

"Terric got there first. The Hunger—it was huge, bigger than a car—I'd never seen one so big, still haven't. It had fed well, was solid as a tank. It leaped. Over Terric. Spotted me. Don't know why. Maybe thought I'd be easier to take down.

"It did something. With dark magic. Got in my head. I couldn't stop it, didn't know the spells, couldn't use magic fast enough to fight it. Once it was in my head, it did something."

He paused for so long I thought he was done talking. Still, I waited him out.

"Did something to me. It wasn't horrible—no, that would have just made me angry. I would have fought. It did something so . . . wonderful. Dark. Beautiful. To me. It was like I was breathing for the first time in my life, like I was finally, fully alive.

"And filled with hunger and power. I wanted Terric. His mind. His soul. His body. I wanted to kill him. Devour him.

"I used the dark magic that filled the Hunger. There was so much. It was so easy. I threw it at Terric, at his soul. I tore him apart."

Pause, then, a whisper, "I laughed while he screamed."

He went silent again, so still, he didn't even blink.

Finally, "Zayvion pulled me off him. Blocked the dark magic I was using, killed the Hunger. Knocked me out. Terric's hair used to be black like mine. Did you know that?"

I shook my head.

"He came so close to dying. The doctors said the only thing that saved him was that our magic matched, blended. Freakish luck. Freakish. It's why they think we're Soul Complements. Because what I did should have killed him. Because he survived me tearing his soul apart.

"When he woke up, the first thing he said was he forgave me. He told me to stop apologizing. That it wasn't my fault. Everyone thought it wasn't my fault. Even Zay. He testified in front of court and counsel in my defense.

"But they were wrong. I might have been pushed into it, but I was the one throwing the punches. It was my fault.

"When they told me we had to test to see if we were

Soul Complements, I said no. Because I owed him that. Owed him his life. Owed him more, really. A lot more.

"He lost his chance to be guardian of the gates because of me. Can't tolerate dark magic anymore. Not after nearly dying from it. It's why he moved to Seattle. He couldn't watch Zay take the job he wanted."

He nodded, and rubbed his fingertips along his jeans, as if wiping off a stain. "It's good we have a state between us now. Good we don't have to work together."

He paused again, then, softly, "I've never been able to get the taste of his soul out of my mouth." Shame blinked and seemed to come back to himself. Seemed to notice I was in the room.

"So you want to know if you and Zayvion have a shot at being Soul Complements? More than Terric and I, more than Chase and Greyson. For one thing, neither of you is a screwed-up killer. That's a step in the right direction."

"Have you ever told anyone about . . . about this?" I asked.

He shrugged, just one shoulder tucking up toward his ear. "They heard what they wanted to hear. They think what they want to think. I know what I was thinking and feeling. I know what I did. Do I regret it? Every damn day. But that doesn't change what I did." He fingered a cigarette out of his pocket, lit it, and exhaled smoke toward the window, which I only now noticed was cracked open.

"You were young. Maybe, what? Nineteen, twenty when it happened?" I asked.

Shame sniffed. "You going to stand here talking about the past all night, or were you actually going to do something to save Zay? 'Cause yakking isn't doing him much good."

Okay, I got the hint. Subject closed. For now.

"I'm going to take a shower," I said.

"Why bother? This is bound to get messy."

"I don't care. First I shower."

"And then?"

"Then I'm going to hunt. My way."

"I'm coming with you," he called as I shut the door.

I didn't want him to, not because of his story, but because he looked exhausted. But I knew there was nothing I could do to stop him, short of getting in a fistfight. Which I'd probably lose. I might not be hurting, but I wasn't at my best either.

I shucked off the pajamas, and got into the hot water. The marks down my arm and hand were dulled to a flat gray. It was strange to see the marks without the metallic shine, without any color or magic in them at all.

But in a way, it made me feel strong. I hadn't always had incredible amounts of magic surging through me. Sure, I was born with a small magic. I paused, concentrating on if I still felt that small weight within me. It was there, candle-flame bright, but not as powerful as the magic I usually held.

Still, that wasn't nothing. And I had a feeling it was a lot more than most people had right now.

I finished washing, got out, got dry, and put on my clothes.

My father had been strangely quiet since we'd hunted Greyson. I wondered if he was still in my mind.

Dad? I thought.

The moth-wing flutter brushed against the backs of my eyes. He was there. A little stronger than he had been before. I swallowed, and tasted the familiar wintergreen and leather of his scents, smelled it in my nostrils, tasted it at the back of my throat.

Still possessed by my dead father? Check.

Small magic still inside me? Check.

Pissed off that some skank and her boyfriend tried to kill my lover? Hells, yes.

I found a brush and pulled my hair back. It wasn't quite long enough to put in a band, but I'd need a haircut soon to keep it out of my eyes. No time for that now. I had a world to save.

I strode out of the bathroom. Shame must have left and returned. He wore a black trench coat. Belted. I had a feeling he was packing a lot of weapons underneath it.

"How you want this to go down?" he asked.

His eyes were a little glossy, like the grips of a fever raged through him. But he was still himself. Still willing to stand beside me and save Zayvion. I probably shouldn't, but I trusted the man, dark past and all.

Was it a bad idea to take a crazy, bloodthirsty Death-magic user on my little stroll around the city? My dad in my head rubbed at the backs of my eyes. Well, I didn't care what he thought.

A phone rang. Mine. In the pocket of my coat that hung over the back of the other chair in the room. I picked it up before it could ring a third time.

"Yes?"

"Allie, this is Detective Stotts. I need you to meet me in Eastmoreland, at Southeast Tolman and Twenty-eighth. Now."

"Hounding?"

"Yes." He hung up.

I hadn't even had a chance to tell him that I was busy getting my vengeance on. Or that without magic, I wasn't going to be any good for tracking spells.

"Problem?" Shame asked. His hands were in his pockets. Fisted, like it was taking a lot of effort just to stand there and not hit something.

"Hounding job. Stotts." My mind raced through possibilities. Stotts knew some things about magic and the crimes involved with it that other people didn't. He knew, for example, that Violet was working on the further development of the disks to hold and store magic, and to make magic less costly. He also knew a few of the disks had been stolen before my dad died.

But he didn't know anything about the Authority. Didn't know that in my spare time I hung around with people who, according to the law, should be locked away.

I'm sure he and everyone else knew magic was down in the city and working off backup spells. Yet, he still called me.

Shame waited. Waited for me to make a decision.

"I need your car."

"I come with it."

"I drive."

Shame snorted. "Like hell." He walked across the room to the door. We made good time down the long hall and the two flights of stairs.

"Why did she have to put us on the top floor?" I asked. It wasn't so much that I was too tired to walk—I was impatient, and the damn stairs just seemed to keep showing up before me.

"It's well guarded. Not just with magic," he said over his shoulder. "And it's as far away from the well as you can get in the building."

"And that's good because?"

"Did you think she was kidding when she said magic would probably come back to life? Explosively?"

No, I hadn't thought she was kidding. But I had thought they'd have some kind of control over it. The thing that spooked me the most was that the Authority, or at least Maeve and Shame, didn't seem very comfortable with how magic was going to react to this emptying, and to the approaching storm.

"I thought you people had a manual for this kind of thing."

He laughed. "*We* have a manual. Magic doesn't."

He took a sharp left, even though I knew the main room was to the right.

"And you're going?"

"Out the door that doesn't have a million people with questions between us and it."

Good thinking.

He was right. There was a door down at the end of this hall, maybe something that had been a staff entrance before. He didn't do any fancy magic, no magic at all, actually. Just opened the door and strode out into the rain.

"What about Terric?" I asked as I followed him.

"What about him?"

"You're leaving him. Maeve said he was sleeping. Is he hurt?"

The memory of him lying on the ground, Greyson chewing on him, flashed in front of my eyes. The memory of him sitting slouched in pain beside Zay, his hand cold against the back of mine, came to me.

"He'll get over it."

"What?"

"If I'm breathing, he's breathing. None of us gets out of living the easy way."

Shame was making good time, his anger steadying his steps. I had to jog to catch up with him.

We got in the car. I glanced back at the inn. A lone figure stood on the porch, leaning against the rail. Terric. He waited, watching us.

Shame started the car. Then Terric turned and walked away.

Chapter Sixteen

Shame pulled out of the parking lot. "Where?" he asked.

"Stotts said on the corner of Southeast Tolman and Twenty-eighth. That's out by the golf course, right? Do you know what's there?"

He thought a minute, turned the car north and toward the bridge. "Isn't that where Beckstrom's labs are?"

"What?"

"Oh, come on. You don't even know where your dad set up labs for Violet's research?"

"Didn't like him, didn't know her, didn't care. Which means no, of course I don't know where the labs are."

"It never came up in board meetings?"

Interesting question. It hadn't come up in board meetings, but Violet had told me the subject of the lab, and more specifically the disks that were being developed there, was causing all sorts of suspicions among the stockholders and higher-ups of the company. So much so, she'd moved in with Kevin because of threats.

I felt like I was working a crossword puzzle with no clues. I should be guessing what was going on, but didn't even know where to begin. People in the company were upset with her for something. The only thing I could put my finger on was that the disks had been used for a lot of bad things. And now Stotts wanted me out at the lab where the disks were made, to Hound something when there was very little magic left in the city.

A break-in? Maybe someone on the board got a judge on their side and was seizing property.

Whatever was going down out there, Stotts had not sounded happy.

"That's a hell of a long time to think over your answer," Shame said. "Try a short word like 'no.'"

"Sorry," I said. "It's just—I think I'm missing something. That maybe Violet said something." I pulled out my notebook and scanned back through the entries. Nothing that immediately looked like a clue. "And no, the lab hasn't come up in any of the Beckstrom Enterprises business I've been involved in. But I'm not the CEO. Violet is."

"And?"

"She told me there was some contention among the board members. They didn't like not knowing what, exactly, she was developing, and why she wouldn't let them get their hands on it. Plus, she moved in with Kevin."

"Cooper? Her bodyguard?"

"She said she received threats. Why don't you know about this? Kevin's a part of the Authority. Doesn't he report in or something?"

"Not to me. Any field agents—hell, all of us—report in to Sedra. She's the mastermind."

Yes, I knew that. I'd just never needed to report to her myself. Things had been really quiet the last couple months. All I'd been doing was training and learning. My teachers reported in for me.

"Do you think they can help Zayvion?" I asked. "Maeve, Jingo Jingo?"

Shame was quiet. "You said he went into a gate."

"Yes."

"He might find his way back. If a gate were opened near his body." Shame took a breath and wiped his hand down his face, as if trying to mop off exhaustion. "Complicated by Jones using light and dark magic, all the disciplines. Opening a gate for him might go bad fast. Or it might help him remember what it's like to be alive and bring him back."

"So why aren't they trying that? Hells, you and I could open a gate."

Shame wiggled the fingers of one hand. "No magic, remember? It takes magic, a lot of it, or a lot of different kinds working together, to open a rift between life and death. Gates aren't easy."

Maybe not, but I'd watched Chase open and close them with a snap of her fingers. But then, she was Greyson's Soul Complement. And they could break magic's boundaries.

I rubbed at my forehead. The left side of my face still hurt. I'd probably be half tanned for the next few months. Since I had my notebook out, I made notes about everything that had happened. City lights, just electric, no magic, washed the pages in white and yellow. I finished my notes and gazed out the window at the magicless city.

Cars that were just cars, nothing shiny, nothing magic, drove past. In the low light of the sky's exhalation into darkness, people walked the streets.

Mostly they looked the same. Oh, maybe a few older coats, maybe more bad hairstyles, thicker waistlines, and a limp or two. But mostly, the kinds of magic people used to enhance themselves were noticeable only close-up—the perfect noses, teeth, complexion, sparkling wit, dulcet voice, and so on.

We'd gotten so used to taking care of flaws with easy fixes. What's a little headache now and then for the illusion of youth? Seeing people with their true faces on was odd. Fascinating. The big noses, laugh lines, thin lips, frowns, crooked teeth—the imperfections somehow caught at the soul of humanity, and left it bare to be seen, the beauty and ugliness. It felt like suddenly we'd become what we were. For good, and for bad.

That lack of magic gave me a glimpse of something I didn't know I was missing. A reality, an honesty, magic could not create. And like seeing a foreign land for the first time, I was caught by the beauty of it.

Lead and glass lines and conduits still wrapped like steel ivy up the outsides of the buildings, crawled up and up, and met at building tops where the gold-tipped spires of Beckstrom Storm Rods stood like beacons to the stars.

But stripped free of Illusion, Glamour, or the comfortable blur magic offered, crumbling brick, peeling paint, rust, and disrepair showed through. The sidewalks were not as clean, the plants not as tended, windows dirty, broken, or boarded. Safety inspections had to be done to assess a building's health without magical enhancements—I'd just been through a barrage of them with the leasing of the warehouse by Get Mugged—so I knew the buildings were stable. They were also old, showing their history, their lives, in every crack and slant.

I loved it.

This was not the Portland I knew. Rust-streaked pipes and mechanical units on rooftops—air conditioners, vents, and the like—sat like squat warts against the sky, changing the familiar horizon. I wondered if Stone was up there somewhere. I hadn't seen him since the fight.

"Have you seen Stone?" I asked Shame.

He licked his bottom lip. Shame still looked like hell, and the anger that had brought him back to life at the inn seemed to be wearing off, leaving a sickly sweat behind.

"You know Stone's an Animate." He looked at me. Waited. I had no idea what he was getting at.

"An Animate is an inanimate object infused with magic," he went on. "Magic puts the life in them. And when magic is gone, there is nothing. . . ."

"No. Absolutely no. You did not just tell me Stone is dead."

"Allie . . ."

"Shut up."

Stone was fine. He was smart enough to track me, he was smart enough to curl up around a backup spell or something. I refused to believe he was dead.

But the more I looked at the city around me, the more dread sank in. There just wasn't that much magic left. Not for generators. Not for illusions. And not for a gargoyle, no matter how smart.

Shame said quietly, "When magic kicks back up after the storm hits, he'll come to." It was sweet, but I knew he didn't think that would happen.

Stone was just a statue. A big stupid rock who left dust all over my apartment and wore my socks on his nose. But he was my big stupid rock. I was going to miss the hell out of him.

I tried not to think about it. Because I didn't want to show up in front of Stotts crying.

Shame drove like he knew right where the lab was. And maybe he did. Maybe the Authority kept the lab on its watched list. But even if Shame hadn't been driving, it wouldn't have been hard to find the place.

Three police cars blocked the street. Beyond them the big white van of Stott's MERC team parked half on the elm-lined sidewalk. A few police officers stood outside the building, which was more of a house, and two more at the street to keep people at a safe distance. I didn't see Stotts's crew: Julian, Roberts, and Garnet.

More police tape, a sullen yellow smear in the dying light, roped off the sidewalk outside the building.

The building really did look like a house out of a storybook. Old hand-placed stone walls scalloped the edges of the sidewalk. The Tudor-style house was set up on the small hill and faced the trees and golf course across the street. At least two stories, the house looked like a home rather than a lab, brick and stucco on arched doorways beneath steeply gabled roofs. The windows, slender and multipaned, had little light behind them.

In the driveway was Violet's Mercedes-Benz.

My heartbeat did double time.

"Stop," I told Shame. "I need to get out."

Why would she be here? I thought she was moving in with Kevin. I thought she was being smart, being safe. Making baby blankets or knitting diapers or something.

Stress is a weird thing. I got out of the car and heard the door slam shut, but I didn't hear the car drive away. I didn't know what the cop asked me when I jogged past her. I didn't feel the police tape skim my back as I ducked under it and made it to the driveway up the walkway.

No blood on the concrete. No blood anywhere that I could see. That was something. Maybe Violet had arrived after the break-in. That made the most sense. Stotts must have called her. Like he called me. To look at the damage inside. To fill out an insurance form or something.

I turned to go into the building.

Stotts's hand landed on my wrist, warm and callused, and brought the world suddenly back to me.

"Stay out of the way." He pulled me to one side, near a line of bushes. Didn't let me get close to the door.

There wasn't any room for me to go anywhere. Men filled that door and came through it with stretchers.

One stretcher carried an unconscious and pale Kevin Cooper. Blood had been wiped off his bruised face, but still leaked in his light brown hair, turning it dark on one side. An oxygen mask fit snug against his face. They moved him past me so quickly, I couldn't see where else he might be injured. But I could smell magic on him. A lot of it, a lot of spent magic.

"Who?" I said. "Who did this?" I was trying to ask who could do this. There just wasn't that much available magic to be able to do this much damage. "How long? When? When did that happen to him?"

Stotts hadn't let go of my wrist. Smart. I'd probably go in there and ruin evidence in this state of mind.

"You're here for that," he said. "To Hound the scene. Tell me what you see. There's more."

And he was right. There was more.

More EMTs, men and women, and another stretcher. This one with tubes and monitors. I knew who it was from the shape of the prone figure even before I could see her face.

Violet.

Dad scratched at the backs of my eyes, no longer a moth-wing flutter, but something made out of sharp edges and teeth.

I exhaled to stay calm and pushed at Dad, needing him in a corner, away from my conscious thoughts, away from seeing Violet on a stretcher. I must have tried to pull away from Stotts too.

"Don't," he said. "Don't get in the way. Let them do their job."

Violet, my dad said. *No. Please, no.*

I pressed my lips together to keep his words from forming in my mouth. He was in my head, but he had no right to use my body. Even if Violet was hurt.

She was in better hands than mine right now. I was not a doctor, and neither was my father. Getting her to the hospital as quickly as possible was the smart thing to do.

As they passed, she opened her eyes.

My dad struggled, shoved at my control. *Violet*, he thought.

"Daniel?" she whispered.

No. Hell no. I didn't care how much they loved each other—I was not going to let my father talk to her, was not going to let him use me or my mouth or thoughts that way, and was not going to stop the EMTs from getting her medical attention.

The EMTs moved swiftly past me. With Stotts's hand still clamped to my wrist, I held my ground while Dad battered the edges of my control. Then the EMTs were gone. Violet was gone, placed very carefully into the back of an ambulance that drove away, lights flashing and sirens blaring. I pulled my hand away from Stotts.

Dad went dead silent. Angry.

Too bad.

Okay. Regroup. First the job. Hounding. Hounding the crime. Without magic. Then checking on Violet.

"Anything you'd like to tell me about this before I go in there?" I asked.

He looked at my expression, puzzled. Then glanced over my shoulder at the ambulance. Maybe at something beyond that. "Violet and Kevin were here when it happened. Violet was semiconscious when I arrived. She can't remember anything."

"Head wound?"

"She's been hurt," he conceded.

Yeah, well, I figured that out all on my own. "Is she going to be okay? Is the baby in danger?"

He looked down at his shoe, then back at me. "They don't know yet."

Fuck.

And the cool wash of my dread and my father's anger melded into something else. Resolve. Whoever had done this, whoever had attacked my wife—I mean my friend—and my unborn sibling, was going to suddenly have a very bad, very short life.

I strode into the building, past the fallen door that looked like it had been blown off its hinges, and into the main room.

Stotts followed.

The first room was a reception area, though there

was no desk. Just a couple small clean couches, a TV mounted on the wall, and a computer and a phone on a table.

I didn't have magic at my disposal. None of us did. I glanced over at Stotts to see if he was uncomfortable with that. He looked calm, composed. Didn't look like having magic or not having magic made any difference to him. Sort of an "If I don't have my gun, I can kill you with my hands" kind of look.

Very cop of him. And it meant he wasn't all that surprised that magic had suddenly died out.

"Do you know why magic's gone?" I asked.

He shook his head. "I'm thinking it might have something to do with that gut feeling of yours. The storm. We've had magic black out on us before. But never this long."

"Okay, so you know I can't Hound without magic."

"I'd just like your eyes on the place."

There were already police officers and other specialists working the scene. Stotts's MERC crew was inside, using a few gadgets that looked like they were low-magic but useful, like the glyphed witching rods, and nonmagical things like cameras and fingerprinting tools. Very old-school police procedural.

I felt out of place—I didn't know what all the stages of investigation would be. All I ever did was Hound magic, track spells, identify casters, and not get involved in the cleanup and meticulous recording of the event.

Stotts had once told me that I was different from other Hounds he'd used, and I saw things in more detail than they did. I guess we were about to find out if that was still true without magic.

I walked through the room, careful not to touch anything, looking at the tables, the couches, the shelves, the walls. I inhaled through my nose and mouth, taking in the scents of metals and plastics, carpet cleaner, and the musty-closet smell of old books.

If magic had been cast here, in this room, I could not smell it.

"How'd the door get bashed in?" I asked.

"Police."

Okay, so that was good. No magical battering ram. "Is there another room?"

I knew there had to be. There had to be a research room—maybe a clean room, a room glyphed and warded and I didn't know what all else—to actually produce the disks, if the disks were made here.

"This way." Stotts led me down a short hall, where windowed rooms lined either side. I followed, tasting the air, listening, looking. I might not have magic, but my senses were acute.

At the far end and right of the hall was a room with a door open. I stepped through the doorway and covered my nose. Magic had been used here. A lot of magic. I could smell the burnt-wood stink of it, hot as red peppers shoved up my nose. I didn't remove my hand, instead breathed through my fingers. This was the lab. This was where the disks were made.

Stotts didn't have to tell me. The magic that was used in here—no, the magic that was stored in here—hung like a flashing billboard that said WATCH YOUR STEP, MAGIC AHEAD.

The room had several long, low working counters sectioning it off, and the walls were bracketed by cupboards and countertops. Toward the back of the room was a wall of little silver-plated drawers, like safety-deposit boxes. Maybe a hundred, two hundred drawers.

All of them were pulled out, broken open, busted.

Drawn forward like a string on a reel, I walked over to the drawers. Black velvet lined the bottoms of the drawers. Glyphs, whorls of glass and lead, were worked into the walls of each drawer, scrolling a repeating pattern around the inside. Hold spells, I thought, maybe Containment. Tricky, intricate stuff. It had taken a fine,

fine hand for that. A hell of a magic user had made these boxes and it was clear they were intended to keep whatever was inside them, inside them.

A flutter at the backs of my eyes, feather soft, brushed harder the longer I looked at those boxes.

And for a second my vision shifted. It was as if I were looking at the boxes through someone else's eyes. My father's eyes. I remembered—or rather I saw his memory of—the disks nestled in the drawers, one disk per box. And I knew that every disk had been fully charged with magic before it had been placed in the box.

Why would anyone store that much magic in one place?

As soon as I thought it, I heard his answering thought. *Experimental. Untested. We were pushing the parameters, calculating the decay rate. Finding out how much magic the disks could hold and for how long.*

How long could they hold magic? I asked.

When I . . . when I was alive, they had yet to degrade. At all.

The reality of what this meant was slowing soaking in. Someone, maybe more than one someone, had more than a hundred disks, all filled with magic.

Hundreds of magic disks that caused no price of pain to use, filled with magic, in a city currently empty of magic.

Holy shit.

My father's grim agreement didn't do much to steady my nerves.

Do you know who would do this? Who would want this? I thought.

Who wouldn't want it? he asked.

Yeah, I got that. When there is no magic, the person who has the remaining power wins. But he had to have some idea of who would know how to break into the lab. Who would know that the disks were here.

If I could Hound it, I'd know. I'd be able to read the

spell used to take the disks, because even to my un-trained, un-police-officer eyes, I could tell this wasn't a standard break-in. Magic had been used.

And I needed magic to Hound.

"Are there any of the disks left?" I asked Stotts.

"Not in the drawers."

"Anywhere else in the building?"

"There hasn't been anything else taken," he said. "We haven't begun looking for other disks. There are no other storage rooms, no other walls like this."

I paced, looking at all the closed cupboards, thinking of all the rooms in the building. There might be a disk somewhere, a reject, a defect, a trial run. How much time did I have? How much time before the storm hit, before Zayvion stopped breathing, before the hospital's backup spells gave out and Violet lost the baby?

Dad? I thought. *Are there any other disks stored here?*

A strange papery scrub flicked at the corner of my mind. Kind of like pages being fanned by a thumb.

There might be, he whispered. *In our . . . office. Down the hall.*

"I need to look down here," I said.

Stotts took my declaration in stride. He was used to working with Hounds. Everyone knew Hounds were quirky at best, and more often crazy. I found the door my dad had remembered, tried it. Locked.

Oh, come on.

"I need in there," I said.

"Why? Crime happened back there."

"Listen—" I looked over at Stotts, realized he had not been in the loop of my conversation with Dad. "Listen," I said a little softer, "there might be another disk in there. And the disks hold magic. I can use that small amount of magic to Hound the scene."

Stotts was already nodding. "I won't ask you how you know there might be a disk in there," he said. "Yet." He tried the latch. "Do you know what this room was used for?"

"Maybe an office?"

He pulled something out of his coat pocket. A key or a lock-picking tool, I didn't know. But whatever it was, Stotts knew how to use it. He unlocked the door on the first try, and pushed it open. He stepped in front of me, blocked my access, and scanned the room, then flicked on the light switch. Fluorescent lights crackled to life, revealing a room filled with mahogany furniture and expensive glass artwork tucked into bookshelves. The desk in the middle of the room probably cost millions and was dead-on for my dad's tastes. So were the luxurious couch, chairs, and wet bar along one wall. The carpet probably cost more than the building I lived in.

Stotts's eyebrows perked up. This room was decadent, but just understated enough to say it wasn't merely money behind the arrangement; it was a fortune.

For her, I heard Dad whisper. *I made it for her.*

Okay, I did not need a lovelorn ghost in my head. Not right now.

Change that: not ever.

You thought she'd like this? Did you even ask her what she wanted? I asked.

Do not—his words were a little louder now—*speak to me in that manner.*

Okay, a pissed-off ghost wasn't going to do me any good either. Especially since he knew where the disks might be.

Where is the disk?

He hesitated and I wondered whether I'd be able to strangle an answer out of him. Considering he didn't have a neck, and I didn't have mental hands, it offered some interesting difficulties.

The shelf.

Terse. Good going, Allie, piss off the dead guy.

I walked across the room to the shelves behind the

desk. Stotts was dividing his time between watching me and taking in the details of the room.

The shelves were beautiful and smelled of polish and something that gave the faint perfume of jasmine blossoms. Books, all leather bound, probably worth thousands, lined the middle shelf. Below that was intricate glass artwork. Lights cleverly positioned in the shelf brought the art to life, glowing deep blues, red, yellow, and smoky gray. Beautiful. I lost a second staring at them, and wondered why they reminded me of magic, of the different disciplines of magic being worked together.

Wondered why they reminded me of Zay.

I swallowed hard. I'd been trying not to think about him. Every time I did, a knot in my throat and a weight in my chest made me want to cry, to go to him, curl up with him, as if somehow touching him and being with him would make the world go away.

As if somehow just being with him would bring him back to me.

I cleared my throat and blinked until the room was no longer blurry. The disk. Maybe there would be more than one. And I could use one to find out who did this, then use the other to go kick their teeth in.

On the top shelf were notebooks, a leather bottle, probably antique, and a lovely collection of crystals.

And one of the crystals looked a lot like a disk.

Well, not exactly a disk. It wasn't a perfect machined circle like the disk in Greyson's neck; it wasn't silver, slick, glyphed. This disk was made of crystal, and looked like it had been carved, magical glyphs scoured into it, deep in some places, barely a scratch in others. It was white, with highlights of soft pink and blue. And it was beautiful.

Did you make this? I asked Dad.

Grew, he said. *We grew it.*

I didn't have to touch it to know it was filled with magic. I could smell the magic in it, a sweet scent like roses in the rain. It looked harmless.

Is it going to hurt me if I pick it up? I asked.

Not that I know of. And if he hadn't been suddenly so curious to see what happened when I touched it, I would have just gone right ahead and done that. Instead, I decided to clue Stotts in on all this.

"I think this is a disk. A prototype of some sort. It's holding magic."

Stotts strode over to me, his loafers hushed against the deep, soft carpet.

"The crystal?" he asked.

I pointed. "That crystal."

"Do you want me to pick it up?"

"No, I just thought I'd tell you what I was doing in case I ended up on the floor or something."

"Maybe I should pick it up."

"Let me. I'm the Hound."

I reached over, careful not to touch the other crystals, and put one fingertip on the disk.

My dad, in my head, chuckled.

Shut up, I thought at him.

Of all the times in your life, it is now that you develop a sense of caution? he asked.

Okay, peanut-gallery dead guy wasn't working for me either.

No buzz, no shock, nothing beneath my fingertip but the slightly oily feel of the magic-infused crystal. I didn't absorb it like a sponge—yes, that thought had gone through my mind, since I usually carry magic—and it didn't explode or anything.

So far, so good.

I picked it up.

If the crystal had been beautiful from a distance, it was absolutely mesmerizing in the palm of my hand. Soft, pink, it didn't seem to sparkle so much as glow against my skin. The glyphs carved or maybe grown into it seemed to shift, slowly, slowly, as they made a snail's-pace path through the crystal.

Are the glyphs moving? I asked Dad.

Growing, he said. *Slowly.*

Not so slowly that I couldn't see it.

Stotts leaned in for a better look. He whistled. "That's amazing."

"It is."

"Does it have magic in it?"

Oh, right. I was here to do a job, not to look at the pretty baubles.

I licked my lips and concentrated on the disk. Yes, it very much did hold magic in it. But it held it in a natural sort of way. The magic didn't feel like it filled every speck of crystal, but there was plenty enough in there for one spell.

It reminded me of the void stones, reminded me of the cuffs we wore to feel one another during a hunt. It felt natural enough, I had a hard time believing it had been made in a laboratory.

It wasn't, Dad said. *We simply enhanced it in the lab.* He was proud of that.

Where did you find it?

He hesitated and I could feel his unease. *In St. Johns. A long time ago.*

Strange. St. Johns had no naturally occurring magic. A magical stone out there didn't make any sense. Unless someone had taken it there, left it there.

Is there more of that I should know? I asked.

No.

That was quick. He was lying. I could taste the bitter wash of it across my thoughts.

Just tell me if it's going to blow up on me, okay? I thought.

"Allie?" Stotts asked.

How long had I been standing there staring at the rock and talking to my dad? "Sorry," I said to buy myself some time to think of what he had last said to me.

He wants to know if it has magic in it, my dad offered with droll patience.

Okay, it was beyond strange to have my dad helping me out at all. He'd never been this helpful in all the years I had known him. It made me suspicious. The man never did something without getting something out of it for himself.

Hound the spell, he said, not angry, just calm and quiet, the way he always sounded right before he got killing mad. *Find out who hurt Violet.*

Ah. Revenge. Now, that I could understand.

"Yes," I said before my silence got out of hand again. "It has magic in it. I think enough for a spell. Maybe just one. I'd like to Hound the safety-deposit boxes. Does that sound good?"

Stotts let out a breath he'd been holding. I had to give it to him. He put up with a lot of crazy to get information out of Hounds, and I wasn't doing much for Hound reputation right now.

"I think so." He motioned for me to leave the room in front of him, which I did, holding the crystal away from my body like it was going to turn and bite me at any minute.

Which it might.

Stotts shut the door and then we were both in the other room again, in the lab. A couple people from the police department, I assumed, were there, taking pictures. Stotts asked them all to leave so he and I could look at the room alone for a few minutes.

They left and I walked around the room, deciding what my best view would be if the magic gave out quickly.

"Were Violet and Kevin in this room when they were attacked?" I asked.

"I didn't tell you they were attacked."

"They were taken out on stretchers. What was I supposed to think?"

"It could have been an accident in the lab."

Huh. He was right. It could have been. But one look at the empty drawers told me it was not.

Stotts knew that too.

"Well, that looks like a robbery to me," I said, pointing at the wall of boxes.

"Anything you want me to do?" he asked.

Since there was no magic, Stotts couldn't even cast Sight to watch what I was doing.

"Nope, I'll do this old-style. I'll repeat everything I see. If you want to take notes, that might be good."

He pulled something out of his pocket. A tape recorder. He held it up, then thumbed the button down.

Good idea.

I calmed my mind, sang my jingle, set a headache Disbursement, then traced a glyph for Sight and Smell. "Sight and Smell. I don't know how much magic I'll have at my disposal, so I don't know how strong the spells will be."

Then I very carefully closed my hand around the crystal and urged the magic out of it and into the glyphs that hovered, invisible, in the air in front of me.

Magic didn't so much flow as uncoil out of the stone and then stretch out into the spell. A tendril of magic stayed hooked in the stone, like a root set deep.

I shook the crystal a little. The tendril, the root, did not let loose. Okay. Strange. But then, I'd never used magic by pulling it out of something like this. Maybe it was supposed to stay attached.

My dad didn't have anything to say about it, and I didn't have any time to waste.

"Using Sight and Smell," I said again. "There was at least one caster here. A man, I think. Give me a minute." I took a couple steps toward the wall of boxes. "There's a spell here, maybe more than one. But they're really tight. Tangled. Like they collided or were crushed. Hold on."

I leaned in closer to one of the spells that clung like

a spit hair ball the size of my head, near the middle of the boxes. "Okay, there's a big spell here. Not Illusion. Something with force. Impact? Oh." It came to me in a rush. "Unlock. Nice. It's masterfully cast," I continued. "Even wadded up and kind of tangled, I can tell someone knew exactly how to throw this spell."

"Blood magic?" Stotts asked.

"I'll check." I took a deep breath, through my mouth and nose to get the taste and scent of the spell at once. And it was not the sweet smell of cherries that I caught. It was the heavy mineral stink of old vitamins.

I knew that smell.

When? Where?

"No Blood magic," I said to give myself time to think. "But I have smelled the scent of this spell before. Have smelled it on someone."

My father brushed the back of my mind. Gently. Like he was thumbing through paper again. It was odd and made my teeth itch.

And then the memory came forward. A memory of my old apartment torn apart, my furniture and belongings broken, trashed. This was the same scent that was left behind. Whoever had broken into my apartment had also broken in here.

"The spell's hard to parse. The casting is really tight. I don't even know how someone could cast magic with the network down," I muttered.

"The disks?" Stotts suggested.

"Maybe." I walked to one side to get a different view on the scene. And that was when I could tell. I knew who cast the glyph because I had seen him recently.

Sedra's bodyguard, Dane Lannister.

Which meant the Authority had broken in here.

Which meant the Authority had broken into my house.

There was another, more frightening, sickening memory attached to that smell, but I could not pull it to the front of my mind.

Dad? I asked.

He did not respond. If he knew where that memory was, he didn't seem willing to kick it forward.

"Uh, I still think it's a man's signature," I said.

"Who?" asked Stotts, the magical police detective who did not know about the Authority, who should not know about the Authority, and whom I should not tell the Authority even existed, much less that its members broke in and stole the disks.

And even that didn't make sense. My father had been a part of the Authority. Kevin currently was a part of the Authority. Violet had a passing knowledge of the Authority.

So why would the Authority break into the lab if they could, as far as I could tell, just ask Violet for the disks, or, at the very worst, tell Kevin to steal them from her?

Maybe he had.

Maybe this spell had only been cast to act like it was cast by Dane.

Which left me one hundred percent confused about what I should tell the nice detective.

So I went into default mode: the truth.

"I think a man named Dane Lannister might have been involved. But the spell is tangled, collapsed. It could be someone trying to make it look like Dane Lannister is involved."

"Anything else?"

"I'd say get another Hound in here to double-check my findings, but since that isn't going to happen, let me do a little more footwork." I checked the spell again. Yep. Still looked like Dane's. "Still seems to be Lannister's signature," I said. I checked the boxes. "None of the glyphwork has been broken." Which meant he had taken the time to Unlock each box instead of just blowing the thing apart.

"The disks were in here. I'd say one per drawer." What else? What was I missing? I looked around the room, and caught the angry red slash of a spell hovering about midway across the room.

That was not Unlock, or Hold, or any of the kinder spells. That was Impact and I could tell the target had been Kevin.

Dane attacked Kevin?

I looked the opposite direction to see if a spell from Kevin was there.

"Allie?"

"Just checking a few other spells. Cast in about the same time period as the Unlock," I said. "Similar decay rate."

Beyond the desk, where maybe Violet had been sitting, was the tattered remnants of a Shield spell.

Kevin had tried to keep Violet from getting hit with magic.

Dane had been here to kill Violet?

"Uh, one of the spells is aggressive. Not sure what kind, but in the category of Impact. Not one I recognize. That's midroom. There's another spell over here, a Shield. Tattered, like it withstood a blow or flux of magic.

"Is this where they found Violet?"

"Yes."

Okay, so my theory about attackers seemed to be holding up.

I walked to the opposite side of the room and looked for anything Kevin might have cast.

Holy crap. Kevin had cast at least a half dozen spells. Hold, Freeze, Impact, something that involved blood and pain, and more. And they had all fallen—no, they had all been drawn—to this side of the room, and smashed together into one big tangled, useless spell.

Kevin had hauled on a hell of a lot of magic—recently, like after the magic had turned off—and it had all been batted aside and crushed like empty beer cans.

The smell of minerals and old vitamins was stronger here.

Okay. I didn't know why Dane and Kevin were fighting. Sedra's bodyguard fighting Violet's bodyguard, but they had both accessed a hell of a lot of magic with the grids down.

Maybe they had disks to drain, but I didn't see any discarded empty disks on the floor.

"Allie?"

"More spells over here. There was a fight. All these spells are collapsed in on themselves and tangled together." I shook my head. "It's a mess, but they still bear Kevin Cooper's signature."

The crystal in my hand was feeling heavy and cold. "Is there anything else you want me to look at, because I think my battery's going dead."

"This is where they found Kevin." He pointed to a place near the door of the room. Like Kevin had been trying to get out and leave Violet behind. Strange.

I walked over to the door without losing my hold or concentration on Sight and Smell.

Death magic. I couldn't smell it, but it cast just enough of a shadow that I knew it had been mixed with dark magic. The only people I'd ever seen wield dark magic were Frank Gordon, who tried to raise my dad's soul from the dead, Zayvion, who used it as well as he used every other discipline of magic, and Greyson, who used it mixed with Blood magic to control Tomi. Since Frank was dead and Zayvion was comatose, that left Greyson.

I inhaled, trying to catch his scent—death and blood and burnt blackberry—but all I came up with was the slight tang from Death and dark magic, and the scent of old vitamins. Beneath that, I caught the notes of Kevin's cologne, a mix of spices, and blood—his blood.

"There's nothing here I can testify to," I started. "Magic was used, but I don't know these spells." I didn't want to tell Stotts it was dark magic. As far as I knew, he didn't know about dark magic. The entire event in the warehouse with Frank and my dad's corpse had been chalked up to some kind of mutated Blood magic. That was not what it had been, but that was what the Authority had wanted people to think it was.

And so that was what the lab tests came back with, that was the official police report, and that was what the causes of death on the four kidnapped girls' death certificates read.

I glanced out in the hall to see if there was anything else beyond the room. Nothing, or at least no spells, that I could see.

The crystal suddenly went so cold it hurt.

"Ow!" The pain in my hand broke my concentration, and the glyphs for Sight and Smell faded.

I almost dropped the crystal, but instead tossed it to my other hand, and then back and forth like a hot potato.

"That it?" Stotts strolled over. He didn't look at all concerned that I'd gone all Hacky Sack crazy.

"Really cold." I tossed the crystal at him, and he caught it.

"Huh." He held it with the fingertips of one hand, and traded off when he couldn't stand the cold any longer, studying it and holding it up to the light. Then he placed it on a clear space on the counter.

I swear I heard the crackling of ice. I looked at the crystal.

Yep. Froze the countertop out in a foot circle.

"Is this something new Beckstrom Enterprises is developing?" Stotts asked.

"It's something we've looked into. I haven't gotten reports of its viability in terms of development, manufacturing, or marketing yet." See, I could lie in business-speak when I had to.

Stotts gave me a funny look. "You have a crystal that

acts like a battery for magic, and you're trying to decide if it's a good idea to market?"

"It's the paperwork I hate."

The ice seemed to be melting some, and I thought the crystal looked a little less white and a little more pink.

Will it recharge? I asked my father.

Yes. Again with the hesitance.

That was good enough for me.

"I'm going to take this," I said.

Stotts raised one eyebrow. "Why?"

"It is legally my property," I said.

"True. Property you didn't know was here until a few minutes ago."

"Let me put it this way—I'm not leaving it here. I don't want anyone to break in and take it, and since it wasn't involved in the crime, I don't see any reason why the police would have claims to it."

"And you're keeping it because?"

"I want it?" He didn't believe me, and I didn't care. "Listen, I used all the magic in it. I don't know how to recharge it with magic, don't even know if it can be recharged. But I want to keep it. If it's Violet's, I'll return it to her."

Stotts sniffed and looked down at his shoe. Man had a mess of problems to deal with right now and me pitching a fit over a pretty rock did not rank up there on his list of traumas he had to plow through. Not with magic out. Not with the backups about to go down.

"Do you know why someone would want to take the disks?" he asked.

"They were filled with magic," I said. "All of them."

"And anyone can access that magic?"

"Yes."

He looked at me and I looked at him. In a city suddenly empty of magic, both of us were probably coming up with a thousand horrific things someone would want to do with a hundred disks full of power.

"I still think a storm, a wild-magic storm, is going to hit," I said. "Maybe it will kick-start magic again."

Stotts grunted and shoved both his hands in his coat pockets, shifting his shoulders as if carrying a new ache. "Interesting theory."

"Do you need me for anything else?" I asked before he came up with questions I didn't want to answer.

Stotts shook his head. "If I do, I'll call." He walked me to the door of the room. "I'll let you know if I find out anything more."

I pocketed the crystal and started down the hall.

"Allie?"

I slowed and glanced over my shoulder at him.

"Whatever it is that you're thinking of doing. Don't. We'll handle it."

I wondered what he saw in me. Was it my anger? My fear? Or did I just have a bad reputation for doing stupid things when magic was screwing with the people I loved?

I didn't answer. I didn't have to. Stotts and I were enough alike, we both knew that when people I cared about were hurt, there was no way in hell I was going to just stand aside and let other people handle the problem.

Chapter Seventeen

It was colder now and darker outside the lab, but at least it wasn't raining.

"Want a lift?" Shame stood on one side of the police tape. Even though he had no magic, he still managed to blend in and look like he was just another citizen out ogling the police and pony show.

I strode down the walk toward him and didn't stop. "Where'd you park?"

"Up a block. What's the hurry?"

I had to press my lips together to keep from yelling. I shook my head.

He got the hint and paced me, then unlocked the car so I could get in. Shame got in the driver's side, which was fine with me. Even though Shame still looked like death on a low simmer, I was angry. And I didn't want to kill us on the highway.

As soon as Shame started the car, a coo called out from the backseat.

I knew that coo.

"Stone!" I unbuckled so I could sit up on my knees and reach back for him. "Where'd you find him?"

"He found me," Shame said.

Stone filled the entire backseat; his head rested on his outstretched arms like he was really tired. But at the sound of my voice, his ears pricked up into sharp triangles and his wings shifted against his muscled back. He tipped his head enough he could look at me and gave me a toothy smile.

"I missed you, boy." I reached back and petted his head.

Three things sank in: one, Stone was cool, not cold, but not his usual cozy temperature. Two, he wasn't moving as fluidly as he should, his motions catching like he was full of gears that had rusted up. Three, his eyes were different. Usually his eyes shone with a sweet kind of intelligence. Right now they were dull, like someone had taken a sandblaster to them and left behind clouds.

"Hey, boy," I said more gently. "Who's my good boy? Who's my big hunter gargoyle? That's right, that's you. You're a good boy." I rubbed his head and scratched behind his ears. He angled his head for a better scratching, but did it slowly. His coo and his happy marble sound were too soft, like all he had left in him was a whisper.

"Stay there, boy, okay? Sleep time."

He gave me a rock-garbled reply and dropped his head back down to rest on his forearms.

"He's not moving very well." I don't know why I said it. It was obvious. Shame knew it. I knew it.

"I'm amazed he's still moving at all," Shame said. "Maybe he has his own backup spell battery in that belly of his."

"Is there anything we can do to help him?" I asked.

"Besides getting magic up and running again?"

"What happens if he runs out before then?" I asked.

Shame just shrugged. "You tell me. No one's been able to pull off an Animate this big for years."

I rubbed at my forehead. I had no idea what would happen. I didn't want to think about it.

"At least we know where he is," Shame said.

True. I could probably get him up into my apartment if I had to. And if he ran out of magic there, at least I'd know someone wasn't breaking him up into gravel or turning him into a table or something.

"You want to tell me where I'm driving?" Shame asked.

"Legacy Emanuel. Someone broke in and stole all the disks."

"All?"

"Hundreds. Charged with magic."

Shame's eyebrows shot up. Yeah, it freaked me out too.

Then he started laughing. "Oh, for fuck's sake. Now? Really? Hundreds of disks on the loose with a goddamn storm bearing down on the city? Perfect. Just perfect."

"Do you know what the disks will do when the storm breaks?"

"Not a damn clue. Might be nothing. Might be a lot. If we see a mushroom cloud suddenly blow out half the damn city, we'll know for sure. Fuck it all. Did you Hound for Stotts?" he asked.

"Yes."

Shame slanted me a look that was pure appreciation. "I'd be interested to know how you pulled that off."

I tugged the crystal out of my pocket and held it up for him to see. It was still cool, but not frostbite cold. "Ever see this before?"

Shame glanced at it. "God's balls, woman. Where did you get that?"

"In there."

Shame made a quick right turn and nearly hit a car that honked as it went past us. He stopped in a lot behind an office building and twisted in his seat. "Give."

Yes, I was hesitant to give it to him. But whom else was I going to trust with this? Whom else could I even ask about it? Maybe Violet. If she were conscious.

I handed it to him. Shame held it like it was made of gold and unbroken dreams. "It's natural," he said. "Who—no, how can this even exist?"

"It carried magic. Enough I could Hound the room."

"Still does. It's weak, thin, but it is refilling, slowly . . . like the heartbeat of the world." Shame licked his lips and swallowed hard. Then he slowly pressed it against his mouth. He closed his eyes and a shudder shook him.

"Shame?"

With visible effort, he lifted the stone away from his lips and held it out to me, without looking at me, without looking at the stone.

"Take it. I'd drink it dry."

I hesitated. Shame wasn't looking good, but the stone seemed to have brought a little color into his lips. Maybe letting him use the magic in the stone would help. "Maybe you—," I started.

"No." He looked away, looked out the window at the dark city. "You don't want me to have that. It will only make me want more." I saw the reflection of his smile in the glass, and it was pure hunger and need, coupled with a willpower I didn't know he had.

I shoved the stone in my pocket and Shame rubbed his hand on his thigh, as if trying to rub off the sensation it had left behind. He pulled a cigarette out of his pocket and held it between his fingers, but didn't light it. He went back to driving like nothing had happened.

Except I could tell his hands were shaking, and he was sweating. Not pain. Hunger.

"What did you see when you Hounded?" he asked as if we were talking about the weather.

This was the weird part. Shame had been raised in the Authority. He knew more political backstabbings and payoffs among the people in the Authority than I'd ever get the inside skinny on. His mother was a voice in the Authority, essentially speaking for every user who trained under Blood magic. He had more connections than Velcro.

If I told him the Authority was behind the break-in, whom would he tell? Did he already know someone in the Authority wanted the disks enough to attack my pregnant stepmother?

There is a reason I am not a spy. I do not do the cloak-and-dagger bit worth a shit. I prefer to lay my cards on the table, and then draw a gun to clear up any misunderstandings.

That meant it was default mode again—the truth.

"Someone from the Authority broke in. Fought with Kevin. Hurt him. Hurt Violet. With magic."

Shame was silent. I watched his body language. Something like curiosity or like he was trying to figure out where that information fit in with other information.

"Could you tell who it was?" Flat, even. He knew how to keep his emotions in check when he wanted to. Wasn't that a surprise?

"Dane Lannister."

Shame frowned. "Seriously?"

I nodded.

"Huh."

"Do you know why he would do that? Couldn't he have told Kevin he wanted the disks?"

Shame took a deep breath, let it out. "I don't know. There are always things going on in the Authority that I don't know about. I haven't heard . . . No, I haven't heard that Sedra wanted the disks."

He stopped at a light, tapped his fingers on the wheel. "Could be a last-minute thing. Don't know why they wouldn't have clued Kevin in. But Violet. Yeah, they might not have wanted her to know. Still, force is usually a last resort."

I snorted. "You people are always throwing magic around. What do you mean, force is a last resort?"

"Us people? You're a part of us too. And it is. A last resort. They used magic?"

"The spells were . . . collapsed. Tangled. Crushed."

Shame pressed his head back into the seat of the car, straight-arming the wheel. "I am so going to ask for a raise. This job blows balls. You want me to take us to Mum's place instead? We can get some answers. Find out what the cool kids are doing."

We were just a couple blocks from the hospital.

"No. I want to see Violet." And if she was awake, I planned to ask her a few questions. Like if she had been making a move on the Authority, trying to strong-arm them into something and holding the disks as collateral. She was smart and she was strong. It would not surprise me to find out the business associates who were angry with her over releasing the data on the disks were actually members of the Authority, maybe even Sedra herself.

And the way Kevin felt for Violet, the love he would not admit to, might just be enough to make him take her side. Might be enough to make him fight Sedra's bodyguard for her.

Love did strange things to people. Left them weak, made them stronger than ever before, or destroyed them.

Shame drove into the parking structure and wound his way up the concrete ramps until he found an open space.

"You coming in with me?" I asked.

He lit the cigarette and sucked down the smoke. "I'm not letting you go in alone."

I stopped, my hand on the door handle. "Why?"

"That's the way it is."

"Talk, Flynn." I wanted to know whom he was working for, or spying for. His mother? Jingo Jingo?

"I owe Zay. For letting you down. For letting him down. I should have known. Seen it coming. Chase is such a bitch." He opened the door and blew the smoke out in a thin stream.

Oh.

"Yeah, well, we all could have done something differently. But we didn't. Now we go forward," I said, "'cause looking back won't fix anything. Stay here—it won't take me long to check on Violet."

"Wrong. Chase and Greyson are still loose. Still on the hunt. Still looking for you."

"They got Zay. They don't want me." But as soon as the words were out of my mouth, I knew it was not true. Greyson wanted my dad, the rest of him that was still inside me. What they did to Zay just got him out of the way so they could do what they really wanted.

"Holy shit," I said. "They attacked Zay because they want to get to me."

"I swear, you are denser than lead," Shame muttered. "Of course they wanted him out of the way to get to you. And they wanted him out of the way because he is the guardian of the gates. The one and only magic user who can use light and dark magic to break the barrier between life and death. Knocking him out means that when the gates blow open—and I'd bet my left ball they're going to—he won't be able to close them."

"There are other Closers," I said. "Terric, Victor, Nikolai, and Romero, more of the Seattle crew."

"None of them use magic like Zayvion Jones. No one does. Not even Victor. Or Terric."

An image, a flash of Chase and Greyson casting magic together, using magic in ways I had never seen, making it go against its own laws, rolled through my mind.

"Soul Complements," I whispered.

"What about it?"

"Chase and Greyson. That's why they could use magic like that. That was the only thing that could hurt Zayvion."

"Part right. Soul Complements let them screw with the laws of magic. But they threw around light and dark magic. And they could do that because Greyson is a Necromorph—half alive, half dead. Whatever he did to Chase so she could do it too—his own Soul Complement . . ." He blew out smoke again. "It makes me wonder how much that bloodsucker would burn in sunlight. He's using a hell of a lot of dark magic."

"No. Greyson didn't use magic. He had to use Tomi to cast Blood magic for him."

"And now he has Chase to act as his hands. Happily ever after, evil-style, in their evil little hovel with the evil little picket fence around the evil little garden of poisonous weeds and dead bugs. Evil cookies, evil nooky—not that I have anything against those last two." He got out of the car and I did too.

"Don't you take anything seriously?"

"No," he lied. "It makes me interesting." He started off toward the elevator that would take us to ground level.

Elevator. Great.

But before I closed the door, I leaned back in the car. "You be a good boy, Stone," I said. "Sleep. Okay?"

Stone cooed but didn't move one granite muscle.

I shut the door. And strode across the parking structure of gray, gray, gray, my boots cuffing a loud rhythm against the concrete ceiling.

Shame waited by the elevator, hood up, his shoulders hunched, his hands in his pockets, the discarded cigarette sending up a tendril of smoke at his feet. He didn't face the elevator doors. He faced me. Good to know he was keeping an eye out for trouble.

Just as I stopped next to him, the doors opened with a horror-sweet ding.

"After you," he said.

Okay, I could do this. I'd done it plenty of times before. "Are there stairs?"

"Fuck stairs," he said. "Too slow. And too damn much work."

I gritted my teeth. Couldn't get my feet to move.

"Need a push?" he asked.

"No."

A hand slammed into my shoulder and a body followed it. I stumbled into the elevator. "What the hell?"

"Your phobia was saying no, no, but your feet were saying yes."

He stabbed the button and stood in the corner nearest the doors, facing me.

"If you ever listen to my feet again, I will end you, Flynn."

He glanced at me, grinned. "Ooh. You're kinda hot when you're angry. I suddenly see why Jones likes to make you mad and then tumble you on the mats."

"Don't. Just don't. Or they'll have to scrape you up off this floor with a dustpan."

He opened his mouth, thought better of it, and instead stood there and whistled.

Whistled. Using up all the air in the tiny, tiny room, filling it up with sound so that there wasn't even room for me to hear my own thoughts. There wasn't enough room for me to breathe. I closed my eyes and tried to picture open fields, blue skies, oceans, deserts. Big horizons, big space, big air.

A hand grabbed my upper arm and tugged, hard, propelling me toward the open doors.

I didn't stumble this time. We were at the street level on a sidewalk covered by the overhang of the parking structure.

Shame made a *tsk* sound. "And you were going to do this alone."

"Alone I would have taken the stairs. You are seriously pissing me off."

"You're welcome."

"What the hell is wrong with you?"

He started off toward the doors. "Good thing about anger. It keeps you going when nothing else will."

He'd done it on purpose. Shoved me when I didn't even want to be touched, irritated me. My heartbeat was up, but other than that, I was thinking clearly. And not at all freaked-out from the elevator ride, though I should be. Usually it took me a couple minutes to shake off the panic from the phobia.

"You're a real jerk, you know?"

He smiled and it looked like it hurt. "I am whatever it takes to get the job done."

We stepped into the hospital and checked with reception to see where Violet and Kevin had been taken. Both had been admitted. Violet was in the prenatal ward three floors up. Kevin was in the intensive care unit, and visitors were not allowed. They were doing what they could to tend his magic-induced injuries with what little magic they had left.

Shit. We wouldn't be able to get in to see him unless we wanted to storm the place. I weighed my options. Sneak in and somehow be lucky enough to see if Kevin was okay, or check on Violet.

Dad pushed at the backs of my eyes. Yeah, well, I knew what his vote would be.

"Think Kevin will be okay?" I asked Shame. We were standing shoulder to shoulder so the receptionist couldn't hear us.

He tipped his head, thinking it over. "If he made it this far, there's a good chance he'll recover. Several of the Authority doctors work here. They'd know him, and know what to do with severe magical injuries."

I nodded. That would have to be good enough for now. I didn't know a lot about Kevin's personal life, like if he had family in the area. I pulled my book out of my pocket and made a note to check on him tomorrow, if I could. I walked back over to the receptionist's desk.

"Where are the stairs?" I asked. She pointed down the hall and I started off in that direction.

"You're kidding, right?" Shame asked. "There's a perfectly good elevator right over there."

"Take the elevator. I don't care."

Shame scowled. "How about I just make you angry again? That coat makes you look fat."

"Even more reason to take the stairs."

"Fucking hell." He sighed dramatically. "I hate you, Beckstrom."

"Hold on to that," I said. "You know, because anger will get you there."

Shame rolled his shoulders and I heard more bone grind than I should. Like a fricking walking corpse, he still had his hood of his coat up, the shadows catching moss green against his sallow skin.

Maybe I should make him check into the hospital. Maybe he was sicker than I thought. Maybe the magic Chase had used on him, and the magic he had used to help me save Zayvion, had done something more permanent than he wanted to admit.

I found the door to the stairs and pushed it open. It was only three flights up, and I did that every day at home. But I was a little worried about Shame.

An elevator probably would be his best choice. "You know I won't get killed between here and the third floor," I said.

"Yep. Because I'm gonna be there to protect you. Walk."

I shook my head and started up the stairs. I did not need his protection. There was no magic, so it wasn't like someone would magically attack me. Which meant I could get killed only the old-fashioned way—with guns, knives, strangling, beating. Okay, maybe it was nice to have Shame with me. I could handle myself just fine physically—even better now that I'd been training—but it never hurt to have an ally in a fight.

We didn't say anything as we climbed. Shame walked behind me, and I listened for his breathing, which remained good, strong, and his footsteps, equal to my pace.

He didn't sound like someone who hovered one breath away from the shambling dead. Shame knew how to handle pain.

"So which doctors are a part of the Authority?" I asked on the second floor.

"Not saying."

"Why? Is it that big of a secret?"

"Enough that I don't want to talk about it in a stairwell with this much echo. Would have told you in a nice quiet elevator, though."

I grinned. "Bitch, bitch, bitch."

We made it to the top of the stairwell and I opened the door, then followed the signs to the reception area.

Shame wasn't breathing hard, didn't even seem like he'd broken a sweat. He did, however, shove his hands in the pockets of his coat and hunch up his shoulders like he was enduring a hailstorm.

I gave him a questioning look.

"It's just . . . babies." He said it like most people say *snakes* or *spiders* or *tax collectors*.

I had no idea what his problem was. "You're afraid of babies?"

"Shut up." He strode past me to the reception desk and, I noted, stayed far enough away that the light wouldn't quite clear the shadows beneath his hood. "Violet Beckstrom," he said. "Could we see her?"

The woman at the counter looked sixteen, the tight curls of her black hair pulled back in a flowered headband that make her deep brown skin burnish gold.

"She's resting. There isn't a restriction on visitors, though. Are you family?"

"I am." I stepped ahead of Shame. "And he's a friend."

"She's been given some painkillers, so she might be sleeping. We'd like her to get as much rest as possible, so if she is asleep, you could come back later." She pointed down one of the halls that branched off from the main hall. "Down there. Room 3243."

"Thank you," I said.

We headed down the hall and I noted Shame walked closer to me, almost brushing my shoulder with his.

"Don't worry," I whispered. "I won't let the scary babies hurt you."

He didn't say anything. Which was weird. I had no idea what had gotten into him.

And then we passed the huge glass window beyond which was the nursery. Shame's body language changed. He went from stiff-shouldered and tense, to relaxed, loose, like a runner who was warmed up and ready for the road.

The emotion that rolled off him was hunger.

Holy shit.

"You aren't afraid of the babies. You want to . . . eat them? What the hell?" I was still whispering, but that did not lessen the horror in my voice.

"It's not that I want to eat them—well, okay, maybe a little." He grinned at me. "Oh, put the Bible down, Beckstrom. I'm not going to hurt babies. It's . . . it's just so much life around here. Life, get it?" He tipped his head down so the shadows cleared his eyes, and I was relieved to see Shamus behind those eyes. Sane, clear. "I'm on some short supply of that right now. And babies are full of fresh, beautiful life energy."

"Tell me you wouldn't."

"I wouldn't. Not in a million years. Not if my life depended on it. Not for anyone. Not for anything. Not ever."

And I knew he meant it. Which was good. I did not want to have to fight him. Again. But I would for babies.

We were still walking. I put my hand on his arm, and could feel the bunch of muscle against bone. He might promise to never take the life energy from the babies, but it wasn't an easy thing to resist.

"Is this because of the fight?" I asked. "What you and

Terric did to help me keep Zay alive? Is it a part of dark magic?"

"No, it's just a part of Death magic. Energy transference, life transference, carried on the magic. And the side effect that comes with giving too much energy before you draw on magic again, or reclaim that energy."

"Eating babies is a side effect of Death magic?"

"Like dry mouth."

"Is a disgusting sense of humor a side effect too?"

"No, that's all me."

"Shame." I stopped. Pulled on his arm.

He pivoted toward me, his head down again, slanting me a gaze though the shadows. "Yes, Beckstrom?"

"Do you need energy? Life energy?"

"Not need. Want." He pulled his arm away. "I couldn't take it anyway. No magic to carry it on. Can we keep walking?"

We could and we did, passing the babies, and stopping about midway down the hall at Violet's room. "You coming in here?" I asked.

"Afraid I'll gnaw on your stepmother?"

I made a face at him and opened the door as quietly as I could. Violet was in the bed. Someone had brushed her hair back, revealing a bruise that covered her forehead and spread palm-wide down the left side of her face. She was in a hospital gown, an extra blanket tucked across her rounded figure, monitors and an IV hooked up to her.

Something inside me twisted, hurt. I felt, more than heard, my dad's moan, his sorrow. It was good enough to know she was alive. Probably better if I didn't go in to see her. Better for me. For my control over my dad. And maybe for Shame too.

Violet stirred, opened her eyes, squinted, without her glasses, over at us. "Allie," she said softly, and a little slurred. "Come in, please."

So much for walking away. I stepped in. "Hi," I said.

"I won't stay long. This is Shamus Flynn. He drove me here."

Shame held up one hand. "Hello, Mrs. Beckstrom. I could step out if you two want some privacy."

What did you know? Flynn had manners.

"It's fine," she said. Violet pursed her lips, as if trying to feel her teeth. "I'm numb."

"Something to help you sleep, I think. Has the doctor talked to you?"

"She said I should sleep." She closed her eyes, and the green lines on the monitor jumped before it settled again. I wasn't sure what the doctors were monitoring, but I knew it had something to do with magic as well as her physical injuries.

"I'll let you rest. I just wanted to make sure you're okay, that the baby's okay."

Violet frowned. "Baby?" She pressed her fingers against her eyes. "They said I might go into early labor." She pulled her hands away from her eyes and cradled her stomach. Her eyes opened and the whites were red and glossy from more than just rubbing. She'd been crying. "Poor little thing. There was so much magic in the room. I can still feel it in me. In the baby." The tremor in her voice gave away her fear. She sounded small. Frightened.

I put my hand on her hand.

Dizziness washed over me. Dad pressed against the backs of my eyes, against the edges of my mind, pushing forward.

I couldn't let him. Couldn't trust what he would say to her. It never went well when he tried to run my life, or my body.

Stop it, I thought to him. *You're dead. Stay dead. It's not going to help her if she thinks anything else right now. Don't mess with her.*

He did not stop pushing.

"I know you're going to be fine," I said to Violet.

"Both of you are going to be fine. The doctors are look-ing after you. Good doctors." I glanced at Shame, and he nodded.

She looked down at her stomach. "I don't want to lose the baby. It's all I have left. Of him. Of Daniel." The last word came out with a longing. "He'd be so angry I hurt our baby." She made a sound that was half sob.

Dad shoved. Hard.

Like falling off a curb, I stumbled and landed in the back of my head. I could still see Violet. Could still hear her, but I could not feel my hand on hers. Which wasn't a big surprise, since I couldn't feel any of the rest of my body either.

"I—," Dad said through me.

No, no no. Don't. Dad, don't, I thought.

"I know," he said, getting the hang of my mouth far too quickly for my comfort, "that I—that he—married you because he saw your strength. You know how much he loves—loved you. You know he would be proud of you. And he regrets—would regret not being here for you, to see the baby, to hold you both."

Sorrow, hope, fear, and regret raged through me. My father's emotions, not mine. And on top of them all was love.

It pissed me the hell off. I was all for happy endings, but not if it meant my dad using me, my body, my mouth, my hormones. It didn't help that he'd never shown this kind of emotion around me before. And now I was crawling with his emotions, and knew, far too intimately, his feelings for Violet.

Give me back my body! I screamed at him. Yes, like a two-year-old getting her tantrum on.

Shame, in the corner of the room, suddenly stood out of the chair and walked over to the opposite side of Violet's bed. He tipped his head a little, letting the light under his hood, almost reaching his eyes. He stared at me, at my dad behind my eyes, and his eyebrows hitched up.

"I think he would be upset," Violet said, still gazing at her belly. "About everything. About me. I've made a huge mess of things."

"Perhaps some things, yes. But not everything. He most certainly wouldn't be upset with you. And he'd be stunned." He swallowed—I swallowed, whatever—then said, softer, "He'd be so very thrilled about the baby."

"Do you think so?" Violet looked up, eyes unfocused but searching for hope, for comfort, for understanding. And I felt my heart, my body, stir with love and desire for her.

Okay: no. I just could not wrap my brain around where this road might lead. I had a complicated enough relationship with her. I didn't need to mess it up with Dad's desires.

"I know so," he said gently. "Trust me, Vi. He is looking down on you right now with nothing but love."

She smiled. "Daniel used to call me Vi."

Shame snapped his fingers. "Wow. Isn't that neat? I have an idea. It's time for us to leave. Now."

It was about time Shame picked up on the weirdness. You'd think someone who dealt with Death magic would have caught on sooner there was a dead guy running the show.

"You're not a part of this family, Mr. Flynn," Dad said through me. "You can wait." And I knew he tried to put Influence behind it, because I could feel the twist and pull on the small magic inside me, but I wrapped around that flame, holding it back, far, far out of his reach. The magic, the small magic, stayed with me and Dad was shit outta luck.

Shame chuckled. "No, I can't wait. And neither can you, Allie. We should let Violet get her rest." Shame put his hand on my hand and licked his lips, smiling with his lips parted.

I felt it.

So did Dad.

Shame's hand was warm, almost too warm, his palm slick on the back of my hand. Very clearly, the tingle of something being drawn out through my skin, like a leech had just stuck onto the back of my hand to suck my blood out, or like a really bad Band-Aid rip, prickled my skin.

Dad did not like it. We both knew what Shame was doing—taking a little nip of him. So much for needing magic to draw on energy. I guess Shame could draw on life—or was it death, since my dad was undead?—without magic.

That made Dad angry.

And distracted.

I shoved him with everything I had.

And fell back into myself, a wave of vertigo doing damage to my knees. I had the presence of mind not to fall on top of the pregnant woman.

No, I had more sense than that. Enough that I pulled my hand off hers, Shame pulling his hand off mine at the exact same time. But just before my fingertips left Violet's hand, I felt the bump of movement in her belly.

"Oh," she said. "Did you feel it? The baby moved." Her words were slurring, and her eyes were only half open now. The lines on the monitor jumped again, uneven, ragged.

Somewhere in the center of my brain, my dad raged.

"I did," I said, my mouth tasting of wintergreen and old leather, and not feeling nearly enough like it belonged to me. "It's wonderful, Violet." I tried to smile, but wasn't sure I did it. "Shame's right. You should get some sleep."

Then there were nurses, striding into the room, moving briskly, doing things with the tubes that ran in and out of Violet. They told me she'd be fine, but needed me to leave so she could rest.

I turned and walked out of that room, leaving Violet and my unborn sibling to their care, and took my father and his pain as far away from them as I could.

Chapter Eighteen

Shame and I made it down to the car without any arguments about stairs. I didn't care if he took the elevator—I needed to stomp, to move, to stretch out and feel my body as my own again. The stairs suited me perfectly.

We made it to street level. I straight-armed the door, and practically ran across the street to the parking garage. Fear, hate, and, yes, anger got me where I was going—anger at my father. For doing this to me. For using me. Again.

I was so done with it. I didn't care what it took—I was going to get rid of him. He wasn't going to stay in my mind and use my body, my thoughts, my emotions, ever again.

You, I thought, *are going down.*

A hand caught my elbow and yanked. Hard. "Slow the hell down." It was Shame, breathing hard, looking even more like death, if that were possible.

"You are going to get yourself killed."

A car, horn blaring, rolled down the parkade ramp.

"That car almost hit you. Allie? Are you in that noggin somewhere listening to me? Or is there another Beckstrom I'm addressing?" Shame's grip was punishing, and the pain cleared my mind.

"I heard you," I said. "Holy shit, Shame. I am so fucked-up."

He blinked, gave me a weird smile. "And?"

I didn't know what to say. Didn't know what to do. Zay was in a coma. Violet could lose the baby. My dad was raging in my mind. The storm was coming, Stone wasn't working very well, and someone out there had disks of magic that could kill us all. I'd forgotten to ask Violet about the break-in, but there wasn't a herd of elephants that could drag me back into her room right now.

How come I had to be the one to fix everything? How come I had to be the hero? I sure as hell didn't feel like a hero.

"No hero does," Shame said.

I must have said some of that out loud.

He tugged my arm again, this time gently, and pulled me into a hug. He was a little shorter than me, thinner than Zayvion—the last man I'd been this close to—but strong, and careful. It was a simple, brotherly gesture. I had to work hard to not cry for the comfort of it.

"You," Shame said, not letting go of me, "are going to save Zayvion. Not because you're a hero, or he's a hero. Not even because you're Soul Complements. But because you love him, he loves you, and you deserve the chance to be together. Whatever that takes. Don't give up on him. Don't give up on yourself. You can do this. All of this. For him. For you."

I inhaled, caught the deep burn of tobacco on his clothes, the spice of cloves beneath it. Shame was half dead, his heart pounding slow and hard, a slight tremble shaking his body. But he was standing there, giving me the strength he had left. So I could save Zayvion. So this could somehow turn out happily ever after.

"Thanks," I whispered. It wasn't enough. There weren't enough words to say how much I needed him to be here for me, this way, right now.

He let go of me, searched my face. I wiped the tear off my cheek, waited for his approval. He nodded.

"You did notice I didn't grope your ass," he said.

I rolled my eyes. "You always have to take a good moment out at the knees, don't you?"

"I don't know what you're talking about." He started toward the car. "I just want it on the record when Jones wakes back up. I did not grope your sweet bits. And I had ample opportunity, what with how you were pawing at me."

"Keep digging, Flynn. Six feet makes a grave."

We got in the car, and Stone turned his head. He was moving even more slowly.

"Hey, boy. Have a nice nap?"

He opened his mouth and clacked. It sounded like his gears were missing a few cogs.

"That's okay." I turned around and rubbed his head. "You rest."

He put his chin back on his arm. Shame started the car, but I stayed twisted in my seat, petting Stone's head.

Shame's phone rang. He dug it out of his pocket. "Flynn."

I had good ears. But I couldn't quite make out the words. I knew who the speaker was, though: Terric.

I recognized his voice, and also I knew it had to be him from the way Shame tensed up.

"Where?" A pause. "Unbelievable. Fine. We're stopping by Mum's place first."

He snapped his phone shut and stuffed it back in his pocket.

"I hope you didn't have plans for today."

"Other than hunting down Greyson and Chase?" I shifted so I was sitting facing forward again and buckled my seat belt.

"Sedra has ordered everyone to go out to St. Johns."

"Why?"

"They're setting up some kind of storm rod, to try to divert as much of the storm as they can and to channel it into one place when it hits. St. Johns, probably because there is no magic there. It's the one place that could handle a huge blast without blowing out the networks. I have to admit, it makes sense."

"You're surprised Sedra is making sense?"

He licked his lips. Stared at traffic for a second or two. "She's been . . . different. I don't know if it's the storm, or your dad dying—which, by the way, I've been meaning to ask you—what the hell happened back there with Violet?"

I rubbed at one eye. "I've told people he's in my head. I've told you. Jingo Jingo doesn't believe me, so no one else in the Authority does—"

"Jingo is a one-man freak show. And he's been lying this entire time about not knowing your dad is in your head. I believe you. After seeing your dad glaring out from behind your eyes? Oh yeah. I'm convinced."

"Good. Now help me get rid of him."

Shame shook his head. "Magic. And not even your pretty pink crystal can hold enough for the kind of magic it takes to draw a soul out of a body. Even if the soul doesn't belong there in the first place. Plus, it will hurt. A lot."

"I don't care about the pain. Greyson did it, and I held up pretty well."

Shame glanced over at me. "Greyson did what?"

"He sucked Dad out of my head." *Should have left you in him. Let him eat you*, I thought.

"So he's really in Greyson?"

"No. He's in me. And maybe some of him is in Greyson."

My dad shifted in my head, as if uncomfortable. That was how I knew it was true. Part of him was still in the Necromorph, in the man who had tried to kill him. Who had tried to kill Zay.

Shame was quiet a moment. "You know how you said you were really fucked a few minutes ago?"

"Yeah?"

"I'd like to change my response to 'and how.'"

"Wonderful. Thanks for that, Mr. Good News."

"If your dad is in Greyson, or a part of his soul is in Greyson, then you are tied to Greyson through him. He's spanning two minds, two lives. It makes for an interesting state of being for him. I can appreciate the advantages, though."

My dad in my head went very still. He listened to Shame like he had just found an expert in the one subject he could not figure out.

Yes, that scared the hell out of me.

"Uh, I'm not sure that you should tell me right now. Dad's listening."

Shame laughed. "You are such a creepy girl. Not that I mind. But I just never expected Jones would go for the whole goth-chick-possessed-by-the-dead-guy thing. Talk about Daddy issues. And I'm not at all sure what that says about Zayvion, psychologically speaking. Tell me, does your dad know when you and Jones are, you know, doing it?"

"Do you want me to puke in your car? 'Cause if you keep it up, I will destroy your upholstery."

Stone, in the backseat, growled.

"And then my gargoyle will eat you."

"Aw, c'mon. A hint?"

"Zay's been helping me find ways to block him."

"Ooh. Nice. Can you block your dad without him?"

"Yes. Most of the time."

"But back with Violet?"

"It's always worse when I get around her. Dad . . ." I couldn't believe I was about to say this out loud. "He loved her. And even though I do not know why, Violet loved him too. So when he sees her, hears her voice, we get into sort of a wrestling match over who gets to run my body."

"Do you always lose?"

"Not for long. We're not going to St. Johns, are we?"

"I don't think skipping out on this party is an option."

"Then you go. I have a Necromorph to hunt."

He wiped his hand over his face, then rubbed his palm over his jeans. The pressure of the building storm was growing strong enough now, I was starting to feel it like a migraine behind my eyes.

"I want Greyson dead," he finally said. "No questions. But if we don't deal with the magic, with the storm, we'll lose the chance to get Zayvion back. Until the wild magic passes, all bets with magic—how it's going to work, when it's going to work—are off."

I crossed my arms over my chest. "I can handle myself. With or without magic."

"I know. And if you're set on it, on the hunt, then I'll go with you."

"That's not how this works. I'm making this decision for myself. Alone."

"That is exactly how this works. You don't go anywhere without me. You don't go anywhere alone. I won't let that happen. Like it or not."

"Get off my back, Flynn."

The corner of his mouth quirked up. "You'd rather I get on your front? What would Zayvion say?"

"He'd tell you to shut up and hunt."

"Planning on it. But even he wouldn't be stupid enough to go into a hunt without weapons. And until we have magic—until both of us have magic at our disposal—hunting Greyson is a waste of time."

He had a point. And it finally soaked through my stubborn head. Magic first. Because once I had magic, was filled with it again, it wasn't going to take me any time to find Greyson and kick his ass.

"Fine," I said.

"Fine," he agreed.

"Why are we going to Maeve's and not straight to St. Johns?"

"I need to pick up a couple things."

I was glad. After having my dad run roughshod over my body and emotions, I wanted to look in on Zay. Tell him I was okay. Tell him he was going to be okay too, and to not give up on us. Tell him I hadn't given up on finding Greyson, no matter what I told Shame.

It didn't take long to get across town to the other side of the river. But even in that short time, the sky changed. Clouds, lots of them, all the shades of gray and black, gathered. Some of them tinted with a watercolor wash of green and blue and burnt orange. There was magic in the sky. And it was coming to kill us all.

Shame pulled up beside his mother's inn. The inn seemed to be doing business as usual. A dozen or so cars were in the parking lot, and when we walked through the front door, the dining room had only a few empty tables. The one thing that was different was I didn't see Maeve anywhere in the room, talking to patrons, or pouring coffee.

One of the other girls who worked the place, Kathy, looked up at us. Shame still had his hood up. He raised his hand in greeting, and she nodded. We walked along the outer edge of the room and through the arch to the hall beyond. I started up the stairs that led to the rooms above.

"You coming?" I asked when I didn't hear Shame's footsteps behind me.

"Downstairs first. See you outside?"

"Five minutes?"

"That should do."

I took the stairs a little faster. If I only had five minutes before I went off to fight a storm of wild magic, I wanted to spend those five minutes with Zay.

I hesitated at the door to his room. Thought about

knocking. Knew it would only hurt more when he didn't answer, so instead, I just opened the door.

The light was dimmer in here, making the strange-colored clouds hanging outside in the darkness seem even more eerie.

Two beds. The one I'd been in was empty and had been remade.

But in the other bed was Zayvion. I walked over to him, trying to be quiet, and feeling stupid about that. I wanted him to wake up. So why was I being so careful not to disturb him?

I walked up to the head of the bed.

Even sleeping, he was a handsome man. In the low light, his skin looked like burnt bronze, his hair a dark tangle of midnight. I brushed my fingers through his hair, then down his cheek. Finally, I brushed my finger over his lips, hoping he could feel my touch.

The cool, steady exhalation of his breath against my fingers gave me hope. He was still breathing. On his own. There was very little medical equipment hooked up to him, an IV, and something that ran under his blanket, to attach to his chest. His skin was warm to the touch.

He looked alive. My sleeping beauty.

But I knew he was not in there, not in his body. And no matter how long his body breathed, without his soul, his spirit, or whatever part of him that had been shoved into the gate between life and death, I knew he would never wake up.

I didn't know how long they would keep him like this. How long until they gave up on him.

Shame said it was possible to open a gate as soon as magic normalized. I didn't know if that would help Zayvion find his way home, but it was all I had to hope for right now. And if that didn't work, then I'd find something else that did.

But first we had to take care of the storm.

"Don't think you're getting out of this," I said to Zay. "You still owe me that horses-on-ice-skates thing. I plan to collect." I brushed my fingers across his lips again, thought about kissing him.

"Just don't die," I whispered. I concentrated on projecting my words, my thoughts, to him though my fingertips. Willed them into his mind, his heart. "Don't give up on me. We're going to St. Johns to take care of the storm. And after that, I am going to find a way to get you home. A gate. If you see a gate open, all you have to do is step through it. I'll be waiting on the other side."

I knew this wasn't a fairy tale. Still, I bent, kissed him on the corner of his mouth, ignoring that, yes, he was motionless, unresponsive, not even a flicker of his awareness stirring at my touch. There wasn't any magic in the kiss, but there was something just as strong: a promise that we were in this together.

I straightened and the crystal in my pocket clunked against the side of the bed. I dug it out.

It was warmer, pinker, the shadows dusty blue. It was filling with magic, though I didn't know how it could collect it when even the best magic user couldn't tap into the cisterns and networks right now. Maybe the crystal had a default mode that allowed it to collect whatever scraps of magic it could find to fill the emptiness.

Maybe it could help Zay. I thought about leaving it here. The crystal might act as a beacon for him.

My dad, who had been wisely silent this entire time, brushed the backs of my eyes gently.

The crystal is passive, he said. *It holds magic and gives it up when tapped correctly. It will not call a soul, save a soul, or hold a soul. It carries magic, deep, natural, but it works no magic on its own.*

I didn't want to listen to him. I was heavy into hating him for what he had done to me. But his thoughts were weary, as if he had lost the hope of making me believe him, but tried anyway.

Will it hurt him if I leave it here?

No, but there are those within the Authority who may take it for themselves.

He was right about that. One of the reasons I kept Stone under wraps was because when the Authority found out I had him, they brought him here and were going to keep him for study. And even though the crystal was smaller, it was no less amazing than the gargoyle.

Dad was telling the truth. And it seemed to be a truth that would help rather than hinder me.

Weird.

That still didn't make it okay for him to run me around like a puppet.

I put the crystal back in my pocket.

"Allie?" Shame pushed on the door. "Ready?"

"Has it been five minutes?"

"More like fifteen." He stepped in and leaned against the wall. From the way he moved, I knew he had stashed more weapons on his body. A lot more.

"Do you know where Zayvion's sword is?" I asked.

"Probably. Why?"

"I want to take it with me."

"This is a peaceful gathering. We're setting up storm rods, or something—Terric wasn't very clear about that. But it's not going to be a fight."

"I'd feel better with a sword on me. As soon as we deal with the storm, and get Zayvion back through a gate, I won't have to make a special stop to gear up before hunting Greyson."

"Thought you might have that in mind." With a little contorting, Shame pulled Zayvion's blade out from the sheath he had strapped to his back.

Peaceful gathering, my ass.

"His knife?" I asked. I took the blade—not the machete Zay usually used on Hungers and for other magical threats, but a beautifully balanced sword, his katana. I'd used it a couple times in practice. It fit my hand and reach better than a machete, but it was harder to convince a police officer why it was in the trunk of a car. So for quick dirty hunts, a magic-worked machete was best.

I don't know where Shame pulled the knife out of, but I was glad he had it on him. Zayvion's blood blade was long, slender, deadly, centered with a beveled crystal and glyphs that were carved into the metal and glass, ash black against the shiny dagger. It was familiar, the first weapon Zay had given me, trusting that with it I would be able to protect myself.

Call me sentimental, but that knife was more romantic than a car full of pink roses.

I tucked it in my belt. Shame handed me the sheath for Zay's sword, which I strapped on my back, before shrugging back into my jacket.

"Anything else?" Shame asked.

"Hold on."

I stepped over to Zay, rested my forehead against his. "Come home to me," I whispered. "I love you."

Magic beneath my feet bucked and I braced against the bed frame to keep from falling. Something, low thunder with the strangest high wail behind it, like a horde of the dead come calling, skittered at the edge of my hearing.

I looked at Shame. "You felt that?"

"The storm," he said. "It's about to break. We need to haul."

I brushed my fingers one last time over Zay's lips. Then I jogged across the room out to the hall. Shame was already at the stairs and heading down. He was also on his phone.

"How much longer?" Pause. "Fuck. Yes, we'll make it."

"How much longer?" I asked.

"Maybe ten minutes. Maybe not." We took the stairs as fast as we could without falling, then used the side door to exit the building.

"Car's here," he said. "I moved it."

Smart thinking.

We ran.

Got to the car, got in, got going.

Stone was sitting up in the backseat, his big face pressed to the window, his eyes searching the sky. He crooned, a lonely sound, and his wings trembled.

"Stay in the car, boy. It's gonna get messy out there."

He crooned again, but didn't try to get out. The big lug was moving better. Maybe because there was magic coming our way, roiling across the sky. Maybe the storm was helping him. Wild magic was, after all, still magic.

Halfway across the bridge, magic rolled again, like a hot wind pushing through the car, through my skin, my bones.

I hissed, and Shame grunted. "Lord. This is gonna be such an ass-kicking," he said. "Ours."

He drove at a terrifying speed, one boot on the gas, both hands on the wheel, eyes narrowed in concentration. I stopped watching the traffic around us as soon as the number of impending collisions got into the vicinity of two digits.

The void stone between my breasts went warm, then pulsed cold. My skin itched.

Over the bridge now, and rolling up to the St. Johns neighborhood. Before we reached the tracks that separated St. Johns from the rest of the city, magic rumbled and rolled again, and I saw the faulty-lightbulb flicker of lightning somewhere high, high above us.

"Do you know where?" I asked.

"The bridge."

"What is it about that bridge?" I scrubbed at my arms, but the itching only got worse. "Too many weird things happen there."

Shame didn't answer. We were over the railroad track and into St. Johns. Even in the darkness, St. Johns looked like it always looked. Magic never prettied it up to make it into something marketers would approve of. St. Johns wore her face bare, and even if she wasn't perfect, she was more beautiful because of her flaws.

Broken-down, homey, unapologetic, St. Johns wore many faces. All of them the truth.

Crossing the railroad track made my teeth hurt. Not like there was no magic in St. Johns, but like there was far too much magic here.

Stone clacked a low growl and rubbed the top of his head against the back of Shame's seat. Stone felt it too. Something was wrong. Very wrong.

Shame took the speedometer down out of death-defying, and worked off the main drag toward the towering green arc of the St. Johns Bridge.

"In the park?" I asked.

"I think so." He got us there in too little time. Parked in the open lot and got out.

I turned to Stone. "You stay here, boy. Sleep, okay?"

Stone's ears flattened, then perked back up. He tipped his head and looked out the window, making the bag-of-marbles sound and then the coo again. He jiggled the door handle.

"No. Don't go out. Don't leave the car." I pointed at him and he let go of the handle. "Sleep," I commanded.

He clacked, then clunked his snout against the window, ears up in triangles.

I hoped he would stay put. I didn't want anyone in the Authority to see him. I locked the doors and stepped out.

The air had so much magic in it, it felt like it was made out of lead. It weighed on my shoulders, legs, and feet, crushing. Shame had lit up and sucked his cigarette down to half ash. His face was tipped toward the sky, his neck exposed, hood fallen away, to let his dark hair fall free from his eyes. Eyes closed, the arc of his body was taut with ecstasy as he drank the magic down.

He held the cigarette smoke captive in his open

mouth, then exhaled, his mouth still open, eyes still closed in rapture.

The air broke under the impact of thunder. Shame moaned away the rest of the smoke, and took in a breath like it was his first, like he could suck down the sky and still not be full.

He opened his eyes. "Fuck yes," he said up into the rain. "That's what I needed. More. Much more of that."

I finally got a full breath myself. "This is not good."

"It's magic. It's never good." Shame grinned at me. "But it's a hell of a lot better than the alternative."

"Not if it's wild magic."

I'd been through a few wild-magic storms before, fast-moving tangles of lightning and thunder and magic. Beckstrom Storm Rods did their job and channeled the strikes of lightning and magic down into the glyphed channels that stored magic throughout the city.

This was different.

This storm had death on its wings.

"Come on," I said.

I jogged across the parking lot toward the center of Cathedral Park, Shame at my side. Above us, thunder broke, the high demonic wail an earsplitting echo. Magic crackled through the sky, tracing out in flashes of glyphs.

Lights on the bridge flickered. A rolling blackout washed over the city downriver.

The void stone at my neck burned.

I ran, but my feet moved mud-slow. My breath came too quickly, too loudly. The void stone flashed cold again as lightning the color of dead roses webbed the sky with wild, elongated glyphs and spells.

Even my feet itched.

What had Maeve said? We were wearing the stones because when magic came back, the stones might help us not burn to death? Nice. And since I held magic inside me, I was in for a world of pain. Maybe Shame had the stone pressed against his neck for another reason. Like to keep him from drinking down too much energy once it hit.

What if magic wouldn't fill me again? What if it was a onetime thing, back when Cody had pulled it through my bones? Maybe now that it was gone, it was going to stay gone, leaving nothing behind but some ribbon tattoos.

I hoped not. I had a lot of things I wanted to do with magic right now, one of them being taking out Greyson. I wanted the magic back. I wanted that power back.

The pathway parallel to the river hooked uphill. Even though it was dark, the trees weren't leafed out enough to hide the flicker of the warehouse and factory lights on the river. I wondered if there were people there. People who were about to get hurt.

"And I repeat: fuck yes," Shame said beside me. "That's beauty." He pointed.

I looked over to where the bridge angled across on huge arched pillars. Magic lingered there. A lot of it. Not from the storm, thundering like a mountain being hammered down. This magic was contained, controlled, almost mechanical in its perfection. I knew the Authority had to be behind that magic. Shame had one thing right: it was beautiful.

And I knew that magic came from the disks. Hundreds of them.

The Authority had broken into Violet's labs and stolen these disks from her. They had hurt her, maybe killed her baby, and hurt Kevin, one of their own. I didn't know anything that would justify those actions. Not even this. But I was willing to tame the storm first and take names for ass kicking later.

Shame strode toward the wall of magic that had been cast in such a masterful Illusion that it mimicked the park perfectly. I started off after him, and pushed through the spongy resistance as I crossed that magical barrier. Someone who wasn't determined would not be able to get through the Illusion—it had a weight and a Diversion woven in it that would repel people and animals.

This, apparently, was a private party.

I don't know what I expected to see on the other side. Something gothic, magic going off like fireworks, maybe wizards' robes and pointed hats and wands, which I had yet to see in all my time in the Authority.

What I saw was even better.

The Authority, all the men and women who were supposed to make sure magic was used correctly, that the common citizen wasn't destroyed by it, that the world benefited from it, stood shoulder to shoulder, creating a circle.

No longer in street clothes, they wore what I could only assume they liked to cast magic in. Maeve had on her leather pants and stiletto heels, Hayden his leather bomber jacket and lumberjack boots. The twins Carl and La wore loose-legged pants and kimono-like shirts. The rest were in a variety of leather, tight- or loose-fitting coats and jackets, none longer than knee-length, and all of them had weapons at their sides.

I expected the atmosphere to be grim. What I didn't expect was the mood behind the magic.

The magic users did not like one another.

The magic users did not like being here, working together.

The magic users were all waiting for someone to make a wrong move.

Angry, suspicious, explosive. Just the kind of situation I liked to stay far, far away from.

There were two places open in the circle. One next to Terric, which I was surprised to see Shame stride over and fill, and one next to Sedra. I supposed that one was mine, though I wondered if it had once been my father's, or Zayvion's.

I crossed the grass uphill, conscious of the body language of everyone who stood still and focused. Even though the general mood was hate, they were, for the moment, each doing their job. They held their hands in front of them, and as I came nearer, I saw why.

At the feet of each of them was a disk. Small enough to fit in the palm of a hand, the disks were silver and black. Since I'd gotten a pretty good look at the one in Greyson's neck, I knew the disks had glyphs carved through them.

The disks gave off a soft pastel light. Magic I could see with my bare eyes rose in wisps, held in stasis by the magic user's hand and will.

I took my place beside Sedra. There was no disk on the grass in front of me.

What? The new girl didn't get to play?

"This completes our circle," Sedra said before I could point out that I didn't have a shiny toy like everyone else.

"This completes our power," she continued. "We stand together facing a common threat. Magic rises in our world, claiming the sky. It is our duty to bring it once again to the heart of the earth."

A few people looked over at her, or pointedly avoided her gaze. Wasn't that interesting? Liddy didn't look at her. Neither did Mike Barham, and half a dozen other people. No, instead they looked at one another.

Uh-oh.

The sky above us clotted with color. Lightning flashed again, shattered the sky with wild glyphs so bright I couldn't blink away the burn. Even flash-blind, I thought I saw a shadow moving back by the trees on the other side of the wall of magic. Short, female.

It was Mama Rositto, the woman whose youngest boy had been used as a Proxy, and almost killed, to cover up my father's murder several months ago. I used to Hound for her, but after her boy had been hurt, and her son James had been thrown in jail, she'd made it clear I wasn't welcome in her life.

What would she be doing out in the park in a storm?

With the Illusion up, she wouldn't see us, couldn't see us. And if we did our job right, she'd go her way, take her walk or whatever it was she was doing, without ever suspecting that the most powerful magic users in Portland were about to bring the sky, and all the magic in it, crashing down in her backyard.

Lightning flashed and thunder exploded so close they joined.

A drop of rain hit my head. Then another.

Great. Why did it always rain when the world needed saving?

The disks around the circle flickered as rain pattered through the rising magic.

I looked around, uncertain as to how this was a storm rod that was going to channel the magic. Unless they intended to channel bits of the magic into the disks at their feet. Even so, there weren't nearly enough disks to contain that storm.

The big, heavy figure of Jingo Jingo lumbered out into the center of the circle. He carried a sack over his back. Lightning struck, painting him pale as a horror-movie Santa Claus. A flash of ghostly faces, children's faces, swarmed around his body, tied to him, clinging to him in sorrow and desperation.

Darkness returned, snuffing out the ghosts.

But I knew I'd see them in my nightmares.

Jingo swung the bag off his back and upended it.

Disks poured out, dozens and dozens, striking one another in sweet glass tones, primal music and magic, ringing in song so pure I caught my breath. Disks and magic poured into a pile, a mountain, a treasure of glittering, beautiful power.

I moaned softly. I wasn't the only one.

There it was—the unattainable dream. Easy magic.

Safely contained, safely used. No price to pay. Ready to do what you wanted it to do. At no cost.

I wanted it to stop a storm. I wanted it to help me open a gate so I could get Zayvion back.

I looked around the circle, at faces brushed in liquid light from the disks at their feet. I saw awe, doubt, greed. I saw anger, and fear. All the good things a human could feel and all the bad, played out across the faces of those gathered.

The Authority, Zayvion had told me, was on the brink of a war.

And someone had just poured a pile of loaded weapons at their feet.

"Allison Beckstrom," Jingo Jingo said. "Come forward now."

"What?" Thunder struck, covering my voice. I shot a panicked look at Shame and Terric, both of whom looked away from the thrall of the disks and at me. They looked as confused as I felt.

"We need a focal point," Sedra said softly next to me. "I had hoped there would be another way. If Zayvion hadn't fallen, he would be the one standing here. I would not have asked this of you."

"Asked what of me? Explain—" Lightning, thunder. I waited them out, or at least until the thunder's volume went down a notch. Tried again, "Explain what you think I'm going to do."

She smiled, and it looked out of place beneath her cool, brittle eyes, as if there were two different people with two different emotions behind that face. "You are going to direct the wild magic. You don't need to wield it, don't need to absorb it. You simply need to Ground it, into the disks."

How had she not noticed that I sucked at Grounding? I thought my teachers reported to her about me. I wasn't even any good at keeping control over the magic inside me and never left home without a void stone anymore.

Volatile was the polite word my teachers used when they didn't think I was listening. You'd think someone would have pointed that out to her.

"I don't Ground."

Her eyebrows flicked up. "You will do so now. If you are the Soul Complement to the Guardian of the Gate, then you will be strong enough. We will divert the wild magic to you, and you will Ground it. Using the disks."

"I'm a lightning rod? A storm rod?" I blinked back rain that trickled into the corners of my eyes. "I tapped into a wild storm and it almost killed me."

"Zayvion wielded all manifestations of magic. It is now your time to prove you can do the same. Prove that you really are his equal." This last bit she said with more anger than I expected. I got the feeling she didn't like me very much.

"Zayvion's had a hell of a lot more training than I have."

"There is only you. If you don't channel the magic, the city will burn, magic will explode, melt the conduits, destroy. People will die. Zayvion will die."

"What? Why?"

"He has been broken by magic. And only magic— dark and light—can make him whole again."

Holy shit. "So if the storm hits, it's going to kill him?"

"If we don't control it, yes." I did not like the pitying smile she gave me. It looked like she wanted me to fail.

Well, screw that.

The entire conversation lasted all of a few seconds. It scared the crap out of me. But I was getting tired of standing there getting wet and arguing about things I knew too little about.

Not knowing what the hell I was doing had never stopped me before. And so far, not knowing what I was doing with magic hadn't killed me.

But this time it wasn't just my life on the line. It was

Zay's life, and the lives of people in the city—Violet's life, her baby's life.

If I failed and magic blew out the conduits in the city, thousands could die.

Maybe some of the fear showed on my face.

Victor, who stood next to Sedra, said, "We will guide you. We will be your hands if you falter, your strength if you fear, your breath if you fall."

That was good and all, but what I really needed was someone to be my sense of self-preservation and oh, I don't know, tell me to run away now and run real fast.

Since that wasn't going to happen, I nodded and pushed my fear as far away as I could. I was good at denial.

I walked out into the center of the circle where Jingo Jingo waited for me.

"You're gonna do just fine, Allison," Jingo Jingo said in his low, smooth liar's voice. "You were born for this, made for this." He smiled, but there was a fevered gloss in his eyes. Even in the rain I could tell he was sweating. Even in the rain, I could smell his lie.

Or maybe I was reading too much into this. Panic will do that to a girl. I took a deep breath, and squared my shoulders.

"What do I need to do?"

Jingo Jingo stepped closer to me and ran his hand down my arm, petting my right shoulder and stroking down to my fingers, which he caught up. It was weird, creepy, invasive. I gave him a look that let him know exactly what I thought about that.

"You're gonna stand here." He guided me around the pile of disks so I stood facing Sedra.

Sedra looked calm and cool as an ice sculpture. Which is to say she looked like she always looked.

Well, that and wet. Lightning flashed, painting ragged glyphs across the sky, and for a second, less than that, I thought I saw something else in her, something under her skin that was dark, twisted.

Panic shot through me. I looked at the other users gathered. There was something wrong with their body language. Too many sideways glances, meaningful looks. Even Liddy, my teacher in Death magic, looked tense, as if she was waiting for her cue.

Sedra might be the head of this parade, but I was pretty sure some of the band didn't want to march.

"All you need to do is hold this," Jingo Jingo continued. He bent, dug through the piles of disks. They were all the same. I didn't know what he was looking for. He finally selected one and placed it in my palm. "And meditate."

Meditate? Oh, yeah. That would be no problem in the middle of a wild-magic storm surrounded by a circle of users—all better trained than me, all giving one another hateful looks—with a big pile of free magic at my feet.

Okay, yes, granted, you had to have a clear mind to actually cast magic, and high emotion destroys the concentration it takes to access magic. But meditation takes time to do well. So if my ability to meditate was what was going to save the world, or at least save Portland, then I was pretty sure we should all think about moving to Seattle.

"Meditate," I said. "Right, then what?"

Jingo Jingo stood in front of me. I could smell his fear, bitter and sharp on the back of my sinuses. And something else—the candy sweet of excitement, anticipation. He licked his lips. He was looking forward to this, anxious, eager. "Then, you are going to do the right thing, Allison Beckstrom. And you won't need me to tell you what that is."

He stepped back, putting rain and space between us. Lightning flashed again and thunder broke the sky to pieces. I had zero chance to tell him how incredibly unhelpful he had been.

Some teacher. Going silent on me when I most needed a clear answer. Bastard.

Okay, I had my disk. It was heavy and cool in my hand. And I had my sword. It was heavy and cool on my back. It shouldn't, but just the presence of Zayvion's blade made me feel better, like a part of him was with me, telling me, calmly, to stop thinking so hard, and just kick some ass.

And that was exactly what I planned on doing. I was about to meditate like no one had ever meditated before.

Yes, that sounded stupid.

I took a deep breath, spread my feet so I wouldn't fall over when the winds picked up.

Just as I began to close the outside world away from my senses, the storm tore open the sky, the air. And the magic beneath the earth rushed into me, and burned through me.

Chapter Nineteen

Too hot, too hard, magic rushed up out of the earth and poured down from the sky to stretch and fill my bones, my skin, my body. There wasn't enough room in my body for me to breathe, wasn't enough room for me to think.

Meditate, he'd said.

Jingo Jingo was such a joker.

I had to clear my mind. Had to direct—no, channel—no, Ground. I was supposed to Ground, and they were going to direct the magic that ricocheted and fractured, leaping above me, above us, above St. Johns, striking wild, random arcs of lightning and wild glyphs that would tear us all to shreds.

We might be using magic, but it was going to use us right back.

I cleared my mind. Sang my "Miss Mary Mack" song. Lost the line when thunder rolled and rolled, and lightning hit so low I felt it in my molars and thought we'd all go up in a crisp. Picked up at the "silver buttons, buttons, buttons" line and held tight to the disk, which hummed with magic, in my hand over the pile of disks.

The wild magic was not me. The wild magic could not change me. It could pour around me, fill the disk in my hand, and fill the other disks on the ground. It could follow the marks, the paths, the ribbons, magic had painted in my skin, my blood, my bones, and use me as a conduit. Magic could slide through me, soft, gentle, and return to the soil, the stones, the heart of the earth, where it belonged.

The reason St. Johns had been chosen for this suddenly made sense. St. Johns was an empty sieve. Magic would flow through it, and into the channels beyond this neighborhood, and fill all the rest of Portland.

That was, if I could Ground it.

I inhaled, exhaled, tasted the burnt wood and hot ozone of fire. The wind lifted, buffeting, hot in the cold, cold rain.

Grounding wasn't a difficult glyph to draw, but making magic follow it, and standing there, steady, calm, and completely focused while the magic used me, was what made Grounding hard. I set a Disbursement, hoping to push off some of the pain for later. Maybe I'd catch a flu in a week or so.

If I survived.

I looked up, at the sky roiling with metallic, psychedelic clouds, stirred by the winds like oil on water, pushed into new shapes, into unnamed hues and colors. Lightning struck, and all the colors of magic flashed gold against the black sky. I'd never felt so much magic so concentrated. At least, not that I remembered.

Even the rain tasted of the oily, metallic heat of wild magic, striking sour on the tip of my tongue, and so sweet at the back of my throat.

Lightning struck again. Thunder roared.

Now. I knew I had to cast it now.

I focused, pushed away the awareness of the magic users around me, most of them chanting over the rush of rain and wind, pushed away my awareness of the storm, of the rain, of the wind buffeting my body.

Raised my hand.

This one stroke, this one line, this one curve—I cast each part of the glyph for Grounding with precise, purposeful motion. Nothing wrong, not a tremor, not a pause.

Then I drew upon the magic from the disk in my hand. It hesitated, and for a second, I thought I had screwed up and was going to suck all the magic in the disk into me, into my bones, blood, and flesh. But the magic sprang free of the disk, and I guided it to fill the glyph for Grounding.

Magic poured into the Grounding, and shot ropes of magic over me. Even though I expected that and braced for it, I jerked. The thick, cold cables of the magic clamped over my shoulders and fell like hundred-pound anchors into the soil, where they plunged deep and hooked. I could not move if I wanted to.

I was now officially Beckstrom the storm rod. And I hated it.

Have I mentioned I am claustrophobic? I tried to push my fear out of the way, tried to ignore the clamping restraints of the Grounding holding me down.

This is why I am no good at Grounding. I freak out within the first three seconds or so. Trapped. Too trapped.

I exhaled, focused on the disk in my outstretched hand. I could do this. Not only that, I would do this. Everything depended on me doing this one thing. One thing wasn't hard. I could do one thing.

Magic leaped into the hands of the users in the circle. I recognized directional glyphs, drawn to attract and guide the magic down out of the sky and into me—or rather into the framework of magic around me, the Grounding I'd just cast.

I breathed evenly, bracing for the onslaught.

Magic would not burn me alive. So long as I didn't take it into me. So long as I didn't lose my concentration. These magic users were professionals. They knew what they were doing.

I hoped.

From the corner of my eye, I saw a figure leap out of the shadows. Two figures. Magic flared. Glyphs turned to flame. The pile of disks at my feet caught fire, magic bursting free.

A wall of heat hit me and I yelled, thinking, *Ground, Ground, Ground.*

No, my dad said. *Let go, Allison, let go!* He shoved at me, tried to take control, but I was nothing if not made of stubborn. I held my place, kept my cool, even though I was being roasted to the core.

Ground, Ground, Ground.

Look, Dad said. *Look around you. Look at the battle.*

Battle? My ears were already ringing from the pounding thunder and magic. I couldn't hear him over all the screaming.

Wait. Screaming?

I hesitated. I was not good at doing what my father wanted me to do. But there was something very wrong.

I looked away from the disk in my palm, holding my concentration in the Grounding spell.

Chaos. The circle was broken. And it wasn't because of the storm.

Magic user fought magic user in a blur so confusing, I couldn't make out who was where.

I blinked hard, trying to clear my vision. Magic poured over me, hot, heavy, cold, biting, rushing down the cables of the Grounding spell that I somehow still held.

Go, me.

But all around me the Authority battled.

I searched for Shame in the melee.

And instead saw Greyson and Chase.

No, no, no. Absolutely no. They could not be here. Who would have told them we were going to be here?

Greyson was more beast than man, on all fours, wide head, fangs, and claw, bone and sinew for legs and arms, and burning eyes. Chase cast magic for him, with him, his Soul Complement and his hands. She was tall, but thinner and paler than just a day ago. Working magic with Greyson, or maybe being Soul Complement to a man who was half alive and half dead, carried a hard price—her humanity.

Her hair hung around her shoulders like a black cape, glimpses of her skin flashes of moonlight in a dark night. Her eyes and her lips were bloodred. She no longer wore jeans and flannel, but instead had on a black dress that skimmed her knees and black boots with heels low enough to make running easy. Or fighting.

And that was exactly what she was doing.

And doing very well.

Just like back at Officers Row, Chase was chanting and weaving glyphs in the air and filling them with magic she pulled out of the storm. Multicolored ribbons wrapped down her fingers and up her arm, where tendrils shot out to anchor in Greyson, feeding him. He was headed my way.

Romero, the family-man killer, launched himself at Greyson, the machete in his hand a blur of magic channeled from the sky.

Greyson fought him, fangs bared, then unhinged his huge jowls and sucked down the magic Romero threw at his head.

Chase clapped her hands together once and a gate sprang up. Greyson leaped through it. Chase slammed her hands together again, and the gate disappeared in a blast of black smoke.

I didn't know how she was doing it. Those gates weren't allowing any of the creatures that haunted the other side, the Hungers, to break through. But Greyson used them as easily as stepping though an open door.

One more clap, and the gate was open again, this time on the other side of the circle. Near Sedra and Maeve. And me.

Greyson tore out of the gate, and ran fast, too fast, a

nightmare of bone and fang and claw. He launched at Sedra.

Sedra stood, cool and angry, hands raised in a block I'd never seen before. Greyson hit the block, and I swear I felt the thrum of that impact at the base of my skull, over the thunder, over the wail of magic in the storm, over the sounds of battle.

Maeve stepped up to Sedra's defense. She wielded a long knife in each hand, blood covering her fingers and the blades as she cut glyphs into the air. She threw magic at Greyson. It wrapped him in dark lightning, filling the air with the sweet smell of cherries. Greyson sucked the magic down. Which was exactly what Maeve had wanted. Still connected by blood to her blade, and her will, Maeve yanked on the spell, tearing a brutal scream out of Greyson.

Greyson stumbled. Gave up his advance on Sedra and turned on Maeve instead. He leaped.

"No!" I yelled. I tried to take a step. The Grounding spell rooted me, anchored. I couldn't let go of the spell, couldn't break it.

Come on. Let go, undo, leave me now, go away, go away, stop.

Lightning struck, so close, rain sizzled. Thunder popped an ear-busting explosion and I tasted blood at the back of my throat.

Wild magic filled me, licked across my skin, catching fire down the ribbons of my arm and hand. Wild magic grew roots in me, different from the Grounding spell. I had felt this before. I suddenly remembered it now. The last time I'd tapped into a wild-magic storm and nearly died.

The crystal, my dad said. Or I think he said it. It was hard to hear anything over the thunder, the yelling, the fighting—worse because someone, I think the Georgia sisters, was supporting the dome of magic, keeping all the sounds we made inside.

I pushed my left hand into my pocket and pulled out the crystal. Deep fuchsia, the crystal was hot, glyphs carved inside it fluctuating with the magic I carried. I didn't know how the crystal was going to help.

Direct the magic into it; use it to Ground. It is organic, unlike the disks, Dad said. *It can act as a Grounder.*

Okay, so all I had to do was recast the Grounding spell onto the crystal. One crystal to handle what me and a hundred disks were barely managing?

It'll explode, I said.

It will hold long enough, Dad said.

Long enough?

For the storm to pass.

Maybe that was his idea of success. As a matter of fact, it probably was. I didn't know what his stake in this was, except Violet's safety.

Put the crystal on the disks, he said.

And that made sense. The excess magic in the crystal would bleed off into the disks, and they could help carry the load of wild magic.

But the Grounding spell wrapped me in concrete. It took everything I had to bend my knees and hold my hand out over the pile of disks. I opened my fingers, tipped my palm. The crystal fell, tumbling down and down. It struck the disks and a sweet, harmonic tone echoed back from the rain

And then the world exploded.

My hands flew up without thought. Well, without my thought. Dad took over and cast a hell of a Shield spell. That kept me from burning to the bone. But it did not keep me from being thrown back ten feet, and landing flat on my back.

Someone above me, in the light, shadows, rain, wild magic, held a hand down for me.

"Move!" It was Victor, my teacher, Zayvion's teacher. He grabbed my hand and rocketed me onto my feet.

All the training I'd done on the mats came into play. I

found my balance and footing in the wet and confusion, and got out of the way fast. Victor had pulled me to one side of the battlefield.

I hurt—my skin stung from the magic burns, or, for all I knew, from lightning strikes. But even with all hell coming down, I did not draw Zay's blade and go in swinging.

I didn't know whom we were fighting, other than Greyson and Chase, and I didn't know why. Everyone was throwing magic and weapons around. This had gone from a fight against the storm to a fight against one another.

"Stay out of the way." Victor turned and ran into the fray.

I wasn't going to do anything until I knew my hands, my body, were my own. I shook my hands, making sure my dad was not using them. It creeped me the hell out when he did that.

You're welcome, his sardonic voice said in the middle of my head.

Shut up. And leave my body alone.

This isn't your battle, he said. *There is so much more you were meant for. So much more you and I could do to make this right. Death isn't the end, nor life the beginning.*

Save it for the encore, I thought. *I am a part of this. My friends are in there.*

You do not know who your true friends are.

I ignored him because, really? Busy trying to figure out how to lend a hand here, and the last time I'd let him tell me who my friends were, I was six. I set a Disbursement, headache, and traced a glyph for Sight. The entire field opened up like I'd just flipped the switch on a floodlight.

The scene was gruesome.

Several things were happening at once. On the compass points of the field, four people had backed off, and now stood with their hands above their heads and forward, feet spread for balance, in some kind of weird yoga pose that was actually sustaining the flow of magic into the shield. The Georgia sisters were three of them—I could tell because they each stood with one hand on their staff, and one extended skyward—and I think Carl, the brother twin, was the other. They were wet, shaking, and chanting, though I couldn't hear their words, and held their focus and concentration with grim robotic determination.

Inside that circle that reached to a domed height maybe six stories above us, at least as high as the trees, was magic. Wild magic pounded in the sky beyond the bubble and fluttered around the bubble like a bee to nectar.

I didn't know what it looked like on the outside, but I could guess. I guessed that it looked like a storm, a regular thunderstorm. Even the best magic users wouldn't be stupid enough to try to tap into the wild magic to cast spells like Sight. So all they'd see was multicolored lightning rolling across the sky in vaguely glyphlike shapes. There were probably strikes in other parts of the town, caught by the Beckstrom Storm Rods, but the flow of magic here would be mostly invisible. Magic is so fast, it cannot be seen by the naked eye. And with plain old ordinary lightning blasting through the sky, I doubted anyone even knew what was going down behind the dome of Illusion in St. Johns.

So long as the four magic users held their concentration and kept the dome intact, this would never hit the news.

Inside the circle was a battlefield. Mostly, it looked like the magic users had chosen two sides. The one against Chase and Greyson and the one for them. With this many people fighting for Chase and Greyson, it was no wonder Greyson had escaped.

And with this many people on their side, I considered

them against me, and responsible for Zayvion's lying unconscious. I knew which side I belonged on. The side with Maeve, Victor, Hayden, Sedra, Dane, Shame, and Terric.

Chase and Greyson worked together, Liddy standing close by them, and not doing anything to stop them.

Over and over Chase called up gates for Greyson to leap through. He tore into magic users, pinning them, and drinking the magic out of them. He was mostly man now, wearing pants and no shirt, but still a wild thing, all muscle and pale skin, his hair long, his eyes more human than they had been, but still filled with an animal's intelligence. No, the intelligence of a killer.

He attacked La, the other twin. She swung her scythe and magic so hard, it should have cut his arm off. But it didn't even nick him. He shoved hands into her chest like he was digging for bones. He tipped his head back, the disk pulsing silver green at his throat, and howled over her screams as he sucked the magic out of her. Her twin, Carl, holding the east side of the dome, yelled out too, but the dome did not waver. He endured.

Big Hayden was having nothing of it. He wore the bomber jacket, but the shotgun and broadsword were no longer over his shoulder.

He fired the rifle at Greyson. Missed his head by an inch. Greyson ducked and rolled, using the unconscious La as a shield. Hayden swung his sword, and a sound wave pushed against my skin as if a hundred voices were calling out in a chant, a prayer, a force. There was magic in that sword—I don't know what kind, but it was old. It wrapped around Greyson, dug into his muscles as he ran, slowing him and leaving lines of blood behind. Then there was a gate, and Greyson was through it.

Hayden was hot on his heels. Before the gate closed, Greyson grabbed a handful of it—of the magic Chase used to create the gate—and threw it like a hand grenade at Hayden.

Hayden sheathed his rifle, and caught most of the magic with his hand, diffusing the magic so that it froze into a cloud of shattered glass that fell and burned the grass at his feet.

Magic should not do what Greyson and Chase were doing with it. They were using so much magic, they should be unconscious by now. Someone had to be bearing the price of their magic use, but I didn't know who it was, although it could be the other magic users on their side acting as Proxy.

Or maybe more magic users somewhere else in the city were standing Proxy. How far did this break in the Authority run? Were they fighting in Salem? In Eugene? Was there an uprising in Washington? California? Or was this just a local war?

I glanced at Chase. Stop her to stop Greyson. The flaw of that plan was that Greyson had now drunk enough Life magic, light magic, to transmute back into the form of a man. Which meant he had hands, and could cast magic as well as any of us. But I knew he wouldn't stay a man for long. Not without a constant intake of magic.

Chase worked the southern end of the fight. Liddy had shifted to stand behind her, one hand on her shoulder, the other drawing spells. Liddy whispered and traced glyphs, pouring magic into Chase, providing her with the magic to give to Greyson.

Liddy was a bad guy. Great. How was I going to get past the teacher of Death magic to get to Chase?

We don't need the Closer, Dad said in my head. *All we need is the beast, to take back what is mine.*

Wrong, I said. *We get the Closer, we get the beast. They're Soul Complements. They're one. And she's going to be easier to take down.*

I glanced around for Jingo Jingo. He might be a freak, but he was good at what he did.

Jingo Jingo was in a deadlock with Maeve. Jingo's Death magic absorbed the Blood magic Maeve threw at him, sucked it down like a well with no end. He strolled toward her, almost as easy as a Sunday walk, nodding as if he understood why she was fighting him, and maybe would regret killing her. I think I heard him humming a song, an old gospel about babies and the devil and bones. Maeve wove spells with blood and blade, not about to back down.

Sedra, nearby, was locked in a cage work of magic like nothing I'd ever seen. It had to be technology, something my dad would have built.

Maybe it wasn't just the disks the Authority had broken into the lab for. Maybe they'd come in and demanded that cage too.

That wasn't in the lab, Dad said. *I developed it years ago. It was taken from me years ago.*

Like something out of Victorian clockwork, the cage was a collection of gears and glyphs and metal twisted into the shape of holding spells. It hinged in every section, as if it could be shaped into any spell, and shaped around any person.

Holy shit. It was a physical carrier of magic, like the disks, but specific to single spells.

This was part of what my dad had been working on. Not just the conduits of magic that could fuel the city. Not just the disks that worked as batteries. But a metal or some other compound that could be shaped into a spell and *become* that spell until the day the magic died.

Using this would permanently change the world.

The cage was constricting, pressing in on Sedra's clothes and moving closer. It was going to crush her to death.

What the hell kind of tech were you making? I thought at my dad.

Do not vilify that which you do not know. All great things can be used for war or peace.

The cage had Sedra frozen completely. She didn't so much as move a hand or speak a word.

Dane, her bodyguard, was doing what he could to hold a slowing spell around her. It kept the cage from collapsing in on her, but he couldn't do anything else.

Shame and Terric fought back-to-back, moving as if they could read each other's minds. It was not just Greyson and Chase and Jingo Jingo and Liddy causing problems. Mike wore the glowing glyph gloves and threw lightning around like it was rice at a wedding. Shame and Terric were counteracting his constant barrage.

La was down. So was Romero. Hayden had finally pinned Greyson back against the wall of magic where Chase couldn't get to him. Greyson was no slouch. He cast magic, light and dark, Life and Death, at the big man. He forced Hayden to spend so much effort blocking, Grounding, or containing magic, he was not making any headway against Greyson.

If it hadn't been real, if it hadn't been my friends' lives on the line, this scene might be beautiful for the amazing skill. Greyson was liquid silver and shadow dancing with the saber he'd found, Chase, his pale, blood-lipped lover, feeding him the power to fight.

Hayden, a mountain of power and precision, took blows that would cripple a lesser man. Dane wove incredible, complicated lacework spells to keep Sedra from being crushed, while Jingo Jingo supped on Maeve's Blood magic like a man with a hunger that had no end.

Maeve's spells painted quick, sensual strokes of Blood magic that wrapped deadly vines around Jingo's soul. Shame and Terric, brothers, Complements, warriors, blades, ax, magic, shouted curses and synchronized death.

It was Jingo who broke the stalemate between the two factions.

He stopped strolling toward Maeve, stopped singing.

He put one hand over his heart and shook his head. I didn't know if it was an apology or a salute. But when he lifted his hand, there was blood on his palm. And a disk.

He lifted his hand from his heart and pointed the disk at Maeve.

He twisted the spell she had anchored into him, and sent it back on her. Mixed with his blood. Mixed with Death magic. Mixed with the magic in the disk. All the souls of the ghostly children who clung to him were set free.

They screamed through the air, rabid, feral, tearing into Maeve like a mob of crows. They covered her, clawing, biting, and lifted her off the ground.

Jingo slashed the disk downward. The ghosts dropped Maeve to the ground, but clung to her with tiny hands and hungry mouths.

Maeve yelled. Pain. Agony. She could not move to break the spell. Could not free herself of the children's souls. And those souls were drinking her dry.

Shame saw it. Terric saw it. Hayden saw it.

And so did I.

Shame ran for her.

So did Hayden.

Greyson ran too. To Chase. To the gate she opened for him. Closed for him. Then opened again. Behind Maeve.

Greyson leaped out of the gate and was on Maeve. He drank down the magic around her, lapped up the children's souls and all the magic they contained.

Hayden and Shame yelled out. They were almost there. Almost close enough.

Greyson stood, faced Jingo Jingo. And disgorged the children's magic, and more—all the magic he had taken from all the people he'd been fighting—straight at Jingo Jingo.

For a second my heart soared. Maybe Chase had told

Greyson that Jingo was a freak. Maybe they were on the good guys' side. Our side.

But Jingo Jingo took that magic, all of it, into the disk in his hand, mixed with his blood, and every discipline and expression of magic. His eyes were wide, desperate, as if this one thing, this last thing, was his only chance. He pointed the disk at the pile of disks and the crystal in the center of the field.

He chanted a spell that made my ears hurt.

Light seared through the air—a hot talon carving a hole through space. Light burst out of the opening, swirled with metallic colors reflected on my arm. A gate between life and death opened.

More than opened, the gate had been made real. Solid. It was made of iron and stone and glass. And magic.

I glimpsed a figure standing in the gate, ghostly thin. A fair-haired boy with eyes as blue as summer. Cody Miller. The Hand who had pulled magic through my bones, the boy who was still alive, and currently living with my friend Nola on her farm in Burns. The boy who had eyes too much like Sedra's eyes. Too much like the eyes of Mikhail, the dead leader of the Authority.

It wasn't all of Cody—his mind had been Closed by Zayvion because he had been deemed too dangerous to use magic. So while his body, and part of his mind, did live with Nola, this part of him, a piece of his soul, a piece of his spirit, his mind, that could use magic, was in this gate between life and death. He'd jumped into the gate when I had been tested into the Authority. He had sacrificed himself to keep the gate closed. And to keep Mikhail, the Hungers, and other horrors of magic out of the living world.

He looked out across the scene. And locked eyes with me. *I can't*, he mouthed. I am good at reading lips. His eyes were filled with sorrow, but also with anger. *I can't stop this anymore. You have to do it.*

He rocked forward, as if something huge had hit him

from behind, but all I could see behind him was a swirl of colors that matched the light from the gate.

He rocked again. And then I saw what bore down upon him. Eyes. Fangs. Claws.

The Hungers.

He was holding them back. Keeping them from entering our world, just as he had kept the gate closed. But now the gate was open, and *real*, he couldn't hold on any longer.

We'd fought the Hungers before, when the gate had opened during my test. Even with all the magic users gathered and on the same side, thank you, we'd nearly lost. I didn't have any hope we would win this time.

All this, all the things I'd seen, had taken up maybe a minute. But it felt like years. I was running, to save Maeve, to try to pull Greyson off her. Shame was still running too.

Hayden got there first. He'd sheathed his sword. Grabbed Greyson by the throat and tore him off Maeve's still body. Pinning Greyson to the ground, Hayden pounded the hell out of him.

Chase yelled out. And Greyson smiled through bloody lips and broken face. Another gate opened— one of Chase's gates. Not beside Greyson. Below him. It swallowed Greyson and Hayden. Chase closed it. I did not see where they reappeared. I didn't have time to look.

Shame, at a dead run, threw everything he had at Jingo Jingo. Jingo, his hand still extended to keep the gate open, staggered.

Shame was good. A master. Even though he had been Jingo Jingo's student.

Jingo turned, faced Shame. Looked surprised. Maybe he didn't know that his student had become so skilled. This would be the end of one of them—that, I knew.

Shame still looked like hell. He'd added a cut across his cheek and a bruise over one eye, and his skin was still sunken against bone. He looked like the walking dead. Like at any moment he would fall. But his eyes told me that it was not the strength of his body that was fueling him.

Yes, one of them would fall. But from the fury pouring out of Shame, it wasn't going to be him.

Shame chanted. He pulled his hands, a blade in each, across his chest, his head tipped down so that only his eyes burned through the ragged, bloodstained curtain of his hair. He looked like a dark angel, head bowed in prayer. And maybe he was. The grass at his feet crackled and seared brown, dead, and began to smoke. He was drawing energy, life energy, out of everything in his range. It was the way of Death magic, a transference of energy.

Jingo Jingo knew it too. He'd taught him.

"Don't, boy," he shouted. "You don't know what's at stake here. You don't understand what we could lose."

"Fuck," Shame said, "you."

He pulled his arms open, as if embracing all the life, all the pain, all the death and magic, in the circle.

I made it to Maeve. I had to pull her out of the way before Shame drank her down too.

I touched her face. She was cold. Too cold, even in the falling rain. I couldn't tell if she was breathing and didn't have time to wonder whether moving her would kill her. I picked her up, not easy, but I was in shape, and adrenaline gave me strength and desperation. Good enough.

I dragged her away, though there was no safe place, finally stopped near one of the Georgia sisters who was holding the east side of the Illusion barrier. The sister, the youngest, I thought, did not look down at me. Did not break out of her hypnotic trance.

That kind of focus was crazy. They should have had her Ground for the group. It was a good thing Sedra hadn't asked me to hold the Illusion. I would have dropped that shit long ago.

I knelt and placed my hand on Maeve's chest. Flashbacks rocked through me. Of Zayvion lying still, of a fight I could not win raging around me, of watching him cross into death. I tried to push it away, tried not to panic. Maeve's heart beat, strong and even. She was breathing.

I didn't know if I could heal her. With the wild magic pouring through the air, I wasn't sure if I should even try. I might kill her.

I glanced back at Shame.

Things were not going well. Jingo Jingo smiled, a flash of white across his dark face, and I added another image to my nightmare list. He shook his head slowly, pitying Shame.

Shame's hands shook as he cast the next spell. A spell Jingo Jingo batted aside and countered with something that sent Shame to his knees.

Where was Terric? Where was the cavalry? There didn't seem to be any end to the storm, to the magic, to the fallen.

I didn't know what to do.

Listen to me, Allison, Dad said in my head. *This battle is not the war. Those who fall will be remembered. But there will be more, many deaths, hundreds.* I saw a flash of Davy's face, of Bea, of Violet, of Stotts, of Zayvion, then a blur of people whom my father knew, some of his ex-wives and business partners, and for one brief, sweet moment an image of my own mother's laughing face; then the images were gone. *Thousands could die if you do not listen to me.*

I'm listening.

Leave Maeve. She is alive. Leave the others. You must release the Hand, Cody, back into this world. He was never meant to hold the gates between life and death closed.

The Authority will kill him. Destroy his soul if they find out, maybe even kill the living Cody too, I said.

No. There is one who will keep him hidden.
Who?

My dad pointed in my head—a strange feeling that made me want to scratch the roof of my mouth. I looked up to the right.

Mama stood on the other side of the wall of magic, all five-foot-nothing of her. Her arms were crossed over her chest and she wore a secondhand raincoat that was two sizes too big, the green hood tightened around her face like a corn husk.

"Mama?"

She couldn't hear me. She was outside the Illusion. Wait. What was she doing there? From her perspective, she was standing in the middle of the field at night in a downpour. Why would she do that?

She owes me a favor, my dad said.

Okay, that was fucking creepy. I didn't know how my dad had gotten her to show up. Didn't know if he'd left something about it in his will, or if he was somehow talking to people when I didn't know it. Like at night when I was sleeping or something. I tried to think if I had done any sleepwalking and came up with nothing.

You are not the only vessel I fill, he said. *You are not the only one who can hear me.*

Holy shit. Could he get any more creepy?

Who? I asked. *Greyson?* Oh, I hoped I was wrong.

It has not been easy, he said. *The beast fights me, but I found a way.* He sounded proud about that.

It made me want to barf.

Dad, or Greyson, or some combination, had somehow talked to Mama. Which meant she knew my undead dad was undead. And she'd agreed to do him a favor.

I didn't know if I should break through the shield and tell her to go away somewhere safe fast, or if getting my body, and my possessed brain, closer to her would let Dad jump the ship. He was stronger here, with the wild magic and the disks. Stronger ever since Greyson had attacked Zayvion.

Was he a part of Chase and Greyson's betrayal?

What do you want? I asked him. Cold sweat washed over me, and I shivered in the rain, even though it was tropical hot inside the shield. Fear, of him manipulating me all this time, of the frighteningly real possibility that he was the one behind the attack on Zayvion, made me want to run far and fast.

But how could I escape that which was inside me?

I want magic in the right hands. And I want immortality.

Two things he'd told me before. If they were lies, they were lies he was sticking to.

Why should I trust you?

Do you want your friends to live?

I looked at Shame again. He was still on one knee, the other foot braced, his hand sunk deep to clutch the grass, the soil, the other raised toward Jingo Jingo, so much magic pouring through him that Jingo was having to take hard steps backward, even though he leaned with all his strength, with all his bulk, into Shame's spell.

Shame shook with fury. He wasn't chanting. He was cursing. And every word drew blood from Jingo's thick skin, sending Jingo's blood to pour down with the rain, and into the soil, where Shame drew the energy and strength out of Jingo's blood, draining Jingo's life energy and throwing it back at him to cut him again.

Holy fuck, that boy was ruthless.

I didn't need my dad. I didn't need to do what he wanted. Shame was taking care of Jingo Jingo. Dane still held the cage from crushing Sedra, though he hadn't broken it yet. Victor was hot in battle with both Liddy and Chase, and Terric had knocked Mike out—with fists, not magic. I couldn't see Greyson or Hayden.

I needed to deal with Cody and close the gate so the Hungers couldn't get through.

Jingo Jingo yelled.

Shame was on his feet now, magic still hammering Jingo's Shield. But Jingo wasn't yelling in defeat. He swung his huge arm to one side and directed the disk and magic at the gate.

Cody screamed. The incorporeal shrill felt like someone had shoved hot peppers in my eyes. His voice, his pain, filled the dome.

For a breath—just that long—everyone stopped.

Except me.

I stood. Ran. Straight at the gate. And caught Cody's spirit as he fell free into this world again. Caught him, not in my arms, but rather, confusingly, horrifyingly, in my mind.

For a moment, I was three people, three lives, three memories. I remembered painting with magic, carving with magic, creating beautiful, beautiful things that broke barriers between life and death, ways for magic to be all disciplines at once.

I remembered inventing technology, formulating glyphs, standardizing spells with a mix of metal and glass that broke barriers between life and death, and made magic follow all disciplines at once.

I remembered my eighth birthday party and the purple sweater my dad bought me. I loved that sweater.

Too many memories, too much. Too crowded. I whined and stumbled backward, trying to get away from the people inside me, trying to escape my own skin, flee my crowded, crowded brain.

People can't possess people. People can't possess people. Zayvion had said it was rare. Said my dad was in my head only because we were the same blood. Cody and I were not related. And yet his spirit—or at least this part of it who could make magic do beautiful, beautiful things—was curled around my brain stem.

There wasn't any room for me to breathe, to think.

Out, out, out!

My back brushed the spongy wall of the Illusion, and I finally heard my father's voice.

Allison. Let him go!

I exhaled, blinked. Magic swirled around me, a curtain of ribbons and fire, a maelstrom all my own.

Good. You are doing fine. Calm your mind.

I shouldn't. Shouldn't listen to him. Shouldn't trust him. But I had loved that purple sweater. He had canceled a business trip to Europe and stayed home for my birthday. He had brought me a birthday cake. And the purple sweater I had secretly loved and mentioned to him only once when we walked by the store.

I did as he said.

Dad used me to cast a spell. It felt like a gentle stroke over my hair, except it was inside my head. And then the awareness of Cody, his life, his memories, his soul, was gone. Instead, Cody's spirit, pale as watercolor, stood beside me.

"Tired," he said in a voice little more than a child's. He was transparent, rain falling through him. He looked like the watercolor people who usually showed up when I cast magic. Or usually showed up if my dad didn't block them when I cast magic.

"I'm sorry," he said. "I thought I could fix this." He frowned, his voice drifting away on the wind. Destroyed by thunder.

"You're okay now." I was surprised at how calm I was. Apparently some part of my brain still functioned. Now that Cody was out of my head, I could think again, breathe again, and not panic again.

Mama stepped forward, just enough that she was through the Illusion. She squinted. It must be brighter in here. It was certainly a bloody mess.

"Come with me now, boy," she said to Cody's spirit.

Which meant she could see Cody's spirit. Which meant she was using some kind of magic to see him.

Which meant she could use magic. A fleeting memory of her hand on my chest, glowing, snapped bright in my mind, then was gone. But the sense that she had more to do with magic than I knew lingered.

"Wait," I said. "Mama, what are you going to do with him?"

"He's safe with me, Allie girl. I'll keep him hidden. Have my own ways, and you won't ask me nothing about it. Tell your father I don't owe him no more." She held out her hand for Cody.

Cody looked at me. "I like her." He smiled.

I had no idea what to say to him. Had no idea what was the right thing to do. Maybe I should try to keep him somehow and return him to his living self.

Cody took Mama's hand, and for a second, I thought I saw her hand glow white, just as lightning struck. I blinked away the flash and Cody was stuck to her by a stream of white light, like the ghost children had been stuck to Jingo Jingo, only Cody didn't look sad about it. He looked relieved, walking to the end of the length of light, then back close to her again. I couldn't help but think of a balloon being caught safely before it floated away.

Mama stepped toward the wall of Illusion, out to the outside world.

Just before he followed her, Cody turned back toward me. "Zayvion," he said. Thunder drowned out his words.

"What?" I asked.

Allison, my father warned.

"Zayvion . . . ," Cody started, the stream of light between him and Mama tugging on him.

Allison, Dad said again.

Shut up, I thought at him.

". . . says he loves you too," Cody said.

"When did he say that?"

"In there." Cody pointed at the gate. "Today."

I looked over at the gate.

And saw a wave of monsters, Hungers, and horrors I had no name for pouring through the gate and onto the field.

Chapter Twenty

There was no time to see how anyone else was reacting to this. There was no time to think anything through. Hungers would tear the magic users apart in seconds. There was so much wild magic in the air, in the sky, in the city, that it would take the shadowy Hungers only a few minutes to become fully solid. And then they would hunt. They would eat magic users and civilians. They would kill.

I pulled Zayvion's sword, and wondered why that hadn't been in my hands all along. A calm washed through me, as if this sword that Zayvion had spent so much time with had been infused with his calm, his strength, his clear, concise ability to deal with a horrifying situation and make competent, lifesaving decisions.

The Hungers, a dozen, two dozen, went from transparent beasts into solid muscled creatures with wide heads, red eyes, and fanged jaws. Magic pulsed down their hides, like black veins, wild magic feeding them, making them strong.

Other things with too many eyes and too many limbs clattered out of the gates behind the Hungers.

Magic users turned weapons and magic on the beasts that howled and charged across the field. But just as quickly as the magic users struck the beasts down, magic, wild magic, poured through the beasts. The black veins along their bodies pulsed with it, and then the beasts stood again, attacked again.

They were not going down and staying down.

A beast leaped for me. I swung the sword, caught the thing midleap, straight through the neck. It fell to the ground, quivered, and lay still.

The blade in my hand went black, then grew bright and silver tip to hilt. Holy shit. Zay's sword had some kind of spell worked into it so that it could drink the magic out of its foe. Maybe it was honed to drink down dark magic.

It is, Dad said. *But you are not trained to use it. You will grow weaker with each strike.*

So tell me how to use it right, I thought.

I can't. He didn't sound happy about that. *I am not the guardian of the gate.*

Here's the thing. I was getting pretty tired of having to pay the price of magic. But I'd do it with grim satisfaction if it meant I could save my friends.

Another Hunger leaped at me. I swung again. Left it headless. It did not rise. The ground beneath my feet swayed and I stumbled as my knees gave out. Okay, he wasn't kidding. It took a hell of a lot of stamina to wield dark magic.

I pushed back up to my feet, into a fighting stance, sword at the ready.

The four beasts nearest me backed away. Like scenting the wind, they all lifted their wide heads. And ran. Past fallen or injured magic users—easy kills—which made no sense. Ran toward Sedra.

A dozen beasts ran for Sedra. Two dozen. More.

Dane could not hold them off and keep the cage whole. He threw a wall of magic at the beasts, but only half of them fell. The rest rushed him, fast. Too fast. Dane disappeared beneath slathering jaws and wicked claws.

The cage around Sedra constricted, crushing her. Sedra screamed—a strangely inhuman yell.

I started off toward her. But the battlefield was filled with beasts. And with each one I killed, I had to pause, catch my breath, and balance before I could raise the sword and stride forward again.

Jingo Jingo answered Sedra's cry. Caught in battle with a beast, he cast magic, the disk clenched in his thick palm, and chanted something that sent the beast to its belly. No. Something that made the beast crouch, then spin to launch at Shame's throat.

Shame opened his arms and laughed, magic caught between his two hands drinking the dark magic out of the creature. But the monster was huge, bigger than a car. It kept coming, no matter how quickly Shame drained it. Shame yelled, anger, terror, maybe even desire, as it broke through his spell and leaped upon him, jaws tearing into his chest.

Terric, on the other side of the battlefield, yelled. "No, no, no!" He swung his axes, cleaving through the beasts between him and Shame, blood and a black ichor covering his face, so much that not even the rain could wash it away as he hacked and sliced. Hungers and the other, stranger creatures with too many hands, too many eyes, and too many teeth fell in pieces at his feet as he cut a bloody swath through them.

I ran toward Shame. Slow. Too damn slow.

Jingo was already striding over to Sedra. Past the slathering pile of beasts on top of Dane, ignoring them, and Dane's screams, like they were of no more concern to him than a pack of puppies. He slammed the disk, full of magic, into the cage that held Sedra. His voice rose above the battle, above the storm, above the thunder. "This will end!"

Copper lightning shot up out of the ground, enveloping them. Then Jingo Jingo and Sedra were gone, leaving nothing behind but a circle of black ash.

Holy shit. I killed another beast. And another. Then pulled the blood blade to hold another off while I tried to catch my breath and strength. I wasn't going fast enough. Shame lay dying beneath that creature. Might already be dead.

A blur to my right caught my attention. Victor, wielding his sword, and I swear not even breaking a sweat, sliced his way toward Liddy, who held a protective spell around Chase. I didn't know why she was protecting Chase, but Chase wasn't looking too good. She looked dazed.

Liddy wasn't looking too good either. She didn't even try to keep Victor from breaking the Shield spell. She stiffened and fell before Victor's blade reached her.

And then I saw why. Behind her hunkered a huge nightmare of a thing. Too many heads and mouths and hands, all bloodred. It pulled six bloody pincers out of Liddy's back and reached for Chase. Chase crumpled as if she'd been hit by a Taser. Victor's sword, which I thought had broken Liddy's spell, instead finished its intended arc and sliced the creature in half.

The creature shuddered, then fell into a pile of quivering flesh. Flesh that started smoking in the rain. Victor grabbed Chase and dragged her away. He ran back for Liddy, but he was late, too late.

The creature went up in a screaming bonfire of flames, so dark, it hurt to look at it. And somewhere in that flame had been Liddy.

This was a slaughter.

Chase coughed and rocked, as if she'd hit the ground from a height and was trying to kick-start her lungs. Blood and rain splashed across her face. That nightmare creature had done some damage.

From the edge of the clearing, I saw another beast moving fast, liquid on four legs.

Greyson. No longer a man. All pissed-off hell-spawn creature, somehow more familiar and less frightening than the Hungers and horrors, coming straight for Chase. He tore through the Hungers, sucking down their life, their magic, and then spewed that magic at the other creatures, boiling them until they burst into flame.

I didn't know where Hayden was. Didn't know how Greyson had gotten away from him. But there was another killer on Greyson's heels. Just as fast. Just as frightening. Coming down heavy enough I could feel the vibration of his stride under my feet.

Stone.

And he looked angry.

Greyson pounded toward Chase, throwing Hungers to the ground, laying a path of destruction behind him.

Allison, my dad said. *Get close to Greyson.*

I intended to do just that. Then I intended to stick Zay's sword in his chest.

I understood the pain Chase must be going through. She still loved Greyson, even though he wasn't human anymore. I could forgive her for siding with him, for wanting to defend him. But I would not let that keep me from killing the bastard.

If you kill Greyson, Dad said, *you will kill the part of me inside him.*

You're not supposed to be alive anyway, I said. *Get rid of him, get rid of you. How is that a bad thing?*

Because without me, you'll never be able to bring Zayvion back.

A chill washed over my skin, colder than the rain. Stone leaped and landed, hard, in the middle of Greyson's back. I heard bones break. Chase screamed as if the pain was hers to share, and maybe it was. She pushed up to her knees, and feet, and stumbled toward Greyson.

Victor did not stop her, too busy with the half dozen Hungers that surrounded him.

Hayden was back, at the northernmost edge of the field, swinging his broadsword like a one-man army, and yelling at the top of his lungs.

Zayvion is trapped, my father said. *They did more*

than push him through the gate. They locked him there. They are using him there. He will never return.

No, I thought. *That's a lie.*

My hand jerked, and I nicked the side of my thumb on the glass and steel blood blade I carried. Zayvion's blood blade. I hadn't moved my hand—my father had.

What the hell? It was a small cut, but blood ran freely from it.

Blood to blood, Allison.

I didn't know what he was talking about, or why it mattered. He drew on the magic in the air, maybe used some of the magic in me, and I felt the tight, intimate tingling of a Truth spell spread through me, spread between us.

Zayvion is locked on the other side of death, my father said, and I felt the truth of it like a fire against my bones.

I thought Truth spells were bad on the outside. Having someone inside of my head bonding through Truth hurt. But it was very, very clear that my father was not lying.

I believe I can free him and send his soul back to his body, back into life. If you regain the parts of me Greyson now holds. And if I cross over into death to find him now. His time there is at an end. He is dying.

I didn't want to hear that, didn't want to feel that truth burning through me.

We can do it later. After the battle. After we win. You can help me later. I didn't care how desperate I sounded. He already knew what I was feeling. Truth spells worked both ways.

No, I cannot.

He broke the Truth spell, or uncast it, or did whatever it is a dead guy who can still freaking cast magic from inside someone else's freaking body can do.

I opened my mouth to curse, but didn't have time. More and more creatures continued to pour out of the gate. Too many for the magic users to deal with, too many to hope to defeat, too many to let loose into the city.

Victor had carved his way across the field to the front of the gate, his hands lifted in a complicated glyph that would close it. Nikolai, the good-looking Russian Closer, stood next to him, killing the beasts that came too near, holding a Shield of magic so that Victor could do his work.

Close the gate. So that there were no more beasts loose in the world.

Close the gate. And trap Zayvion.

Close the gate. Sealing Zayvion's death.

Maeve was still on the ground, unconscious, but Sunny knelt next to her, keeping the beasts away with wicked knives.

Shame was also on the ground.

Terric had destroyed everything between him and Shame, and beheaded and de-limbed the Hunger that had attacked Shame. Terric now crouched next to Shame, one hand on his chest, glowing with magic that sank into Shame and poured out of him into the ground, as if Shame were a sieve, broken, unable to carry magic, life, breath.

I couldn't tell if he was breathing. Terric was crying, his teeth bared in fury, his ax raised and crackling with black licks of magic as creatures circled them, came too close, and died on the edge of his blade. The blood on one side of his face was finger-painted in the glyph for life and I knew it had been traced there by Shame.

Shame was dying. Maybe he was already dead. I didn't have the wrist cuff. I couldn't tell if his heart still beat.

The gate was about to close. There was no more time to make good decisions. There was only time to make a decision.

Whom to save?

Zayvion had once told me I was not a killer. I'd

proved him wrong. I had killed. But right now, it was life I was trying to hold on to.

I ran toward Greyson, caught the attention of too many creatures, and hacked my way through them. Months of training and sheer fury drove me on, Zayvion's sword drinking down the magic, the energy, of the beasts. It was draining me, but I was pulling on magic from the sky, wild magic that licked and bloomed and caught fire in my blood, my bones, and fed me strength.

I channeled the storm. And now the storm raged in me.

Too bad for the beasts. Too bad for anyone in my way.

Closer, my father said.

I made ground as things born of death's nightmares leaped at me, tearing at my magic, tearing at my flesh. Something, a claw or a fang, got through, sliced my thigh. Something else raked down my back. I felt the hot pump of blood mix with the hard-falling rain.

Then I was on Greyson.

Still pinned beneath Stone, he was more man than he had been. And I knew why. Chase lay next to him, frozen, her hand clasped with his. She was alive. I thought she was. And she was pouring her life out to sustain his.

Sometimes love made you stronger. And sometimes it made you crazy.

Greyson looked up at me. "There is still hope."

"Not for you. Give me back my father, you bastard." I swung the sword.

My father shifted in my head, stretched like electricity crackling behind my eyes. He pushed at my brain, my mind, my head.

My sword halted midswing.

My father's ghost stood next to me, his hand blocking my blade. "Taking his life with this blade will kill you," he said, from outside my mind.

I didn't care. I had a lot of fury and magic holding me up. But there was also a lot of screaming in the back of my head that had been going on for a while. I knew I was ignoring a lot of pain. Maybe ignoring too much pain.

"Get out of my way," I said through clenched teeth.

"Allison." My father stepped closer to me. I caught the scent of him, wintergreen and leather. His voice was gentle. "There is no time for revenge. Not if you want life to win."

How much time did it take to kill someone?

And that was when I felt it. The storm was passing, the rain lifting. Wild storms ended as quickly as they hit. Soon there would be no more wild magic to hold me up. I glanced up, away at the city, crouched in magicless darkness.

Lights flickered on, blazed. Magic caught again like a flame to a wick, and exhaled life and safety into the city. We had done it. We had channeled the wild magic away from the city. The storm was passing.

More than that, the wells and networks were filling fast. I could feel the deep tingle of familiar magic wrapping up inside me again, a heavy warm weight that stretched out against my skin, all pleasure, no pain.

I could easily access that magic, even out here in magicless St. Johns. But it was obvious Chase, lying still, eyes closed, hand clasped with Greyson's at my feet, struggled to reach magic. To keep him alive.

My father let go of the sword, and bent over Greyson. Stone growled. My father paid no attention to him. Instead, Dad traced a glyph in the air, a serpentine line that glowed pure white gold. He caught it up on his hands, where it pressed into place like gauntlets a king might wear. My father glowed with that light, as if the magic wrapped him in its vestments.

And then he pressed his hand into Greyson's head.

Yes. *Into.*

Greyson went absolutely still, and Dad said something that sounded like an old language. A blessing more than a curse.

The gold lines of magic grew stronger and filled my dad with more light. He stood, and was more solid than he had been, though I could still see Stone and Greyson through him.

He regarded me for a moment. "Good-bye, daughter." He turned toward the gate.

A rumble shook the ground. I turned. The gate, trapped by Victor's spells, began to collapse.

Hayden was cutting a swath through the beasts toward us. He'd be here, on top of Greyson and Chase, in a second.

And out of the corner of my eye, I saw Terric stand and swing his ax, killing another beast, while he poured magic, less than before, into Shame. Terric was exhausted. The easy magic, the wild magic, was nearly gone.

Without it, Shame would die.

I spun, Zay's sword still in my hand, and ran for the center of the field, for the pile of broken, blown-apart disks that no longer held magic, where the gate still shimmered in the air, growing smaller as Victor wrapped it in massive lines of magic that webbed it so that no more creatures poured out.

I didn't want the disks. I wanted the crystal. Found it, glowing pink with magic beneath the burnt silver disks. I picked it up and could almost taste the sweetness of the full, heavy magic it carried like a perfume on the back of my throat.

"Terric!" I yelled.

He glanced over. I threw the crystal to him, willing it with mind and magic to find him, reach him. He caught it with the hand that was channeling magic, life, into Shame.

His eyes widened. And then he was on his knees, his ax discarded at his side, pressing the crystal to Shame's chest with both hands, as if it were a new heart for a broken toy. He bent and pressed his forehead to Shame's, whispering to him.

No time.

My father strode toward the gate. Close enough he could step through, but Victor's lines blocked him.

"He must let me pass," my father said.

Victor was focused, caught in a trance of sheer will, sweat peppering his face, his arms shaking as he chanted the spell and forced the gate between life and death to close. He was wielding a hell of a lot of magic with very little resources.

He did not see my dad. He did not know he was sealing Zayvion's death forever.

There was no cavalry to come to our rescue.

But I didn't need a cavalry to save Zayvion.

I strode over to Victor. My teacher, Zayvion's teacher, who might even have been a father figure to Zay. I put my hand on his shoulder and used Influence so that he would understand me and obey.

"Wait until I pass through. Then close the gate behind me."

"Allie," he gasped. "It is suicide."

"Zayvion is the guardian of the gates and I am his Soul Complement. No one's going to tell me I can't bring him home."

Someone yelled. I thought it was Shame. He had told me I couldn't go anywhere without him.

He was wrong.

I glanced over my shoulder. Shame was barely standing, eyes wide in horror or anger, one hand extended toward me. Terric stood behind him, one hand clasped with his, the other arm wrapped around Shame's waist, holding him up, holding him back.

"Allie," Shame yelled. "Don't!"

I didn't listen. I held up one hand. A wave. A farewell, and I turned away. Shame was in good hands. Maybe the best hands he could be in. Terric's hands.

If there was ever going to be a chance to bring Zayvion back, it was now.

The shadow of a figure in flight flashed above me. Stone.

The big rock landed with surprising grace at my side.

I sheathed Zay's sword across my back, and glanced down at Stone, all muscle and wing and fangs. He tipped his head to look up at me, ears perked into triangles.

"Stay," I said. "I have work to do."

Stone growled, then crooned like an out-of-tune pipe organ. His wings pressed against his back and he took a step toward the gate.

Fine. I was running out of time. I didn't know if Stone could walk into death and return alive. Hells, I didn't know if I could walk into death and come out alive. Didn't know if I could find Zay's soul and drag it back with me into the living world.

But I sure as hell was going to find out.

"Are you ready?" I asked my dad.

He frowned. "Where are you going?"

"To save my man." I put my hand down on Stone's head. My father smiled. I didn't know why. Maybe he was angry.

"No," he said, reading my thoughts. "Impressed. You know you can't survive in there without me."

"I didn't say I was going alone." I didn't trust him. Sure, he talked a nice Truth spell, but once on the other side, he might change his mind about saving Zayvion. I wouldn't chance that.

Dad took his place at my right, and Stone stood at my left. Without another look back, I walked through the gates of death.

Read on for an exciting excerpt from
Devon Monk's next Allie Beckstrom novel,

MAGIC AT THE GATE

Coming in November 2010 from Roc

Death had seen better days. Vacant, crumbling buildings, a brown-red sky, and slick pools of black oil stretching out along the sidewalk of what I was pretty sure was supposed to be Burnside Boulevard. The city—and it was very clear we were in Portland—looked like a dump. If this was death, I wanted to meet the marketing team that had dreamed up both the fluffy-cloud-golden-harp thing and the eternal-fires-of-burning-hell shtick.

Because this place was broken and empty. Achingly so.

"Allison?" my father, next to me, said.

He was fully solid now, no longer ghostlike at all. A little taller than I, gray hair, wearing a business suit with a lavender handkerchief in the pocket. Death didn't seem to bother him one bit.

And it shouldn't have. He belonged here.

He squeezed my arm, his eyes flicking back and forth, searching the details of my face. "Can you breathe?"

Of all the dumb questions. "Of course I can breathe. Let go of me."

His lips pressed together in a thin line and the familiar anger clouded his eyes. He pulled his hand away from my arm.

There was no air. No air in my lungs, and none to breathe. I tried not to panic, but, hey, this was death. I knew I'd be lucky to get out of here alive. And I had to get out of here alive. Zayvion was here, somewhere, his soul sent here, his body in life, in a coma.

This was my one chance, my only chance, to save him.

The wild-magic storm might have passed, but the very real danger of my never seeing Zayvion's beautiful eyes, hearing his gentle voice, feeling his touch, set off a sharp panic in my chest.

Well, that and not being able to breathe.

Dad put his left hand in his pocket, tucking away something. Then he crossed his arms over his chest and watched me gasp. Stone-cold, that man.

I shut my mouth and glared. Yes, I was that stubborn. My vision darkened at the edges.

Could you pass out in death? I was about to find out.

Stone growled and stepped toward Dad, fangs bared. That's my boy. Stone's normally dark gray body was now black, shot through with lightning flecks of blue and green and pink, as if he were made of obsidian with opal running beneath the glassy surface. He shone, his eyes glowing a deep amber.

"Touch the Animate," Dad said. "You should be able to breathe again."

Since it was beginning to dawn on me that passing out and leaving my dad conscious might be a really stupid idea, I put my hand on Stone's head.

Air—good . . . well, if not good, serviceable, smelly air—filled my lungs. I hacked like a smoker on a three-day bender. My lungs hurt.

"You are in death." Dad hit lecture mode from word one. "A living being crossed into death. There is so little chance you could have survived that, Allison. No one can step into death if they are fully alive. And yet here you stand. It does make me curious. What part of you is dead, my daughter?"

I didn't know. My sense of humor, maybe? My tolerance for his being a jerk? Or maybe because my Soul Complement was in a coma and his soul was already in

death—that counted. I was too busy coughing and trying to breathe to be philosophical.

He shook his head, dismissing the question as easily
as he dismissed me. "To survive you will need to stay
in contact with something that is neither fully alive nor
completely dead. Something that exists in a between
state. A filter between life and death."

"You're dead." I finally managed to exhale. "All dead.
Why could I breathe when you touched me?"

"That answer is complicated." He looked up and
down the street, then at the building next to us, as if getting his bearings, and started walking down the street.

I followed him, and Stone somehow sensed the need
to stay under my hand. There was no one on the streets
with us, no wind, no rain. When I glanced up, it was nothing but terra-cotta sky and hard white light.

"Tell me you're dead," I said.

"Very much so. That doesn't mean I'm not without
resources."

Which meant part of him, some of him somewhere,
was alive. Great. I did not trust my dad. I never had. For
good reason. And that very calm, trustworthy face he
was wearing made me twitchy.

"Where are you alive? Why?" I asked. "Who's helping you?"

"That is not important."

"Yes, it is. What is your angle in all this, Dad? I have
lost track of whose side you're on."

"I am on magic's side. To see that it falls into the right
hands. My motives are not yours to question."

"I'll question your motives until the day I die. Again.
For reals."

"This is real," he said quietly. "Very real. If you are
to survive, you need to put your stubbornness aside and
listen to me."

"Oh, I just love that idea."

"Love it or not, your options are limited. Living flesh

does not travel well in the world of death. I believe if you stay in contact with the Animate, it will filter the . . . irritants of death long enough for you to accomplish your task."

He made it sound as if he were teaching me the ABC's and knew there was no way I'd ever make it to Q.

He stopped and glanced back down the street the way we'd come. "Faster would be better."

He grabbed my arm and propelled me down an alley. I shook free of him, my other hand still on Stone's head, and looked over my shoulder.

Watercolor people. And not the nice kind. Unlike the other Veiled I had seen in life, these ghostly people barely resembled people. With their twisted bodies and sagging faces, they resembled movie zombies more than ghosts. They also looked solid.

And hungry.

Stone growled.

The Veiled heard him, turned our way, sniffing, scenting, crooked hands tracing half-formed glyphs, as if they could use magic to find us.

"Veiled?" I asked.

"Quiet," Dad said.

Stone's ears flattened. He stopped making noise but his lips were pulled back to expose a row of sharp teeth and fangs.

Dad traced a glyph in the air and magic followed in a solid gold line at his fingertips. I wasn't using Sight, yet magic was clearly visible. That wasn't how it worked in life. Magic was too fast to be visible. Here, it was slow and fluid.

He finished the glyph. Camouflage glittered in the air like a filigreed screen. He whispered a word and the glyph stretched and widened, creating a swirling shell around us. I swallowed, but could not taste anything. That was different from in life too. Magic didn't smell or taste here.

Or maybe I just wasn't dead enough to sense it.

The Veiled were almost on us.

"This way," Dad whispered. He rolled his fingers, catching up the lines of the Camouflage glyph and balancing it on his open palm. He pushed his palm outward in a sort of traffic-cop *stop* motion and the spell moved with us, keeping us hidden.

Impressive.

Dad's mouth set in a hard line and his eyes narrowed, as if casting magic and maintaining the spell wasn't easy. Still, he stormed down the alleyway—not once looking back—strong, confident.

And for a second, just a second, I saw my dad as a heroic figure. The epitome of what a magic user should be. The mythic wizard who knew the hidden strengths of magic and his own soul. Even in death, my dad stood tall and kicked ass.

"Walk or be eaten," he said.

Okay, so much for the hero bit.

I picked up the pace and Stone padded along beside me.

The Veiled stepped into the alley behind us and shuffled over to where we'd been standing. They didn't follow us. A few dropped to their knees, patting the sidewalk as if they'd just lost something, while others ran their hands along the brick wall, mouths open. They leaned against the building and sucked at the wall as if they were starving for even the slightest drop of magic it might contain.

It creeped me out. I walked faster, holding tight to Stone's ear.

"I did not want to enter this way," Dad said, "but bringing you along has changed my approach. Why must you challenge me in every way, Allison?"

"I'd be happy to help," I said as pleasantly as I could muster, "if you'd tell me where Zayvion is so I can get the hell out of here."

He stopped at the other end of the alley. More Veiled blocked our passage. These stared at us as if they could see right through the Camouflage my dad still held.

That wasn't good.

I put my hand on the hilt of Zayvion's katana, which was sheathed on my back.

"Don't draw the blade."

There wasn't a lot of room in the alley. I was mostly behind him. I didn't know how he'd seen me reach for the sword.

"I'm not going to wait until they jump us."

And just like that, the Veiled rushed toward us.

"Do you trust me?" he asked without looking back at me.

"No."

"That's unfortunate."

My dad broke the Camouflage spell—and I mean it shattered and fell like glass exploding.

Then he spun and stuck his hands into my chest.

Into. My. Chest.

It hurt. I inhaled. Exhaled. Yelled. Couldn't move to draw the sword, draw a spell, draw a breath.

Stone launched at him. Then I couldn't breathe *even more*.

Dad was fast. He pulled his hands free, pulling magic—pink and silver and black—out of my chest and pointing at Stone, who halted in his tracks and stepped on my foot, so I had at least some contact. Dad cast a glyph out of the magic—my magic—and threw a metallic, sparking fireball at the Veiled.

The explosion lit the street and carved hard shadows down the alley.

The Veiled screamed, an unholy sound that echoed out and out and seemed to reflect off of the sky as if it were a low ceiling. It was too big a sound, too much sound, in too small a place.

Their scream vibrated somewhere deep inside of me

where I couldn't get away from it, making their pain a part of me, my magic a part of them.

No, no, no.

I reached for Stone, for my dad, for anyone, any*thing* to hold on to to make this stop. Then Dad was standing in front of me, his hand over the old bullet scar just below my collarbone.

"Breathe, Allison. Breathe."

I gasped. Got some air down. Tasted something sweet against my tongue, and the cool, rough bricks of the building against my back.

"What. The. Hell," I said.

"Light and Dark magic, through Death magic," he said evenly, not moving away from me. "A transference. I took from the magic within you, and now I give you back the magic of death."

So that was the bluish glow coming from his hand.

"Wait. What? You are not putting dead people in me." I pushed at his hands, but it didn't do much good. I was very, very tired, and he didn't seem to have any problem keeping me pinned against the wall.

Why was I was so tired?

Could it be because I was in death? And my father had just ripped magic out of my chest? And right before that, back in life, I'd Grounded a wild-magic storm and fought a bunch of crazy magic users, all the while killing Hungers and other nightmarish creatures while trying to save my friends' lives?

Yes. That would be why. I'd had a hell of a day and the adrenaline of the battlefield was wearing off, leaving behind the very real horror of what had happened.

Zayvion was in a coma. Shame had almost died. For all I knew, the crystal I'd given to Terric had been only a temporary reprieve for Shame. Jingo Jingo betrayed everyone, nearly killed Maeve, nearly killed Shame, kidnapped Sedra. Magic users had turned against magic users. Liddy, my Death magic teacher, was dead. Chase and Greyson might be dead too. And La, and Joshua, and probably more were hurt. Violet was in the hospital. Kevin too.

The Authority wasn't cracking; it had broken. Sides had been taken. The war was on.

Whoever came out on top would rule how magic was used by the common citizen, and by the Authority. Whoever came out on top would control all the magic the public knew about, and, worse, all the magic they didn't know about. There was a lot of power at stake here. Plenty enough to kill for.

And I was here, dead. With no one but my gargoyle and my dad to help me find my way home. Where were my ruby slippers when I needed them?

ALSO AVAILABLE

FROM

Devon Monk

MAGIC IN THE SHADOWS

Allison Beckstrom's magic has taken its toll on her, physically marking her and erasing her memories—including those of the man she supposedly loves. But lost memories aren't the only things preying on Allie's thoughts.

Her late father, the prominent businessman—and sorcerer—Daniel Beckstrom, has somehow channeled himself into her very mind. With the help of The Authority, a secret organization of magic users, she hopes to gain better control over her own abilities—and find a way to deal with her father…

Available wherever books are sold or at penguin.com

ALSO AVAILABLE
FROM
Devon Monk

MAGIC IN THE BLOOD

Working as a Hound—tracing illegal spells back to their casters—has taken its toll on Allison Beckstrom. But even though magic has given her migraines and stolen her recent memory, Allie isn't about to quit. Then the police's magic enforcement division asks her to consult on a missing persons case. But what seems to be a straightforward job turns out to be anything but, as Allie finds herself drawn into the underworld of criminals, ghosts, and blood magic.

"Monk's writing is addictive, and the only cure is more, more, more!"
—*New York Times* bestselling author
Rachel Vincent

Available wherever books are sold or at penguin.com

Magic to the Bone

"Brilliantly and tightly written ... will surprise, amuse, amaze, and absorb readers." —*Publishers Weekly* (starred review)

"Loved it. Fiendishly original and a stay-up-all-night read. We're going to be hearing a lot more of Devon Monk."
—Patricia Briggs, *New York Times* bestselling author of *Bone Crossed*

"Highly original and compulsively readable. Don't pick this one up before going to bed unless you want to be up all night!" —Jenna Black, author of *Speak of the Devil*

"Gritty setting, compelling, fully realized characters, and a frightening system of magic-with-a-price that left me awed. Devon Monk's writing is addictive, and the only cure is more, more, more!"
—Rachel Vincent, *New York Times* bestselling author of *Rogue*

"An exciting new addition to the urban fantasy genre. It's got a truly fresh take on magic, and Allie Beckstrom is one kick-ass protagonist!"
—Jeanne C. Stein, national bestselling author of *Retribution*

"The prose is gritty and urban, the characters mysterious and marvelous, and Monk creates a fantastic and original magic system that intrigues and excites. A promising beginning to a new series. I'm looking forward to more!"
—Nina Kiriki Hoffman, Bram Stoker Award–winning author of *Fall of Light*

"Monk's reimagined Portland is at once recognizable and exotic, suffused with her special take on magic, and her characters are vividly rendered. The plot pulled me in for a very enjoyable ride!"
—Lynn Flewelling, author of *The White Road*

Praise for the Novels of Devon Monk

Magic in the Blood

"Tight, fast, and vividly drawn, Monk's second Allie Beckstrom novel features fresh interpretations of the paranormal, strong characters dealing with their share of faults, and . . . ghoulish plot twists. Fans of Patricia Briggs or Jim Butcher will want to check out this inventive new voice."
—Monsters and Critics

"[A] highly creative series about magic users in a world much like our own, filled with greed and avarice. I love the character of Allie and she is just getting better and stronger as the series continues. . . . If you love action, magic, intrigue, good-versus-evil battles, and pure entertainment, you will not want to miss this series." —Manic Readers

"One heck of a ride through a magical, dangerous Portland . . . imaginative, gritty, sometimes darkly humorous. . . . An un-put-downable book, *Magic in the Blood* is one fantastic read." —Romance Reviews Today

"This series uses a system of rules for magic that is original and seems very realistic. . . . The structure of the story pulled me in right away, and kept me reading. There's action, adventure, fantasy, and even some romance."
—CA Reviews

"Ms. Monk weaves a unique tale of dark magic that will keep readers at the edge of their seat[s]. *Magic in the Blood* is so thoroughly described that the creepy bits will have you thinking of magic and ghosts long after you've finished the story. Fast moving and gripping, it will leave you wanting more." —Darque Reviews

". . . . y Allie Beckstrom . . . . e first. . . . It's . . . . . t!"
—RhiReading

continued . . .